For an instant Holt thought about turning back. He tried to convince himself that the animal had continued deep into the Knollbarrens, no longer a threat to Oxvale. Yet the memory of the wolf in his own pasture burned in Holt's mind, and he refused to give up his pursuit. The beast had been there once—he could think of only one way to ensure that it didn't come back.

The clatter of a pebble alerted him, and he spun quickly. The fierce predator crouched at the lip of the gully where a second earlier there had been only trees and sky. Even in the instant of recognition the Daryman was awed by the wolf's size—it was larger than even the biggest deerhound.

In a flash of movement, the animal's legs uncoiled and the shaggy gray body sprang into the air. . . .

Quest Triad
Douglas Niles

Other FIRST QUEST™
Young Readers Adventures

First Quest™
Books

Pawns
Prevail

Book I of the Quest Triad

Douglas Niles

PAWNS PREVAIL

©1995 TSR, Inc.
All Rights Reserved.

Cover art by Paul Jacquays

First Printing: May 1995.
Printed in the United States of America
Library of Congress Catalog Card Number: 94-68136

9 8 7 6 5 4 3 2 1

ISBN: 1-56076-854-1

TSR, Inc.	TSR Ltd.
201 Sheridan Springs Rd.	120 Church End, Cherry Hinton
Lake Geneva, WI 53147	Cambridge CB1 3LB
United States of America	United Kingdom

**For all First Daughters,
and especially Rhiannon, Katie,
Allison, and Molly.**

Prologue

The temperature in the Hall of the Immortals was, as always, perfect. A soothing wash of light spilled indirectly through tall windows into the vast, marbled chambers. Even the odors were ideal—the scent of lush blossoms perfumed the gardens while the aroma of freshly baked bread wafted through the kitchens and dining chambers.

Yet still, amid all this perfection, Dalliphree was bored. The faerie buzzed her wings listlessly, flitting down a wide corridor. Columns of white stonework lined each side, and in a swirl of gossamer wings, she swooped back and forth between these pillars.

Whirling carelessly around one of these obstacles, Dalliphree bumped into someone's chest and bounced backward onto the floor.

"Ouch!" declared an outraged voice.

"Ouch yourself!" she retorted, climbing to her feet and rubbing her bruised hindquarters. She scowled upward at an old man who stood more than twice her own height. "Why don't you let a person know you're there?"

The elder scowled back, his forehead creased with wrinkles and his dark eyes flashing. Though his head was mostly bald, a long gray beard extended as far as his belt. Now those bristling whiskers quivered with indignation.

"If a person would use the *middle* of the hall, like everyone else, then *another* person wouldn't *have* to look out behind every pillar!" he said stiffly.

"Want to play a game, Pusanth?" Dalliphree asked. She hopped upward and, with a buzz of her wings, rose to meet the other immortal eye-to-eye.

"Don't change the subject," griped the old man. Then he glanced again at her, interested in spite of himself. "What kind of game?"

"A mortal game—a wager," the faerie said slyly.

"Perhaps I would play. What kind of mortal game?" Pusanth inquired.

"One with two plays for each of us," Dalli replied without hesitation.

Pawns Prevail

"A powerful game," the sage murmured, not displeased by the stakes.

Dalliphree nodded quickly, her light red hair bouncing around her pixie face. She knew that Pusanth would not plunge into the contest without first giving it careful thought.

Indeed, playing the mortal game gave pause to even the most liberal of immortals. In the purest sense of immortal code, *any* interference in the lives of mortals was taboo—they were supposed to let the short-lived creatures go about their years without immortal meddling.

Yet the mortal game allowed some minor exceptions to this prohibition. Each immortal player drew one or two tokens before the game, each of which allowed one "play" in the game—minor adjustments to the life of a mortal. These plays were strictly controlled, as each immortal tried to use his tokens to advance the fortunes of his chosen mortal.

"Who will you choose for your mortal?" asked the sage.

"Oh, I don't know," Dalliphree chirped with an exaggerated shrug. "She'll be rich, I know—probably a princess. And beautiful and fabulously clever—oh, and the men will just *die* for her—!"

"She sounds like *all* of your mortals," Pusanth retorted. Nevertheless, he sat himself down on a marble bench at the side of the hall and stroked a finger through the long, curling hairs of his beard.

3

"Well, *so?*" Dalliphree was indignant. "Doesn't *everybody* have their favorite piece in the mortal game? Don't we use the same kind of pieces over and over and over? You always have some fuddy wizard, or know-it-all sage! You choose someone with as many brains as you can fit into his wee little skull!"

Pusanth bit back his retort, knowing the faerie was more than a little right.

"Very well," he said after a few moments' careful consideration. "This time my mortal will be different. He will begin bereft of riches, lacking family station or status. He will have no formal training, no teacher to prepare him for the rigors of the contest."

"Interesting," Dalli admitted, secretly pleased that Pusanth would give her such an opening advantage. "My own mortal shall be schooled in all the skills, of course. Naturally, her family will bring tutors from across the world."

"Naturally," murmured Pusanth, slightly mocking.

"Well, why shouldn't they?" demanded the faerie. "After all, those poor mortals only have fifty or sixty years to live!"

"Such a terribly short amount of time. . . ." Pusanth admitted.

"Let's draw now!" Dalliphree squealed, buzzing down the corridor. Pusanth followed, his sticklike legs propelling the frail body with surprising speed.

They emerged into one of the elegant gardens. Rosebushes, heavy with blossoms, filled the dewy air with perfume while immaculately groomed grass rolled like a lush carpet over the ground. In the center of the garden, they reached a deep, lily-lined pool where gleaming goldfish darted through the water.

"Me first!" cried the faerie, settling at the shore of the crystalline pond. In her hand she held one of the blossoms from a red rose. Carefully she plucked a petal and placed it upon the still waters.

A long goldfish emerged from the shade of a lily pad and gently nudged the rose petal with its snout. Dalli quickly snatched up the blossom and flipped it over in her hand to read the words that had appeared there. Her face was creased by a sudden pout.

"What is it?" pressed Pusanth. "What play did you get?"

"A gust of wind!" huffed the faerie. "I don't know what good *that's* supposed to be!"

The elder sage immediately dropped a petal of his own into the water, and another fish came over to give the flower a nudge. When he removed it, his brow wrinkled in concentration. "Green leaf," he muttered. "I can make plants grow."

"That's better than wind," Dalliphree snapped, jealous. Still, she repeated the process, drawing her second token, and this time she squealed with delight. "A bee sting! I can *use* that—and *look!*" Her voice rose in excitement.

"What is it?" demanded the bearded man, suspiciously.

Dalliphree triumphantly showed him her petal. "It says here that I get an extra draw!"

"What? Oh, I suppose it does—as if you don't have enough advantages already! Go ahead and draw your extra play."

"An artifact!" the faerie cried, her face growing serious as she examined her third and final play. Her voice was hushed, awestruck. "I get to make an artifact!"

"What? Let me see that!" Pusanth grabbed the token and grimaced. The artifact play was extremely rare and extremely powerful, for it allowed an immortal to create a mighty tool and give it to her mortal pawn. Though such objects often required a hidden cost to the mortals who used them, artifacts could be employed by mortals to gain great influence and power.

Pusanth groaned. He knew that the artifact token was the most powerful play in the mortal game, and it seemed terribly unfair for Dalli to get one as her extra play. Muttering in frustration, he dropped another blossom into the water. When he read the symbols on the other side, his eyes squinted into a crafty gleam.

"I drew the seven directions of chaos!" he exclaimed, his own voice rising in triumph.

Dalli's eyes widened with dismay, but she carefully concealed her reaction. The chaos token was one that could change the play of any other token, and she knew that it represented a threat to her plans. Still, she didn't want Pusanth to know how much she was worried.

"Now, the bet," she said.

The waters of the pool began to swirl, and soon in the calming surface, the two immortals beheld a vista of rolling hills, green woodlands, lush pastures, and a multitude of lakes and rivers.

"We will play in Karawenn," Pusanth declared.

"It doesn't matter to me where the mortals live," Dalliphree agreed with a shrug.

"The terms, then?" suggested Pusanth.

"She possesses all as birthright . . . yet in her lifetime she shall gain far more," Dalliphree intoned solemnly.

"He will begin with nothing," replied Pusanth, *"but by his own hand shall he rise as high."*

And so the mortal game began.

* * * * *

The Sphere of Entropy was the realm of death, of darkness and decay. Here seethed the forces of corruption and hatred. Here, too, dwelled those creatures who wielded hurtful power through the worlds of mortals and immortals alike. With no care for growth or beauty or kindness, creatures of entropy sought only to destroy.

Among all the spheres, Entropy was the true center of evil, and the heart of chaos. Powerful and far-reaching, the tendrils of entropy had wormed their way into many other spheres, seeking power.

Thus, when the tokens of the mortal game were drawn, the tight connection between chaos and entropy resounded like a drumbeat in the dark sphere. The sound brought a message and a summons. The power of the chaos token, as it entered the mortal game, thrummed through entropy—a call that could not be ignored.

In the darkest reaches of entropy yawned a deep cavern, utterly black and lightless, filled with the stench of poisonous gases. From this pool of mire, a huge head slowly rose. The black, oozing form of the nightshade emerged from the slime and pressed its midnight limbs against the hard stone walls around it. Though eager to spread its black wings and fly, the beast could only spit its hatred and fury into the dark.

It was trapped, for now.

But soon it would be free.

1
The Wolf

A bush beside the pasture abruptly rustled and cracked. Holton Jaken whirled, expecting a company of armored riders to charge noisily through the undergrowth. His long dark hair spun in the air about his shoulders, and the huge sword gleaming in his hands was ready to meet the attackers, ready with its razor-edged blade. . . .

His heart sank when he saw Besserel. Sad brown eyes blinked at Holt from the tangle of bushes, and the big cow lowed softly. Delighted to see her friend, Bess pushed forward, mooing more loudly and nudging Holt with real affection.

Pawns Prevail

Sighing, the tall young man disappointedly dropped his hands. No attackers, just a cow. Of course, he'd known all along that his 'sword' was no more than a stout walking stick, but for a brief moment the knotted oak had seemed to glow like steel in his hands. His mind had pictured the face-plates of the helmeted riders, the snorting nostrils of the huge chargers. . . .

The lanky young farmer sighed again. He had grown bored of these woods around Oxvale, perhaps because he knew the land so well. Though he was unusually tall, he could move through the forest with natural grace. The bow and quiver he carried on his back swung within easy reach of his hands in case a rabbit or pheasant offered itself for dinner. Of course, rabbits and pheasants weren't brigands and chargers.

The cow mooed again, and Holt scratched around her horns with the end of his staff. Surprisingly, Bess didn't stop to enjoy the attention. She pushed past him, lowering her head and plodding along the trail that led back to the barn.

"Hey!" cried Holt, pulling his foot away from a trudging hoof. "What's your hurry?"

The cow's rust-colored back and flanks shivered as if she were trying to shrug away a cloud of pestering flies. Yet it was early spring—even in the bottomlands, flies wouldn't be a problem for a month or more. Holt hurried after Bess, clapping a

Douglas Niles

hand on her shoulder while he walked beside her.

"That's okay, old girl," he said affectionately to the lumbering cow. "There's some oats back in the crib if you want 'em." Then Holt noticed that the cow still shivered, and he paused in concern. "What is it—something spooking you?"

Besserel continued walking, and he knew she would follow the path along the stream until she came to the yard.

Something lurked in the valley, something Bess feared. The young Daryman turned back to the underbrush. Bess's trail was easy to follow—for some reason the cow had blundered through a dense thicket rather than take the more winding route of the streamside path. In growing concern, Holt trotted along, wondering what had driven the cow to such anxiety.

He reached a wide, soggy meadow, one of Besserel's favorite grazing spots. Muddy hoof-prints clearly indicated where she had taken her morning feeding. She had waded far into the muck to reach a lush clump of clover. Holt laced his boots tightly, then followed the cow's tracks into the meadow. With the support of his stick, he took long steps, sinking to his ankles in the soft loam. At the clover, he paused to look around.

Another set of tracks moved through the moist field, just beyond the leafy cluster. Water had settled into the depressions, showing that the prints had been made before Bess's visit to the field. Yet the presence of the tracks had frightened her into hurrying back to the barnyard.

Pushing through the clover, Holt knelt beside the marks. The soft ground had settled around them, obscuring the shape of the feet. Still, the black scars in the moist, green earth were deep and big enough that he knew they had been made by a large creature. Holt easily followed the tracks back to their source, a pine grove at the edge of the meadow.

Amid the cool shade of the pines, the ground was drier. Here Holt got his first clear look at the prints. One in particular stood out in detail, and as he recognized it, his hands instinctively reached for the long ash bow at his back.

The footprint had been made by a wolf.

Holt had never seen a wolf print, much less a wolf, but in his eighteen years he'd heard them described countless times by the older farmers. The five claws, the four pads, were reminiscent of the fox and dog tracks he'd seen many times before—except that the print before him now was *much* larger than any canine's foot he had ever seen. Placing his hand over the muddy depression, he could not entirely cover the track.

Karawenn was a big land, Holt knew, and he believed there was room here for both wolves and men. Yet normally the gray predators stayed in the far reaches of the Knollbarren wilderness. Only in times of danger did they wander down to the farmlands and settled places. Holt knew that sixteen years earlier his father and the other men of Oxvale had staved off an invasion of wolves in league with human and monstrous lords, routing the creatures so solidly that they had not threatened the vale since.

Did the appearance of a wolf now mean that trouble again threatened the land? Perhaps, but that question went far beyond Holt's present concern. He had to decide what to do about *this* print, *today*.

The wolf's tracks were clear, and he believed that he could follow the trail—though if the hunt took long he knew his father would begin to worry.

He thought of going back to the farm and telling the older Daryman of his intent, but quickly discarded that idea. The farmsteads of Oxvale were several miles away from these low pastures, opposite the direction taken by the wolf. He would waste precious time, and his father, Derek Jaken—who had lost both of his legs before Holt was born—would in any event be unable to help with the tracking or pursuit.

The trail was already several hours old—Holt couldn't give the wolf an even greater head start. His only choice was to begin, right now, following the carnivore's faint spoor. Derek wouldn't worry *too* much, since Holt often took off for several days of prolonged hunting in the 'Barrens. The one difference, he reminded himself, was that this time his quarry could hunt him in return.

The thought gave him a tingle of excitement—and a shiver of fear. Carefully he removed his bow from its sling and strung the long, supple weapon. Only then did he look at his quiver. It held four long, straight shafts, each tipped with an arrowhead of sharp steel. The weapons had served him well against rabbits, pheasants, marmots, and even deer. Somehow, however, they seemed very inadequate when he considered using them against the creature that had made these prints.

Yet here, again, Holt had no real choice. If the wolf settled residence around here, how much time would pass before it killed someone's cow? For any farmer in Oxvale, Holt knew, such a loss would be catastrophic. He wouldn't—he *couldn't*—allow that to happen.

Carefully he studied the trail of the wolf. The animal had apparently pushed its way into the meadow in order to reach the bank of the stream. After drinking, and thus leaving the tracks for Besserel to find, it had returned to the shelter of the woods.

But where had it gone from here?

All his hunting skill came into play as the young Daryman bent over the tracks. Away from the streamside, the ground remained dry, covered with dead leaves, and for long moments he could see no sign of the wolf's path. A tuft of gray fur, hooked to a wild rose thorn, gave him his first clue.

Spotting tiny signs of the wolf's passage along a winding game path, Holt followed the trail carefully. With a sense of relief, he realized the animal had been moving away from the valley bottom. The cows of Oxvale were safe, at least for the time being.

Perhaps the wolf had even decided to return to the Knollbarrens. That large, rugged wilderness offered plenty of hiding places, but Holt reasoned that if the animal got away without difficulty, it would probably be back. Stubbornly he clung to the trail, working into higher ground where broad-limbed oaks with ancient, gnarled trunks ruled the wood.

The trail veered toward the foot of a rocky bluff, and Holt's eyes narrowed as he studied the ground. As if seeking to conceal its trail, the animal had scrambled up from the forest path to bound along the trackless expanse of broken rock.

Shadows of the hills lengthened around him as Holt pressed on. He found more faint signs—footprints, fur, once a pile of droppings. Larger bluffs rose around him now.

Something scurried through the brush beside the trail. Holt whirled, bow and arrow raised. Fur flashed, and he shot, his arrow piercing a plump rabbit. It was no wolf, but at least he would have supper. Unfortunately, as Holt tried to remove the arrow, he snapped the shaft. Though he saved the arrowhead, he was left with only three usable arrows.

He decided to stop and rest for the night, quickly gathering wood and building a fire. Near the camp he found dandelion greens, tubers, and mushrooms. Flavored with chives, they gave him a bountiful supper with enough leftovers to provide breakfast in the morning.

Relaxing beside the remnants of his small fire, Holt wondered why the wolf had chosen now, this year, to come down from the 'Barrens. It had been more than a decade since the last battles of the Troll War had been waged. During that conflict, which had lasted for more than fifteen years, marauders and monsters had threatened Karawenn. Yet since the Stand of the Darymen, which Holt didn't remember because he had been merely two years old, no wolves had been bold enough to come to Oxvale. He felt, keenly, the menace presented by the beast he was tracking, and he resolved to catch and slay the animal before it could return and perhaps kill a cow or calf.

His fire faded to ash, but just before he slipped off to sleep, he was startled by a pale, greenish glow in the woods. Then he chuckled—it was only phosphorescent lichen, the shy, leafy plant that flourished in regions of darkest shadow. Often he

returned. Seeing no wolf, he turned back to the trail. The clattering of a pebble alerted him, and he spun quickly.

The fierce predator crouched at the lip of the gully, where a second earlier there had been only trees and sky. Even in the instant of recognition the Daryman was awed by the wolf's size—it was larger than even the biggest deerhound.

In a flash of movement, the animal's legs uncoiled, and the shaggy gray body sprang into the air. Raising the bow while the beast was in midspring, Holt shot and then tumbled to the side, away from the snapping jaws.

The steel arrowhead struck the wolf's shoulder—and bounced off! The animal landed, snarling, while the Daryman desperately scrambled backward. Holt fumbled for another arrow as the wolf crouched, growling ominously. Nocking the shaft, he drew the string to his cheek and let the arrow fly. Again the shot struck true, this time in the wolf's brawny chest—and once more the steel arrowhead bounced off of that shaggy pelt to fall harmlessly on the ground.

What was wrong—he *saw* his shots strike their targets! Holt snatched up another arrow, realizing it was his last. Grimly nocking the missile and biting back his frustration, he stared furiously at the growling predator.

The wolf bared white fangs, snarling. For a

moment Holt hesitated, taken aback at the sight of the creature's eyes. They glowed like cherry-colored embers, smoldering with rage, radiating pure hatred. The unnatural sight struck Holt like a physical blow, driving him backward.

Again the wolf snarled, crouching. The fierceness of the monster's gaze weakened Holt's knees. Gritting his teeth, he made sure his hands didn't tremble as he drew back his last arrow. Holt aimed carefully as the wolf's muscles bunched for the spring. He shot at the chest but at the last second the beast turned its head away. The missile struck the animal's muscular shoulder, once again rebounding harmlessly.

The wolf lunged, and Holt saw cruel triumph in those burning eyes. Drawing his skinning knife, Holt scrambled behind a large rock and flailed madly at the snapping jaws. The blade scraped across the wolf's scalp, not penetrating the thick hide any more than the arrows had. White teeth flashed, and the human jabbed again, striking the animal's tongue. The wolf yelped and jumped away, blood trickling from its mouth.

Holt dived past the creature, darting along the floor of the gorge, and the wolf bounded in pursuit. Seizing one of his arrows where it had fallen to the ground, Holt whirled and slashed with the knife, again aiming for the mouth. The animal spun away so that the blade struck its shaggy flank and skidded harmlessly off.

Only its mouth, Holt thought quizzically as he scrambled atop a rocky knob and spun about. Now he had an idea about the wolf's weakness. Drawing back his arrow, Holt jerked suddenly, pretending to release the shot. Again the wolf ducked away, protecting its face. Only when it turned back and leapt, jaws agape, did Holt let the missile fly.

The arrow soared into the animal's maw, between the gaping jaws. With a gasping yelp, the wolf dropped, thrashing. Tumbling back to the ground, it fell to the side, chest rising and falling with quick pants. The feathered tail of the arrow emerged from between those horrifying jaws. Red eyes glared balefully at Holt for a moment, and then the hateful color faded to a more natural yellow. Finally even that dulled to gray, and the shaggy flanks fell still.

Only then did Holt fully realize his weakness. His legs threatened to collapse beneath him, so the Daryman sagged into a sitting position on a nearby rock.

Holton needed several minutes to recover his strength, and calm his spinning mind. In time he set to work. He probed with his knife and found that, now, he could cut the animal's leathery coat. Skinning the carcass and retrieving his precious arrowhead, he started back on the trail to Oxvale.

2
Home Fires

Holt followed the most direct route back to Oxvale, skirting the rising bulk of Mount Rustwind. Even carrying the heavy pelt, he reached the lip of Oxvale's green valley the day after he had slain the wolf. As the sun set, he paused on a rocky outcrop, enjoying the view of neat farmsteads below. Although many abandoned farms on the village outskirts were overrun by weed and thicket, whitewashed barns and stone-walled cottages clustered in lush pastures along the meandering stream. In the middle of the vale a placid millpond reflected a sunset of orange and red.

Pawns Prevail

Though weary from the march and hungry after several days of scavenging food, Holt checked the lower pasture on his way back to the cottage. He knew that Besserel and the other cows would be up in the barn already for evening milking, but only when he was satisfied that nothing disturbed the farm did Holton start up the trail to the farmstead. His father, who spent his days in a wheeled chair, was remarkably capable around the house and barn, but the legless farmer couldn't get into the pastures and fields.

It was nearly dark when he reached the little cottage. The shutters stood open to the warm night, revealing the cozy glow of lamplight within. Holt heard conversation from inside and recognized his father talking with—or more accurately, listening to—their neighbor, Nowell, son of Nowscon. Holt and most of the other Daryfolk knew him as Nowell the Aching since he always complained of pains whenever a nettlesome task needed doing.

Setting the wolfskin down outside, Holt pushed open the front door. He saw his father's weathered face, suddenly creased by a grin of relief. Derek Jaken's broad hand rose in a wave of greeting to his son, and he swiveled his chair as Holt settled wearily onto a stool.

"Where have you been these past days!" cried Nowell after realizing that Derek intended no rebuke for his son. The neighbor was a stooped tub of a man, who walked with a limp and stood with a crooked back. His hands were gnarled, with fingers that twisted like the roots of a tree.

He took a pained breath before sputtering further recriminations. "You left your father here by himself! A farm to tend, and him with no legs! With butter and cheese ready for market, and ice melting in the storerooms? And not just your own, but the whole valley's! What about the rest of—"

"I saw wolf prints along the stream," Holt said. "I followed the trail into the Knollbarrens."

Nowell fell silent, looking hesitantly at Derek Jaken, who frowned at the news.

"It's been a long time since a wolf has come to Oxvale," Jaken observed solemnly.

"Near twenty years," Nowell agreed, "since they fled into the 'Barrens for good—I thought!"

"This one won't be back," Holt promised, privately skeptical about Nowell's part in the Troll War. "I've got his skin outside." He thought of the wolf's last hateful glare, those eyes seeming to glow like coals, but he dismissed the vision, attributing it to his overactive imagination. He would say nothing about that to his father—and certainly not to Nowell the Aching.

"The spring cheeses . . ." their neighbor griped. "They'll be past their peak if you don't get them to the market. You should have gone two days ago!"

"I'm sorry," sighed Holt. He had forgotten that

he'd promised to make the market trip for the village. In past years the three-day journey had been made by Mill, son of Miller, but since the elder Miller had died last winter the younger had inherited the full workload at the mill. The prospect of another journey after only a short night's rest made Holt feel even more tired. Yet he knew his duty to his father and his village. "I'll be ready to go first thing in the morning."

* * * * *

"It hasn't been easy, these eighteen years," Derek said quietly as the two Jakens finished their late evening meal. "You know, when your mother passed on and you were just a hungry toddler—and me stuck in this chair—I feared you'd not grow to manhood."

Holt, stuffed with hearty oat porridge and a pheasant from his father's snares, put down his spoon. Despite Nowell's complaints, Holton reflected that his father had managed to cope pretty well in his absence.

"I've had a good life," he said, embarrassed by his father's bluntness.

"Goin' after that wolf, and killin' it . . . you made me proud."

"It was something anybody else would have done," Holt protested. Again he thought of those

27

coal-red eyes, and wondered if he were telling the truth.

Derek smiled gently. "You're the only young man in Oxvale—the only *healthy* man. You've borne a lot of burdens."

"I don't see them as burdens," Holt replied. "I've had the chance to hunt . . . to fish, and to build. And if I do my share of the work, it's only because you and the other men sacrificed so much more during the Troll War."

"Still, I wish I could've given you more . . . some schooling, a chance to learn a trade. . . ."

"I can run a farm, make cheese . . . mill grain, lay the stone for a house! Didn't I shape the beams and build that barn with my own hands? I think I know all the trades I need to know," Holt declared.

Again Derek smiled, but there was a trace of sadness in the expression. "I'm not sure those skills will serve you in Vanderton."

"I can take care of myself in the city. It can't be worse than the Knollbarrens!"

"Don't be so certain, lad. The dangers in Vanderton are different than those in the wilderness—different, but no less real."

"Besides, I've been there before," Holt said defensively.

"But it was years back, and you had Nowell and Mill, son of Miller, with you. Now you'll go alone. . . ."

"With the full wealth of three month's labor," concluded the younger man. "And I'll fetch the worth of that cheese, you can be sure!"

Derek held up an apologetic hand. "Don't take me wrong. I know you'll do the best for Oxvale of any man here. It's just that, well—I feel for you! I wish it didn't have to be this way. If you could have been born later, you wouldn't have all this to bear—"

"And if I'd been born earlier, I'd have perished in the Winter of Tears, just like all the others," Holt shot back. "I was born when I was, and if that makes me the only young man in the village, then so be it!"

"There's a lot of wisdom in what you say," Derek agreed. "I know this as well: if your mother had lived beyond that bleak winter—if she were here today—she would be very proud of you."

Squirming uncomfortably, Holt wondered why his father pressed these unusual thoughts on him tonight.

"Tell me about the wolf," Derek said.

Holt described the discovery of the tracks, the pursuit, and the fight.

"Did you see its eyes?" his father asked deliberately.

Any icy shiver ran along Holt's spine. Dumbly, he nodded.

"A warwolf," Derek said grimly. "This is very

bad—it means that there are matters of the Troll War that remain unfinished."

"What kind of 'matters'?" asked the son, sharing his father's obvious unease.

"Ah, let's talk of other things," Derek Jaken said, shaking his head stubbornly. "D'you know the Highland Sharp cheese is especially good this year?"

"I thought it would be," Holt agreed, knowing his father would comment no further. "Though Nowell probably had something bad to say about it."

"Even Nowell, chronic complainer that he is, has pronounced it the best in recent memory—almost as good as his own," the older man disputed with an easy grin.

"I don't know why you listen to him!" Holt said scornfully.

"Even Nowell has a good side—many good sides," Derek replied, gently chiding his son. "Don't be too hasty to condemn your neighbors."

"But Nowell? You heard how he talked about you—like you're helpless or something! I don't know why you—"

"That's *enough!*" barked Derek, and Holt immediately fell silent. "Perhaps it's because Nowell remembers me when I was a whole man—how can I *not* seem helpless to him now?"

Though he knew that his father had lost his legs

during the early campaigns of the Troll War, Holt had never learned the cause of Derek's misfortune. Neither his father nor any of the neighbors would discuss the matter with Holt. Now, hearing Derek talk about Nowell's memories, the questions all came back. But Holt could not speak.

Instead, they quietly tidied up the cottage together before turning in. Lying in the darkness, listening to his father's snores, Holt couldn't keep his eyes closed. At first his mind was occupied with all the things he'd need to do to make his trip to Vanderton—oil the harnesses, check Old Thunder's shoes for wear, grease the cart wheels, load the cheese from his own farm and the neighbors'. . . .

Still planning, he closed his eyes in exhaustion. When at last he did fall asleep, he tossed and turned restlessly, disturbed by dreams in which a wolf with red eyes chased his heavily laden wagon down the road.

3
A Road to Market

Dawn barely colored the eastern skyline when Holton made his way to the barn. Derek already sat beside Besserel, collecting a bucket of milk. Terressa and Cici, the other two cows, patiently waited their turns.

In the cellar beside the barn, Holt found the cheese he and his father had made over the winter. Carefully thumping each wheel with his finger, he selected only those that had fully aged. About three dozen of the heavy wheels, all told, were ready for market, and he carried these, two at a time, to the big farm cart waiting in the yard.

Pawns Prevail

" 'Morning, Holton my boy!" The hearty voice called from the lane, and Holt saw Codwell the Elder wheeling a full barrow. "Got room for a few more wheels?"

"Sure, you're early enough to get them the best spot!" Holt replied as the wiry farmer—their second-closest neighbor and an esteemed citizen of Oxvale—brought his own small bundle to the cart.

Codwell kept only one cow. His high status as a Daryman was attained because he owned the best bull in all the commons. Holt had tended the animal many times and admired as much as he feared the snorting nostrils, the powerful neck, and the proud, tapering horns.

"A fine day for market," came another greeting as Hag Biddlesome approached down the Hightrack. Holt didn't know the crone's age, but Hag had been a very old woman when he first became aware of the world around him. Now her rail-thin body, robed in a soft woolen cloak, stooped forward from the weight of her own cheese.

Helping her with the load, Holt remembered how, in the early years of his life, Hag had often helped his father with household chores. Her stern voice and the rap of her bony knuckles had been all too common as she forced Holt to learn the basics of sewing, cooking, weaving, and other boring pastimes.

Hag pressed a package into Holt's hand, and the

aroma of fresh-baked eggbread teased his nostrils. "A little something to carry you on the road," said the old woman, her thin hand touching him on the shoulder.

"Can somebody give me some help with this?" Nowell the Aching shouted from the far end of the lane. He sat on a stump beside his small wheelbarrow and rubbed one knee piteously. Holt resignedly trudged down the track and trundled his neighbor's barrow back to the cart.

By this time the others had gathered. Karl Fisher brought his small wedges of sharp, rock-hard cheese. Karl's nets provided bass and trout for the village, and even his cheese retained a suggestion of that fishy flavor. Holt knew that, pound for pound in Vanderton, it fetched the best price of any Oxvale cheese.

The Wilbert brothers, three old men who worked a large, common farmstead across the river, brought their own barrows, and several farmwives hauled their loads from the upland steadings. The Daryfolk chatted quietly, offering Holt advice as he lashed each new bundle to the cart. Fully loaded, the stack of cheeses rose as high as his head, and Holton knew that it would be a long, slow plod to Vanderton. As the sun crested the treetops, he felt a growing urgency to be on his way.

His father, meanwhile, had fed and harnessed Old Thunder. The huge horse tromped reluctantly over to the cart, standing between the traces while Holt lifted the brace and latched the buckles. The two-wheeled cart rocked slightly backward, but the load was well balanced and securely bound in place.

"A day to town, a day to sell, and one more to return," Hag said, wagging a finger at him. "Don't waste your time in any of those smoking houses!"

"I won't," Holt promised. He cast them a wave as he started down the lane.

Though the cart had a high, narrow seat, the young Daryman preferred to walk—at least to start out the journey. Besides, the load was heavy, and he felt a certain amount of sympathy for Old Thunder. The horse, muddy yellow in color, was stubborn and irritable, but Holt knew that the big gelding would plod along tirelessly through the day. The least Holt could do was spare the steed the extra load of his weight.

Thunder's broad hooves, surrounded by shaggy fetlocks, thumped to the road. Curls of dust puffed upward with each clopping step. The spring weather had left the road dry and the sky clear, and Holt relished the steady pace of the walk and the budding greenery around them.

Soon they reached the valley of the mighty Tannyv River, where the bluish-green water provided a sparkling contrast to the dark, lush foliage crowding its banks. The road meandered for many miles, always in sight of the sunlit ripples that glittered like emeralds on the fast-flowing water.

The Tannyv cut through this wide, pastoral valley, collecting the runoff from the highlands and the wilderlands beyond. Joined by tributaries spilling from the Knollbarrens to the east, the river swelled quickly for the final portion of its progress to the sea.

The city of Vanderton, capital of the realm of Vanderthan, would lie on the far bank of the river. Holt recalled the towering heights of Castle Vanderthan, smooth walls of white marble reflecting so brightly that even in starlight the great fortress was visible for miles. The King of Vanderthan was widely hailed as the mightiest monarch in all Karawenn—except of course for the High King of Humankind, who ruled from his distant palace at the foot of the Trollheight Mountains. Though Oxvale was removed from the main highways of the Vanderthan realm, the Daryfolk had always been loyal to their noble rulers. Unlike folk in the larger towns, however, the Daryfolk had no local lords of their own.

Idly Holt wondered what life in the palace was like for the aged king and his lifelong queen? It was an existence very foreign to his own, he imagined—but not a life he would choose. He knew that the king and queen had a daughter, and his imagination stretched enough that he felt a little sorry for the princess, First Daughter of Vanderthan. No doubt she lived a life of social rules and restrictions. Perhaps she'd never even had the chance to walk the River Road!

Occasionally Holt paused to rest at the bank of the river, first eating Hag's eggbread down to the last crumb and later chewing on the tough hardtack that was his usual trail ration. At each stop, Old Thunder found a clump of clover or wild oats and munched contentedly until the Daryman was ready to go on.

Time flowed nearly as quickly as the aquamarine waters of the mighty Tannyv. Old Thunder plodded, looking neither right nor left. Sometimes the big gelding grunted and strained to pull the cart over ruts, but most of the time he just lumbered along.

By late afternoon Holt's muscles grew weary from the steady, slow pace, but when they came around a bend and the full glory of Castle Vanderthan rose before him, his fatigue fell away like an old cloak. A slanting ray of sun lit the alabaster fortress like a beacon. From the highest towers, two pennants of royal blue trailed in the gentle breeze. Seeing the crown and scepter on each of the banners, Holt knew that the king and queen were in residence. The sword-and-shield banner that indicated the First Daughter's presence at the castle was not raised. Perhaps the princess did get to go out on this splendid day, thought Holt with a measure of satisfaction.

The River Road descended through several sharp curves as it approached the bank of the Tannyv. Before the city of Vanderton, the river narrowed. A long, single-tracked bridge spanned the gorge, allowing the farmers of Oxvale and other valley settlements to reach the city without a long detour to a ferry crossing.

Wide enough only for a single cart, the bridge surface hung nearly a hundred feet over the surging waters. Sheer walls of rock plunged away, forming a deep, steep-sided channel below. Heavy chains supported the bridge, and though the span swayed slightly in the breeze, Holt enjoyed the sensation of height as he led Old Thunder onto the worn planks.

With a tingle of anticipation, Holt pictured the teeming lower city of Vanderton, mentally planning for the upcoming night and day. He would find an inn with a stable, rent a cheap room, and keep a careful watch over his cheese. Excitedly he thought of tomorrow's market—the bustle of buying and selling, an eye kept alert for thieves, and the growing weight of coin in his purse. With a little good fortune, this load of cheese would provide money enough to last the farmers of Oxvale through the summer.

Carefully he guided the horse along. He watched

Pawns Prevail

the cart wheels to see that they remained on the road planks, which rose several inches above the bed of the bridge. The sound of rushing water buffeted him like a strong wind, and ahead the castle loomed even higher. Lesser structures of the upper city, including the mansions of nobles, the royal mint, and the great columns and fountains of Vanderton's public squares, surrounded the castle walls and keep.

Holt's heart quickened with excitement and anticipation; in another few moments he'd be among those buildings, and the life of the city would be his.

* * * * *

A rose petal token fluttered on the surface of the immortal pool. A play was made in Immortal Hall; on Karawenn a wasp buzzed angrily upward, looking for the cause of its ire.

4
The Princess

Halfway across the bridge, the normally placid draft horse, with a sharp whinny of annoyance, lurched to one side. Holt saw a wasp buzzing away from the gelding's ear, and reached for the bridle to pull Old Thunder's head around.

But already one of the cart wheels teetered at the edge of the planking, and when Thunder again leaned toward Holt, that wheel slipped downward, lodging between two of the trestles below. The horse, startled again by the sudden resistance, pulled harder.

Holt's heart sank as he saw the wheel bend on

its axle. With a loud *snap,* the mounting bracket gave way, and the cart dropped to the planks. Twisted partly sideways, the disabled wagon wedged itself firmly between the two rails of the bridge. Thunder yanked and reared, straining to pull free, but that only jammed the cart more tightly in place.

"Easy, old fellow," Holt soothed, placing a hand between the draft horse's snorting nostrils. "We'll get you out of here—just you settle down, now."

How to get the wagon loose was another question. In despair, he studied the situation. Perhaps, using the tongue of the tracings as a lever, he could pry the cart free from its jammed position. But then there was the broken wheel to deal with. In fact, he wasn't even sure if the big horse would be able to drag the load.

Resignedly, he looked at the massive stack of cheeses. He would have to carry them, one sackload at a time, to the end of the bridge. Then he'd have to find someone to guard them while he got the cart repaired. And after that . . . he could see that he wouldn't be getting to bed anytime early tonight.

A steady cadence of hoofbeats thrummed through the bridge at Holt's feet. Unnoticed by him, four armored riders had approached, rushing down River Road. They cantered onto the end of the bridge, then skittered to a halt behind the

Douglas Niles

obstacle of Holt's wagon.

The first rider wore gleaming plate-mail armor, including a shining helm with a lowered faceplate. Despite the bulk of the metal covering, the person seemed slight, smaller than Holt would have expected of a knight. Two other horsemen wore chain-mail shirts and open-faced helmets. They pressed forward at the flanks of the leader, while the fourth rider, a small fellow mounted on a pony, hung back.

The leader's leather-gloved hand reached up to push back the visor of the helm. Holt gaped at the smooth, haughty face of a young woman. Her high cheekbones accented the sharp gaze of her green eyes, while strands of golden hair coiled around her cheeks, unruly enough to spring outward from the warlike helmet. Her features might have been lovely in different circumstances. Now, framed by the metal helm, her appearance was cold and formidable.

"Move this wagon, farmboy—*now!*" barked the woman in a tone of command that banished all thoughts of beauty and grace from Holt's mind.

"It's stuck," he explained. "The wheel broke. As soon as I get my cargo unloaded, I can pull it out of—"

"We have no *time!*" spat the woman. She turned to the two men who flanked her. "Korth, Ferrill—dump it over the side."

Pawns Prevail

The two men dismounted and started toward the rear of the cart while Holt stared in disbelief. Surely she was joking!

"You can't!" he burst out as the men reached for the rear of the cart. "That's a whole winter's—"

"Mind your tongue, farmboy!" snapped the rider. "I can and, in the name of the Crown of Vanderthan, I will! We're on business more important than you can comprehend."

Holt wanted to leap at the warriors, to push them away from the cart. Yet the swaggering confidence of Korth and Ferrill convinced him that any such resistance would be madness.

"You don't understand! This cheese is all the produce of my village—you can't just throw it away!"

The young woman remained silent.

"Best take hold of your horse, lad," the man-at-arms called Korth said. His voice was not unkindly, but his gestures were firm as he seized the back of the cart.

Old Thunder reared, and Holt seized his reins, hauling hard as he tried to settle the jittery steed. The stack of cheese lurched, and frantically the Daryman unsnapped the harness connecting the horse to the cart.

Numb with disbelief, he watched the two burly guards lean against the load, pressing the cart upward until it balanced on the railing. Several

Douglas Niles

squares of cheese tumbled free, and impulsively Holt scrambled forward and seized one bundle.

The wagon toppled over, plummeting quickly to the turbulent river below. Holt wanted to cry out as the water splashed upward. Wheels of cheese bounced into the air as the cart splintered into pieces, and then the cheese, cart wheels, and wreckage vanished beneath the frothing surface.

"Now, stand aside!" said the woman. Her tone had lost its anger, though it was no less firm.

"Who are you?" asked Holt, still numb.

"Stand aside for Princess Danis, First Daughter of Vanderthan!" declared Korth.

The Daryman was forced back to the railing as Danis put the spurs to her steed and the war-horse charged forward. The two guards, swiftly mounting, followed.

Only then did Holt get a good look at the fourth rider. He saw bushy sideburns and wide, rounded cheeks. The fellow, no bigger than a child, had the features of an old man—a halfling, Holt realized. The little person shook his head sadly, and then galloped after his companions.

Trembling, Old Thunder followed Holt to the end of the bridge. The Daryman looked down, bitterly thankful that the cheese he had salvaged was the high-priced sharp of Karl Fisher.

Then he looked up at the castle, where the four riders already thundered over the drawbridge and through the open gates. The third pennant, banner of the sword and shield signifying the First Daughter's presence, rose up the high flagpole above the keep.

Holt thought of the lost cheese, the wasted months, and he knew that he couldn't let things stand as they did. Nodding his head in firm determination, he made up his mind. He pulled himself onto Old Thunder's broad back, and gently urged the horse into an ambling walk.

They reached the first corner, where a riverside lane led toward the vast market plaza of Low City. Here Holt turned uphill, toward the castle.

5
Castle Vanderthan

"Ho, men! Stand alert for Lord Knight and his bold charger!"

The guard at the castle gate cried a mock warning to his fellows, and the small company laughed appreciatively at the lanky farmer on dusty, shambling Old Thunder. The horse clopped across the drawbridge toward the open gates.

The laughter died as the guard who had spoken sauntered into the gateway, barring Holt's passage into the castle. "Surely you took a wrong turn, lad—this is Castle Vanderthan. The waterfront slum rows are down the hill there."

Pawns Prevail

Through the arched gateway Holt looked in wonder at the white walls of the keep itself, as well as the ornate hedges and fountains of a formal garden. His attention turned to the guard who blocked his path. The man, his round head capped by an upside-down bowl of a helmet, sneered up at him.

"I pray, Lord Guardsman," Holt began, swinging down from Thunder's broad back. "I've come to speak with your castle cook about some cheese— cheese I can claim in truth to be the best in all Karawenn!"

"Bold words," said the gatehouse guard skeptically. Still, he all but drooled as he looked at the bundle in Holt's hand. The other men-at-arms, a half dozen or so, crowded forward for a look.

"Good warriors!" said Holt. He drew several more chunks of Karl Fisher's cheese from his satchel. "Try these—and you'll agree to give me passage to your kitchens!"

" 'Tis good, I'll grant," smacked the first guardsman. The others mumbled their agreement around mouthfuls of sharp cheese. Within moments the samples had disappeared.

"Very good, even," the watchman continued. "But we can't give you passage to the kitchens— that's the main keep, and you've got to be invited." He grinned maliciously.

"Perhaps this will serve to get me an invitation,"

47

Douglas Niles

Holt offered, thinking fast. He pulled another piece of cheese from the dwindling sack. "Here's a sample for the chief cook, with another waiting for the man who takes it to him and brings back my passage into the castle!"

"Let me take it!"

"Give it here!"

Six burly men pressed forward, but the chief spokesman bellowed over their offers.

"*I'll* go!"

"Many thanks, Lord Guardsman," Holt said, offering the bundle with a deep bow.

"Keep an eye on this lout," the fellow commanded, snatching the cheese and marching into the castle.

The other guards, disappointed, turned back to their post in boredom. Several picked up a pair of small, cubelike stones and began to roll the objects on the floor, cursing or exclaiming at the results. Holt eased Old Thunder into the shade of the gatehouse. In the courtyard of the castle, beside the neat hedges of the great garden, he saw a rail fence and several haystacks flanking a weathered plank barn.

"Can I take my horse to the stable?" he asked. "That way I won't keep the cook waiting when I get word."

Two of the guards looked at each other over their dice and shrugged. "Go ahead—just get back here in a hurry!"

All but trotting across the courtyard, he led Old Thunder into the large barn that stood near the gatehouse. Sleek racers and tall, snorting chargers occupied many of the stalls, though none of the steeds was quite so large as the draft horse. Holt quickly found an empty corral, and Thunder began to munch on a pile of hay as the Daryman closed the gate behind him.

Looking around quickly, Holt saw several doors out the far side of the stable. He ducked through one of these, out of sight of the gatehouse, and hurried past a long hedge. His heart pounded as he turned a corner, hoping he was out of sight of the gatehouse guards.

Only then did he see that he had entered the formal garden. Tall hedges surrounded him, and through gaps, he saw several bright flower beds.

He heard voices. Several young men, wearing sleek jackets and silken leggings, rushed around a corner of the hedge. Their hair fell in carefully curled ringlets around their cheeks, and they looked disdainfully at Holt as they hurried past.

Cautiously pressing onward, Holt felt acutely conscious of his long, unkempt hair. He looked at the ridges of dirt under his fingernails, the mud that spattered his boots and his oft-patched leather trousers. Combing his fingers through his hair, he at least forced the unruly locks behind his ears as he continued forward.

Hedges taller than his head rose to each side. The lofty spires of Vanderthan Keep climbed, clearly visible, into the sky, allowing him to keep his bearings as he worked his way through the garden.

He came around a corner where a side passage opened up. The hedges curved outward to circle a large reflecting pool, and the Princess of Vanderthan stood near the edge of the water. She had removed her helmet, apparently just moments earlier since her hair still clung to her perspiring forehead. Her sculpted face was locked in an expression of determination.

Before her paced the elderly halfling Holt had seen on the pony. That worthy gentleman wrung his hands and bobbed back and forth so quickly that the Daryman feared he would soon wear a trench into the ground.

A third person stood in the garden, his back to Holt. The young man recognized the chain-mail armor and long black hair of the guardsman Korth who had ridden at the princess's side. The warrior's sword still swung from his waist.

"Where *is* he?" demanded the halfling. "We summoned him *hours* ago—as soon as we lost the trail!"

The young woman was not listening. Instead, she stalked back and forth beside the pool, her face frowning in frustration. "I can't believe Papa won't see me now! What's so important about that treaty that he can't take ten minutes to hear my news?"

"Now, now, my dear—the king can't just dismiss the Ambassador of Bedford. Why, it might start a war!" The halfling tried to soothe the princess, apparently without success—she continued to pace and frown.

A fourth figure suddenly popped into sight next to Princess Danis, and Holt gasped at the nature of the newcomer's arrival. The white-whiskered man hadn't walked or run into the clearing—he hadn't even dropped out of the sky! He had simply popped into view and hovered there, his hands clutching something over his head. He now blinked in befuddlement through narrow, rounded spectacles as he swung back and forth several inches above the ground.

The fellow clung with both hands to a large metal hook. The other end of the hook was a bolt that was attached to absolutely nothing, as if it had latched onto the sky itself! The swinging motion slowly subsided, and the man released the hook and tumbled into a sitting position on the ground. He wiped his glasses as he scrambled awkwardly to his feet.

"Hello? Is that—oh, I see that it is! How nice to see you again, my dear!"

"Yes, Tellist, it's me," Danis said in exasperation

that was nevertheless affectionate. "We've been waiting for you."

"What in all Karawenn *took* you so long?" squealed the halfling, marching up to the older man's belt and staring at him.

"Well, now, that's a long story—a *complicated* story, too," said Tellist. He turned to the long hook and lifted it upward, unhitching it from its invisible support. Folding the device numerous times, he reduced it to a small bundle that he put in his pocket.

Tellist was a tall man with a wispy beard and thin strands of hair stretched tightly over his balding pate. Watery eyes squinted through his silver-rimmed glasses as he made a great effort to remember. "I received your summons right on time—certainly the magical wind chime worked just the way it was supposed to. Though I suppose I should work with the bass tube—it was ringing a bit flat. Yes, that's—"

"If you *don't* mind," snapped the halfling. "We're here to discuss the problem of the warwolves, not the wind chime!"

"Gazzrick's right," the princess said.

"And I was explaining about the problems I had getting to this meeting about the warwolves!" replied Tellist frostily. "If that's not relevant, I don't know what is. Now, as I was saying, I arrived at the waterfront by mistake. Folks there were excited—seems there was a whole float of cheese coming by, like magic. In fact, they wanted me to see if it was magic, but it wasn't—that's *part* of what kept me."

Danis placed a restraining hand on the sputtering halfling, as if she sensed that the fastest way to get to the discussion was to allow the befuddled magic-user to complete his preamble.

"Then, since I had teleported to the wrong place, I had to learn that darn spell all over again so I could teleport up here. And that, as you know, takes me a few hours."

"The waterfront is a fifteen minute *walk* from here!" sputtered Gazzrick Whiptoe.

"Why, so it is! I must remember that next time," noted the wizard.

At the reminder of his lost cheeses, Holt stepped forward, determined to speak up, to demand payment for the cargo. But some hunter's instinct held his tongue, and instead he watched, still partially screened by the hedge.

"Now, *I* didn't see any warwolves," Tellist offered. "But I take it somebody else did?"

"There've been two sightings. One came down from the highlands," Danis explained. "It killed a herd of sheep along our border with Bedford. The royal huntsmen have tracked it into the hills—it seems to be heading back to the wilderlands."

"And the other?"

Pawns Prevail

"Down in the Tannyv Valley—only a dozen leagues from here," Danis asserted. "No one knows where it came from—and now it's disappeared. We've lost the trail!"

"Right." Tellist's voice became crisp, authoritative. "Then the best thing to do is wait!"

"Wait?" Gazzrick cried. The halfling's round face reddened. "That's *madness!* We've got to do *something!*"

"It's an emergency! I wanted to tell Father that we should muster the militia," Danis said urgently. Holt noticed that the others grew quiet when she spoke. "We raced back here as fast as we could—but he won't even *talk* to me!"

"He's busy in a treaty conference," Gazzrick explained helpfully.

"Tut, tut," cautioned the magic-user, holding up a frail-looking hand. "We mustn't be hasty. This wolf, I believe, is the portent that we've awaited . . . for um, well, for a long time. Now's not the time to overreact."

"Calling out the troops is a *sensible* precaution," Gazzrick argued. "At least we'll be ready for the wolves if they attack!"

"Oh, I don't think they'll do that. Not yet, anyway." Tellist scratched the wisps of hair on his head, as if trying to coax some decision from his brain. "No, I think that it won't be long before we get a sign—an indication as to what this is all about."

55

Douglas Niles

"A sign from *whom?*" demanded the halfling.

"Why, the immortals, of course. At least, one of them."

Holt was wondering what the old man meant when a burly hand seized him by the shoulder.

"What are *you* doing here?" demanded Korth, nudging Holt forward, toward the startled trio in the garden.

"It's the farmboy with the cheese cart!" exclaimed Danis, her jaw dropping in surprise.

"Well, don't be shy, lad," Korth encouraged, squeezing his hand a bit. "Why are you here?"

"I—I came because it wasn't fair, what you did!" Holt stammered, finally squirming free of the guardsman's grip. Tugging his shirt back into place, the young Daryman did his best to stand straight and firm. "That cheese was the work of a whole village, over a long, cold winter," he went on. "It's all we have to trade! I would have gotten it out of your way—you could even have helped," he added, turning to Korth. "Now I ask that you don't send me home empty-handed."

"How did you get in here?" demanded Danis, taking a step toward Holt. "I told you—we were on an urgent task. We couldn't waste a minute!"

The Daryman held his ground. Gazzrick, Holt noticed, had cast his eyes down to the ground. Now he raised a fist to his mouth and coughed gently, catching the eye of the princess. The halfling nodded meaningfully toward the Daryman.

The princess studied Holt, and he couldn't help but squirm under the scrutiny. Her eyes seemed incredibly bright, and he felt as though all his flaws were revealed to them. She looked away, apparently lost in thought, and then turned to Korth.

"I authorize the treasury to compensate the farmboy for his cheese," she told the guard captain. "See if you can work out an accounting." The matter dispensed with, she turned back to the magic-user and the halfling.

Holt was elated by her decision, and emboldened by his good fortune.

"About the warwolf. . . the one in the Tannyv Valley," he said, hesitating only slightly. "Could it have wandered up to Oxvale?"

Danis bit back a sharp reply. "Perhaps," she said grudgingly.

"The trail was leading north when we lost it," Gazzrick noted. "If the beast had turned away from the river it could have gone right around Oxvale."

"Did you *see* it?" The voice of the princess was cold, demanding.

"Not there," Holt replied. "I tracked it into the Knollbarrens. There I not only saw it, I killed it!" he concluded proudly.

"What?" demanded Gazzrick, surprising Holt by

the depth of his consternation.

"You'd best watch your tongue, lad," said Korth warningly. "Lies will get you nowhere but the dungeon!"

"I killed it, I tell you—hunted it down and brought the skin home with me!"

"What did you use—the enchanted blade of your heroic ancestor?" snapped Danis. For some reason the scorn in her tone hurt worse even than the loss of the cheese.

"I killed it with an arrow," Holt said evenly, trying to control his anger.

"Throw the arrogant farmboy out!" Danis cried, turning her back to Holt. Korth seized him by the collar and started toward the gatehouse.

"Wait—my payment!" protested the Daryman.

"I make no payment to liars!" shouted the princess.

"It's the *truth!*"

"Stop now, lad—or it *will* be the dungeon," said the guardsman gently, prodding Holt around a corner of the hedgerow.

Squirming free from the man's burly hand, the young farmer stared furiously at him. "I'm not lying!" he insisted.

Korth's mustache drooped in an expression that was not unsympathetic. "You don't seem like a liar," the guard admitted. "I think you actually believe what you're saying. But whatever you killed, it wasn't a warwolf."

"How can you say that?" demanded Holt as they continued toward the stable. "Why don't you believe me?"

"It's the warwolves, son," said the man. "You see, they have the magical protection of entropy—the dark force. Their fur is a magical barrier—it protects them against even a slight cut into the skin. Even the strongest man can't thrust a lance through that coat. . . . I don't know how you could kill one with an arrow."

"I shot it in the mouth!" Holt said bluntly.

Korth paused, his eyebrows raised. "Pretty amazing shot for a farmer," he murmured.

"I *did!*" Holt's face flushed.

"In that case you'll just have to take it as a lesson, lad—next time you see the First Daughter of Vanderthan, try not to get her mad."

Furiously, Holt turned away. If he had anything to say about it, there wouldn't *be* a next time.

* * * * *

The artifact of the immortals was made. A splendid thing of gold and gemstone, a crown, created as a most treasured possession and intended for the First Daughter of Vanderthan.

When the artifact token was played, the crown sailed through the spheres, plunging toward its destiny upon Karawenn.

Before it could land, however, the chaos token entered the pool. The flight of the artifact went awry, as the effects of chaos rippled through the spheres of the Immortals, the mortal world, and even into the desolate realm of Entropy.

There, in the bleak center of darkness, a cage was opened . . . and a power freed.

6
Skysign of an Immortal

A blinding flash of light brightened the garden, as if the sun had suddenly pulsed with brilliance.

"Brimstone's beard!" cursed Korth, raising a hand to shield his eyes.

Holt looked upward, squinting into the blue sky, and clearly saw the source of the flash. An object brighter than a star streaked overhead, leaving a lingering trail of sparks and smoke. The shooting star blasted from west to east, quickly disappearing beyond the horizon. In its wake the pathway sparkled, glaring and pulsing with an intensity that paralyzed Holton in awestruck wonder.

In another instant, a thunderous boom rocked the air like a physical force, the sound reverberating with gut-pounding power until it slowly faded to an echo. Only then did the ground shudder, lurching underfoot for one quick moment, as if something immensely powerful had seized and shaken the world itself.

"By all the spheres—what *was* that?" gasped the guard captain.

"It was like a shooting star—but a thousand times as bright!" declared the Daryman, his despair of a minute earlier replaced by awe.

They heard cries of commotion from the castle walls, and guards at the gate rushed into the courtyard, staring in wonder at the trail of smoke that slowly vanished in the sky.

"I've got to get back to the princess," Korth said abruptly. "You get your horse and ride for home— and if you know what's good for you, you won't look back!"

"I *did* kill a warwolf!" Holt insisted stubbornly.

Korth sighed and shook his head. "Whether I believe you or not just doesn't matter," he declared. The guard broke into a trot toward the garden, leaving Holt alone.

Miserably, Holt watched Korth go. The Daryman's anger had faded, replaced by a bleak sense of failure and despair. The spectacular comet had momentarily taken his mind off his dispute with Danis Vanderthan. Now he realized that he would be forced to return to the village and report that his neighbors had wasted half a year's work. It galled him further to realize that his appeal for compensation had been denied only because he hadn't kept silent about the warwolf. He had only stated the truth, but it seemed there were times when even the truth was best left unspoken.

Holt mounted Old Thunder, and the big horse clopped through the courtyard and past the guards in the gatehouse, who had quickly returned to their game after gaping at the trail in the sky. Evening settled around the town, and the Daryman thought for a moment of bartering his remaining square of cheese for a night's lodging. He couldn't bring himself to squander the precious remnant, however, so instead he guided Old Thunder back across the narrow bridge. There was no sign of wreckage in the water or along the banks below—the cheese had probably floated all the way to the sea by now.

Following the road just far enough to get beyond the noise and torchlight of the city, Holt turned Old Thunder loose to graze and found a grassy bower where he could spend the night. Clouds rolled across the stars after sunset, and intermittent showers soaked and chilled him until the gray and soggy dawn.

The sun emerged listlessly. Depressed, Holt decided to put off his return journey for a while, drying his bedroll and tunic while he caught a few perch from the river. His camp was screened from the road, and though he heard a few carts and some playing children go by, he didn't see anyone.

By the time his clothes were dry, half the day was gone, and since he wasn't expected home until the morrow he found it easy to mope away the afternoon at the riverbank.

Hoofbeats called his attention to the road, and curiosity compelled him to peer through the bushes—though he remained concealed behind a mossy stump. Princess Danis herself galloped past, accompanied by Korth, Gazzrick, the magic-user, and three men-at-arms. The sight of her reminded Holt of his failure, and sent him miserably back to his fishing pole. As if in cruel spite, the perch ignored him for the rest of the day, and he ate a lean supper.

The following day he started early for home. The trip back to Oxvale seemed to take twice as long as the journey to the city. How could he break the news of his disastrous mission? Though he anguished over this question throughout the long ride home, he couldn't arrive at any satisfactory answer.

The Oxvale road led upward from the river valley,

and in time he crossed through the familiar meadows of the lower pastures. As soon as he passed the farm of Nowell the Aching, he sensed that something was wrong—something more sinister than the loss of their winter's cheese. Nowell's shutters were tightly closed, and heavy bolts secured the barn doors.

Prodding Old Thunder into a lumbering canter, Holt hurried home. There, too, shutters and doors were closed and bolted, though as he dismounted in the yard the front door of the house flew open.

"Thank the spheres you're alive!" cried Derek, wheeling along the planking of the front walk.

"Father! What's wrong?"

"It's wolves! A whole pack came through in the night!"

"Was anybody hurt? What did they do?" he asked, dreading the answer. He should have been here—why had he wasted time yesterday?

"Codwell's bull was killed," said Derek. "As for us, Besserel and Tess are in the barn—but Cici didn't come back this morning. Codwell's gone to look for her now."

The thought of Codwell's mighty bull slain was too stunning for Holt to comprehend. He'd always pictured the animal as the ultimate pillar of strength in the valley. Yet if it could fall prey to these savage predators . . .

"Where are the wolves now?" asked Holt.

Douglas Niles

"Seem to have moved on this morning," Derek replied. "Going east—like they was following that comet."

Now Holt noticed Nowell the Aching, tentatively coming down the lane, peering this way and that as if he expected a pack of wolves to emerge, snarling, from the bushes of the front garden.

"I see you made it back," Nowell acknowledged. "At least there's *some* good news."

"Don't count on it," Holt warned.

"You haven't heard the worst," Derek told his son, his voice dropping ominously. "The *graveyard* was desecrated at the same time. Whatever came through here was strong enough to dig up each grave."

"And the bodies have been stolen!" Nowell added with a shudder.

At that moment Codwell came around the barn. The old man's boots were covered with mud, and he carried a stout walking stick. If the loss of his bull had affected his spirit in any way, the fact didn't show at first glance.

He looked at Derek and shook his head.

"The wolves got yer cow down by the creek," he said bluntly. "Cici gave 'em a bit of a run, but they caught up to her in the soft ground."

Holt's throat tightened with grief, but in another moment he felt his hands trembling in fury. He was gripped by a sense of violation, as if life itself had conspired to treat him unfairly.

"Were the tracks going east?" Derek asked.

"Sure enough," replied the old Daryman.

Hag Biddlesome arrived, and Holt told the tale of his misadventures in Vanderton. Then Karl Fisher came up from the river and the young Daryman told it again.

"Well, prove it with the wolfskin!" urged Karl indignantly.

Holt shook his head in frustration. "She wouldn't even listen to me, I'm sure. But I promise—I'll pay you back for the losses, every one of you," he pledged. "I don't care how hard I have to work, or how long—I *will!*"

"That's not necessary," Nowell said quickly. "It wasn't your fault."

"I should have done *some*—"

"Now stop that," Derek said firmly. "Say, son, why don't you go out and get some wood, and I'll heat up a kettle of tea. Then we'll talk some more."

Dejectedly, Holt went outside. His neighbors' charity touched him, but at the same time he knew all too well that none of them could afford the loss.

At the woodpile, Holt heard hoofbeats behind him and whirled in surprise. A tall horseman had cantered into the yard, and Holt immediately recognized the flowing black mustache and eyebrows of Korth, captain of the palace guard.

"Hello, Daryman," offered the captain, reining in

his horse and dismounting. The expression on his face was no less surprised than Holt's.

Despite his recent experience, the Daryman was pleased to see the warrior—though not quite sure why. Putting down his armload of wood, Holt raised a hand in greeting.

"I never learned your name," Korth said with a wry chuckle. "Now I'm guessing it's Holton, son of Jaken."

"That's right. How did you know?"

"One of your good neighbors, up on the heights. I came to Oxvale looking for a guide . . . someone who knows the Knollbarrens. The fellow gave me the name of Holton Jaken."

Derek, his wheeled chair pushed by the limping Nowell, came out of the house and along the planks of the walkway. Holt introduced them to the captain of the guard.

"He's the one who threw me out of the castle," he added, mostly in jest.

"Well, it seems he had reason!" Derek exclaimed, surprising his son. "After all, you told him a tale of killing a warwolf like you expected him to believe it!"

Korth looked shrewdly at the elder Daryman. "Do *you* believe him?" asked the warrior.

"I *know*," Derek replied quietly. "I saw the skin—there's the head, mounted over the door."

"You did what you said, sure enough," Korth

granted. "No normal wolf has side whiskers like that—not to mention the size!"

"You said you needed a guide through the Knollbarrens," Holt remembered. "What for?"

The warrior grew serious, drawing down those heavy brows in a fierce scowl. "A matter of some urgency," he began. "And for which I'm willing to pay."

"Is it the princess?" guessed the young Daryman.

"Aye. You'll remember the shooting star. Well, that crazy wizard got an idea into his head—said that it was the sign her highness had been waiting for. But it didn't come to the castle—instead, it landed off to the east."

"In the Knollbarrens?" Holt said wonderingly. He remembered the ground shuddering beneath his feet, imagining the quake as the distant impact of some cosmic portent. The idea staggered his senses.

"The princess decided that we would journey to the site. Once in the 'Barrens, we found our path blocked at every turn—by cliffs and gorges, or rivers too deep to ford. I left the princess with a strong party—they sought a way around a deep gorge. She sent me to the nearest town to seek a guide. If you know these Knollbarrens as well as your neighbor said, I offer you the job."

"What will the princess say when she sees me?"

The thought of serving Danis Vanderthan did not appeal to Holt.

"I'm willing to vouch for you," Korth said—not exactly answering Holt's question. "I helped dump your cheese, so I guess it's the least I can do. At least it's a chance for you to get paid."

Holt bit back a wry laugh as he tried to imagine Danis's frustration. No doubt she had made life miserable for the entire entourage. Getting lost in the Knollbarrens seemed a just fate for the arrogant princess, and a part of him would have been content to leave her out there.

Yet another voice within him wanted to help her. Perhaps it was the satisfaction of being needed, or more likely, the chance to gain some payment for the loss of the cheese cart. For some reason he found himself remembering the flash of her green eyes, the graceful curve of her cheek. Yes, Holt realized, he *wanted* to take on this task— in no small part because he would see Danis Vanderthan again.

"What are you authorized to pay for your guide?" he asked.

"The fee is . . . negotiable," Korth cautiously replied.

"My services will cost the same as a cartful of fresh cheese."

"Steep wages," grunted the warrior.

"But just wages, as well," Holt added.

Pawns Prevail

Korth muttered something, stroking his thick black mustache. He turned and took a step back toward his horse, as if he intended to depart. Then he spun on his heel and planted his burly fists on his hips.

"I would say ten pieces of gold—or a hundred of silver—would have fetched the worth of that wagon," the captain of the guard calculated.

"It would have brought thirty gold in an easy day!" Holt protested.

"Impossible. The very best I can offer is twenty."

"For twenty I'll be your guide," Holt said with a grin. He knew that it would have taken a long day of weary bargaining to make anywhere near that much from the cheese.

"We have a deal," Korth agreed. "Can you provide your own horse?"

"Old Thunder's been to the Knollbarrens a time or two," the Daryman replied with a nod.

"It's too late to start out now. Why don't you be our guest for the night?" Derek offered. "I've got tea boiling, though we can certainly find something a little cooler as well. Most of the neighbors are here anyway, so we'll just set out another plate. You can start for the 'Barrens first thing in the morning."

"Agreed!"

Inside the cottage the captain of Vanderton's guard listened raptly as the Daryfolk described the grave robbers and wolves. By late evening the better part of Oxvale had gathered in the Jaken cottage, and if it got a little crowded as the hours moved toward dawn, there was no one who preferred solitude.

7
Into the Knollbarrens

"Here's six gold—all I've got with me," Korth said, handing the shining coins to Holt. "The princess will make good the other fourteen. You have my word."

"That's fine," the young Daryman agreed, reminding himself to hand the money to one of the villagers before leaving.

They met in the morning sunlight outside of the cottage, ready to take to the trail. Korth cinched the saddle on his restless charger while Holt carefully packed rope, tinderbox, bedroll, and extra arrow shafts into Old Thunder's voluminous saddlebags.

"Looks like you're planning to migrate," the warrior observed with a wry chuckle.

"It doesn't hurt to be prepared," the young Daryman replied seriously. Regardless of his companion's impatience, Holt refused to be rushed through his preparations.

Derek Jaken had wheeled out with them, and Nowell the Aching and Hag Biddlesome also came to see the two off. Nowell brought a long, burlap-wrapped bundle, which he handed to Derek. Holt's father rolled forward with the object in his lap.

The son recognized the outlines of a sword, the blade protected by a plain leather scabbard. Derek's chair came to a stop, and the elder Daryman raised the weapon, hilt first, toward Holt.

"We thought you might find some use for this," Holt's father said gruffly.

"I've been keeping it—but it kind of belongs to the whole town," Nowell explained.

"How long have you had this?" asked the younger man in surprise.

"Since before—*years* before—you were born. As a matter of fact, it's belonged to the village for a very long time. I'd hoped that we Darymen would have no further need of swords. . . . I fear that my hopes were in vain."

"Because of the wolf?"

"Because of the *eyes* of the wolf," Derek replied grimly. "I pray that you'll have no use for it, but if you do . . ."

Holt nodded silently, uncertain what his father meant, but touched by the gift. He took the worn hilt and drew the weapon from the scabbard, revealing a blade that was neither smooth nor especially shiny. The surface was a mottled gray, pocked with irregular marks. Still, the edge was sharp and the weapon had a solid, sturdy feel.

"Thank you," he managed, though his throat had gone suddenly tight. Awkwardly he buckled the scabbard to his belt.

"Your sword?" Korth said, as he came around the side of his eager horse. The worn hilt looked dull and plain in the sunlight. "It has seen some use."

"Not by me. It was a gift from my neighbor and my father."

Korth looked back at Derek and Nowell, nodding as if an opinion had been confirmed.

"Here," the younger Jaken said, handing the coins to his father. They'd already talked about using the payment to make up for the lost cheese, and Derek would use a fair hand in sharing it among the Daryfolk.

"Have you got a saddle for that horse of yours?" asked Korth when Holt led Old Thunder from the barn. In answer, the Daryman brought out the loose flaps of leather that served him as a seat on Thunder's broad back.

"As long as we don't cross swords with anyone, you'll be okay," Korth laughed good-naturedly. "Of course, the first good blow will knock you flat on your backside!"

"I know how to hang on," Holt retorted, flushing from the warrior's joke. He knew that this was no war saddle—that the draft horse was no knightly charger—but it rankled him to have the fact rubbed in.

As if he sensed the younger man's discomfort, Korth turned to Derek Jaken. "Thanks for the wonderful meal—and the roof over my head," the guard captain said warmly.

"Nothing but simple country fare," the Daryman protested.

"Nevertheless, it was a feast that would have put many a noble's kitchen to shame. I thank you for sharing it with me."

After bowing deeply, Korth swung into the saddle of his sleek, chestnut-colored charger. The animal kicked eagerly as Holt finished cinching the buckles on Thunder's saddles. He'd never before appreciated how impractical the multiple fasteners were, but now they seemed to cost him precious extra time. Eventually, however, he, too, was able to mount.

Pawns Prevail

With a final nod, Korth whirled his stallion. The horse galloped off in a cloud of dust, and Holt had barely time to wave good-bye before Old Thunder followed.

They soon slowed to a fast walk, but Holt was surprised by how quickly they passed over the lip of Oxvale's valley and entered the tangled ways of the Knollbarrens.

"The princess sought a way around that mountain," Korth said, pointing to the rusty dome of the 'Barrens' highest peak. "She tried to discover passage to the north."

"She didn't find it," Holt said confidently. "That's Mount Rustwind. On the far slope the summit is split by a gorge that runs twenty leagues or more to the northwest."

"I'm sure she had the sense to turn back," Korth said, though concern rippled beneath the calm veneer of his voice.

Holt snorted. "Good sense was not the foremost trait I saw in the princess," he observed wryly.

The gruff warrior shook his head, his expression a trifle sad. "She's not as bad as . . . well, as she was that day. At heart she's a good girl, and very concerned about the welfare of her father's kingdom. Unfortunately, you—or, to tell the truth, your cart—got in the way of that concern."

"*Oxvale* is a part of her father's kingdom! I still don't see how she could—"

"It was the warwolves, lad. The sighting of those beasts is bad news for all Karawenn, and the princess knew that. She had tried to track the one to the north and it eluded her—eluded all of us." He looked at Holt squarely. "Except maybe you."

"I didn't know anything about a warwolf," Holt objected. "I thought I was hunting a threat to the herd."

"And so you were," Korth agreed with a hearty chuckle.

By nightfall they reached the foot of Mount Rustwind and made a camp in a forest clearing. Though in the past Holt had always traveled the Knollbarrens alone, he now enjoyed the company of the gruff warrior. They settled around a cheery fire and devoured a brace of pheasants that had fallen to Holt's arrows. Korth quickly fell asleep, but Holt spent some time trying to polish the blade of his sword. Eventually he gave up, however, conceding that the stony gray color on the blade was there to stay. He, too, fell into a sound sleep, and both trail riders rose with the dawn.

Before noon they crossed the trail of several riders. "All right, guide," Korth said, indicating the prints as he turned to Holt with a friendly challenge. "Let's see what kind of tracker you are."

The Daryman dismounted and inspected the prints. "This print—with a fine horseshoe—is from the princess's charger. There's the pony Gazzrick rode. . . . And let's see, this set looks like an old nag who walks with a limp. The wizard's horse, I presume."

"Not bad," Korth allowed with a nod.

Holt remembered the party he'd seen ride by him on the road, and he decided to embellish. "These three war-horses are a black, a chestnut, and a roan—a mare and two geldings. Let's see, one's ridden by a husky fellow with a brown mustache. Another has a tall rider—one who carries a silver buckler and short sword."

Korth gaped at him, then scowled suspiciously. "Pretty vivid tracks, I'd say," he growled.

Holt laughed good-naturedly. "Actually, I saw you ride by on River Road three days ago," he admitted. "But there's no question this is her party."

Korth huffed. "You had me going for a second there," he admitted.

"I'd guess they came back this way after being blocked by the gorge," Holt speculated. He looked at the spoor of the horses. "They probably passed here yesterday, so they've got a pretty good start on us by now."

The two riders followed the trail at a fast trot, hoping to make up some of the distance. The pathway sloped around the lower ridges of Mount Rustwind, climbing gradually toward the heart of the wilderness.

They came over a ridge and saw a sheltered valley. A placid lake mirrored perfectly the surrounding crags, and a cluster of hardy pines formed a grove along the near shore. Sunlight sparkled from a long waterfall, where runoff from Rustwind's summit thundered from the heights into a frothy brook that fed the blue waters of the lake.

The trail of the royal party led straight to the woods. "I'll bet they made camp there last night," Korth suggested.

Cantering now, they hurried down the long slope toward the valley bottom. Holt was pleased to see that Old Thunder easily matched the rapid pace of Korth's sleek charger. Soon they drew up before the edge of the pine grove, spotting the narrow trail where the princess and her companions had entered the woods.

Korth led the way, and as Holt followed, he heard the warrior give a shout of alarm and spur his horse forward. Thunder raced along the path, forcing the Daryman to duck his head against a barrage of branches and pine needles.

They galloped into a clearing and reined back. A quick glance showed Holt that a brutal fight had occurred there. In two places large, dark stains marked the ground. Holt's eyes took in the scene of bloodshed while Korth leapt to the ground, cursing. The warrior found the remains of broken arrows, and Holt indicated the drag marks extending from each of the stains.

"Two large men were slain by arrows, the bodies dragged away," guessed the Daryman.

"Shot from ambush!" the captain muttered bitterly, indicating trampled brush where the attackers had apparently concealed themselves. "Without even the chance to defend themselves!"

"But *who* attacked them?" demanded Holt. "There's no one living in the Knollbarrens!"

"Someone's visiting, then," Korth said grimly. "These arrows weren't shot by any warwolf."

Looking in the brush around the camp, Holt found a quiver containing some two dozen arrows. The Daryman slung the pouch from his belt after showing it to Korth, who declared that it hadn't belonged to any of his men. Next they found a broken sword near the far fringe of the wood. The blade was crusted on both edges with dried blood, and it lay next to another large stain on the ground.

"Jareth's weapon. He was a good man," the warrior declared. "It looks like he made them pay."

"But what about the princess? Or the halfling and the wizard?" asked Holt, still examining the brush. "I don't see any—wait! There's tracks—looks like several riders. Yes! Here's her charger and the halfling's pony. And even the limping nag that Tellist rode."

Korth swung back into his saddle, and they

started along the trail. "It looks like they rode fast—making an escape while Jareth held the attackers back, bought her a few more seconds," the warrior observed bitterly. "And paid with his life, judging from the amount of blood on the ground."

He cursed privately, his big hand closing around the hilt of his own sword. Holt saw the warrior's knuckles turn white with tension and fury.

"Three bloodstains . . . but where are the bodies?" Holt wondered.

The warrior shrugged. "We'll find that out when we get our revenge," he stated grimly.

"The three who escaped made it out of the woods at least. Look—here's where they broke into the open," Holt observed.

Korth led the way, cantering forward with his eyes intent upon the path. The trail climbed away from the lake, toward a series of rocky ridges across their path. They crested the first of these, and Korth cried out in alarm.

"Look out—above!"

Holt looked up to see something flash in the sun. Instinctively he ducked as slender shapes buzzed past his head. Arrows! He saw three bowmen standing behind the crest of the low ridge, already drawing fresh missiles to their weapons.

"Throw down yer arms and yer miserable lives'll be spared!" cried a voice from a looming knob of craggy rock. A tall man, his face surrounded by a bristling mane of orange-red beard and hair, stood atop a ledge above them and leered savagely down.

Holt stared upward in surprise while Korth bellowed in outrage. "Dare you attack like a man—or do you need to skulk in the brush like an assassin?" he demanded.

"A pair of foolish wretches!" laughed the red-bearded bandit. "It'll be your last mistake, friends—to try and stand before the men of Serge Blackthorn!"

Hooves thundered as five horsemen raced from the cover of the rocky knob, pounding toward the two riders. The attackers brandished swords, whooping savage cries of battle. The red-bearded man leapt downward, mounting a huge horse and galloping after his men.

Korth put the spurs to his own horse, and the snorting charger sprang past Old Thunder. For a second Holt stared in surprise as the warrior met the charge of six men, hewing to the right and left with his sword. One of the attackers fell from his saddle and the other five hauled back, cautious in the face of Korth's courage.

"Flee, lad!" cried the warrior. "Remember your mission!"

The trio of archers again released their missiles. All three shafts slashed toward the captain, and Korth grunted in sudden pain.

Pawns Prevail

"No!" Holt cried, despairing as he saw an arrow jutting from the warrior's right shoulder. The attacking riders closed in again, but the guard captain, controlling his horse with his knees, dropped his reins and wielded his sword with his left hand.

"Go!" Korth shouted furiously.

The captain's skill could hold the riders only for a few moments, Holt sensed. The Daryman twisted back and forth, torn by an agony of indecision. Finally, his throat tight with humiliation and shame, he kicked Old Thunder—*hard*—and pulled the reins toward the downhill path to escape.

The big horse snorted indignantly and stubbornly turned in the opposite direction. Thunder sprang up the steep slope like he thought he was some kind of mountain goat. Appalled, Holt hung on for dear life.

Quickly the incline proved too extreme, and the big horse wheeled sideways and galloped downward, straight toward the bowmen. One of the archers fired, the arrow carving a nick out of Holt's scalp.

Lowering his massive head, the gelding pounded toward the ambushing bowmen. Holt scrambled to draw his sword, almost dropping the weapon in his excitement. Securing his grip, he slashed it through the air as Thunder leapt nimbly over rocks and shrubs.

Frightened—more by the gigantic horse than

Douglas Niles

the sword-wielding young rider—the archers turned and sprinted for the shelter of the nearby clump of rocks. Holt whacked to his right, knocking one of the men to earth, while Thunder's heavy hooves smashed another one. The third threw down his weapon and scrambled up the steep face of the rock-studded knob.

Holt and Old Thunder raced down the mountainside. Korth broke away from the melee, galloping after them. The burly warrior slumped in his saddle, desperately struggling to stay mounted as his charger drew even with Holt.

The Daryman's first look convinced Holt that the captain had been sorely hurt. Korth's face was pallid, his lips tinged with blue. Risking a look behind, the Daryman saw that the bandit riders hung back, apparently tending to their own wounded. Holt reached over to seize the warrior's reins and pulled both horses to a stop.

Twisting his mouth in a grimace of determination, the warrior tried to speak through his pain. "Find her!" he gasped. "Without delay—you *must* find her!"

Korth leaned in his saddle, and Holt leapt to the ground, barely in time to catch the warrior as he collapsed. As gently as possible, Holt eased the big man down.

"It's not as bad as that!" declared the Daryman. "Just rest a bit—we'll get you back on your horse, and take to the trail together!"

"*Go!*" hissed Korth, so forcefully that the warrior gagged in a fit of coughing. When the spasm subsided, a froth of pink bubbles lay on his lips.

"Listen," whispered the warrior, his voice soft but steady. "She *needs* you now. She doesn't know it, but you'll have to convince her . . . *ride,* man!"

A flash of movement drew his attention, and he saw that two of the bandits had crept into bow range. Now they drew back and shot.

Springing to his feet, the Daryman ducked away from an arrow that arced toward his chest. Old Thunder whickered nervously.

"I'll get you to shelter!" Holt barked, his eyes still sweeping the heights.

Only when the guard captain didn't answer did he turn around. Immediately he realized that Korth was in need of no further shelter—one of the arrows had plunged downward, straight into his heart.

Holt heard hoofbeats approaching again, and suspected that Serge Blackthorn and his riders were emboldened by the death of their dangerous foe. He held no illusions that his own skills would allow him even the limited success Korth had achieved should he try to carry on the unequal battle. Instead, he could only reach out a hand and gently close the brave warrior's eyelids.

Tears of frustration burned his eyes as he pulled

himself back to Old Thunder's saddle. The black-garbed captain lay forlorn and alone, but already the mysterious horsemen pounded into sight. They spurred their steeds to a gallop at the sight of Holt's inactivity.

"*Go!*" shouted the Daryman, the command to his horse a cry of anguish and a curse. Old Thunder sensed his urgency and raced from the scene of battle, quickly leaving the ambushers in the distance.

From the top of the next ridge Holt looked back. His last view showed him Korth's body, as Serge Blackthorn's men lifted the corpse to the back of a horse. The Daryman counted a full dozen of the bandits, with half of them mounted. Why they wanted the corpse he couldn't imagine, but the fact struck him as a grotesque indignity. He remembered, with bitterness tinged by fear, that they had carried away the bodies of their earlier victims as well.

In another moment, the file of bandits and their inert burden disappeared from sight.

8
Tellist Tizzit

Holt numbly straddled Old Thunder's broad back, allowing the horse to choose their route. A sense of failure smothered him like a shroud. Eyes downcast, shoulders slumped in defeat, the young Daryman paid no attention to the possibility of pursuit or ambush.

The horse trotted around the lower slopes of Rustwind, moving away from the band of cutthroats and at the same time pressing farther into the Knollbarrens. Fortunately, the bandits seemed content with their lone victim, making no effort to follow Holt along the rugged mountainside.

Douglas Niles

Vividly Holt remembered Korth's death, and his own terrifying sense of helplessness. He should have done *more!* A chorus of voices told him that the warrior's fate was Holt's fault, and with each step away from the scene, the volume seemed to grow louder.

What courage had enabled the man to charge into the enemy riders, one man against six? Now in Holt's memory Korth became a nearly legendary figure of gallantry and courage—and the Daryman a pathetic wretch who couldn't even provide a decent burial for his companion.

Again he thought about the band's eagerness to cart away the dead man's body. There seemed to be no good reason for such an action. Holt could imagine them looting a corpse's clothing, though the notion renewed the fires of his outrage. But why would they want the body itself?

With a chill, he recalled the Oxvale graveyard, where the bodies had been literally dragged from the earth. He wondered, with growing fear, if a connection existed between the two events.

He even considered doubling back, sneaking up on the band. He pictured Old Thunder charging into their camp while he slashed to both sides with his sword. Revenge!

Suicide, more accurately, he told himself. Tears of frustration stung his eyes. As much as he wanted to avenge Korth's death, there was nothing he could do about that fact—for the time being, at least.

"Get to the princess," Korth had commanded. At least, Holt resolved, he could try to do that—and he would succeed.

Holt looked up to see the eastern portion of the Knollbarrens opening before him. The steady horse had carried him halfway around the red-brown dome of Rustwind. With a quickening of his pulse, Holt saw the tracks of the charger, pony, and nag, and realized he remained on the trail of the princess and her party.

"Good job, old fellow," he said warmly, clapping the big horse on the neck. "Even when I'm sitting here feeling sorry for myself, you stay true to the task."

At least the trio seemed to have escaped the reach of the bandits, Holt thought. He pictured the princess—no doubt once more clad in gleaming armor—trying to make her way through the wilderness. Neither the pudgy halfling nor the befuddled wizard, he suspected, would be a great deal of help.

Holt resolved to reach Danis Vanderthan and inform her of Korth's fate. With bandits abroad in the 'Barrens, Holt would need to guide the party back to Vanderton. A new sense of purpose before him, his despair lifted like a windblown storm cloud.

Douglas Niles

The eastern 'Barrens were the most remote part of the wilderness. Holt had explored many of these valleys, though he had preferred to hunt closer to Oxvale. Still, on several occasions he had journeyed all the way to World's End—the great cliff at the edge of Karawenn. There the land fell away in a dizzying precipice, finally vanishing in a misty haze far below. The great plunge marked the uncrossable border of the world, several days' travel to the east of here. He knew that to his right and left were other parts of the Knollbarrens that he'd never seen—indeed, places about which he'd never even been curious. Then as now, it had seemed right to stick with the more obvious trails.

He followed the path down a wide valley where steep granite cliffs rose to the right and left. Old Thunder walked beside a shallow stream, sometimes clopping through the water when brush or rockfalls formed barriers close to the banks.

The tracks departed from the stream and started toward the crest of a nearby ridge. Snorting from the effort, the gelding began to climb, cutting back and forth between several of the dark, looming cliffs.

A tremor passed through the ground, and Old Thunder froze, feet squarely planted. Abruptly a terrific *crack* split the air. The sound came from the other side of the narrow gap, perhaps a quarter mile distant. There a great sheet of rock broke from the cliff, toppling free to plummet down the steep slope. Gravel and dust exploded outward, sending rubble zinging through the air. An occasional piece struck the ground very close to Holt.

The horse stood placidly as the stony landslide crashed and rumbled. Huge boulders smashed into the valley, still some distance from the trail, while trees splintered like matchsticks from the crushing force. A few small rocks tumbled in the wake of the great slide, and a cloud of dust lingered in the air as silence once again fell across the valley—silence broken only by the lingering echoes, thundering back and forth through the distance.

"It's a good thing we weren't over there," the Daryman observed softly, awed by the power of the rocky cascade. Old Thunder nickered appreciatively. Holt had seen numerous slides during his time spent in the 'Barrens, but never one of this magnitude. Nor had a landslide ever crashed so close to him, though even here he had not been in any real danger.

Again he turned Old Thunder's steps toward the upward trail. He vaguely remembered this ridge as one he'd followed in a previous journey. The other side, he remembered, fell fairly steeply but remained passable. The slope descended into a forested valley with plentiful water and game.

Reaching the crest, he saw that his memory was correct—a thick carpet of pines covered the valley floor, while numerous lakes and ponds reflected the perfect blue of the sky.

He started down, but almost immediately encountered an unexpected obstacle. The tracks of the three riders, which had been following a fairly obvious trail, reached the edge of a deep, wide gorge and vanished. Tracks and trail both disappeared at the lip of the chasm, and both resumed on the far side.

Holt approached the gap cautiously. The crack sliced across the face of the ridge between two jutting knobs of rock. A steep cliff blocked passage on the uphill side of the gorge, while a sheer drop plummeted away below.

How had the princess and her two companions crossed? Holt saw no sign of a bridge, and the gorge—forty or fifty feet wide—was far too broad to jump. And even if it hadn't been, the tracks showed that the princess and her companions had approached the chasm at a *walk,* not the gallop that would have preceded a desperate leap into space.

"Some kind of *removable* bridge?" he wondered aloud.

His common sense told him that the idea was completely impractical for a gap this wide. He found the barrier completely baffling. A few moments' scrutiny of the rocks to either side told him that he would have to backtrack to the far side of the ridge and find another way to cross. The detour would cost him hours, at least.

Yet there was nothing else to do. With a discouraged sigh, he pulled the reins around, and Old Thunder spun awkwardly on the narrow trail. Stones flew from the horse's wide hooves, clattered down the path, over the lip of the gorge.

There they stopped, suspended in the air.

Astonished, Holt leapt down from the saddle. Grasping a handful of pebbles, he cast them into the chasm—but they *bounced* at the top, and then came to rest. He kicked dust and gravel into the gap, and the debris spread across a solid, unseen surface. Gradually the Daryman saw the rough outlines of the mountainside.

Even then his mind refused to accept the truth. Only when he reached out a foot and stubbed his toe against solid ground—ground that he *couldn't* see—did he understand.

There was no gorge, no gap in the land before him. Instead, a section of the mountainside had been made invisible. The trail meandered right across this unseen patch. He felt biting chagrin when he realized that, though the barrier was in fact no obstacle at all, he had almost spend several hours trying to find a way around it.

On foot, Holt picked his way across the invisible trail, leading the reluctant gelding. At first the sensation of walking on air was dizzying, but by his third step the faint outlines of the ground began to appear around him. As he became more familiar with the terrain, the invisibility faded away, until soon the mountainside looked as if it had never been enchanted.

The rest of the descent passed smoothly, and soon the dense, dark boughs of the pine forest embraced them. Cool, moist air surrounded the trees, and the Daryman felt as though he had entered a huge, humid cave. Holt ducked under the first of the long-needled limbs, but quickly decided to dismount. The princess and her companions had done the same, he deduced from the footprints in the dirt of the forest trail.

The small, heavy-soled boots of Danis herself had led the way, followed by the diminutive shoes of the halfling, Gazzrick. Holt looked for the third set of tracks, from the wizard, and after a few more steps concluded that Tellist had separated from the party before the princess reached this forest track.

Abruptly he remembered the magical chasm, and the hairs on his neck prickled upward in supernatural alarm. Another thought chilled through him—the landslide! Could that, too, have been a trap the wizard designed to frighten pursuers off the trail?

A sizzling bolt of energy crackled through the air over Holt's head, sputtering into the bole of a pine tree and exploding in a cascade of sparks and fire. Old Thunder reared in alarm while the Daryman threw himself facedown on the soft loam of the forest floor. Another bolt, and a third, hissed past him, until the tree trunk across the trail from Holt had been very thoroughly charred.

The blazing magical arrows had originated from a dense clump of pines beside the trail. If the forest were any drier, Holt realized, both he and his attacker would have been caught within an inferno. Fortunately, the wet ground and damp limbs resisted the sparks and flares.

Several moments passed with no resumption of the attacks. Was this, too, the work of Tellist? Probably, Holt decided.

A figure darted around the trunk of a tree, and Holt caught a glimpse of a balding pate above a bright, multi-colored robe.

"Tellist!" he shouted. "Wait! I'm here to help you!"

Branches rattled behind Holt, and he whirled, sword raised. He saw the startled figure of the magic-user. Tellist stumbled backward, again disappearing behind a tree.

More noises rattled to the right and left, and Holt crouched in alarm, trying to protect both sides. Astonished, he saw Tellist diving away to the right, but when he heard a noise and spun left he also saw the magic-user thrashing through the

brush over there. In another instant the sounds of flight faded, and the Daryman heard only his own gasping breaths.

Four different Tellists—and four different directions! Holt groaned in dismay, completely baffled.

Old Thunder nickered softly, lowering his head and clopping past Holt, ambling along the trail. Holt followed, reasoning that this way was as good as any. In a few moments, he heard muttered sounds in front of him. Lashing the horse to a tree, he crept cautiously forward, using all of his hunter's skill to move silently.

"Tut, tut—he knew my *name!* By the seven stars, this is . . . well, dear me—this is *most* upsetting! If only my horse hadn't wandered off! The creature was *most* ungrateful, I should say!"

The words came from around a bend in the trail, and Holt pressed forward. He saw the balding magic-user stalking down the trail, hands clasped behind his back. Tellist shook his head, talking to himself.

"How did that bandit learn my name? Oh, this is just a fine pickle—a fine pickle indeed!"

Holt noticed three more magic-users, each identical to Tellist. The trio marched through the brush to the side of the trail, mutely following the example of the central wizard. Only that figure spoke, however.

"Well, I've botched this *quite* nicely!" The old

man's voice was close to despair.

"Tellist! Wait—I'm a friend!" shouted Holt, trotting after the wizard

With a startled yelp the figure on the trail darted to the right, while the other three images made off in different directions. This time, however, Holt kept a careful eye on the genuine Tellist and rushed forward to catch the mage by the elbow.

The wizard made a final attempt at escape, vanishing from sight abruptly and twisting out of the Daryman's grip. Tellist's footprints appeared in the muddy ground, and in moments the wizard's invisible boots were covered with so much dirt that Holt had no trouble leaping after him. Even so he could only stop the magic-user by jumping on Tellist's invisible back and forcefully bearing him to the ground.

"Wait! I'm Holton—the guide! Korth came to get me!"

The wizard slowly appeared, flat on his stomach with the Daryman straddling his back. His spectacles had fallen off, and he fumbled through the dirt for them. Finally, exasperated, Holt went to get the glasses and handed them back to the mage. Perching them on his nose, Tellist blinked suspiciously at the younger man.

"If the captain of the guard went to get you, why didn't he come back with you?"

Pawns Prevail

"He did—part way. He's dead." Briefly, Holton described the journey, the battle, and its tragic outcome.

"Tut, tut," said the mage, sadly. "Captain Korth was a good man. Those scoundrels!"

"I've been following you by myself since then," Holt continued. "But where's the princess and Gazzrick?"

Tellist looked pleased with himself. "I sent them on ahead while I tried to delay you—well, not *you*, really, but the bandits we thought were chasing us. That is, I thought *you* were a bandit, which is why I guess I *did* try to delay you—only as I said, it wasn't really you—"

"I understand," Holt said. Another brave man sacrificing himself for the princess, he thought bitterly. "That landslide was frightening," he offered as consolation. "It almost did scare me off."

"Oh, well—that wasn't supposed to scare you. Actually, it was supposed to kill—well, not *you*, but—"

"It was a little too far away to do that—I'm thankful!"

"Well, yes, I guess it did work out for the best, didn't it? Still, it vexes me that my spells went awry. That's the way of it sometimes—but not often." Tellist picked himself up and dusted off his clothes.

"You see, magic is really quite handy," he

explained. "Take our plan, for instance. As a wizard, I, Tellist Tizzit, have the power of teleportation. Therefore, my plan was to hold up the bandits long enough for the princess and Gazzrick to get a good head start. Then I will simply pop to our meeting point."

"You planned a rendezvous?" Holt was delighted. "Where will they be? I'll ride there immediately, and meet you!"

"Oh, er, yes . . . " Tellist's voice trailed off in some embarrassment. "Well, normally that would be a simple matter—only this time, it seems, well, we didn't really have time to set up a meeting. I went off in such a hurry, you see. . . ."

"You have no idea where they are?" Holt guessed.

"Actually, that seems a terribly blunt way to put it. But in the literal sense of the words, I suppose it's true."

"Can your magic help us find them?"

"Well, as I said, magic is a terribly useful thing. Why, for example, I have a spell that will hasten our movements considerably. I could cast it on both of us, and we should move like the wind!

"Of course," he added, "the spell can be reversed to slow somebody down. Perhaps I should have cast it on the princess and Gazzrick before they left—then we should have an easier time catching them! But no, that's not very practical for running away, now, is it?"

"You had a horse—do you know where it is?"

"Ah, a splendid animal! Fleet as the wind, sure-footed as a mountain goat . . ."

"Where *is* it?"

"Oh, er . . . well, I suppose it got hungry. I forgot to tie it up when I came back to stop the bandits, you see."

Holt left the wizard to his prattling while he walked back to get Old Thunder. Returning to Tellist, he pulled the magic-user onto the horse behind him, and together they set off along the trail of the princess.

9
Knollriders

"Magic, you see, is quite the most remarkable thing in the world," Tellist explained.

The wizard currently rode astride Old Thunder's haunches, though Holt had already been forced to stop several times when the absent-minded mage had let go of the Daryman's belt and fallen heavily to the ground. Each time, however, Tellist had scrambled back up without interrupting a sentence.

"After all, it has uses for building—for moving and lifting all sorts of things. Enchantments can enhance the beauty of a garden, or improve the value of a statue. Why, a spell can get you some-place else in the blink of an eye!"

"So I heard," Holt said with a chuckle. "But doesn't it take you longer to learn a spell than to make a short walk?"

"Well, if you want to be particular," Tellist said peevishly. "It's true that once a wizard casts a spell, it vanishes from his mind until he can study it again—*re*learn it, so to speak. But that's at worst a minor inconvenience!"

"Why don't we use magic for *everything,* then?" inquired the Daryman.

"The pursuit of magic is a very demanding pro-fession," the wizard said haughtily. "Few are those who can master even its most elementary tech-niques—and but a tiny fraction of that number can progress to the more splendiferous enchant-ments."

"I take it you fall into the latter category?"

"My dear young man, *naturally.* No apprentice mage can teleport himself, or bring a landslide off the top of a mountain—just to name a couple of examples. There are countless others. Even invisi-bility is a gift beyond the powers of the beginning mage. Or take—"

"I think I understand," Holt interrupted. "Only a few people have the talent to become wizards."

"A *very* few. I tell you, it is the most subtle of all skills. Why, the studies alone are enough to put off

Douglas Niles

all but the most diligent of scholars. And the risks! There are some stories I could—"

"I'm sure there are," Holt agreed wholeheartedly. "But if you don't mind, I've got to pay a little more attention to this trail if we're ever going to find Danis and Gazzrick."

"Now that's *just* the kind of thing I'm talking about," Tellist rattled on. "A skilled magic-user needs the intelligence to be able to carry on a conversation while at the same time remaining carefully alert to every detail of his surroundings. Not a thing happens within range of my senses that I don't immediately notice! Over on the other side of that stream, for example—did you note that black-tailed warbler, high in the oak—"

"Stop right there!"

Holt, who had been vainly seeking some sign of the bird, reined back in astonishment as a short, bearded figure stalked onto the trail a dozen paces ahead of them. Tellist gasped, and then slid over the tail of the horse to thump heavily to the ground.

"Who are *you?*" demanded the Daryman, sizing up the stranger. A bristling beard almost hid the fellow's broad, scowling face. A pair of bowed legs held booted feet firmly planted on the ground, and though the stranger's arms were long and his shoulders broad, the whiskered warrior was no more than four feet tall.

Pawns Prevail

"Don't make me do something I'll regret," the dwarf said ominously. "Tell me—*now*—why you're riding around in the 'Barrens!"

To punctuate his words, the stocky warrior lifted a heavy warhammer. The steel head of the weapon looked chipped and tarnished, and the shaft was worn. Still, the dwarf held the hammer with the casual familiarity of many years' use.

"We're . . . looking for someone," Holt declared. "Why do you threaten us?"

"What better to do with grave robbers and thieves?" growled the dwarf.

"What?" demanded the outraged Daryman.

"Tut, tut," cautioned Tellist Tizzit, raising a skinny hand. "That seems a rather rude conclusion, my good dwarf."

"Don't bother to deny it. First, the graveyard of my village is robbed, bodies snatched from their mortal rest! Then we see the tracks of horsemen, leading into the Knollbarrens . . . men who kill out of sheer savagery and carry away the bodies of their victims! And now I find you—on a horse!"

"*Lots* of people ride horses!" insisted Holt.

"Well, you're the horsemen I tracked this far. Now, make ready to fight like warriors!"

The Daryman considered making a rush at the dwarf, hoping that the hammer of the footman wouldn't be as effective as the rider's sword. Still, he wasn't certain that the dwarf was an enemy—

in fact, it sounded as though he sought the same group of bandits that had slain Korth.

"Look here," Tellist interjected. "This reminds me of an historical incident during the Troll War. A company of King Bankar's warriors, Army of Bedford, marched through the Trollheight Mountains. There, they met a band of King Kalright's dwarven warriors. A fierce battle followed, with many killed on both sides."

"And?" inquired the dwarf sourly after a long pause.

"And what?" replied the wizard. "Once you're dead, you're dead. I should think that would be obvious!"

"Why did you tell the story?" sputtered the stump-legged warrior.

"Oh. Merely because the two forces, Kalright's and Bankar's, were both in the mountains looking to fight trolls."

"Those grave robbers," Holt blurted, "they've killed many—including a brave companion of mine within the last day."

"Enemies of yours, too, eh?" The dwarf scowled more fiercely than ever, but after a moment Holt realized that he was thinking. "Well, now that you mention it I'd have to say you don't look like the kind of scurvy lot that would muck around with the dead. Yup—I trust my judgment on a thing like that!"

Pawns Prevail

"Are you down here from Graywall?" Holt asked as he dismounted, knowing of the dwarven community in the northern fringe of the Knollbarrens. The dwarf fell into step beside the Daryman and the wizard, while Old Thunder followed at a plodding walk.

"Aye," the dwarf asserted. "Fenrald Falwhak's the name. I'm the warmaster of the village—not that we have much of an army, of course. Still, when this bad magic lot came through the other night, I was the one who got sent to check it out."

Holt introduced himself and his companion, then described his experience with the bandits. Finally he told of their search for the princess and her halfling companion.

"Haven't seen sign of 'em," Fenrald said with a shake of his head. "Though it sounds like the 'Barrens're more crowded than I'd of thunk."

" 'Thought' is the word," Tellist noted.

"Shhh!" hissed Holt, holding up his hand for silence. Old Thunder came to a stop as his companions clamped their mouths shut and listened.

First they heard the clopping of hooves on rocks, and soon the creak of harness and saddle grew audible.

"Comin' from the trees, there," Fenrald said, pointing with certainty toward a clump of aspens. The leaves shimmered silver and rustled in the faint breeze, though not loudly enough to conceal the sounds of the mysterious riders.

"Here—we can hide," urged Holt, pulling Old Thunder into a low hollow behind several thick pines. He left the horse and crawled beneath the dense limbs, peering cautiously into a meadow on the other side. Fenrald and Tellist joined him, though the wizard muttered about the thorns so loudly that the Daryman feared he would give away their position.

In another moment, a file of riders emerged into the clearing. The horsemen followed a trail along the valley bottom, below the companions but not very far away. Ten scruffy bandits rode along the winding trail. At the rear of the column several mules plodded along, each laden by the weight of a bulky bundle.

With a shiver of apprehension, Holt realized that each of those bundles was a limp, lifeless body. The corpses were draped over the backs of the mules like so much baggage.

"There's your grave robbers," the Daryman said very quietly.

The dwarf, his face locked in a bitter scowl, nodded. He gestured for Holt and Tellist to follow him, and the trio withdrew to the far side of the pine grove. Keeping his voice low, Fenrald suggested a plan.

"We can take 'em! There's only ten—and I can handle at least six. That leaves two apiece for you."

Holt's heart surged with excitement for a moment; then, in light of reality, it sank. The dwarf's boast notwithstanding, he felt very uncertain of his ability to 'handle' even one of the burly swordsmen, not to mention a pair. Before he could object, however, the wizard shook his head.

"Tut, tut. My spells will no doubt claim at least eight of them as soon as the battle is joined. By a simple calculation, that leaves one for each of—"

"You're dreaming!" sputtered the dwarf, trying with limited success to hold his outrage to a whisper. "If you get a pair of them, I'll—"

"They're getting away!" Holt hissed urgently. He saw the lead rider's horse trotting into the forest on the other side of the clearing.

"Let's count up after the fight," the dwarf suggested pragmatically, springing to his feet. He pointed at Holt. "You ride along the streambank, get in front of them. I'll chase after the rear. When they see you, I'll attack."

"I shall teleport across the valley," Tellist suggested. "I can strike them from the high ground over there."

"Good. When the lad shouts the warning, we hit them from three sides!"

Holt tried to suppress the trembling in his limbs as he untied and mounted Old Thunder. The wizard muttered a quick, unintelligible word and blinked out of sight, while the grim-faced dwarf, clutching that worn and battered hammer, slipped into the bushes and worked his way silently after the column of riders.

The big draft horse splashed quickly through the stream and then trotted steadily up a game trail. Holt hoped they paralleled the path of their quarry as the bandits moved along the other side of the valley. He couldn't see them through the trees, and the gurgling stream drowned all sounds of their passage, but he knew that the same concealment would work for him as well.

After a few minutes of riding, the valley floor began to climb, and the Daryman knew the time had come to begin the ambush. Turning Old Thunder toward the stream, he urged the horse through the thicket and into the shallow water. Misgivings arose, but he thrust them aside—he would follow Fenrald's plan and hope for the best. Vividly he remembered Korth's heroic death; he was surprised that his grim determination for revenge gave him courage.

The gelding's heavy hooves splashed curtains of spray to either side, and then Old Thunder carried him up the far bank, plunging toward the place he guessed the bandits to be.

Hearing shouts of alarm through the trees, Holt knew that his estimate was correct. In another moment Thunder broke from the trees and reared to a stop in the trail. A hundred paces away the lead bandit saw him, and immediately spurred his horse into a gallop.

The man was Serge Blackthorn himself. The red-bearded rider, a cruel grin splitting his face, pounded closer. Holt drew his sword, surprised as Old Thunder snorted aggressively. The big horse leapt forward, carrying the Daryman straight into the bandit's charge.

Where were his companions? The question vanished in a chaos of thunder and steel. As the bandit chieftain raised his sword, Holt lifted his own blade in an awkward parry. Before the weapons clashed, Old Thunder swiveled sideways, forcing a broad shoulder into the bandit's smaller horse. The lighter animal stumbled away, and Holt stared in shock as Serge Blackthorn flew from his saddle to crash into the brush.

A sharp metallic *bonk,* followed by a curse, told him that Fenrald and his hammer had attacked the rear of the bandit column. In the confusion, Holt saw a scar-faced rider charging toward him, and he swiveled toward the new threat.

The bandit's face was twisted into a hateful grimace; the man wanted, with almost beastlike intensity, to hurt him. Instinctively Holt parried the bandit's wild swing, keeping his own sword low; then, as the attacker rode past, the Daryman stabbed him in the side. With shocking abruptness the dead rider tumbled from his saddle and lay still.

Douglas Niles

Other horsemen rode toward him, eager to avenge their comrade. Thunder pulled through a sharp turn and galloped away, drawing the bandits in pursuit.

"For the Falwhak beards!" The lusty battle cry rang through the woods, and Holt caught a glimpse of Fenrald. The dwarf leapt onto a rock, swinging his hammer at a pair of bandits. Pursuing horsemen quickly blocked Holt's view of the dwarf, but the Daryman heard a chaos of smashes and curses from that quarter.

His pursuers drew closer, and he risked a look back, seeing four mounted bandits on his tail. Desperately he urged Thunder into the stream, running up the gravel bed of the channel. The horse splashed through the water, but soon the brook turned into a narrow gorge. Sheer stone walls rose to either side, and the bandits closed off any retreat. Pressing forward, Holt and Thunder came around a bend, and saw that the upstream path was blocked by a small, turbulent waterfall.

Wheeling in the trap, Holt raised his sword. Curiously, he felt no fear—only a sharp bitterness at the unequal odds that would likely spell his death.

Then he saw Tellist. The wizard stood on a rocky promontory above the river. As the riders splashed toward Holt, the magic-user raised his hand and barked a sharp, commanding enchantment.

The Daryman's hair stood on end as lightning

crackled through the air. A sizzling bolt of energy exploded from Tellist's fingertip. But Holt's momentary elation turned to despair as the magical lightning bolt streaked past, far above the heads of the charging bandits.

Fiercely kicking Old Thunder's flanks, the young farmer urged his mount forward. Before the beast moved, however, a splintering shock boomed through the narrow gorge. Tellist's lightning bolt had struck the gorge wall, which exploded in a shower of boulders and debris.

Thunder reared back, panicked by the noise, and a cascade of stones crashed into the streambed. Three of the bandit riders vanished underneath the slide, leaving only the fourth to complete his charge. That swordsman, his face locked in a villainous sneer, hacked at Holt with a battered blade.

Desperately the Daryman deflected the blow, though his attacker's weapon scraped the skin from his wrist. Maddened by rage, the bandit reached back for another swing, and Holt stabbed furiously. The tip of his sword struck the man in the chest, and soundlessly the bandit dropped his axe and tumbled backward from his horse. His body disappeared beneath the shallow water.

Holt heard more crashing on the bank, and he urged Thunder into a gallop. The horse clambered over the pile of rubble and raced back to the site of the ambush, where the Daryman found Fenrald surrounded by four circling riders.

The dwarf still brandished his hammer. Fenrald hurled the weapon at one of the bandits. In a whirl of metal it left his hand and flew outward to strike the fellow a hard blow on the head. With a groan the man slumped in his saddle. More amazing to Holt was the action of the hammer after the blow. The weapon reversed its flight, soaring back through the air and returning to Fenrald's hand!

At Holt's approach, the bandits pulled away from the scrappy dwarf, wheeling their horses to start back down the trail. A flash of streaming red hair whipped past, and the Daryman knew that Serge Blackthorn had scrambled back into his saddle. Only one of the bandit horses held back—a shaggy creature that whinnied nervously over the motionless body of its rider.

"After them!" shouted Fenrald, raising the hammer for another toss.

At that moment, the air in the wilderness valley was split by a chiming, resonant chord. Musical notes rose upward like holiday bells, ringing through short melodies and beautiful scales. The sound finally faded to an echo, though shivers crept along Holt's spine for several moments afterward.

" 'Tis the Chimes of Summoning, sounded by the princess!" cried Tellist Tizzit, his face blanching at the sound. "She's near—and she's in danger!"

10
Shadow of Nightfall

"You know, that actually worked quite well," Tellist remarked breathlessly, clinging to Holt's belt on the back of Old Thunder. Fenrald, mounted on the captured bandit pony, rode beside them. The three companions thundered eastward, horses at full gallop, yet the wizard spoke with scholarly detachment.

"*What* worked?" demanded the dwarf, bouncing up and down in the lurching saddle.

"Why, the Chimes of Summoning, of course.

That's the sound we heard—we can still hear, actually."

Holt was about to disagree when he realized that, even above the din of pounding hooves, the echoes of that tuneful call still resonated. The noise drew them toward a point in the unseen distance.

"I gave them to the princess as a gift, you see— *oof!*" Tellist was forced to hang on as the horses scrambled up a steep embankment. On the highland tundra the steeds stretched forward and fairly flew across the stubbled grass.

"She can only use it in direst emergency, of course. But it's designed to call me to her rescue. Distance mutes the volume, but it was quite loud. . . . I say, that means we can't be terribly far away from her!"

"If I understand you, it also means she's in danger!" cried Holt, leaning flat against Old Thunder's heaving shoulder. Never in his life had he ridden so fast.

"Tut, tut—that's right," noted Tellist, a frown creasing his bouncing features.

"And we've got bandits somewhere behind us!" shouted the dwarf, sourly addressing the wizard. "I thought you were going to take out eight of them!"

"Or six for you?" demanded Holt in exasperation. "I'd say we were lucky to get out of there with our lives!"

Pawns Prevail

They pounded across the rolling crest of a broad plateau. The horses grew winded and gradually slackened their pace to a steady lope. The ringing notes of the chimes echoed in the air before them.

"The lad's right," grunted the dwarf. "My plan was bad—we split ourselves up and underestimated the foe."

"Er, I'd be forced to admit my own—tut, tut—my own guilt in the matter," Tellist said awkwardly. "It seems we each tried too hard to outdo the other—"

"Magic and muscle *both* have their place," Holt declared, pointing toward the vista opening below. "Right *here!*"

The plateau had begun to descend, and the Daryman indicated the broad valley before them. Ringing more urgently than ever, the chimes swelled to a crescendo.

"There she is!" Tellist gasped.

The companions saw two riders on the flat, brushy ground of the valley floor. A sleek black charger and a short-legged pony, both stumbling with weariness, carried the pair this way and that. Though the setting sun cast the valley into shadow, the shining plate armor of the princess gleamed atop the stallion, and the shaggy steed of Gazzrick Whiptoe bucked and bounced beside her.

"What's that?" shouted Holt. He saw movement in the shadows beyond the princess—gray shapes loping tirelessly, closing in on the desperate riders

119

from both flanks.

"Wolves!" Fenrald grunted.

Holt and his companions reached the edge of the broad plateau. A wide, smooth hillside descended before them, leading to the flat and brushy valley bottom where Danis and Gazzrick fled for their lives.

"They're making for the high ground," Fenrald observed, pointing down the ridge to their right.

Holt saw that a series of rocky outcrops jutted upward from the crest of the ridge. The two riders below made for one of the highest of these promontories.

"Come on!" Holt urged, starting Thunder along the crest. "We'll meet them up here!"

The horses again flew into a gallop. Wind whipped their faces as the three riders coursed toward a meeting with the desperate pair below. From atop her panting steed, the princess hacked at the wolves with a long, gleaming sword, while Gazzrick chopped back and forth with a hook-bladed dagger. Even in the fading light Holt could see that both weapons were slick with blood.

Danis and Gazzrick saw the trio coming to rescue them and veered more directly up the gradual slope. The wolves fell back to lope patiently in the wake of their quarry.

The young woman's snorting charger carried her to the crest of the ridge, with Gazzrick's pony straining behind. Holt got a quick look at Danis's flashing eyes, her mouth set in a line of determination. She guided the charger with her knees, ready to wield her sword to either side.

Those green eyes blinked in momentary surprise as the princess recognized Holt; then she whirled, the black horse springing to the front of her four companions. The wide-eyed halfling, his long sideburns trailing backward from the speed of the ride, did not have to urge his pony to race alongside Old Thunder and Fenrald's sturdy steed.

"This way!" cried the princess, waving a commanding hand as her fleet charger slowly outdistanced the others. Old Thunder's nostrils flared, the big horse puffing in determination, but the long run had taken its toll. Now the gelding stumbled, and Holt reined back.

In moments the princess reached the base of a rocky knob on the hillcrest. Her black horse scrambled upward without hesitation. The others followed, their steeds more cautious in picking a route up the steep promontory. Holt and Tellist dismounted, the Daryman leading Old Thunder by the reins, wincing in fear each time the gelding's big hooves knocked a rock loose.

Finally they joined the others at the top of the rocky knoll. He admitted that the princess had chosen a very defensible spot. Though the sides were steep in all directions, the top of the granite

Douglas Niles

outcrop was relatively flat, broad enough for the horses to gather in the middle while the riders spread out to watch all the approaches from below.

"They're not coming after us!" Holt exclaimed hopefully, seeing that the wolves circled around the rocky knob but made no attempt to climb.

"Cowardly curs!" snapped Fenrald Falwhak. "Fear, that's what it is—they won't attack this many of us!"

"It would seem, however," Tellist observed reluctantly, "that they're not about to let us go, either."

The Daryman then realized that the wolf pack had encircled the entire outcrop. He watched as the animals settled to their haunches or flopped to their shaggy flanks, panting. Everywhere yellow eyes focused on the companions, and the animals took care to form a ring with no gaps.

"Of course they're not coming after us—but it isn't cowardice," Danis declared. "They're simply trapping us, and waiting."

"For what?" Fenrald demanded.

"You'll see soon enough." The princess dismissed the dwarf with her eyes, turning to Tellist.

"It's good to see you alive—I feared for you!"

"Oh, posh," Tellist said. "I wasn't in a moment's danger, I assure you. My plan worked like a—well, to tell the truth, there may be a bandit or two we missed. . . ."

"We broke off our pursuit when we heard the

122

chimes," Holt explained.

"And you, farmboy," the princess said, turning to him with raised eyebrows. "Why are you here? I find it hard to believe you're still seeking payment—"

"*Korth* hired me," Holt interrupted furiously, struggling to stay calm. "He said you needed a guide—but I suppose you have things well under control!"

Danis flushed at his sarcasm, and for a moment the pair glared at each other. Neither broke the silence until a sudden concern flashed across the woman's face.

"Where is my captain?" she asked.

"He's dead, Princess," Holt said softly, suddenly ashamed of the bickering. "Slain by the same bandits that killed your guardsmen."

"He died bravely," she replied. It was not a question.

"He charged six by himself and felled at least two," the Daryman confirmed.

"You were with him?"

"Aye, Princess—his last command was that I reach you."

"Then his passing was as Korth would have wanted it—a hero's death," Danis said. Only a mist glowing in her eyes, distant as a daydream, betrayed any deeper emotion.

"I never learned your name, farmb—Daryman," the princess remarked suddenly.

Douglas Niles

"I am Holton Jaken, Your Highness."

"On the trail I'm Danis to my companions," she replied, surprising him. She turned to the dwarf. "And you're a traveler who found more trouble than he bargained for?"

"I came *looking* for trouble!" blustered Fenrald. Then his expression sobered. "Seems I found plenty." He told the princess and the halfling about the plundering of Graywall's burial ground and his quest to confront the grave robbers.

Holton described the similar attack against Oxvale.

"The bandits that attacked us," he added, remembering his earlier speculation. "They've taken the bodies of each man they killed. There *has* to be a connection—they're clearly the grave robbers."

As they spoke, Danis's eyes had drifted back to the valley below. The sun had already fallen behind the western ridge. Her posture tightened.

"That explains one thing," Danis said grimly after the Daryman concluded his tale. She pointed into the shadows of the valley floor. "Look, there."

Squinting into the darkness, Holt saw something moving. As his eyes adjusted to the reduced light, he saw a band of figures walking toward them, through the short brush. Rusty helmets rested on several of the heads, and swords, spears, and other weapons were clutched in rigid hands.

Pawns Prevail

But there was something vaguely inhuman about the appearance of these warriors. They moved with a jerky, awkward gait, more like marionettes than people. And they seemed very gaunt, almost frail—like stickmen rather than real warriors.

With a sickening chill, Holt understood why: these were not humans, though once they had been. Now the shambling warriors were the mere remnants of humankind—skeletons summoned from graveyards and forced to march mindlessly in an army of evil!

"By the Dark Sphere!" gasped Fenrald, reaching the same understanding as Holt. As the rank of skeletons drew closer, the companions saw that some of the undead warriors were short, broad shouldered, and bowlegged in physique—dwarven remains stolen from the biers of Graywall.

"We first came upon them this morning," Danis explained. "We rode away, barely beyond their reach. The wolves tracked us, but I suspect they only marked us for the real enemy."

"But—but *how?*" Holt wondered, horrified by the unnatural foe. "What power can make the dead walk?"

"Entropy, of course," Tellist noted conversationally.

The answer meant nothing to the Daryman, but he didn't feel like pursuing the discussion in the face of the advancing foe.

Pawns Prevail

"Here they come," Gazzrick said grimly.

At the base of the ridge, the skeletons spread into three long ranks—twenty or so of the undead in each. Marching abreast in a military formation, the first of these started up the slope, advancing steadily toward the rocky outcrop where the companions waited. When that rank was halfway up the hill, the second formation of bone-limbed warriors started upward.

"I say we attack!" Fenrald Falwhak declared, pressing his fingers around the worn haft of his warhammer.

Holt gaped at the dwarf, while the halfling sputtered in surprise. "We're at least a little safe up here!" Gazzrick protested. "And you want to go down there?"

"We're not as safe as you think," argued the dwarf. He pointed.

The first rank of skeletal warriors had ascended the broad ridge and now reached the base of the rocky knob. Those in the center of the line halted, while the left and right wings advanced to join the wolves encircling the bottom of the little hill. The army of skeletons proved large enough to almost completely encircle the outcrop, leaving only a narrow gap down the back side. The first rank then continued to advance upward, each undead using one hand to help climb while the other brandished a rusty weapon.

Douglas Niles

"Attacking—that makes sense," Danis decided. "Mounted, we can fly through each rank. Lancer will open the way." She indicated her eager, black war-horse, then turned to the three newcomers. "We learned this morning that they're not fast, but neither do they seem to get tired. We'll hit them quickly—just remember, don't stop for anything!"

The princess seized the reins of her charger and started on foot down the treacherous trail toward the gap in the skeletons' first rank. Holt helped Tellist into Old Thunder's saddle, then took the reins and led the horse after Danis. Walking their ponies, Gazzrick and Fenrald hastened downward.

Immediately the undead shambled toward them, trying to close off the escape route. Holt hurried forward, Old Thunder skipping and skidding down the steep, rocky slope. A skeleton lunged, bony fingers reaching for Danis, but she deflected the monster with a slash of her sword. The skeleton fell back a step, but then raised its spear and thrust forward.

Metal whirred past Holt's head as Fenrald's hammer smashed into the undead warrior. The figure toppled, and the weapon flew back to the stocky dwarf's hand.

Scrambling down the steep slope, cursing the growing darkness, the Daryman pushed through the line of undead. A skeleton clattered toward

Holt, but he chopped furiously with his sword until it fell.

From the saddle, Tellist chanted a spell, and Holt cringed as he imagined the climax. To his surprise, the enchantment cast a glowing outline around the forms of many skeletons, making them easy targets. Quickly Holt chopped two into pieces, clearing the immediate threat from their right.

More skeletons lurched forward beside sleek, darting wolves. Spooked, Thunder plunged suddenly down the trail, pulling Holt off his feet. The Daryman clung desperately to the saddle until the big horse halted at the base of the steep knob, with the broader slope of the plateau falling away beyond.

On this nearly level ground the companions mounted quickly. Tellist grabbed Holt's belt, and they turned toward the smooth, descending slope.

The second and third ranks of skeletons advanced up the hill toward them, though the more distant undead were barely visible in the darkness. Other skeletons and the wolf pack still pursued them from behind.

"Charge!" cried Danis as Lancer thundered forward. The others followed, whooping and screaming as they plunged downhill toward the ghastly warriors.

Holt ducked and dodged, whirling to face corroded spearheads and vacant eye sockets as Old Thunder pounded through the undead. Sickened by horror, the Daryman chopped with his sword, cracking the skull of one skeleton. He felt a tearing cut in his leg, and the big horse whinnied in pain, and then the companions had thundered past.

The final rank of skeletons closed to meet them, but the horses gained unstoppable speed during the downhill gallop. Holt felt a fierce exhilaration, raising his sword and aiming for another bony face. The skull's teeth clenched in a humorless grin as the blade slashed outward.

Abruptly full blackness cloaked the riders, like a weightless curtain that had dropped to mask all light. Old Thunder stumbled, unable to see the ground, and Holt flew through the air. He crashed to earth, gasping for breath as his sword flew from his hand.

The cloud of darkness lifted, though the night seemed blacker, more menacing than it had before. Holt saw Tellist crawling around on his hands and knees, muttering about his spectacles. Then the Daryman's eyes widened in horror as a huge shadow loomed behind the wizard, rising and spreading outward like a storm cloud to block out sky and horizon.

"What in the spheres is *that?*" gasped Danis, equally horrified.

The black shape grew taller than a mounted man, spinning out weblike arms to ensnare Tellist Tizzit. Wolves gathered around it, lunging and snarling toward the companions. Holt nocked an arrow to his bow, aimed at one of the beasts, and let fly. The missile struck the wolf, who yelped in pain, cringing back from the fight. But two more creatures charged forward to fill the space, and the black shape swept down to engulf the wizard.

Staring at the billowing darkness, numb with horror, Holt nevertheless managed to aim and shoot another arrow. The missile disappeared into the cloud with no more effect than a shot into a smoke cloud. The tendrils thickened about Tellist.

From the cloud of darkness emerged Fenrald Falwhak, sudden and huge, mounted on his pony. He reached down with a brawny hand and plucked Tellist from the ground, lifting him by the scruff of his neck and throwing him across the withers of the laboring steed. "Let's *go!*" urged the dwarf, galloping past, the wizard flopping like saddlebags across the horse.

The others turned and followed swiftly away. The slavering animals and the remorseless skeletons clustered around the great black shape did not immediately pursue. The monster's hatred, an inaudible but piercing shriek, resounded through the night and froze Holt's blood in his veins. Even after the miles, the terrifying aura of that black, evil presence seemed to linger at their shoulders and in their minds.

11
Fatal Fog

The companions rode through the night, following faint pathways illuminated by a half moon. The wolves gave chase at first, but the horses outdistanced the snarling carnivores, and after an hour, Holt saw no sign of pursuit. When Danis slowed to a walking pace, the others reined back, exhausted. Holt felt as though his bones had been rattled loose in their sockets.

Avoiding the dense forest, the riders followed the more visible paths through meadowlands and open woods. The moon set after midnight, and finally the company halted, dismounting and allowing the horses to graze.

"What *was* that thing?" asked Holt, giving voice to the fear that had driven him through the night. "It's like it was there, but it wasn't *really*."

"I think I can make a guess," Gazzrick said soberly. "It is a creature not of this world—a being from another sphere."

"The Sphere of Entropy?" suggested Tellist Tizzit. "*That's* the force that animated the skeletons, commanded the wolves to gather."

"Indeed. I sensed in that black cloud a great vacuum, a hunger that wanted to suck the very life from us. Only entropy can create such an overwhelming power—and fear."

"And it is the comet, the skysign of the immortals, that gave it entrance to Karawenn," Tellist concluded triumphantly, as if securing victory in an academic debate.

"What do you mean by *sphere* and *entropy?*" demanded Holt. The terms were meaningless to him, though he had heard the former word used in a number of well-known curses.

"The spheres represent all kinds of life, everywhere. And entropy is the enemy of life throughout the spheres—always it seeks to kill, to destroy," offered Gazzrick.

"How do you know so much about it?" Holt pressed.

Gazzrick waved a hand dismissively. "I've been a

tutor to the family Vanderthan for . . . well, for a long time," he said. "I hope I've learned *something* in all those years."

"But what *is* that creature . . . of entropy? What does it want?"

"There's no time for explanations—or guesses—now," Gazzrick said with a shake of his head. "We've got to be off again, moving!"

Holt would not be deterred so easily. "How is it connected to Serge Blackthorn?"

"I can't answer that," Gazzrick said in exasperation.

"I think it seeks the same thing we do," Tellist explained, nodding as if the spoken sentence had confirmed his unspoken suspicion. "I have mentioned my conviction: the shooting star we chase was an artifact of the immortals carving its path through the sky—it has drawn this being of entropy to Karawenn."

"That makes our business more pressing than ever," Danis declared. "Gazzrick's right—we must be mounted immediately and on our way!"

Holt looked around. The nearby trees were outlined in pale starlight, but since moonset, the ground at their feet had vanished into a murky pool of shadow. The faint trail they had been following disappeared with the moon, and any attempt to move would get them hopelessly tangled in the terrain.

Pawns Prevail

"Prin—Danis," the Daryman said, speaking carefully. "I was hired as your guide. I have to point out that we won't be able to see the path before us—if we press on now, we'll only make our travels harder in the morning."

"But time presses! Didn't you see that thing—that black *force* in the air?" she snapped.

"I know it's urgent," Holt replied. "But we're all tired—a little rest during these dark hours will triple our speed at dawn!"

For a moment he thought she would push the argument or ignore his advice. But then she nodded. "You sound like Korth—I can picture him saying the same thing. Very well—we'll take cycles of watch, just in case the wolves, or worse, close in." Danis looked at Holt. "Do you know where we are right now?"

"In a general sense," the Daryman replied. "Rustwind lies to our northwest, no more than twenty-five miles away. The Knollbarrens continue to the east for a long way from here—though the drop at World's End is sudden."

"The skysign's course took it east by northeast of Vanderton," Danis said. "I take it we're north of that line, now?"

"We can make it up in half a day's march," Holt assured her. "We'll start out south and veer toward the east later in the day."

"Very good. Now we should get some rest—but

135

everybody stay ready to move in a hurry." The princess unrolled a thin bedroll. Then she paused and turned to Holt.

"How much did Korth offer you to serve as guide?"

"We arranged for twenty gold—he paid me six in advance."

Danis went to her saddlebags and solemnly counted out some coins. She brought them to Holt. Her expression was distant, sad he thought, as she gave him the money. "The account is paid," she declared, staring into the Daryman's eyes.

"Thank you," he said, though he got no satisfaction from the payment. For some reason he wanted to give the money back, to show her that he was capable of service for honor alone . . . but his memory of his neighbors' need rendered that course impossible. He would take the money because he owed it to Karl Fisher, Hag Biddlesome, and all the rest.

"Now let's get some rest," huffed Fenrald Falwhak. "I'll take the first watch."

* * * * *

The dwarf poked Holt in the shoulder, awakening him as he clapped a rough hand over the Daryman's mouth. "Wake up!" whispered Fenrald. "But be quiet about it—we've got company!"

Scrambling upward, Holt blinked the sleep from

his eyes. He reached out and found his sword next to his head where he had left it. Meanwhile the dwarf woke Danis, Tellist, and Gazzrick.

The predawn darkness pressed close, though a faint trace of pale light showed along the eastern horizon. Fenrald, they saw, had maintained the entire watch throughout the hours of their too-short rest.

"I smell wolves," the dwarf whispered. "They're coming downwind toward us—be here soon, I'd reckon."

Stumbling about in the darkness, the companions made far too much noise; every cracking twig gave an additional clue to their pursuers. Hastily they threw their equipment onto the horses. Fumbling with his bridle and reins, Holt was glad he'd left Old Thunder saddled. He'd wanted to release the horse, but if he'd done so he would be abandoning his saddle right now. He barely had time to adjust the bridle before Fenrald warned that the enemy was virtually upon them.

The band of pale sky to the east had expanded slightly by the time they were ready to move. The companions could see each other in the shadows— and beyond those shadows, they saw more movement. It was too late to make a clean escape.

"Tut, tut. Has anyone lost a dog?" muttered Tellist Tizzit, squinting at the canine form slinking toward him.

Crimson eyes glowed hatred from the darkness.

"Warwolf!" cried Holt, seizing the magic-user by his shoulder and pulling him onto Old Thunder's haunches.

Metal flashed, and Fenrald's hammer leapt outward. Holt heard the *thunk* of a heavy blow, and the great warwolf snarled ferociously but backed away.

Other shapes moved in the darkness. Skeletal limbs and ribs appeared, clean bone glowing white against the backdrop of night. Holt shuddered reflexively at the eyeless sockets and leering skulls. Upon clumsy leg bones the undead warriors shambled steadily closer.

"Take flight!" cried Danis, gesturing toward the pathway. The princess drew her gleaming steel sword, her charger prancing toward the advancing skeletons.

"Your Highness—you *must* escape!" cried Gazzrick Whiptoe, bouncing up and down on his pony's back.

"Fly, child! Now!" cried Tellist, clinging to Holt's belt. "I don't mean actually *fly*, you understand," he added. "Just flee!"

"They're right!" Fenrald snapped. "*Go!* I'll hold them for a few minutes!"

Cursing, Danis put the spurs to her horse and thundered up the path, Gazzrick close behind. Old Thunder reared and whinnied as Holt looked back, his heart pounding in fear as he saw the horrific faces of the attackers and the lone dwarf who stood against them. The Daryman remembered the faithful guard, Jareth—no doubt he, too, had intended to catch up to the party.

"Tut, tut," muttered Tellist as Holt spurred Thunder back toward the fight.

Relieved that terror hadn't caused his hand to tremble, Holt urged his big horse forward, toward Fenrald's side. The dwarf's hammer flew outward, smashed a skeleton, and rebounded. Another of the undead approached, but Old Thunder reared and brought his heavy forehooves down in a crushing blow. The skeleton collapsed, a splintered pile of bones.

Bony fingers reached for Holt, and he slashed blindly with his sword, shuddering. The unliving hands clutched at his legs. His fear gave him strength, and the Daryman's battered blade hacked into his attackers, knocking them down in both directions.

Old Thunder reared again, whinnying in pain as a great wolf sank its teeth into the gelding's haunch. Holt slashed, gashing the creature between its yellow eyes. The animal dropped, yelping, to the ground.

"We've held them a few minutes by my count!" the dwarf declared as a fresh row of skeletons lurched forward. "Let's get out of here!"

The two horses wheeled and galloped along the trail. Grateful that the forest remained open and uncluttered around them, the three riders quickly left the horrifying attackers behind.

"Any sign of that black thing—the cloud?" asked Fenrald, casting a worried glance over his shoulder.

"No—but it would've been hard to see in this light," Holt replied.

Dawn continued to creep across the sky. The last stars blinked out, and the pale blue in the east brightened to a promising, fiery glow.

They came around a corner in the trail and almost smashed headlong into Danis, who was racing back along the pathway with the halfling galloping behind. The pair had apparently been returning to the fight.

"What are you *doing?*" howled Fenrald. "You were supposed to get away!"

"I know," snapped the princess, wheeling Lancer in front of Old Thunder. "Now, let's *all* take that advice!"

Galloping up a shallow slope, they saw the valley spread behind them in the growing daylight. The huge form of the warwolf led their pursuers, while numerous gray wolves loped after. Farther back, skeletons shambled forward among the scattered trees.

"Trouble ahead!" squeaked Gazzrick, pointing toward the ridge.

Pawns Prevail

A group of horsemen appeared there, leading a train of mules along the trail. The head rider shouted in alarm, as surprised as were the companions by the abrupt meeting. He had a shock of red hair and a bearlike, bearded face.

"Serge Blackthorn's bandits!" Holt cried. "They're the men who killed Korth!"

He brandished his sword, shouting a cry of outrage.

"For vengeance!" shouted Danis Vanderthan, veering toward the band of cutthroats.

Though Serge Blackthorn's bandits at first pursued the companions, the outlaws soon showed no stomach for this fight. Instead, following the example of the flaming-haired leader, they spurred their horses into a gallop and fled obliquely away from the companions.

"They're heading toward the wolves!" cried Gazzrick in amazement.

"How can they not see them?" Holt wondered.

"They *do* see 'em," Fenrald grunted.

The five companions slowed to a halt at the crest of the ridge, looking back into the steadily brightening vale. The bandits, leading nearly a score of mules, trotted straight toward the company of skeletons. Wolves circled to either side as the horsemen stopped.

Serge Blackthorn dismounted and swaggered toward the undead company. Despite the bravado of his posture, however, Holt saw that he kept his fingers clasped tightly around the hilt of a dagger.

Suddenly the Daryman understood what was happening. "He's taking them the *bodies!*" he gasped, his voice choking in revulsion. "That's why they collected them after the fights—Korth, Jareth . . . the others!"

"No!" Danis Vanderthan's voice was a whisper of pure horror. "They *can't!*"

But already they saw the other bandits unstrapping the lifeless forms from the backs of the mules. Blackthorn paced back and forth before several skeletons, as if he were waiting for someone—or some*thing*. The undead and the wolves abandoned, for the moment, their pursuit of the companions. Apparently this meeting was something they, too, had sought. The shadows thickened beneath the trees, and then, rising like a cloud of black smoke, the creature of entropy appeared. Its vapors coalesced into a fog that drifted toward Serge Blackthorn.

The bandit lord took a step forward. Then something in the appearance of the smoke caused him to halt. His dagger fell, unnoticed, to the ground.

With a scream of terror, Serge Blackthorn spun on his heel. He tried to run from the black shape, but he moved slowly, as though his limbs were mired in mud. One agonizing footstep plodded to the ground. The fog crept closer, tentacles reaching like fingers along the earth. After an excruciating pause, the man took another step, but now the tendrils wrapped around his ankles. Serge Blackthorn's scream rose to an even higher pitch as the smoke wrapped his legs, his waist, his chest. . . .

At last the smothering smoke wrapped around his face, and the bandit lord vanished from sight, swallowed by the deadly mist. The only reminder of his presence was the echo of that horror-filled scream, resounding from the encircling heights.

12
Life in the Spheres

Holt led the party along the gravelly bottom of a streambed. For an hour they had followed the splashing brook—an hour during which they had left no sign of their passage. The companions trailed in a file behind the Daryman, with Fenrald Falwhak riding well back and watching the rear. The princess, mounted on Lancer, continually reined back the powerful horse in order to allow the Daryman to select their trail.

They reached a place where the smooth surface

of a wide, flat boulder extended to the water's edge. Holt nudged Old Thunder, and the big horse lumbered upward to clop across the stone. The others followed, and though water sloshed across the slab during their passage, the sun immediately began to evaporate the evidence of their route.

Across from the expanse of rock, Holt found a stretch of dry ground. Brittle grass grew in tufts, leaving large patches of bare dirt. Here, too, they passed without leaving obvious footprints until they reached the next stream. There, once again, the Daryman led them along the waterway, generally working north and east.

Holt used every trick he knew to conceal their trail. They doubled back, they dismounted and brushed over their tracks, and they followed the clear, shallow streams wherever possible.

Despite the bright sunlight, a chill lingered in Holt's body. The memory of that black shape lurked like a stubborn nightmare. His last view had been of those fingerlike tendrils encircling Serge Blackthorn. The bandit's terrified screams had shaken Holt, but the image of that embrace itself had been unspeakably menacing, sinister.

As Holt approached a grove of aspens, a flock of crows fluttered raucously into the air. The Daryman's hand went reflexively to his sword. Several minutes passed before his hands stopped shaking.

Without rest, the five riders pushed through the

long day. The magic-user straddled Old Thunder behind the Daryman, and though Holt felt Tellist's grip weakening, the wizard made no complaint. Gazzrick Whiptoe was pale and drawn, swaying in the saddle from exhaustion, but neither did he suggest that they halt. Later, when Fenrald rode in to report no sign of pursuit, the Daryman noticed that the dwarf kicked and stretched painfully, trying to work the cramps out of his legs.

As they left the lofty summit of Rustwind behind, the Knollbarrens descended to the east in a tangle of ravines and valleys. Many of these were choked with rocks and deadfalls, and finding a passable route became a greater challenge. Holt had very rarely been this far east, and he had no specific knowledge of their path. Still, he felt confident that by following one of the larger streams they should be able to make good progress.

Danis called a halt as sunset cast its first chill shadows. They found a flat shelf of rock on the stream bank and gathered beneath the shelter of an overhanging cliff. Holt, sore and cramped from the hours in the saddle, watched with amazement as the princess sprang nimbly from her mount.

"What about pursuit?" Danis asked Fenrald, who rode in a few minutes after the rest of them.

"Still no sign," the dwarf grunted. "I'd say the Daryman did a pretty good job of hiding our trail."

"Good." The Princess of Vanderthan removed

her helmet and looked around. "We can't risk a fire. We'll rest here for the night—until we get enough daylight to start moving."

With groans of relief, Tellist and Gazzrick climbed down from their mounts. Fenrald cast a long glance up the stream, as if he still feared some evil presence lurking out of view.

"What *was* that thing?" Holt asked again, voicing the question that had disturbed him all day.

None of the companions offered any answer.

"Does anyone know what's going on?" he demanded. "Blazing comets in the sky . . . black fog that can scare the wits out of you? It looked to me like that fog *killed* Serge Blackthorn!"

Gazzrick cleared his throat, looking at the wizard as he spoke tentatively. "Tellist, what do you know of shades?"

The magic-user shuddered. "Tut, tut—nasty creatures, they are. Of course, they dwell in the Sphere of Entropy—but one *could* be summoned here, I suppose, if there were a force of sufficient power. . . ."

"Power such as an artifact?" the halfling wondered.

"Quite so!" Tellist Tizzit exclaimed.

"The comet!" Holt remembered. "You said that you thought *that* was an artifact."

"Indeed," the wizard agreed. "I have known for a long time that the House of Vanderthan has had the blessing of immortal guardianship. My divinations have enabled me to tell with reasonable certainty that Danis would receive an artifact from her immortal sponsor, very soon. That shooting star was it—no doubt about it!"

"I think, perhaps, we have become involved in an affair of the immortals," Gazzrick Whiptoe offered slowly. "In a way, that puts us in great peril—but offers, also, great prospects for reward."

The wizened halfling cleared his throat. As he pondered his explanation, the weariness of the long ride seemed to fall from him like a dusty jacket. He paced back and forth, while one pudgy finger scratched at the whiskers on his cheek.

"You see, normally the immortals are prohibited from any involvement in the affairs of us mortals. They dwell in their own spheres and have no concerns with short-lived beings such as ourselves."

"Do immortals truly live forever?" interjected Holt, quickly fascinated.

"In a manner of speaking, yes." Gazzrick paused and paced for a moment. "Of course, they can be destroyed by each other—much as one mortal can take another's life. But immortals are not subject to aging, disease, or any of the other risks that we lesser beings face."

"You sound like you know a lot about these folks," Fenrald Falwhak suggested, rubbing his cramped legs as he sat on a driftwood log.

"Well, I have devoted many decades of study to

matters of the spheres," the halfling admitted with a modest little cough. "The affairs of immortalhood are as known to me as to any person. I have personally held great artifacts, and more than once have I dealt with visitors from other spheres."

"Gazzrick Whiptoe served my grandfather as the royal scholar sixty years ago," Danis noted with amusement. "He was my father's teacher, and for the past ten years, he's been a harsh taskmaster to me."

"Now, my dear—I have yet to meet the person who could be a harsh taskmaster to you!" Gazzrick objected with a wave of his hand.

Danis chuckled wryly at the remark. Though Holt heartily agreed with the halfling's sentiment, he carefully suppressed his own smile of amusement. Gazzrick Whiptoe's continuing explanation forced any further thoughts of humor from the Daryman's mind.

"That dark cloud we saw—we all felt the evil within it! That mist, I believe, is the essence of a powerful *creature*—a nightshade."

"You mean a monster, like a warwolf?" Holt asked.

"The nightshade is far worse—a being that comes from another sphere and seeks a way to exert its power in our world."

"From the Sphere of Entropy?" suggested Tellist Tizzit.

"Precisely." The halfling's face creased in a deep frown.

"What is entropy?" Holt wondered again. He suddenly felt that his life in Oxvale had kept him very sheltered from the important matters of the world.

"It is the force of darkness and decay—of ultimate death," Gazzrick stated grimly. "Whereas all other forces seek, at least in a general sense, to create, entropy seeks only to destroy.

"To accomplish that destruction, the forces of entropy will expend great power, cause entire worlds to be racked by war and plague. Whole legions of dark creatures labor in this evil cause, leaving horror and despair wherever they go!"

Holt knew that his land, Karawenn, was a much bigger place than he could ever hope to see. This talk of 'worlds' made his head swim!

"Many of these creatures are mere, mindless tools of darkness," the tutor explained. "Such as the skeletons and the gray wolves who answer the primitive summons of their evil masters."

"But not warwolves?" Holt guessed.

"Nay—they are true creatures of entropy. They grow stronger as they destroy, and their power bends the lesser wolves to their will. But even the warwolves are not masters—they are merely lackeys of the true evil."

"The cloud . . . ?" Now the Daryman sensed why

he had found that bodiless mist so terrifying.

Gazzrick nodded. "Among the mightiest of evil's servants are the nightshades. They dwell in the Sphere of Entropy itself and can only move to another world with powerful aid. And even then, the transition is not complete."

"What kind of aid?" inquired Fenrald.

"The greatest tools of the immortals are their artifacts." The scholarly halfling continued his lecture. "And this, I believe, is the reason for our current predicament. As Tellist says, there is a good chance that the shooting star was just such an artifact."

"But you said the . . . nightshade's transition is not complete?" Holt wondered. "The nightshade is not that black cloud?"

"No—that is merely a projection of its real power. It might be that the killing of Serge Blackthorn, or some other act of bloodletting, will let the creature assume its full form. Then, it will likely seek the artifact that drew it to Karawenn in the first place."

"Of course it will!" Tellist interjected impatiently. "I've been saying that for *days!*"

"I don't suppose you claim to know what the artifact is?" snapped the halfling sarcastically.

"Oh, I should suppose it's some accessory to rulership—a scepter, perhaps—or a crown. Tut, tut—I certainly can't say with any certainty."

Douglas Niles

"It's a crown," Danis said, her voice soft with wonder.

The others looked at her in astonishment.

"I've dreamed about it—ever since I was a little girl," she said. "I can tell you the number of points—describe the emeralds and diamonds in their settings. . . ." Her words trailed off.

"That's it, then!" declared Tellist delightedly. "The Crown of Vanderthan—and it lies waiting for us, somewhere to the east!"

"I hate to bring up another problem," Holt said awkwardly, "but World's End lies to the east of the Knollbarrens. If the artifact came down in that direction, if it went too far, it could have missed Karawenn completely and plunged into the mists at the end of the world."

"No! That's impossible!" snapped Danis, but her eyes widened in fear.

"Tut, tut—I'm afraid it is *quite* possible, my dear," countered the wizard, wagging a finger.

"I felt the ground shake when it landed!" the princess insisted determinedly. "That wouldn't have happened if it had gone over World's End."

"That's right!" Holt declared.

"Not at all," Tellist pointed out, as stubborn as Danis. "Sound could have created the boom we felt—a trembling of the *air* instead of the ground!"

"I refuse to believe that," the Princess of Vanderthan declared. "There is a destiny laid on that artifact, and its fate is not to be lost over the brink of World's End!" She glared at Tellist so furiously that the wizard bit back whatever remark was about to emerge from his lips.

"We have little choice but to search," said Gazzrick Whiptoe. "And pray to the spheres for the fortune to find it before the nightshade does!"

They heard a rattling of stones from the embankment overhead, and then a smattering of debris fell to the ground. Fenrald reached for his hammer, but cramps seized his legs, and he doubled over with a gasp of pain.

Danis leapt to her feet, sword bared, as Holt fumbled for his own weapon. A man climbed down the bank toward their camp, but as they watched, he lost his grip. The figure tumbled downward, thudding onto the ground and lying still. Slowly, the princess and the Daryman lowered their blades.

"It's one of the bandits!" cried Gazzrick, recognizing the scruffy fellow from Serge Blackthorn's band. The man's skin was blistered and pasty white. Ugly red pox scarred his cheeks and hands, as if he had been scoured by some virulent disease. His eyes bulged in horror, and he stared madly from one of the companions to another.

"What is it?" asked Danis, sheathing her blade and approaching the bandit. The man recoiled in terror as she reached out a hand. "Don't be afraid."

"*Cold!*" gasped the man, making the word an explosive curse. "It was . . . *so cold!*"

The bandit's eyes bulged as he stared madly at the companions. "It *took* them . . . took them . . . all . . . dead."

Then his back arched, and his body grew rigid, and his breathing choked away to nothing. Though the fellow's eyelids remained open, Holt knew that his eyes could no longer see.

13
Sír Ira Hsíao

Despite the arrival of daylight, the bandit's bizarre appearance and death shrouded the companions in a dark gloom. Trembling, Holt pulled his cloak tightly around his shoulders, not certain whether the morning was unusually cold or his mind shivered from the memory of the wretch's last words.

So cold. What did he mean? The Daryman could imagine no realistic answer, though a variety of horrifying possibilities danced around the fringes of his mind. Foremost among his fears, he suspected that the chill was somehow connected to

Douglas Niles

the horrifying darkness that had drifted, cloudlike, in the wake of the skeleton warriors—the nightshade, as Gazzrick and Tellist had called it.

For a long, grim day they pressed eastward. In stretches Holt took pains to conceal their trail, but in other places they opted for speed, cantering down broad, winding valleys as their course took them toward World's End. Throughout the day they saw nothing except the occasional crow that flew, cawing irritably, upward from their path.

Near sunset they entered a forest of tall, broadleafed trees. The rugged heights of the Knollbarrens lay, for the most part, behind them. Gentle, tree-covered ground led downward in a series of steplike plateaus to the east.

The Daryman led the way along a wide trail in the forest. Danis on her charger trotted easily behind Old Thunder. A pleasant breeze whiffed past them, and the slanting rays of the sun penetrated the leaves in dappled patterns.

"Who . . . who goes there?"

The question, hooted in an almost musical cadence, emerged from a cluster of trees before them.

Holt drew in his reins, surprised as Danis impulsively pressed past him. The princess wasn't wearing her helmet, and her hair sparkled like spun gold in the sunlight.

"Who questions me?" she cried. Her hand rested

on the hilt of her sword, though she didn't draw the weapon.

"I say," came the hooting voice, this time speaking in clipped tones. "We don't tolerate horses around here. Dogs and wolves are bad enough, you know. I really must insist—"

"Show yourself!" commanded Danis. "Who are you?"

"I should be delighted to show myself to such a beautiful maiden as yourself!" Now the voice was smooth, fawning. "It's not often that we're graced with such a lovely and charming visitor!"

Still suspicious, Danis was nevertheless mollified enough to lift her hand from her sword. Shading her eyes, she peered into the foliage of a massive oak.

Brown wings beat, and Holt saw a large, barrel-shaped bird float outward to settle on the lower branch of a nearby tree. Huge, wide eyes studied them, and Holt stared back at the largest owl he had ever seen.

The animal seemed to sense its own magnificence, for it puffed out its chest and preened for a moment, as if to heighten its grandeur.

"Now, to *whooooom* am I speaking?" inquired the bird, his beak primly pronouncing the words.

"I am Danis Vanderthan, High Princess of Vanderthan. This is my entourage," announced the young woman.

Douglas Niles

Holt flushed, insulted that her companions were dismissed thus. Still, none of the others seemed bothered, so he scowled and remained silent, slouching in his saddle.

"I am Sir Ira Hsiao," replied the smooth-spoken bird. "I am pleased to inform you that you have reached the borders of my domain. My friends, the crows, warned me of your imminent arrival."

"*Your* domain?" sputtered Fenrald Falwhak. Danis turned to glare at the dwarf while the owl blinked with irritating patience.

"There *are* no dominions in the Knollbarrens!" Holt added, eager to come to Fenrald's rescue. He ignored the princess as she turned her frosty eyes on him. "I've spent a good portion of my life in this wilderness, and never have I met someone who claims a part for himself!"

"Humph!" snorted the owl, amusedly tolerant. "Perhaps you don't know them as well as you think! After all, I've never seen you here!"

"Well, not right in this part. . . ." Holt was ready to argue, but already the owl ignored him, turning back to the princess.

"And you, my dear," Sir Ira observed graciously. "It's entirely too rare that we have such an illustrious—and dare I say *well-bred*—visitor as yourself. I know that it's a trifle late for tea, but I *do* hope you can join me for dinner."

"I'd be delighted," Danis replied with a polite

nod of her head.

"Your entourage is welcome to rest in my glade," said the owl, bowing his entire body by rocking forward on his tree limb. "While you and I take this opportunity for a genteel conversation."

The owl fluttered to a nearby tree, indicating with a gracious sweep of his wing the trail that the companions were to follow. Holt waited in astonishment for Gazzrick or one of the other companions to object to this waste of time. The halfling met Holt's eyes, but raised his shoulders in a shrug of helplessness. Danis was already following Sir Ira's lead.

Finally the Daryman decided he had to speak. With a kick, he urged Old Thunder into a trot, hastening behind Danis's charger.

"Your Highness," he said in a tone of icy politeness. "There is the business at hand—such a delay won't help us accomplish our task! It's nearly sunset—we have to press on!"

"I've considered that," Danis replied, her voice cold and stern. "But this will be worthwhile. Now, be quiet about it."

Holt's jaw dropped. "*What?*" he exploded. "I'm not your land-bound serf! Now you want us to wait while you stop for a *tea* party? That's just *stupid—and* it's a waste of time! If you don't—"

"Now see here!" declared Sir Ira Hsiao. "That's no way to talk to this royal lady!"

The owl waved a wing, and Holt's words died in his throat. The Daryman felt a sudden, terrifying weakness, and his muscles collapsed limply. Swaying in his saddle, he toppled to the side as the reins dropped from his nerveless fingers.

"Whoa, lad!" The outstretched arm of Fenrald Falwhak prevented him falling to the ground while Tellist clasped both arms around the Daryman's waist to hold him in the saddle. Holt gasped, breathing but unable to speak or even groan.

"What did you do?" growled the dwarf to the owl, his tone grim and a burly hand clutching the haft of his hammer. Mounted on his sturdy pony, Fenrald rode beside the Daryman, reaching up to hold him in Old Thunder's saddle.

"Just a little spell of holding," said the owl dismissively. "He'll be back to himself in a few minutes—though perhaps he won't be *quite* so rude. Now, where were we?" Sir Ira said with a little bow to Danis.

The princess had been staring at Holt. The Daryman's head lay against Old Thunder's withers while Fenrald and Tellist steadied him in the saddle. Momentarily, a flash of concern showed on the princess's features, but after the owl's reassurances she seemed to give the matter no further thought. Turning back to Sir Ira, she resumed their chat. The owl glided easily from tree to tree, leading the companions along a wide, flower-lined pathway.

Pawns Prevail

Holt rode miserably. He tried to clench his fingers, to kick a leg—even to spit—but his muscles refused to respond. The saddle dug into his belly, and the hairs of the horse's mane tickled his nose, but he could do nothing about his discomfort—nothing except stare at the ground and fume.

By the time he felt some slight sensation returning to his limbs, the sun had set. The little party had ridden through an arched gateway framed by a dense thicket of flowering bushes. Holt pushed himself upward in the saddle to see that they had entered a wide, grassy meadow. Flowers bloomed in a riot of colors, and an immense, cone-shaped pine tree rose from the center of the space.

A large, furry animal ambled toward them on all fours. Holt first thought was that it was a short-legged bear, but then the creature rose on its haunches, and the Daryman saw that it resembled a woodchuck, but was far larger than the most massive hedgehog.

"Perinal, Deritik—see to the horses of our visitors," said Sir Ira. "I suppose we'll have to let them into the meadow—for a short time." A second huge woodchuck appeared—a female, though Holt wasn't sure how he knew this—and reached up to remove the bridle and saddle from Danis's charger. Squatting upright, the creatures were taller than Gazzrick or Fenrald.

Douglas Niles

"My lady, if you'll come this way." With his wing the owl indicated the stately pine in the middle of the clearing. "Oh, and the rest of you shall find water and fruit in the grotto—Perinal, please show them where."

The plump creature chattered pleasantly, dropping to all fours and bounding through the grass toward a clump of flowering lilac bushes, while Deritik continued to unsaddle the mounts. The four companions followed Perinal. In spite of his sour mood, Holt was impressed by the fragrant blossoms; elsewhere in the 'Barrens the shrubs were still weeks away from flowering.

Meanwhile, Sir Ira flew toward a middle branch of the big pine tree, and Danis walked to the trunk. Holt caught glimpses, through the dense foliage, of the princess climbing a circling stairway around the thick bole of the tree. Platforms supported a number of unwalled rooms, so that the huge conifer seemed to be a virtual mansion. The wizened owl came to rest on a stout limb about halfway up.

"This place is really quite remarkable," murmured Tellist as he looked around in amazement. "Tut, tut—quite remarkable indeed. I wonder how it came to be."

"I've heard a legend," Gazzrick offered as the four companions followed the ambling woodchuck toward a glittering grove of aspens interspersed with angular, gray boulders. "It dates back many centuries—to a time when the Knollbarrens was a place of elves and giants."

"Elves and giants in the 'Barrens?" Holt said skeptically. "I've never seen any evidence of that."

"It's true. At least, *I* believe the legend," Fenrald noted seriously. "It was during the early years of Graywall, when the dwarves wanted only to be left alone. The stories say the giants and elves fought each other in a war so savage that both sides were wiped out."

"And then there's the rest of the legend," Gazzrick supplied. "When the elves were gone, it's said that animals moved in to some of their most hallowed places. Perhaps this is one of them."

Holt had to admit that the explanation made a certain amount of sense. He knew that he'd never explored this part of the 'Barrens on his own—in fact, he'd never even been *curious* about it.

The grotto proved to be a small, moss-lined niche in a rocky depression. The pool of water in the center of the niche stood so still that the liquid reflected like a mirror. Perinal chirped and bobbed his head toward the grassy bower, an obvious request for the companions to make themselves comfortable.

Holt sat on a mossy rock shaped like a comfortable chair, and chuckled as the huge woodchuck hopped back to help its mate. Looking around the grotto, he noticed berries growing along the shore. Like the flowers, these were ripe much earlier than those in the rest of the Knollbarrens.

Nearby, the solitary pine where Sir Ira and the princess visited jutted upward like a proud staff, its lush limbs waving like feathered banners in the breeze. Holt admitted to himself that he'd never imagined a place like this to exist in the Knollbarrens. He watched the two woodchucks as they carefully combed the horses, using the short claws on their forepaws. When they had tethered the mounts, tying knots as nimbly as any sailor, they hopped toward the pool. Often one of the creatures stopped to nuzzle or scratch the other, and Holt found their affection strangely touching.

Yet when his gaze shifted to the pine tree, his anger at the princess and the unusual owl flared upward again. He thought of her enjoying a pleasant dinner while her companions sat outside, and he wanted nothing more than to quit this place.

After returning from the pasture, the two woodchucks settled themselves beside a round hole beside the pool—apparently their burrow. From that spot, they watched the companions with clear, glittering eyes. When Holt looked at Perinal, he imagined he saw sympathy—or pity—in the animal's gaze. Ridiculous, he told himself. He looked to the sky and tried to guess the time.

Pawns Prevail

The sun had set perhaps two hours before. Low in the eastern sky the full moon crept upward. Now it cast clear shadows of the companions and the surrounding trees. From the grotto, Holt could see a bright light glow high in the branches of the giant pine, illuminating a large platform, a long table and several chairs. Gold sparkled in the lantern light, the gold of Danis's hair. Through the still night air came the soft clink of elegant glassware and china.

"They're probably having roast pheasant and jam!" Holt said angrily. The plump berries around them, which should have been a treat, looked bitter and shriveled to him now.

"Now, now—you mustn't be so hard on her," Gazzrick Whiptoe said. "She *is* the princess, after all."

"But why do you let her treat you like this?" demanded the Daryman.

"Tut, tut," cautioned the wizard. "We'd best lower our voices. It's *awfully* peaceful here. I'd hate to think that we've introduced a disturbance. Mark my words—this is a place of power . . . a very special place. We're lucky to have found it."

"Lucky?" Despite his indignation, Holt whispered. "I was magicked—"

"Now, that was a simple spell of holding—as Sir Ira told you, I might add. There was no harm done, and it *did* make things a little more . . . shall we say, *peaceful?* Just for a time there, anyway."

165

"It's in the past." Fenrald's husky voice entered the fray.

Irritated, Holt spun on his heel away from his companions. He saw the tall pine, needles glowing almost blue in the moonlight.

Then he felt an awful, bone-piercing chill, as if the air itself had turned to ice water around him. The bandit's words came into his mind—*so cold*.

The freezing sensation swept over Holt's companions at the same time. Fenrald cursed. Gazzrick gasped in amazement, while Tellist stammered something unintelligible. The two woodchucks squawked in alarm, scuttling into their burrow.

Instinctively, the Daryman looked up. A huge shadow swirled downward to blot out the top of the pine tree. Holt had a momentary impression of two massive wings spreading outward, as big as the sails of a ship. Even more awe-inspiring than the size of the thing was its all-encompassing *darkness*.

The light in the dining platform winked out. They heard a scream and the crash of dishes, followed by a much louder *crack*.

"It splintered the tree!" Holt cried, watching the upper half of the giant conifer snap free and tumble toward the ground. The earth beneath his feet heaved from the impact, and, horrified, he wondered if the princess had plunged to her death.

Pawns Prevail

The shadow broke from the tree and soared toward them. Those *were* wings—bat wings, each big enough to smother an Oxvale cottage! Holt staggered backward as the massive creature dived straight for him. Fumbling numbly for his sword hilt, he saw a blunt, eyeless face—and yet he *felt* the beast's keen awareness of them all.

Under the bright moon, the gargantuan bat-thing seemed to suck the light out of the air, casting a growing shadow. Holt's feet stuck to the ground, only because he couldn't think to move them. His hands clenched, empty, still a few inches from the hilt of his sword.

"Light!" cried Tellist, suddenly—as if he'd been struck by a great idea. In the next instant, a bright flare of illumination sparkled in the air, directly before the diving nightshade.

The creature swerved to avoid the brilliant glare, and Holt heard Danis cry out from the platform, near the top of what remained of the splintered tree.

"Sir Ira? Where are you?" The voice penetrated the night like a crackle of thunder, and the huge bat veered back toward the remains of the great pine.

"Danis!" Holt cried. "Get out of there!"

Now his sword was in his hand, and he sprinted across the smooth lawn, racing for the tree. He saw movement in the limbs of the evergreen as that great

167

shadow spread overhead, blotting out the moon and the sky. Underneath the monster now, Holt felt the terrible, icy chill suck at his skin, as if the creature sapped the very warmth from the world.

"Jump!" shouted the Daryman as he reached the sagging boughs of the great evergreen.

Danis leapt from the wrecked platform, plunging through the supple pine branches.

The nightshade wrapped the top of the tree in an embrace of total death.

The princess plummeted toward Holt, who sheathed his sword and tried futilely to catch her. They both crashed to the ground, but the next moment, Holt got to his feet and reached down to help her up. She remained limp and motionless. Clenching his teeth grimly, Holt roughly hoisted the princess over his shoulder. Turning, staggering beneath the extra weight, he stumbled toward the rock-walled grotto.

Wood splintered behind him and great limbs crashed to the ground as the tree trunk split asunder. The turf heaved underfoot with the concussion of the blast. Lurching unsteadily, the Daryman struggled to remain upright on the rippling surface as he hauled the stunned woman toward their companions.

He pitched forward at the edge of the grotto. Strong arms embraced them as Fenrald and Gazzrick lowered Danis to the ground.

Pawns Prevail

But already that great shadow turned from the ruined tree. The eyeless face stared straight into the grotto, and massive wings once again reached out to embrace the sky.

Desperate chirping attracted Holt's attention. The huge woodchucks, trembling with terror, squatted outside their burrow. Deritik bounded inside while Perinal hopped excitedly, still chirping. Frantically gesturing with its woolly head, the creature summoned them toward the earthen hole.

"In there!" cried Holt. "They're offering us shelter."

They carried Danis to the hole, which was barely wide enough for Fenrald's broad shoulders.

"You first—pull her in after you!" barked the Daryman to the dwarf. The stocky warrior nodded and disappeared feetfirst through the hole. His hands grasped Danis by the shoulders, and the princess quickly vanished. Gazzrick and Tellist dived after as Holt looked up to see the massive shadow reaching down from the sky.

The woodchuck chattered. Holt turned to the hole, scrambling headfirst after the wizard. He pulled his feet into the burrow, scurrying along the dirt tunnel, trying to make room for the other woodchuck.

But the outside of the burrow vanished in a cloak of utter darkness. Tendrils of icy cold, like invisible, invading serpents, penetrated into the

169

depths of their shelter. Perinal chattered once more, a sharp, furious bark that mingled defiance and despair.

The sound twisted into a horrifying shriek of pain, until finally the only thing Holt heard was the crashing cadence of his own pounding fear.

14
Elkhorn

The dark, close-pressing walls of the burrow wrapped Holt in a cocoon of fear, threatening to choke, to smother him. More truthfully, he thought, it was the intensity of his own panic that tightened his throat and made each breath a rasping effort.

"Come on," Fenrald urged in a rasping whisper. "There's more space farther in."

Gradually the companions crept downward, gathering in a circular chamber. Their surroundings remained utterly dark, but by sound and touch they learned that all of them were present. Holt and the dwarf pulled Danis with them. The

Douglas Niles

Daryman tried to arrange her comfortably, but was shocked by the stillness of her body, the chill of her flesh. Only a faint pulse fluttered at her throat.

At the mouth of the burrow, Deritik chattered hopefully for several minutes, finally whimpering when it became apparent that her mate was not coming. She curled in a corner of the burrow, her restless sleep punctuated by whines and barks of misery.

Holt and Gazzrick sat to either side of Danis, listening as the princess's breathing grew more labored. Gradually they noticed that her skin grew increasingly warm.

"It's a bad fever," the halfling announced, concern tightening his throat. "We've got to do something!"

"Against the magic of *that?*" Fenrald growled. "Fat lot of chance we'd have!"

"The nightshade's complete now," the halfling noted, his voice quivering. "We'd only seen its essence before. Now its full presence has entered Karawenn—probably because it feasted on the life-forces of those bandits. It's lucky for us the shade's physical form won't fit down this hole. If it were still a fog, we'd all be dead now."

Frightened that the nightshade might be listening above, Holt replied in a whisper. "How long will it stay out there?"

"It didn't much care for Tellist's magic light. We

172

can hope that sunrise will drive it away," Fenrald said grimly. "We *have* to hope that—or expect to starve in here!"

Holt tore a rag from his tunic and soaked it in water from his flask. Pressing it to Danis's forehead, he tried to keep her cool. Every so often, she kicked reflexively or groaned faintly, and he took these as encouraging signs.

"You saved her life." The words from the dark, spoken by Gazzrick Whiptoe, took Holt by surprise.

"Aye, lad," Fenrald added. "Trying to catch her, then carrying her to the grotto—that was a display of courage I'll not soon forget."

The Daryman shrugged awkwardly. "I just had to do *something*."

For the first time since the nightshade's arrival, he remembered how angry he had been at Danis. His rage seemed like a trivial thing now, insignificant compared to the awful presence that stalked Karawenn. He imagined the nightshade swooping down upon Oxvale, knew that no one there would dare stand against it.

And even suppose someone did, he thought bitterly. What would courage gain a man against the nightshade? Nothing but an early death. He shivered reflexively as he remembered the vast, sweeping *size* of the thing. Now he knew how a mouse felt when swooped upon by an eagle.

173

"I'll have a look outside." Fenrald moved toward the tunnel, and for the first time Holt noticed the faint illumination of dawn creeping into the burrow.

They waited for what seemed like an eternity until the dwarf crawled back to the lower burrow. "It's clear as far as I can see. Sun's full up by now. We have to hope the nightshade's a beast of the darkness!"

None of them felt sure, but they could see that the alternative was to remain indefinitely in the burrow. "Let's try to get as far away from here as we can by nightfall," Holt suggested, crawling after the dwarf.

Soon, blinking in the daylight, he stood and stretched his back and legs to work out a multitude of painful cramps. The clearing, once Sir Ira's pastoral preserve, looked as though it had been ravaged by war. The great tree had been splintered into fragments, many the size of huge beams. These lay scattered like matchsticks, jutting into the soft dirt and tearing the meadow with deep gouges.

The companions eased Danis out of the tunnel and stretched her on the soft grass beside the pool, under the shelter of a lush berry bush. Holt was shocked by the pale cast of her skin. Her body was limp, almost lifeless. Red spots had broken out upon her face and hands, and they all remembered the hideous pox that had scarred the dying bandit who had found their previous camp.

"What can we do?" cried Gazzrick Whiptoe, wringing his hands. He turned to Tellist. "Your magic—?"

The mage shook his head sadly, placing a consoling hand on the halfling's shoulder. "You know as well as I do, my friend, that wizardly powers are useless for a need such as this."

"Look, here," Fenrald noted grimly. He knelt beside one of the berry bushes at the pool. Where plump, lush fruit had previously grown, withered bunches of rotting, grublike clusters now dangled.

Gazzrick went to his saddlebags to remove some hardtack and cheese and was dismayed to find that the bread had rotted into mush and the cheese was covered with a pungent mold. "The nightshade spoiled all the food," he observed, gray and sickened by the growing evidence of the monster's power.

"Any sign of the owl?" Holt asked as Fenrald came back from the ruined tree.

The dwarf shook his head. " 'Course, he might be pinned under ten tons of lumber, and I wouldn't know it," he announced grimly.

"Who could imagine such poppycock? Perish the very thought!"

At the words, spoken from a tree atop the grotto walls, a surprising wave of relief swept through

175

Holt. "Sir Ira!" he called. "We're down here!"

"Of course you're down here!" snapped the owl, floating through a graceful spiral and coming to rest on a rock above the shore of the pool. "I've been listening to you chatter for the last ten minutes!"

"Spyin', eh?" Fenrald bristled. "I've a good mind to—"

"You've got a mind, but I should hardly call it a good one," Sir Ira retorted. He stalked toward the companions, fixing his round eyes on Holt and the dwarf. "I was simply keeping an eye out for the nightshade."

The dwarf gulped and fell silent.

"As you've deduced, the beast departed with the dawn—probably to rest for the day." Sir Ira fixed them all with his baleful glare. "You chaps have a very potent enemy—you're lucky to have survived with your lives. Unfortunately, it's just the kind of trouble one has to expect when humans start mucking about. Now, I suggest you get—"

"We're not as lucky as you think," Holt declared. He pointed to Danis, lying concealed by the berry bush.

"Oh, dear," clucked Sir Ira, hopping from the rock to the ground. He waddled to the princess, stooping forward in concern. "Tsk, tsk—this is terrible!"

"We *know* that!" Gazzrick replied in exasperation. "I'm afraid that any attempt to travel might kill her!"

But the owl didn't appear to hear. Bobbing forward on his short legs, Sir Ira stared into Danis's face—almost as if he studied her eyes through her closed lids. Slowly, very gently, the owl stroked a broad wing across the woman's face. As the feathers passed, the pallor left her skin, and was replaced by the bronzed glow of vitality. The red spots faded into her normal, healthy complexion. Color seemed to flow from the silken feathertips as the wing passed down her motionless body. Danis began to breath easily and deeply.

Abruptly she yawned, stretching her arms as she sat up. For a moment she blinked at the companions, and then her eyes widened in memory— and horror. Mutely she looked at the wreckage of the tree, at the gouges in the once-pristine lawn of the clearing.

"I—I'm sorry," she said to Sir Ira. "All this is our—is *my* fault. If I hadn't come here, you wouldn't have suffered like this!"

"Now, stop talking nonsense!" declared the owl, stalking up to Danis and scowling sternly. His eyes evenly met the sitting woman's. "That nightshade took a dislike to me right away—and don't tell me it was all your doing! Why, he could have killed me almost as easily as he got you! I daresay it's just like one of you Big Folks to think he came here because of you! Remember, entropy is the enemy of animals as well as humans."

"It was *horrifying*," Danis admitted with a shudder. "The last thing I remember, the tree was coming apart around me. I must have fallen fifty feet! And that thing—that nightshade—came swooping after me!"

"It would have claimed you, Princess, if not for the heroism of the Daryman," said Gazzrick pointedly.

"Aye—the lad . . . well—caught you and carried you all the way to the grotto," Fenrald added.

Danis looked surprised. She regarded Holt curiously for a moment. Whatever her thoughts, her face softened into a smile. "Thank you," she said.

Holt bowed stiffly. Once again his indignation came pouring back, and he flushed at the memory of her arrogance. No doubt such a rescue was no less than she expected from her 'entourage,' he thought.

If Danis took any note of his reaction, she didn't let on. "What about the horses?" she asked the group in general.

"They're safe," Fenrald Falwhak announced. "They broke free and sheltered in the thicket back of the meadow. I found 'em there this morning."

"Then we'd best be on our way," Danis decided. She looked at Holt. "Still to the east from here?"

"If that's where Your Highness believes our goal

to be," the Daryman replied icily.

She frowned slightly at his tone, but then turned to Sir Ira. The owl had flown back to his rocky perch and squatted above them on the lip of the grotto's wall.

"You've helped me already—far more than I can properly give thanks—yet I would ask another favor of you," Danis said to Sir Ira, her voice humble.

"You have only to speak, and if it lies within my power . . ." The owl concluded his offer with a dramatic bow, his right wing gracefully sweeping below the stout belly.

"Last night I described to you the crown we seek. Do you have power that might help us know whether we're on the right path—whether indeed it lies before us at all?"

"I have some ability in that area," announced the owl, strutting along the lip of rock. "And, in fact, I anticipated your request, performing the spell of location during the night. The answer to your question is this."

The owl paused for dramatic effect, checking to see that everyone paid attention. He was not disappointed.

"The artifact lies at the brink of World's End—but not beyond. I have despatched crows to report back with more details. I hope to hear within a day or two."

"Thank you again," Danis said with a bow of her own, "for your healing power and your information. I'm afraid, however, that our business is too pressing to allow us a day or two to wait." Then she turned to the companions. "We ride!"

"Ahem. I should consider it an honor if I might be allowed to accompany you," declared the owl.

"Of course! The honor would be ours!" Danis was clearly delighted with the suggestion.

"The crows will find us," Sir Ira noted. "And then we'll know more."

"For a start, it'll be enough to reach World's End," Danis suggested. "Do you know these valleys, Sir Ira?"

"Why, my dear—like the back of my wing! I've soared over them all; I know the trails and traps better than any human ever will!"

Holt watched the exchange, feeling useless. His initial dislike of Sir Ira had passed, but for some reason the knowledge that they'd have the owl's company drove his mood lower and lower.

Throughout the day they followed the winding valleys eastward. Holt had never visited this part of the 'Barrens before, but that didn't seem to matter now—Danis had ceased to ask for his opinion about their course. Now that the owl flew before them, choosing their path, it seemed that his services as guide were no longer needed.

By paying attention to the location of the sun,

however, he gradually realized that Sir Ira's course led them somewhat north of east. Finally, as the great bird soared toward an oak that towered on the slope of a nearby ridge, Holt pushed Old Thunder up to the side of the princess.

"The owl told us that the crown lies eastward," he declared. "Ask him—why does he lead us to the north?"

She turned to him, irritated, but then her forehead creased in thought.

"Sir Ira," she called. "Where do you take us?"

The owl glided back to land on the low limb of a nearby tree. He bobbed his head sagely at Holt. "The sun sinks toward setting. I lead you to a place where—with luck—we'll be able to spend the night free from the threat of the nightshade."

"What place?" demanded Fenrald.

"A . . . valley. It lies just beyond this ridge. It is well screened against evil, and if you reach its borders by nightfall you will be safe from outside threats."

"*Out*side threats?" Holt didn't like the sound of that. "What about the valley itself?"

"That's where luck comes in," replied the owl stiffly before taking wing once more toward the ridge.

"I don't like it," Fenrald announced, scowling. "There'll be more enchantments ahead—mark my words!"

"Spend the night here then," Danis declared crisply. She started her charger up the slope, Gazzrick following immediately. With a helpless shrug of his shoulders, Holt went along, and the grumbling dwarf fell in at the rear.

As they crested the ridge, the Daryman had little difficulty believing that they looked upon enchanted ground. The valley below was broad and rimmed by sheer cliffs—except for a gentle pass descending at their feet. At least a dozen waterfalls spilled from the surrounding heights, several of them outlined like ivory pillars in the light of the setting sun.

The valley floor was a mixture of wooded groves and open, flowery glades. Spring water reflected like mirrors from numerous pools, while several larger ponds provided homes to graceful swans and busy, bobbing ducks.

They started down the wide trail before them, flanked by a wood of tall trees and dense underbrush. As they reached the valley floor, Holt noticed huge deer tracks in the soft dirt. The impressions of the cloven hooves, he thought, must have been left by a stag the size of a horse!

Lancer reared back in sudden panic. The princess fought to control her frightened mount and grabbed for her sword. Gazzrick's pony bucked the halfling onto the ground while, anxiously, Holt drew his own weapon and pressed Old Thunder forward.

Pawns Prevail

"Halt, humans!"

The command boomed through the air, the sound alone enough to bring the horses to a full stop. Holt, straddling huge Thunder, found himself eye-to-eye with a massive creature that stood on its own hind legs.

"You are trespassers in the valley of Elkhorn!" bellowed the gigantic fellow, who brandished a massive spear in an upraised right hand. Yet though it had hands and walked upright, the being was not human in shape. A pair of massive antlers jutted from the sides of its head, and the nose protruded into an animal-like snout. The torso, shoulders, and arms were like a man's—a huge, brawny man's—but its waist tapered into the legs of a massive, powerful deer.

With a shock, Holt looked at the massive hooves of the creature's feet, knowing immediately they must have made the tracks he'd seen moments earlier.

"Trespassers, I say!" repeated the monster, the bellow of its voice lessening slightly. "And as such, you will have to fight to pass!"

15
Battle Glade

"Fight?" asked Fenrald Falwhak with a snort. "I'm afraid you're overmatched, friend. You're a big one, that's sure—but we're five against one!"

"Aye, *fight*," growled the stag-man, his voice a snarl as menacing as any bear's. "But not five to one—oh, no!

"I tell you, dwarf, this is not a war in which the biggest army wins. It is a duel of nature, in which the champion of your herd must face the defender of this valley. I, Elkhorn of the Vale, am the latter; which of you is the former?"

Again it was Fenrald who answered for the companions. "I'll take that challenge!"

"Wait!" Danis spoke sharply. "Tell us, Lord Elkhorn—why should we grant you this duel? Do you think you could prevent us from passing should we decline to fight?"

The creature snorted again in clear disdain. He gestured with a hairy hand to the woods around them. Already the companions saw that the thorny branches of the undergrowth had intertwined, creating a high barrier that fully encircled them.

"Only upon my command will the woods release you!" boasted Elkhorn.

"Sounds like you need a lesson in manners," growled the dwarf. Fenrald swung down from his saddle and marched toward the looming forest giant. Though he stood less than half as tall as his foe, nothing in the dwarf's gait suggested a moment's hesitation or doubt.

"Weapons—or bare hands?" inquired the dwarf, hefting his hammer while he eyed the stag-man's huge, bone spear.

Elkhorn cast his weapon aside and crouched, his huge arms spreading to the sides like the limbs of a tree. "The natural weapons of the elk centaur are fine for me—you make your own choice."

Fenrald shrugged and passed his hammer up to Holton. "Keep an eye on my weapon for a few minutes—this shouldn't take me long!" Next the dwarf tossed his helmet, chain shirt, and gauntlets to the ground beside his horse.

"To the first fall—or to the death?" inquired Fenrald, his tone unconcerned.

"I'm not a killer—we fight until one of us is thrown to the ground," replied Elkhorn.

Spitting on his hands, Fenrald rubbed his palms together before turning to meet the looming Elkhorn in a wrestler's stance. The dwarf hesitated for a moment in feigned uncertainty, then suddenly dived through the air, somersaulted past the stag-man's hooves, and bounced to his feet to deliver a sharp kick to the back of Elkhorn's knee.

The creature bellowed in pain and frustration, whirling and lowering his head to gore the dwarf with those huge horns. Fenrald tumbled to the side, sweeping a leg into the stag-man's ankle. With another roar, Elkhorn dropped heavily to one knee, but then heaved himself up and lumbered after the dodging dwarf.

Feinting in one direction, Fenrald again reversed his course and caught the lumbering stagman off balance. A swift punch to the ribs followed by another kick in the knee set the creature staggering. The dwarf crouched and then sprang upward, driving his head into the monster's gut.

"Oof!"

With an explosive grunt, Elkhorn doubled up and collapsed to his hands and knees. The great antlered head swung back and forth groggily, and Fenrald closed in with another barrage of blows. Finally, with a gasp, the stag-man fell on his face and lay, groaning, on the ground.

The companions cheered the dwarf, and Fenrald swaggered back to Holt to claim his hammer. Meanwhile, the elk centaur rose to his knees and rolled to a sitting position. The Daryman looked around and noticed with growing apprehension that the thorn barrier still enclosed them.

"It seems we have a winner," Danis proclaimed as Elkhorn lumbered to his feet. "Now fulfill your bargain—open the fence and release us."

Instead the creature glared at her with stubborn, bloodshot eyes. Elkhorn's gaze shifted to Fenrald, and the creature nodded in an expression that might have been respect.

"Beat I was," he admitted. "But this match doesn't count."

"What?" demanded the dwarf.

"Explain this treachery!" Danis declared sharply. "We fought your duel—don't try to change the bet after you've lost!"

"No treachery," muttered the stag-man with a stubborn shake of his head. "But I challenged the best man among you to a fight. Your dwarf put up a good battle—but he can hardly be called a man."

"That's not fair!" cried Holt, outraged at the blatant shift in the elk centaur's challenge.

Douglas Niles

"Fair or not, I stand ready to face whichever of you men dares to meet me! If none do, then you shall not pass."

Holton bit his tongue before letting himself explode in further fury. He shrugged resignedly, pulling his feet from his stirrups and preparing to dismount.

He was shocked when Tellist Tizzit let go of his belt and sprang from Old Thunder's haunches. The frail wizard tottered toward the elk centaur.

"A man, it must be? Tut, tut—that would be me, I expect—that is, if you have the stomach for another fight."

Elkhorn's nostrils flared in a rumbling snort, and the creature pawed the ground with one broad hoof. "I have the stomach for it—do you have the arms?" he asked with a tight smile curling his animal muzzle.

"Oh, indeed—I don't think this will be a matter of arms. Or stomachs, for that matter," Tellist said with a dismissive wave of his hand. "Now, we fight until the first one falls, is that correct?"

"Aye." The elk centaur settled into his fighting crouch.

"Now, let me see. Tut, tut—how did that go again?"

Elkhorn scowled as Tellist scratched a few fingers through his thinning hair, trying hard to remember something.

" 'Tis a strange stance for fighting," the creature observed.

Tellist appeared not to have heard. Abruptly, he snapped his fingers. The hulking giant took a step forward, and the magic-user extended a bony finger.

"Magicus—arachnoid!" cried Tellist Tizzit.

The elk centaur charged, but at the same time strands of wiry goo shot from the mage's finger. The strings extended to Elkhorn's torso, wrapping his brawny arms, circling his powerful legs. Spinning out a fast-growing spiderweb, the spell trapped the big creature in a cocoon of sticky fibers.

Roaring in fury, the huge creature tumbled to the ground, twisting and kicking, unable to break free from the web.

"Foul! No fair!" howled the elk centaur.

"Tut, tut. I heard nothing about a rule against magic," said the magic-user pointedly. *"I* certainly thought it was fair."

Snorting and huffing, Elkhorn rolled across the ground. "Get me out of this!" he bellowed.

"Now, that's no way to act," chided Tellist. "After all, we fought a duel—and you lost. Now, I think—"

"I didn't *lose,*" cried the stag-man, his voice a high-pitched scream. He forced himself to a sitting position, though his limbs were still trapped. "Do you think you'd have won if *I* used magic?" he demanded, sulking.

189

"My dear fellow, I don't see what you could have done," replied the mage.

Abruptly Elkhorn's nostrils flared, and a puff of white smoke emerged, billowing outward in a cloud that surrounded the startled magic-user.

"I say—*ulp!*" Tellist's voice choked, suddenly silenced, engulfed by the smoke. As the white cloud dissipated, Holt stared in alarm, looking for his companion. Tellist Tizzit had disappeared!

"Where is he?" shouted the Daryman, leaping from Old Thunder's back. As the rest of the cloud floated away, he saw a small squirrel crouched on the ground, staring with wide eyes at the horses and riders around him. The animal raised a pair of trembling paws in a gesture of pleading.

"By the spheres—it's Tellist!" cried Danis, kneeling before the squirrel and taking the tiny creature into her arms. "What have you done to him?" she demanded, facing the still-imprisoned centaur.

"I have demonstrated my own magic," declared the stag-man, stiffly. "Now, if you will be kind enough to release me, perhaps there is one man among you willing to put up a fair fight."

"Can you change him back?" Holt asked suspiciously.

"As soon as our duel is done," pledged the elk centaur.

Elkhorn squirmed free from some of the sticky webbing, while Holt chopped more of the strands

with his sword. In a few moments the hulking
creature had regained his feet.

"Now, we fight!" snorted the elk centaur.

Holt handed his sword to the fuming dwarf and
turned to face the hulking creature. He suppressed
his misgivings about the fight—he knew he couldn't
wrestle like Fenrald or enchant like Tellist. Still, if
his guess about the elk centaur was right, he
wouldn't have to.

The Daryman's head rose no higher than the
monster's belly, and as he looked at the strapping
arms and shoulders of his opponent, Holton felt a
sense of true inadequacy. Nevertheless, he planted
his feet and prepared to grapple.

Elkhorn snorted and pawed the ground, circling
warily. The young man feinted a lunge, provoking
no reaction from the elk centaur.

Abruptly the creature lowered his antlered head
and charged. The broad skull caught Holt in the
belly, driving the wind from his lungs. Gasping, the
Daryman rose into the air. His arms flailed wildly,
clutching at nothing. Spiraling through a graceful,
airborne cartwheel, Holt watched ground, trees,
and sky circle through his vision.

He smashed to the dirt on his back, and for several moments he couldn't draw a breath. His
vision clouded, and his lungs strained until finally
he pulled a rattling gulp of air into his lungs.

As Holt's eyes cleared, he saw the brute face of

Elkhorn, peering down at him. The centaur blinked in concern, but when the Daryman started to breathe again, the creature's expression turned to fierce triumph.

"I am victorious!" he bellowed, the sound ringing from the heights surrounding his valley. "The champion has bested the visitors!"

His bones creaking, Holt sat up. He hadn't intended to win the fight, but neither had he suspected that he would lose it quite so fast. Now he could only hope that his guess about Elkhorn's reaction would prove correct.

It was.

"Now, we *feast!*" cried the stag-man, prancing about the companions.

"What?" Danis demanded.

Holt rose stiffly and limped to the woman's side. "He wanted to fight—and to *win,*" he whispered. "To pass, we merely had to fight, and *let* him win."

The princess looked at him, more than a little impressed, he thought, as Elkhorn retrieved his bone spear and brandished the weapon over his head. The wall of thorns around them melted away.

"Oof—tut, tut."

Danis gasped as she suddenly found herself cradling a full-size Tellist Tizzit in her hands. Blinking in consternation, the magic-user dropped to the ground and then stood, feeling himself all over as if wondering if part of him still remained in squirrel form.

"You're as good as your word," Holt admitted, stiffly stretching his creaking limbs. "This means you'll let us pass through your valley, right?"

"Pass *through?*" The elk centaur was indignant. "Not until you've shared my hospitality!"

Without further argument, the creature led them to a wide, grassy glade. Flowers surrounded them in a profusion of colors, and numerous sections of ancient tree trunks formed small tables and chairs. Even in the growing dusk, the clearing was well lighted by the illumination of the stars.

The companions found the seats, in a variety of sizes that fit everyone from Gazzrick to the lanky Holt, to be remarkably comfortable. There was even a perch that allowed Sir Ira to rest beside one of the stump tables.

Something stirred among the bushes around them, and the Daryman gasped as he saw a beautiful, childlike maiden approaching him—without walking! She floated several inches above the ground.

Then he saw the buzzing, gossamer wings, and he felt a deep sense of awe. A sprite! Naturally, he'd heard of the tiny woodland folk, but in all his explorations of the Knollbarrens he'd never seen one.

Now he saw no less than a dozen of the tiny, winged people. None of them would have reached Gazzrick's shoulder if they'd been standing, and their tiny bodies seemed frail and wispy. Nevertheless, each sprite carried a heavy tray of food or a pitcher and goblets of drink.

"Are you the champion?" the faerie asked Holt shyly, tucking one foot behind the other and looking up at him through silken eyelashes.

Fenrald spluttered indignantly while Gazzrick chuckled.

"Um, no," the Daryman admitted.

"But you fought Elkhorn!" the faerie continued, wide-eyed and awestruck.

Danis watched the two of them, her face locked in a frown. The Daryman remembered how he'd felt when Sir Ira had usurped his role as a guide, and he enjoyed the sensation of their reversed roles.

"You know, I certainly did," he declared with an expansive wave of his hand. Giggling, the faerie swirled away to chatter with her comrades.

Elkhorn built no fire, but somehow the glade remained as warm as a snug living room—though a cool, star-filled sky hung overhead. Holt had not realized how famished he was until he started to eat. The sprites brought out breads, cakes and fruits, roasted corn, butter and cheese. The pitchers contained the juice of various delightful fruits, many of which the Daryman had never tasted before. A large goblet for the dwarf was topped by thick, creamy foam.

The elk centaur explained with pride that each

of the foods was native to his valley. "Many of the fruits, in particular, can be found nowhere else in Karawenn!"

"Splendid—truly splendid!" agreed Sir Ira around a mouthful of moist cake.

"Tell me," Holt asked, as they settled back to let their food digest. "How far is it from here to World's End?"

"You can make it in half a day's ride," the elk centaur replied. "Going to have a look off the end of Karawenn, are you?"

"After a fashion," Danis interjected before Holt could reply. He flashed her a dark look—he hadn't intended to reveal their true mission, but obviously the princess feared he would.

"Well, then," continued the stag-man. "You'll want to turn south when you get there. It won't take too long of a ride to bring Thunder Deep into view."

"Thunder Deep?" Holt was awestruck. "I thought you'd have to travel fifty miles to see that!"

"Not on a clear day. Why, that's a sight—" At the princess's questioning gaze, he explained, "That's where the waters of the ocean plunge into the bottomless gorge of World's End. Everyone should see Thunder Deep at least once in his life."

"It's a place that stays with you once you see it," Holt agreed.

"You've seen Thunder Deep?" Danis asked him. Having refilled her glass with sweet juice, she sat on a stool beside him.

"Just once. A few years ago, on a long trip when I traveled most of the 'Barrens."

"Why do you like to spend so much time here?" she asked. He wondered if the princess made fun of him, but her manner seemed serious—and interested.

"I . . . I guess I just like to hunt," he replied, suddenly struck stupid by her attention.

"It's not to get away from people?" she probed with the hint of a sly smile.

"No!" he protested. He didn't want her to look away, but he couldn't think of anything to say. Then he wondered: was she right? Holt felt his face flush, grateful when Danis finally turned to Gazzrick.

"Why are there no human settlements in the Knollbarrens?" she asked the halfling. "After all, the land seems fertile and well watered—the climate is hospitable."

"At one time, there *were* towns throughout these hills," Sir Ira noted before the tutor had a chance to speak. "Though they were realms of elves, not humans."

"As I was about to say," Gazzrick snapped, "*giants* dwelled here, along with elves."

"Why don't we see any sign of them?" the princess inquired.

"Though they reigned here for more than a

thousand years, the elves built homes and halls of wood—" hooted Sir Ira quickly. "They had many sanctified and magical places. The Glade of Wisdom, for example—or a place called the Vale of Strength. They constructed nothing of the stonework so favored by you humans, or the dwarves, so nature quickly reclaimed the elven places after they departed."

"And the giants mainly lived in caves and huts for all that time. Near the end of their dominion, they created one place of note—a castle," the halfling added. "I believe it still stands, someplace in the Knollbarrens."

"It does," Holt supplied. "If you mean the Castle at World's End. I've seen it—though I've never been tempted to get close. It's a *spooky*-looking place!" He well remembered the massive structure of twisted towers and shattered, tumbling walls, perched on a pinnacle of rock at the very brink of Karawenn.

"Indeed. Though it was known as Graytor Castle in its early days," the owl added. Since Gazzrick didn't immediately interrupt, Sir Ira continued. "The castle wasn't really the giants' idea anyway. They were enslaved by a mad wizard—a sorcerer who had prolonged his life unnaturally by tapping into the forbidden powers of entropy. It seemed that the mage had discovered a powerful focus of magic in Karawenn—a rock that he called the Source Lodestone. This was a great boulder buried far underground. It's said that the stone glowed like a small moon, brightening the whole cavern. With the lodestone, the wizard was able to weave spells of great power. One of these enchantments he used to enslave all the giants in the realm.

"And he forced them to build the castle?" guessed Holt.

"Correct. The structure was raised directly above the Source Lodestone. From this fortress, the sorcerer could exert his power across all Karawenn, and he began to spread disease and drought —two of the favorite tools of entropy. He held sway in Graytor Castle for more than a century, sustained by the might of his potent boulder."

"The elves were his first enemy," Gazzrick interjected, taking over the narrative. "And though their own land was at risk, they created a great enchantment to eliminate Graytor Castle and the wizard— a spell so powerful that it actually cracked off the end of Karawenn and tumbled it into World's End! Fully a half mile of the cliff broke away, which should have carried the castle to its doom."

"But the elves hadn't reckoned with the power of the Source Lodestone," Sir Ira resumed. "And when the land fell away all around, the lodestone protected the castle and the ground upon which it stood."

"So that's why it stands alone like that, on the rock that sticks out from World's End," Holt guessed.

Douglas Niles

"Precisely!" The owl puffed out his chest. "And the power of the stone allowed the wizard to slay great multitudes of elves. The survivors left the Knollbarrens forever, for their grief lay too deep for them ever to forget the pain they had suffered there. Ultimately, humans stormed the castle in a battle that killed the wizard and all his giants."

"Humans participated, true," Sir Ira remarked. "But the animals also played a great role in that campaign. Panthers, wolves, hawks—even raccoons and rats joined ranks against the evil sorcerer!"

"Vanderthan's troops fought in that battle," Gazzrick said. "It was about four hundred years ago, in the early years of the kingdom. In fact, legend has it that a company of Darymen from Oxvale led the first wave of the assault," he said, with a nod toward Holt.

"I know for a fact it was the panthers who were first over the wall," sniffed the owl. "Not counting the eagles and crows, of course, who made up the *true* first wave. Though I'll admit I've heard that one human warrior penetrated to the very depths of the caverns beneath the castle. There, after he lost his weapon, he broke off a piece of the Source Lodestone. It was with that sliver of the magical rock that he slew the wizard."

"Stories and legends," Danis laughed. "That still doesn't explain why there's not a town or even a roadhouse for a hundred miles!"

"In the absence of the elves, the enchantment of the 'Barrens came to the animals," the owl continued seriously. "The Glade of Wisdom became my own secluded valley, a place of quietude and study—"

"And as for the Vale of Strength—" boomed Elkhorn, who had listened raptly to the tale, "why, you are all sitting in it!"

"Perhaps for reasons we don't fully understand, mankind has been content to leave the 'Barrens alone," Gazzrick said.

"And pray we have the wisdom to keep it that way," Danis replied softly. Holt studied the princess, surprised to see that she was genuinely moved by the legendary tale.

Holt leaned back, feeling more pleasantly comfortable than he had since leaving Oxvale. The talk of magic places tingled his blood, while the evening air warmed his flesh and soothed the worries from his soul.

At last the elk centaur showed them soft, grassy bowers where they could spend the night. The pleasant aura of restful sleep already surrounded the companions as they made themselves comfortable upon ground more lush than the deepest mattress.

As he drifted into slumber, Holton Jaken welcomed a sleep that was untroubled by shadows or dreams.

16
Thunder Deep

The morning dawned to chirping songbirds, a clear blue sky, and early warmth, which promised a summerlike day. Holt threw back the blanket of his bedroll and stretched, amazed at the comfortable softness of the grassy loam.

Nearby, Fenrald rose at the same time. "I can't believe it!" declared the dwarf, springing to his feet and flexing his limbs. "Nary a cramp or a pain! I'd like a cartload of this grass for my mattress back in Graywall!"

"It's just the good dirt, as laid down by the pattern of the spheres," said Elkhorn, his deep voice providing a natural accompaniment to the sounds of the woodland morning.

The stag-man ambled forward with Danis holding onto his arm while Sir Ira circled overhead. The princess looked refreshed, her hair combed into golden waves. The owl's feathers had filled out, no longer showing the ravages of battle.

"We'll have to get onto the trail," Danis said wistfully, looking at the flowered meadow. Hundreds of new blossoms had opened with the dawn, a profusion of violet, red, and yellow blanketing the ground.

"It will be my honor to escort you to the borders of my vale," announced Elkhorn with a deep bow.

Looking at the elk centaur, Holt could hardly recall the formidable, snorting beast that had met them at the valley's edge on the night before. Now the antlered head bobbed with cultured grace, and the brawny hands offered the handshake of a good friend.

"Next time I hope we don't have to wrestle." Holt couldn't resist the joke.

Elkhorn bowed solemnly. "Your courage was an example to make humankind proud. It was only my greater strength and size that allowed me to prevail."

"You're kind to say so," Holt acknowledged, privately agreeing in full with the centaur's sentiments. Still, he would be glad to return to this

Douglas Niles

place, even if it meant another bout with the stag-man.

The horses, looking sleek and well rested, pranced about eagerly after they were saddled, and quickly the companions mounted. Sir Ira sat upon the horn of Danis's saddle, proudly preening his feathers as the charger pranced along. The elk centaur loped before them, leading the group through a winding maze of paths and trails in the thickly wooded floor of his valley.

Soon the trail climbed, following a hidden gully until it reached a ridge at the lip of the verdant valley. Here Elkhorn bowed again, looking Danis full in the eyes.

"I hope you find that which you seek," he said solemnly.

The princess, who had carefully avoided referring to their quest, was too flustered to ask his meaning. Instead, she nodded quickly and clasped the elk centaur's brawny hand.

"We thank you for your hospitality," she said. "Would only that all Karawenn was as peaceful as your valley."

"It's only peaceful once you gain entrance," the stag-man reminded her with a deep chuckle. "But your visit has brightened it more than I can say."

At the brink of the vale, they encountered several trees full of cawing crows. Sir Ira lofted himself into the branches and spent a few minutes in cackling conversation. When he glided back to the companions, he settled to Danis's saddle with a jaunty skip.

'"They tell me that the skeletons are well back from us—we've gained at least a day's march on them. Of course, they still seek the trail, but it seems that your guide did a splendid job of masking our tracks."

"What about the nightshade?" Danis inquired.

"These chaps know nothing of that—but it *is* a creature of the night, so we should be safe for the time being."

After their farewells, Holt led the companions onto the eastward path, which meandered through pleasant woodlands. Though the trees prevented them from seeing much of their surroundings, Holt took comfort from the fact that they were well screened from observation. The game trail was narrow, but large trees choked out undergrowth, and throughout the morning they found the going comfortable and easy.

Then, without warning, the forest opened before them, and they stood at the brink of the world.

World's End, the great precipice at the edge of Karawenn, plunged away from them. The line of trees ended in a rounded lip, and beyond hung blue sky in a full arc. Below the level of the ground, a white mist swirled in pale tendrils, finally collecting into a vast bank of cloud, far down the plunging embankment. The cliff began as a down-ward-sloping hill, but the grade increased dramatically until it dropped away in a sheer precipice. Though the incline directly below was screened by the upper lip, they could see to the right and the left that it soon became a surface of dark, smooth rock, vanishing downward into infinite mists.

The company stood for a moment, taking in the majestic sweep of the view. Sir Ira soared overhead, swooping down the cliff for dizzying seconds. He wheeled slowly, gaining altitude in graceful loops.

"I—I hadn't imagined it would be like this," Danis said, quietly awestruck.

Holt looked at her in surprise. It hadn't occurred to him that she would not have seen World's End sometime in her eventful and privileged life.

"It never fails to move me," Fenrald Falwhak admitted, his voice unusually hoarse. The Daryman, too, felt a stirring of emotion somewhere between dizziness and awe.

"An amazing vista," Tellist Tizzit remarked. "I remember one time—I took on the body of a bird and flew outward as far as I dared. Such a limitless expanse of sky—I believe it could extend forever."

"It does," Gazzrick Whiptoe observed pointedly. "Like the life of an immortal, it is unbounded by restrictions such as death and time."

"The crown?" said Danis, apparently shaking off her awe. "Which way do we travel from here?"

"According to Sir Ira, our best chance lies to the south," Holt said, pointing along the top of the precipice. "There's a good trail, if I remember correctly."

His memory served well, and the three horses and Gazzrick's pony fell into an easy walk along the brink of infinity. In an uncharacteristic display of exuberance, Sir Ira soared and bobbed along beside them.

Though the trail remained well back from the steep part of the cliff, the ground sloped away dramatically to one side. Over and over, Holton's eyes were drawn to the immense, limitless vista—he found himself forcing his gaze forward, just to make sure he stayed on the best path.

"How far to Thunder Deep?" asked Danis, pressing Lancer forward to trot at Old Thunder's side.

"A long way—two score miles, at least. Still, we should be able to see it on the horizon after we go a little farther." He pointed along the cliff before them. "You see those high clouds up there?"

Danis nodded, squinting at the billowing white tufts that towered into the sky.

"There are always clouds over Thunder Deep— the mists of the waterfall rise into the air, and then rain right back down again."

She looked at him with interest. "Have you

spent a lot of time here at World's End?"

"I've been here a few times—on long hunting trips, mostly," he said. "It's a place where a person can spend long, thoughtful hours."

"You're right about that." Danis sighed, allowing her eyes once more to sweep across the vast gulf of space and sky that yawned beside them.

For a moment Holt was struck with the realization that his companion was in fact a very beautiful young woman. The distant smile across her face, the wonder reflecting in her eyes, combined to give a cast of innocence and delight to her often-stern features. The Daryman had to remind himself that Danis was a ruthless and strong-willed leader—otherwise, he might have found his heart announcing decisions his mind was not prepared to accept.

The princess appeared not to notice his confusion. Still, she rode beside him for a long time, delightedly pointing out features of the view or applauding the aerobatic antics of the great owl as Sir Ira circled and spiraled off to the left.

Toward evening they came around a promontory, and as Holt had expected, the view before them opened all the way to Thunder Deep. Danis gasped in wonder.

Thunder Deep was a waterfall—but it was a fall that dwarfed any river's cataract into insignificance. At Thunder Deep, the ocean itself fell into oblivion, plunging into the bottomless abyss of World's End. The falls were still many miles away, and the rays of the setting sun struck the vast, spilling surface of water, sparkling like a million diamonds. Holt wondered—as he had every time he had beheld this incredible cataract—where did all that water come from? The answer to that question lay, together with so much other knowledge, in the spheres of the immortals.

"We should camp where we can see it," the princess announced, mindful of the waning daylight, but reluctant to leave the magnificence behind.

"It's often breezy beside the cliff—we might find it warmer if we went a little way inland," Holt suggested.

Danis shook her head, once more the commanding figure of nobility. Holt shrugged and started looking around for a likely camp. Sunset fully cloaked them before he'd found a wide, flat shelf that at least was sheltered by a few stunted cedars. In the nearby rocks, the dwarf located a narrow cave mouth that they could use as shelter in the event of the nightshade's return. None of them wanted to consider that possibility, but the presence of the large, deep shelter was comforting to them all.

Contrary to Holt's prediction, the wind died away completely with the coming of night. They sat around a small fire, listening to the booming cadence of Thunder Deep and watching the stars emerge into view. Weary from the long day, they nevertheless felt the accomplishment of a good march.

But they each knew this was not an enchanted grove.

The rapid plunge in temperature provided the only clue to the nightshade's attack. A shocking, icy wave wrapped them in stunning chill and brought back the full horror of the creature's first assault.

Holt sprang to his feet, unaware that he'd drawn his sword. A tiny corner of his mind asked him what use the weapon would be against the massive, winged terror—but his grip remained ironlike nonetheless.

"Scatter!" cried Danis, her own blade gleaming in the firelight as her eyes flashed skyward.

"There!" shouted Fenrald Falwhak.

Holton saw the stars in a vast section of sky vanish, as if swallowed by some colossal horror. His knees trembled, but he determined to stand and die bravely. He pushed Danis toward the narrow cave they'd marked earlier. "Flee!" he yelled.

"Hold there, beast—tut, tut," Tellist Tizzit declared, fumbling for something in his robes. He pulled out a silvery device that Holt remembered was the mage's skyhook. Apparently that was not what he sought. "Hang it!" he snapped, absently swinging the bracket upward to leave the hook dangling in the air.

The massive wings spread overhead. The horses pitched and bucked, pulling loose from their tethers and scattering into the night. For a moment, Holton thought that the nightshade was diving straight toward him.

"Princess—quickly!" Gazzrick Whiptoe pleaded. With an anguished yelp, Danis turned and sprinted toward the narrow cave. The nightshade veered in its dive, plunging after the woman's unprotected back.

"Here it is!" announced Tellist delightedly. None of the others looked to see what he'd found, but abruptly a dim illumination glowed through the camp. The wizard himself shined faintly, like he was covered all over in phosphorescent dye!

"Oh, dear—this isn't quite what I intended!" Stammering in surprise, the magic-user scratched his chin, trying to figure what had gone wrong.

But the illumination had done its damage, for the nightshade's dive shifted slightly. As if drawn by the feeble assault, the beast veered toward the glowing magic, allowing Danis and Gazzrick to scramble into the cave.

"Look out!" Holt cried as the nightshade's black claws reached out for the magic-user. Fenrald threw his hammer with a rough curse, but the weapon's blunt strike seemed unnoticed by the monster.

Instead, those horrific claws reached out, knocking the glowing magic-user heavily to the ground. The huge, batlike shape settled onto the man's squirming body. Massive wings spread like ink-black canopies over the dwarf and the Daryman, then those powerful membranes pressed downward, crushing Holt to his knees. Blindly he stabbed, but the leathery skin proved too tough for his blade. With a rush of wind the nightshade took to the air.

As it soared over the bottomless plunge of World's End, Holt saw the limp, motionless form of Tellist Tizzit clutched in those horrifying claws. Only the wizard's Skyhook remained behind, dangling uselessly in the air.

17
Castle at the End of the World

The second onslaught of cold caught Holt peering out the mouth of the cave. Darkness shrouded the vast sky of World's End as the deeper black of the nightshade swept close.

"It's back!" he hissed, turning to stumble along the winding, shadow-cloaked passage.

The others had already gathered in a larger chamber, two dozen paces from the cave's mouth. A flickering light—Gazzrick had thought to make a torch—showed the Daryman the way. At his heels the icy shawl of the nightshade brought frost to the air of the cave.

"What's that?" asked Danis, sniffing. She coughed.

Poisonous gas abruptly surrounded the companions, gagging throats and burning lungs. Invisible yet biting, the toxin filtered into the air, penetrating in a sinister cloud from the mouth of the cave.

"The nightshade's venom!" sputtered the halfling before convulsing into a spasm of coughing.

Holt's eyes stung, and his vision clouded. A sense of utter despair claimed him—how could they fight a beast that could make poison in the very *air*?

Only Fenrald kept his head. "Higher!" he spat, through the muzzle of his scarf. He seized the helpless halfling by the shoulders and started to climb toward the back of the cave. Danis picked up the torch Gazzrick had dropped.

A narrow crack led upward from this large chamber. The dwarf scrambled up a series of step-like stones, and as the others followed, they gradually reached a dome of breathable air. They collapsed on a sloping cave floor strewn with sharp stones and boulders, gasping, choking, gagging—but still alive.

The companions huddled in a niche near the cavern ceiling. Though the killing cloud of the nightshade lingered for many hours in the main portions of the cave, the gas was too heavy to reach their hiding place.

Each, during the sleepless night, remembered Tellist Tizzit's humor and, in the end, his courage. The wizard's valiant self-sacrifice was all that had gained for the rest of them the time to reach this minimal shelter. Holt wondered whether the wizard's final spell had been a mistake or a courageous tactic to draw attention away from the rest of them. If only for his own peace of mind, he chose to believe the latter explanation.

As gray dawn poked outward from the east, Holt and Fenrald cautiously emerged from the rockbound shelter. With faint hopes, they scanned the cliff to the sides and the precipice below the campsite.

Aside from the skyhook, which still swung unsupported in the air, they found no sign of Tellist Tizzit. Sir Ira soared to the north and south, and even dived along the plunging cliff until the owl was a mere speck below, but when the bird returned he, too, reported no sign of the courageous mage.

"A brave man," remarked Fenrald, his voice husky.

"Aye," Holt agreed.

"And far wiser than he appeared," Gazzrick Whiptoe noted somberly, coming up behind the pair. "Indeed, his mind was an asset to all of us."

"He shall be missed—sorely," Danis added as

the princess, too, came to stand at the brink of the world and gaze at the slowly expanding dawn. Gently she reached up to the skyhook, lifting it slightly so that it collapsed into her arms—just as if she had unlatched it from some invisible beam.

Holt looked at her, wondering if she meant that Tellist's powers would be missed, or if she felt the same emotional vacancy that tore at his own heart. Though the eyes of the princess misted over with tears, her face remained set in tight lines of determination.

"He's bought us another day," Fenrald suggested gruffly. "Let's make the most of it."

Of the horses, only Lancer and Old Thunder had remained in the area. Holt quickly tracked the two mounts to a grassy clearing and led them back to the party.

"The two ponies are gone," he announced. He didn't speculate as to their fate, though he desperately hoped they had run wild and not fallen prey to the nightshade.

Loud squawking suddenly surrounded them, as a flock of crows settled along the nearby rocks.

"Oh, I say—that's for me," Sir Ira noted, fluttering over to hoot and cackle with the crows. In a few moments he soared back to the companions.

"They've given me a definite answer," he said, hesitantly. "Though I'm not certain the news is good."

Douglas Niles

"What is it?" demanded Danis. "Did the crown disappear into World's End?"

"No, not quite. But close. You see, the crows have it from good authority that the shooting star crashed to ground in the courtyard of Graytor Castle. The force of its fall took it through the portcullis and into the keep itself."

"What 'good authority' knows this?" asked Holt.

"Rats, actually. They're about all that live in the castle now, and they saw the whole thing."

"Of course!" Gazzrick said, snapping his fingers. "It must have been attracted to the Source Lodestone! Otherwise it *would* have been lost!"

"So the crown lies in an abandoned castle," Danis declared. "I'd say that's *splendid* news. Let's get going immediately."

"And hope that we're the first ones there," Holt muttered, quietly enough that only Fenrald could hear. The dwarf looked at him and nodded grimly.

The princess mounted Lancer, and Holt helped the halfling and dwarf straddle the big draft horse. Walking would suit him, he announced, and it was the truth.

He led the way along the cliff-top trail, checking frequently to see that his sword remained loose in its scabbard. The sun soon burned off the early haze, and they were bathed in bright light for most of their way. Even that brilliance, however, could not dispel the cloud that glowered within each of them.

218

Pawns Prevail

Despite his despair, the Daryman pressed forward at a fast walk. Another night out in the open could prove disastrous. Fervently he hoped to discover the crown today, praying that the artifact's power might then provide *some* protection against the scourge of the nightshade.

The terrain rose and fell in a jagged series of low, rocky hills. Many of these were covered with trees, and tangled gullies filled with boulders and deadfalls blocked passage between the heights.

Holton knew that Sir Ira, who circled overhead in lazy spirals, claimed that the crows had provided accurate information, but the Daryman could not avoid being skeptical of that boast. Yet when he remembered the healing touch of the owl's feathers on Danis's face, he began to wonder. Still, despair hung too heavy on him for hopeful thoughts to dispel the gloom.

They came around a long promontory that had blocked their view of the continuing cliff. Now the precipice curved back to the right, and as the view opened up Holt stopped, awestruck by the sight. Behind him the riders reined in with gasps of astonishment.

"What *is* that?" wondered Danis.

Though he couldn't see her pointing finger, Holt knew exactly what she meant. The tall castle rose in the distance, perched on the very lip of World's End. Slender towers spiraled upward from dark,

moss-scarred walls. Still far beyond, the vast water-fall of Thunder Deep stretched across the horizon, the turbulent waters vanishing far below in a haze of cloud and mist. The roar of the great falls came to them clearly from more than a dozen miles away.

"The Castle at World's End—like Sir Ira told us," Holt said.

"Where we'll find the crown," Danis announced, her voice full of conviction.

They picked up their pace, enlivened by the vision. As they approached it, the castle quickly grew in size and detail.

"The years haven't been kind to it," Holt observed, seeing that the tops of several towers had crumbled away. Gaps where the parapets lay in ruins gave the impression that the castle wall was a tooth-studded lower jaw.

"It would naturally be subject to decay," Gazzrick noted. "The tale I remembered dates back far —well before even my grandfather's time."

"How old *are* you?" Holt blurted. "You said the legend was centuries old—*my* grandfather was born eighty years ago!"

"I'm—that is, I will be one hundred forty years old next winter."

Danis chuckled, amused. "Gazzrick's just past middle age for a halfling. What would you think of an elder elf—some of them can live for five centuries!"

Holt flushed, once again feeling every inch the country fool. It was Fenrald who came to his rescue by changing the subject.

"Say, lad—can you get a look at the castle's foundation? The way the cliff bends out, just there?"

Holt squinted, his hunter's eye quickly picking out the feature the dwarf had mentioned. It was the dwarf's experience, he reflected ruefully, that gave the jutting terrain meaning.

"It's not really *at* the lip of World's End," he agreed. "More like a peninsula, jutting out from the cliff—"

"Into a sea of sky!" Danis exclaimed. "I see what you mean!"

"The wizard's castle," said the halfling, "over the edge of the world . . ."

Soon they got a better view of the strange fortress. It stood upon a promontory of land that stuck outward from the main cliff. The base of that foundation plunged downward, lost in the mists below. A narrow ridge of stone connected the castle to the main bulk of Karawenn, but in places this pathway looked to be a jagged and knife-edged crest. Holt wasn't at all certain that the companions, let alone their horses, would even be able to reach the ruined structure.

And if they did, would they find the artifact they sought? From this close, the place looked as though it had been abandoned for decades. Trees and bushes flourished among the ruined stones, but there were no other signs of life. Yet could the precious crown have sat there, undisturbed, since reaching Karawenn a week before?

Danis took a turn at walking in the afternoon, allowing the footsore Holt to mount her horse while plodding Old Thunder continued to carry Gazzrick and Fenrald. The princess left her chain mail shirt and steel helmet lashed to her saddle and jogged along with surprising endurance. Soon they stood in the afternoon shadows of the forest that grew along World's End. The ruined fortress, on its rocky peninsula, rose before them.

From this vantage, the place looked more decrepit than they had suspected, though they could tell that it had once been spectacular. Even now, the castle rose into the sky with massive, awe-inspiring grandeur. A circular outer wall studded with towers surrounded the courtyard and keep. In the wall a single gateway gaped vacantly, facing them at the far end of the narrow ridge.

Yet nowhere was this curtain wall intact to the top. In places it had collapsed nearly to ground level. The towers were of varying heights, but all terminated in broken, irregular stones. Even so, some soared far higher than the biggest tree. Holt found himself wondering with amazement how lofty they must have been in their prime.

Within the wall a single structure rose

upward—the keep. This monstrosity stood, a mountainous pillar of stone, far above the highest of the outer towers. At the top, the remains of a huge parapet now crumbled at the edges. The circular keep boasted an odd external stairway, which spiraled in a huge series of stone steps down the outside. The stairway extended from the top of the tower down behind the curtain wall, though the companions couldn't see if it reached all the way to the ground. The outer edges of many steps had crumbled, but none of them seemed to have broken away altogether.

Holt, studying the broken ridge crest, observed, "We'll never get the horses across." Sheer walls plummeted away to either side, and many jagged rocks lay loosely balanced on the knife-edge of the path.

"Lancer will wait in the forest near here—what about Thunder?" Danis asked crisply.

"He'll have to," Holt said amid a torrent of misgivings. Still, he believed as strongly as the rest of the companions that they had to reach that castle. And he wasn't willing to tie the horse up—there were too many threats that might lurk in the woods. The Daryman avoided thinking of the other danger in restraining the horse—that he might not return, and Thunder would be doomed by his tether to starve.

Carefully, he removed the bridle, saddle, and

saddlebags from the big horse. Old Thunder blinked placidly as Holton patted his shoulder and scratched his nose. Mindful of precious daylight slipping away, the Daryman still took time to find his faithful steed a nearby glade in the woods, where thick grass and clover abounded.

"I'll be back for you, old fellow," Holt said, awkwardly clapping the horse on the shoulder. "You'll wait for me, won't you?"

Lancer, meanwhile, had galloped into the forest as soon as Danis had released him. "Don't worry—he'll come as soon as I whistle," she assured Holt.

With the sturdy dwarf leading the way, they started onto the perilous pathway. To the right and left, the world dropped away to an infinite abyss. Now, afternoon shadows darkened that vast expanse, obscuring the clouds that seethed constantly below.

The ridge descended steeply over a series of steplike boulders. Some teetered as the companions crossed, but none of the rocks tumbled free. Fenrald led at a crawl, working over a broken stretch of loose stone before climbing back to the original level of the crest. For a few steps the path was good—smooth, and nearly four feet wide—but then it crumbled away. With extreme care, the little party worked its way across the rough stretches, and though several times rocks tumbled to one side or the other, no one slipped or lost a grip.

The group finally gathered before that yawning gateway. Sir Ira awaited them, perched on the lip of the promontory as the companions climbed the last, broken stretch of the ridge.

"I say," remarked the owl. "This is a good time to have wings!"

Not bothering to reply, Fenrald stalked past him and looked up at the looming arch. "These were *big* gates!" he observed with a low whistle.

There was no sign of whatever portal had once stood in this opening. The gateway itself was at least forty feet high and nearly as wide.

"Giants built this, you said?" Holt asked Gazzrick. "It sure looks big enough!"

Awestruck, they walked through the gateway onto the relatively smooth surface of the interior courtyard. In places, the flagstones had cracked or been forced upward by sprouting bushes, but for the most part, the huge space was open and vacant. The keep rose like a mountain before them. A huge iron grate formed a barrier across the only entrance they could see.

"Look here!" cried Holt, his tracker's eye immediately catching sight of discoloration in the plaza floor. He pointed to a long gouge chiseled in the stones, running from southwest to northeast. He found another, shorter groove, hooking to the left, and then several skid marks—all forming a long curve toward the massive portcullis.

Pawns Prevail

"Do you think it was the crown?" asked Danis, fearfully examining the scars. They had obviously been scored by a terrific force.

"Shouldn't the marks be in a straight line?" Holt wondered.

"Yes," Gazzrick agreed. "That is, unless the artifact was being *drawn* somehow, by a power that pulled it to the side. . . ."

"That magic boulder you talked about?" Holt speculated.

"Precisely." Gazzrick beamed, as if the Daryman were his student and had just passed a difficult examination. "The Source Lodestone. Indeed, if the stone was strong enough to bring the artifact to ground here in the castle, it was strong enough to curve its course." He pointed at the arched scrapings in the ground.

"Whatever it was, it hit the stones hard—and not longer ago than the last week," Holt estimated. "It bounced a few times, then rolled between the bars. . . ."

"Into the keep," Danis concluded, "like the rats supposedly claimed."

The princess crossed to the huge portcullis and peered into the shadows within. Though the entrance was easily four times higher than a human, the portcullis bars had gaps of no more than six or eight inches between. The iron and oak grid would take days to hack through.

Douglas Niles

"We won't get in that way. Let's look for another opening," Fenrald suggested. "We've got about two or three hours of daylight left."

"Excellent suggestion," Sir Ira agreed. He flexed his wings. "I'll have a look at the higher reaches."

The others agreed to remain together for safety's sake. Hurriedly they circled the mighty keep, probing along curving walkways and small courtyards, investigating outer cellars and stone huts. Yet nowhere did they find hint of a doorway leading into the keep itself.

With its forbidding portcullis and strange spiral stair, the keep did not invite visitors.

Finally, around sunset, they gathered again before the great portcullis. Sir Ira glided down to rest on one of the huge steps. The keep itself blocked out the evening sky before them, rising like a small, incredibly steep mountain into the night.

"Only thing I can think is to use one of these big beams as a battering ram," Fenrald remarked, gesturing to several huge, iron-banded timbers that lay scattered about the courtyard. " 'Cept we'd need about thirty or forty of us just to lift one," he added sourly.

"The only door I saw is a trapdoor on the top of the keep," Sir Ira announced. "It looks like you'll have to climb."

Holt's heart sank as he looked upward. "That'll take all night!"

"What's that!" hissed Fenrald, also looking skyward.

A black, winged shape soared across the face of the moon.

"It's the nightshade!" sputtered the halfling.

"Too small," Holt disputed, surprised that his voice sounded so calm. "And it's close—we'd feel the chill already."

Indeed, the batlike shape soared over the castle wall and circled their heads. Though it was too small to be the nightshade, it was still a monstrously huge creature—bigger than a great eagle. Danis drew her sword as the creature swept closer, while the owl flopped to the ground and took shelter in the midst of the companions.

In the dim light, eyes blinked from the beast's fur-lined face. Foxlike jaws, surrounded by tufts of white whiskers, snapped as the bat swept passed.

"I've never seen the like of *that* before," Sir Ira clucked, peering skyward from between Holt's legs. "It's certainly not a regular denizen of the Knollbarrens!"

"It may not be the nightshade," Gazzrick whispered. "But the resemblance is close—that's sure to be one of its servants!"

Holt, who had just had the same thought, pulled an arrow from his quiver and shrugged his bow off his shoulder. Nocking and drawing in one fluid motion, he let fly—but the bat seemed to sense his attack, and veered sharply as the missile left the bow. The arrow whistled harmlessly into the night, while the bat rose into the darkness and flew away.

"Gone to warn its master," Fenrald said grimly.

"Then we've got to get into the keep!" Holt declared with a despairing look at the huge, spiral staircase.

Grimly, the companions started for the bottom step.

18
Blackstair

The first step of the huge staircase rose nearly waist-high to Danis and Holt, which meant shoulder-height for the dwarf and the halfling. Nevertheless, they started to climb, scrambling up one stair after the other as they ascended the great spiral into the sky.

"Oof—it's not hard to believe this was made for giants!" grunted Gazzrick, crawling laboriously over another step.

"Why is the stairway on the *outside* of the keep?" Holt wondered, boosting the halfling to the next platform.

Douglas Niles

"Defense?" Fenrald suggested. "The giants could sit on the top and dump rocks on anyone trying to get in."

Each step was as long as a dining table. Though the outer edges had crumbled into ruin, the stairway remained intact where it was connected to the keep wall, and the companions could only pray that this condition continued all the way to the top. Holt's biggest fear was that they would climb for hours only to find that a full section of the stairway had crumbled away. They would have no choice but to turn back.

Full darkness cloaked the heavens in a sparkling blanket of stars, with the moon—now just past full—well advanced on its nightly climb above the eastern horizon. The companions pursued their own climb with grim determination, and quickly rose above the level of the outer castle wall.

Here they paused to catch their breath, knowing they had covered only a small fraction of the entire ascent. The walls of the keep rose above, with the stairway continuing its spiral into the vault of the sky overhead.

"How many hours will this take?" wondered Holt, giving no thought to stopping for a night's sleep.

"Keep going," grunted Fenrald. "We'll find out soon enough."

Pawns Prevail

"Can we make it before the nightshade gets here? That's *my* worry!" Gazzrick noted.

Despite the fact that, as the shortest, the halfling had the hardest task of them all, he resolutely scrambled from one step to the next and pulled himself up.

Sir Ira circled the tower as they climbed, often swooping in to hoot reassurance and encouragement. Thunder Deep roared in the distance, and when the wind curled around they felt droplets of mist on their skin. Licking his lips once, Holt tasted salt and knew that the mist rose all the way from the plunging waters of the ocean.

Higher they ascended, until they looked down on the crumbling towers of the castle's outer wall—and past those walls into the plummeting abyss of World's End. The thin ridge connecting the castle to the main bulk of Karawenn seemed a frail thread from this height, almost insignificant.

As the moon rose higher, casting the abyssal mists in a hazy, milky light, Holt could not suppress the feeling that they climbed a castle perched atop the clouds. The sensation was especially strong when they traversed the stairway on the far side of the tower, where nothing but vast space lay below.

The moon had already begun its descent toward the west when the companions collapsed, gasping, to rest on a lofty step. Sir Ira settled onto the stair above them.

"More than halfway, now—there's some good news," the owl murmured. "And nothing's stirring at the top."

"And there's a way into the tower there?" Fenrald asked again, rubbing his aching legs.

"To be sure—a large trapdoor in the platform. It's closed, now, but I know one of you chaps will figure out a way to get it open."

Too discouraged by current obstacles to groan at the thought of a future challenge, Holt rose to his feet and wearily hoisted himself up the next step. The others followed, continuing their arduous ascent into the sky.

The Daryman wondered about Old Thunder. Was the big horse wandering back home? Did he flee in terror from wolves or other wood-stalkers? Holt felt a terrible sense of responsibility, but he was forced to shrug the feeling aside.

Frequently they scanned the heavens for some sign of the nightshade or its apparent servant, the giant bat. They even began to hope that they had been wrong—that the animal had *not* gone to tell the beast about their location. Yet they all sensed that this hope, however much they desired it, was futile. Instead, all they could do was try to reach the top of the tower and find a way into the castle before the nightshade found them.

Pawns Prevail

By the time pale dawn streaked the eastern sky, they began to believe that they might make it. The companions had climbed so high above their surroundings that the twinkling of the stars provided sufficient illumination to light the stairway. Holt's hands were rubbed raw, and his knees and legs ached from the constant and repetitive labor. He could imagine that Danis was at least as worn out, and that the dwarf and halfling must be in even worse shape. Yet none of them uttered a word of complaint.

"One more spiral," Sir Ira finally announced, his voice full of encouragement. "Just keep your chins up and all that for a trifle longer, and you'll be there!"

Invigorated by the news, the companions scrambled up step after step. Here, near the top of the lofty keep, the stairs had suffered more decay than below. Many of them had crumbled away to within a few feet of the wall, and for the last spiral the companions advanced in single file, remaining as close to the keep wall as possible. Danis led the way, followed by Holt and Gazzrick, with the dwarf in his usual position as rear guard.

Looking down, Holt shivered with a feeling that if he fell now, he would soar fully beyond the curtain wall and into the abyss of World's End. The notion made his head spin, and for a moment he had to cling to the wall to restore his balance. The sensation passed quickly, and once more he turned to the climb.

In a few more wearying, bone-straining steps, the companions scrambled onto the flat, crumbling platform that had once been the parapet atop the grand keep. The outer rim of the parapet—including the wall that had once surrounded it—had completely decayed. Still, even the timeworn patches only revealed other layers of stone. Nowhere could they see any gap allowing access into the keep.

True to Sir Ira's word, however, they found a massive trapdoor lying in the direct center of the platform. Fenrald quickly walked over for a look, and then spun toward the owl, his face locked into a dark scowl.

"Why didn't you tell us it was made of *iron?*" he sputtered. "How in the spheres did you think we'd ever be able to *lift* it? What do you think we are— giants?"

"I say, old boy—no need to get apoplectic, now," chided the unperturbed owl. "Iron, did you say? Hmm, that sounds a bit on the heavy side, now, doesn't it?"

"There's *got* to be a way!" declared Holt, unwilling to consider the prospect that their long climb might have been made in vain. "How heavy can it be?"

Fenrald looked at him scathingly. "Oh, I don't know—certainly no more than a few tons!"

Pawns Prevail

Holt paid no attention to the fuming dwarf. The Daryman walked over to inspect the trapdoor himself. The portal was a square, perhaps six feet on a side. A large ring was bolted near one side of the door, while two hinges on the opposite side showed that the trap was designed to open upward.

Thick, studded bolts and steel straps connected nine plates of iron into a solid—and tremendously heavy—barrier. Ignoring the dwarf's look of amused contempt, Holt seized the handle and lifted. His back wrenched in pain, and the door refused to budge.

Grumbling pessimistically, Fenrald crouched beside him, but even between them they could only rattle the door slightly in its frame. There was no room for Gazzrick or Danis to add their strength.

"The skyhook!" cried Danis suddenly. She reached into her knapsack and pulled out the hook and its attached pulley. "Can we use the rope? At least we'd be pulling *down,* then!"

"It just might work," Fenrald said, scratching his beard as he looked at the sky over the trapdoor. He uncoiled his long rope and threaded one end through the skyhook's pulley.

Danis hoisted the device, flinging it through a loop in the air. "Hang it!" she cried, mimicking Tellist's words.

The hook caught in midswing and hung suspended, the pulley dangling about eight feet over the ring of the trapdoor. Holton tied a secure knot, lashing the line to the door.

Fenrald seized the end of the rope while Holt, Gazzrick, and Danis all took hold of the line farther up. As a group, they hauled.

The door lifted upward a few inches. Grunting and straining, the four companions pulled desperately. Holt's boot slipped on a loose stone, and as he lost his balance, the door slammed downward, tugging the other three forward.

"It's *still* too heavy!" groaned the Daryman, close to despair.

"Wait." Fenrald looked at the lip of the parapet, where several huge flagstones jutted outward. A kick of his boot wobbled one of the stones in its socket. "This might give us the extra weight we need."

Ignoring the dizzying space yawning just below, the dwarf knelt on the stone and wrapped his rope several times around the oblong chunk of rock. Soon he stepped back, but wasted no time admiring his handiwork.

"Now we've got to knock it loose," he declared. Holt chiseled at the edge of the stone with his old knife while Fenrald lent his battered hammer to the task. In moments, the stone rocked dangerously toward the edge.

"Back!" cried the dwarf, springing away from the lip. The Daryman scrambled behind, conscious of the flagstone toppling free.

The rope snapped taut, and the rock fell a little farther, lifting the trapdoor several inches from its frame.

"*Now* we should be able to lift it," the dwarf asserted, spitting on his hands and reaching for the rope.

The now-familiar wave of cold swept across the tower top, chilling blood and warning the companions of the nightshade's imminent arrival.

"*Go!*" cried the dwarf, hauling desperately on the rope. The door lifted several more inches, leaving a gap perhaps a foot wide.

Danis and Gazzrick quickly disappeared through the gap. Sir Ira dived after them. Holt saw the stars black out overhead, and knew that the massive beast swept downward, eager for the kill. He cast an agonized glance at Fenrald Falwhak.

Veins bulged in the dwarf's forehead. Grunting, he hauled with all his weight on the line. "*Go*—by the spheres!" Fenrald gasped. "I—I'm losing my footing!"

"No!" cried Holt.

But even as his mind revolted, the Daryman's feet carried him to the trapdoor. Blackness closed overhead as he plunged through, grasping the edge with his fingers. His feet swung free into space.

"Fenrald!" he cried, trying to find a way to brace up the door. "Hurry—come here!"

He heard the dwarf curse as Danis and Gazzrick pulled Holt to safety on a narrow platform.

The Daryman looked up toward the narrow gap between the trapdoor and its frame. For a moment, he thought he glimpsed a knuckled hand and the dwarf's desperate face outside the opening. Then the door slammed downward, leaving them in chill darkness. Holt's anguished cry of dismay slowly faded into utter, hopeless silence.

19
Into Darkness

Thick shadows shrouded the interior of the massive keep, but Holt's eyes—already attuned to the night—discerned a few details of their surroundings. He, Danis, and Gazzrick huddled on a narrow ledge at the top of a flight of stairs. The stairway descended into a large, circular room that occupied the entire top of the keep. Sir Ira flapped darkly below.

"Here—help me bolt the door!" gasped the halfling, struggling to move a heavy iron bar beneath the hatch.

Holt hesitated, unwilling to lock the noble dwarf

outside with the nightshade.

Danis's hand settled gently on his shoulder, her voice firm. "We cannot waste Fenrald's sacrifice."

Holt nodded in the darkness. Together, they seized one end of the shaft and pulled it through several rings in the bottom of the trapdoor, firmly barring the portal in place. Just as the bar settled in the rings, the heavy barrier rattled upward, the nightshade yanking against it with tremendous force. The bar showed no sign of bending. For now.

Holton forced his attention down toward the huge room—studying the steps, the dust-coated floor, the many columns lining the inner wall—*anything* to keep his thoughts from Fenrald Falwhak. But, try as he might, these attempts proved futile. Finally he collapsed against the wall, no longer able to hold his emotions at bay. A sob rose from his throat, and he turned, ashamed, from his companions.

A hand came to rest on his shoulder. He looked up to see the shadowy form of Danis, Princess of Vanderthan, her own eyes wet with tears.

"We shall find the crown," she said quietly. "His death will not be in vain."

Holt remembered other brave men, all fallen in the quest for this unknown artifact—a thing none of them had ever so much as *seen*. Not long ago he had wanted to blame Danis for each lost warrior. Yet now, he could not bring his bitterness to bear against the princess. Instead, he felt her conviction.

They *would* find the crown, and the sacrifices of Fenrald, Tellist, and all the others would have meaning and impact now and for the ages!

"Where do we go from here?" he asked, grimly forcing his grief into a dark and shadowed corner of his mind.

Something flashed by them in the darkness, and Holt instinctively flinched before he recognized Sir Ira. The owl settled to the edge of the platform beside them.

"It seems our only choice is downward," stated the bird, puffing out his chest and stretching. "Bit of a sticky affair, flying around in here."

"Will the trapdoor hold?" Gazzrick looked nervously at the iron portal overhead.

"I don't think the nightshade can lift it," Holton said with more confidence than he felt. "And the sun will be up soon—that should keep it off the trail during the day."

"I suggest that we shouldn't wait around for confirmation," Sir Ira remarked.

"My advice is to make haste away from the beast, and the only way to do that is to go down these stairs."

"No!" Danis commanded. "We will go down—but not because we're running from the nightshade! Remember—we seek the Crown of Vanderthan, and it lies within these walls!"

"Right now I don't care why we're doing it—but

let's get going!" Gazzrick encouraged, starting for the top step.

Like the outside staircase, these steps had been designed for giant strides. Now, at least, they could jump down the individual drop-offs, which proved considerably easier than climbing—though harder on their knees.

The companions knew that the sun must be ascending into the sky beyond the tower. Chinks in the thick stone walls of the keep allowed an occasional beam of light to penetrate—the bare minimum of illumination needed to see where they were going.

Quickly descending to the floor of the huge room, Holt saw another stairway continuing downward. Like the steps they had just descended, the lower flight curved around the wall of a circular room, spiraling all the way down to the floor. At the foot of this next stairway he saw another shadowy gap in the floor—apparently a continuation of the steps through additional levels below.

The columns around the fringe of the room loomed like great tree trunks, and many showed signs of ornate carving and intricate design. The Daryman was too numb to show any interest in these creations; instead, he quickly started down the stairs to the next level, urging Gazzrick and Danis to hurry behind. Sir Ira glided below, circling through the lower chamber ahead of his foot-bound companions.

"This looks just like the place upstairs," the owl reported as the trio reached the floor of the next chamber. "But I saw some more stairs over here. . . ."

"So let's keep going," Holt declared, ignoring the wonders of stone carving and giant craftsmanship that soared to the ceiling all around.

"Wait—let's take a little time to rest," Danis suggested. He looked at the princess, surprised by the wan cast of her skin. Silently, he nodded, and the trio made themselves as comfortable as possible on the dusty floor. The pace of the day and night of flight caught up with them then, and each nodded off for a short period of restless sleep. When they rose again, none of them felt invigorated, but neither did they want to remain in place any longer.

Six times they descended into, and through, the large chambers, each time finding a matching room below. All Holt could think about, when he did stop to consider the grandeur of their surroundings, is how much Fenrald would have been impressed—or what Tellist might have speculated about the place's origins.

Standing at the top of the final leg of the stairway, Holt saw sunlight spilling into the chamber below—illumination marked by a shadow pattern of square grids.

Douglas Niles

"I think this is the ground floor," he announced. "The late afternoon light is coming in through the portcullis."

The room they now entered proved to be larger than any of the chambers above, as the walls of the tower flared outward at its base. They saw a massive stone chair mounted on a pedestal in the center of the room, and a host of carved gargoyles perched high up on the walls, looking down at the huge hall. The pedestal was a block of solid marble supporting the ornate chair perhaps twenty feet above the floor of the room. Steep steps—human, not giant-sized, for once—ascended to the front of the throne. Curved arms and a high, sweeping back must have considerably enhanced the magnificence of whoever sat here.

"This was the wizard's throne room," Danis declared. "Looks like he could gather his host of giants around—and still loom above them all!"

"Any sign of the crown?" Holt asked brusquely.

"We know it came in here through the portcullis. Let's have a look around," the princess suggested. She advanced across the floor, walking through the grid pattern of shadows cast by the portcullis, and approached the mighty throne.

"Not bad, for someone who wants to impress a bunch of giants," she speculated from the base of the steps. Thoughtfully she walked around the pedestal, as if inspecting an object in a museum.

Pawns Prevail

Meanwhile, Holt examined the rest of the great throne room. First he checked the portcullis, seeing that it did in fact lead to the courtyard outside the keep. He saw the gouges made by the artifact and calculated that it must have rolled into the room, past the throne, into the shadows on the far side.

Beyond the castle, the sun had descended almost to the western horizon, and Holt realized that they'd been scrambling up and down the keep's stairs for nearly a full day. It galled him to think that they'd climbed a thousand feet into the sky and then back down again just to reach this place a few steps away from where they'd first met the iron bars of the gate.

He followed the apparent track of the crown across the chamber and past the pedestal. The floor beyond the throne was made from tightly interlocked slabs of black granite. Holt took several steps across the floor before some premonition made him stop. Kneeling to reach forward, his heart pounded with surprise as he realized that, a few inches in front of his feet, the floor dropped into a vast, steep-sided pit—a hole so dark that it almost perfectly matched the black marble.

Carefully he backed away, calling a warning to his companions. "There's a *big* shaft going down over here—I can't see how far down it goes, but watch your step."

"A hole? Of course," Gazzrick speculated. "It must lead down toward the caverns of the Source Lodestone. That rock was supposed to be far underground."

"It figures that the wizard would build his throne right on top of it," Danis said.

Holt wasn't listening. Instead, he looked back at the portcullis, following the imagined path of the Crown of Vanderthan. "For whatever reason the wizard put the hole there," he announced grimly, "it looks like that's where your crown ended up."

He expected an outburst of anger from Danis, and was surprised when she sighed resignedly. "Is there any sign of a way down?" she asked.

As his eyes adjusted to the dim light, Holt tried to discern the answer. "Yes—I think there's a flight of stairs down the wall. I can't see how deep this pit is—but something seems to be glowing, very faintly, down there."

"The Source Lodestone?" asked Gazzrick hopefully.

"I don't think it's any one boulder," Holt replied. "The glow seems to come from all over, like it's a carpet spread over the cave floor."

"Can your spell of location help us out?" Danis asked Sir Ira as the owl perched sagely at the edge of the pit.

"Sorry about that," he replied. "But I just tried it. The crown could well be down there, but, well—

Pawns Prevail

I couldn't tell. There's a very powerful source of magic that seems to screen out my lesser enchantments."

"The Source Lodestone, no doubt," Gazzrick suggested.

"Quite likely," the owl agreed.

"In any event, this looks like a good stairway," Holt noted. The flight of giant-sized steps led straight down into the pit, flanked by high stone banisters on each side. Perhaps a hundred feet down it reversed its course around a wide landing, continuing until it vanished into the darkness.

"At least it's not another spiral," Danis said wearily.

Sir Ira glided into the depths to investigate, while Holt studied the faint, glowing patterns scrawled across the floor of the deep pit. "The light reminds me of the phosphorescent lichens you sometimes find in caves, or sunless places in the deep forest," the Daryman suggested.

"We'll be able to see better after the sun goes down," Gazzrick noted, gesturing to the wash of twilight that still spilled across the throne room, ruining their night vision. The halfling looked outward through the portcullis. He squinted, then gasped in alarm. "Look! The skeletons of the nightshade!"

Holt stared in dismay at the ghastly, fleshless figures that clawed their way across the knife-edged ridge to the castle. One or two tumbled free as he watched, but the other undead ignored the loss of their comrades. Steadily they advanced, the first leering skull-faces already appearing at the castle gate. Numerous gaunt shapes lurched into the courtyard.

"At least the portcullis should hold them out of the keep," the halfling said, eyeing the grate critically.

"And there's no sign of the nightshade!" Danis added.

"It's still light—but only for a little while," Holt reminded the companions.

"Let's not wait around to see how long," Danis snapped. "We've got to find the crown!"

"There's a big cave down there," Sir Ira reported, winging his way upward again. "I couldn't see any sign of the crown, but there's lots of passages leading downward from the cave floor—it could have rolled down any one of them."

"Any sign of the Source Lodestone?" Gazzrick asked. "It should be glowing very bright—easy to find in the underground."

"Afraid not, old chap," the owl replied. "No sign of a big, bright boulder."

Danis found the top of the steep stairway and began to descend, followed by Holt and the halfling. As they dropped below the level of the throne room floor, the darkness closed thickly about them.

Pawns Prevail

Conversely, the pale illumination below became more apparent.

"It *is* lichen," Holt said. "But brighter than any I've ever seen."

"Perhaps the Source Lodestone enchants it—increases the phosphorescent effect," Gazzrick speculated.

A loud thump rocked the great castle. The crashing sound was quickly followed by another, and a third.

"What's that?" Holt wondered, suddenly sick with apprehension.

A regular cadence of pounding began to thrum through the huge walls of the keep. The sound came from far above them, and it rang with metallic resonance.

"A battering ram! The skeletons are hammering at the portcullis!" Danis declared.

Holt remembered the big, metal-capped beams in the courtyard and agreed that she was probably right. Despairingly he looked at the lichen-covered floor of the pit—it seemed a long way below them. Already the pounding increased in cadence, as if the creatures sensed success near at hand.

"All we can do is hurry," he declared determinedly. "If the nightshade comes in here, I don't want it to catch us on these stairs!"

They leapt down the steps, rashly hurrying toward the cavern floor spreading below them.

Douglas Niles

They had no sooner reached the rocky surface when a great rending sound shrieked overhead, ringing through the caverns with continuing echoes. Vividly Holt imagined metal bars bending, giving way before the inexorable pressure of the ram.

"The gate—they're smashing it in!" Gazzrick declared. "The nightshade will be here in no time!"

Gasping for breath after the arduous descent, the Daryman looked around. The cave floor was large, greater in diameter than the shaft leading up to the throne room. The ceiling curved overhead in a great dome. The pale light of glowing lichens revealed numerous caverns descending from the floor of this massive chamber. The artifact could have tumbled into any one of them.

"Come on!" Holt urged, indicating one of the tunnels leading downward. "Let's get in there—at least we can stay ahead of the shade for a little longer!"

"No!" Danis declared forcefully. "I'm through running! We can't wait for the next dawn because down here there won't be a dawn. If the night-shade is after the crown, we haven't any time to waste in finding it. We'll conceal ourselves until it passes, then get on with the search for the crown!"

20
The Tutor of Vanderthan

"Your plan is bold, to say the least," admitted Sir Ira with a nod of his broad, feathered head. "Perhaps even a trifle rash. Are you sure you don't want to continue—?"

The pounding above rose to a crescendo of tearing metal and shrieking hinges.

"No!" Danis declared, her tone cutting off any further argument. "Now, let's find a place to hide."

Holt stared at her, thinking her scheme was madness. Yet rationally he knew that if the crown was truly powerful, they could not let the shade attain it first.

"I noticed a fairly deep niche over there," Gazzrick said, pointing to the upward sloping cavern floor.

"Indeed—I saw the same thing," Sir Ira noted. "A bit small, though—why don't the three of you take shelter there. I can get myself to a ledge on the cave wall up above."

Quickly Holt and Danis scrambled up the slope and into the shadows where the dome ceiling angled down to meet the floor.

"Here it is!" announced the Daryman, eyeing the narrow, dark opening.

Climbing up behind them, Gazzrick gasped, "That's the place."

The niche was about eight feet deep, with a slab of rock hanging low overhead and barely room for the two humans to crawl inside.

The loudest crash yet resounded from above, followed by a sinister, portentous silence.

"Hurry!" cried Sir Ira, perched on a rock nearby and looking nervously upward. "Get in!"

Gazzrick Whiptoe waited on the sloping floor a little distance away. "Danis—Your Highness! Do as he says, please!" begged the halfling.

"Come on," she demanded, gesturing him upward.

"I have a better idea," whispered the halfling,

remaining below the niche. "You two go in here, and I'll find a place a little distance away."

"No!" The woman's face, even in the pale light of the glowing lichen, blanched. "You get in here, too—we'll make room!"

"It—it just makes sense," the tutor argued, surprising Holt with his stubbornness. "That way we have some room to maneuver if . . ." He didn't have to articulate what everyone feared.

"*No!*" Danis repeated, stamping her foot angrily.

Darkness shrouded the entrance overhead, and they all sensed the nightshade's presence.

"The beast is in the throne room!" Holt said. "Come on!"

He ducked down and clambered into the niche, rolling onto his stomach so that he could see into the large cavern. Danis stood stubbornly as Gazzrick started toward a clump of shadows some distance away. Reluctantly the princess knelt and crawled in beside the Daryman. Abruptly, the halfling turned back.

"Dear Danis," he said quietly. "If something happens—if we don't have the chance to—"

"Don't!" she cried, her voice choking.

"It is my great honor to serve you, to serve all the Vanderthans—and I would ask that you remember me well. Farewell!"

The halfling scampered across the rough cavern floor. In moments he disappeared behind a cone-shaped stalagmite.

Danis tensed beside Holt, and he placed a hand on her shoulder, silently urging her to remain hidden. He realized with surprise that she was trembling with suppressed emotion.

"Wait," he whispered. "We'll find him as soon as the monster passes through."

The princess lay without speaking. Several times she turned her head toward Holt, and he wondered if she wanted to say something. She never spoke. Instead, Danis blinked back the moist film that caused her eyes to glow even in the dimness.

Holt found a strange tightness growing in his own throat. He wanted to offer the princess words of comfort, but his mind sought without success for the right thing to say. Should he tell her that he was confident their quest would succeed? Even that basic statement would have been a lie, he realized.

The horrifying chill filled the cave like the sudden coming of winter. Immediately afterward, the massive, dark shape soared down through the vast opening overhead. Tendrils of icy air seeped into the narrow niche, quickly numbing Holt and Danis's feet and legs. Beyond, the horrific, colossal bat-creature settled like a vulture atop a stalagmite near the entrance of the cave.

Two smaller forms darted through the air, soaring

in tight circles about their master. Holt's heart sank further as he realized the monster now commanded at least two giant bats. Every day the beast added new allies to its awful force!

While the bats soared and swooped, searching the vast cavern, the nightshade resided on the spire like the wizard lord enthroned of old. Despite its immobility, Holt sensed that the creature, too, was searching for them—seeking with some sense other than the eyes it did not possess.

The Daryman tried to still his heart, to slow his breathing until he realized he held a single lungful of air for a minute or more. Even his thoughts, he feared, might give him away—the monster's presence loomed so awful, so mighty, that Holt wondered if his own brain could betray him.

Don't think! He tried without success to deaden his mind, but his agitation only increased. He sensed Danis growing equally tense beside him. Her breath caught in a stifled gasp as the beast's fur-covered, eyeless face swiveled in a slow circle toward them.

That vacant visage turned on the pair of humans. The monster froze. The great wings unfurled. Danis clenched her fingers around Holt's arm, squeezing painfully—but still the Daryman made no sound. The grotesque face—horrifying in its lack of features—remained locked upon them.

The wings pulsed downward, and in a swirl of

wind, the huge creature rose from its stalagmite perch. The two giant bats swept downward, one to either side, as the beast's wings flapped again. It lurched into the air, climbing toward the niche where the pair tried desperately to remain concealed.

A clattering of stones rattled through the great cave. The nightshade turned toward the sound, and Holt groaned silently as he saw Gazzrick Whiptoe. The halfling broke from the shadows, and now streaked toward one of the great cavern mouths that led deeper into the earth.

"Wait!" Gazzrick howled into the empty darkness. "Wait for *me!*"

Instantly the monster's flight veered. One great wing came up, and the beast swooped with shocking speed toward the sprinting halfling.

Danis gasped audibly, then turned and buried her face against Holt's arm. He felt her warm tears, but he could not tear his eyes away from the awful scene before him.

The beast dropped to the ground, burying the halfling beneath a smothering cloak of black wings and death. One final shriek, filled with unspeakable terror, rang through the cavern. Then all was silence. The two giant bats circled distractedly in the center of the cavern, as the nightshade's horrible bulk cloaked what remained of Gazzrick.

The Daryman blinked back his own tears, awed

by the halfling's courage. Though Gazzrick had
played the terror-stricken wretch, his last act had
been motivated by heroic selflessness.

Yet now, hunched on the ground, the nightshade
again raised its head. That eyeless face turned
about the cavern, and the Daryman knew that the
beast's original quarry had not been forgotten.

Movement flashed overhead, and Holt watched
a winged, feathered shape dive between the two
giant bats. The Daryman's heart swelled at
another example of sheer courage—Sir Ira twisted
past the bats, ignoring slashing claws and snapping teeth. Hooting madly, the owl swept down one
of the lower caves, and the bats soared after. The
Daryman couldn't be sure, but he wondered if he
now saw three of the huge mammals swooping
after Sir Ira.

The cries and hoots of the owl grew louder, ringing back and forth through the cave in a resounding cacophony. Even after Sir Ira disappeared, the
sounds of his agitated voice emerged from the
darkened tunnel. Noises rang through the cavern,
resonating and echoing even more loudly than
their original source until, in moments, the entire
cave rang with chaotic sound.

Holt's eyes turned back to the nightshade.
Hunched like a buzzard over the place Gazzrick
had fallen, the beast looked this way and that,
apparently confused by the echoes in the cavern.

Finally, the monster's face turned toward the darkened cave yawning at the far end of the chamber—where Gazzrick Whiptoe had drawn it with his sham flight. The beast hesitated, as if still suspecting that its prey remained hidden. Yet it seemed unable to focus its search amid the ringing noises in the chamber.

The black wings spread, darkening half the cave, and then the awful creature took wing. It rose from the ground and soared into the dark passageway, vanishing deeper into underground Karawenn. As though drawn from the chamber along with the nightshade, the hooting and flapping of wings abruptly stopped.

For several minutes Danis and Holt remained concealed and silent. They saw no sign of the owl, nor of the bats that had flapped downward and out of sight. The chill of the nightshade's passing still lingered, but the immediate icy grip of the air had begun to fade.

"I—I'm sorry," Danis said softly. She wiped at her face and turned away from Holton. "Gazzrick. . . ." She could say nothing more, instead lowering her head and shaking with suppressed sobs.

Holt wanted to touch her shoulders, to offer her comfort, but his hands remained frozen at his sides. Instead, he cleared his throat awkwardly. "We'll find the crown—I *know* we will," he said softly.

Pawns Prevail

She looked at him, frightened and unsure. Tears gathered in the corners of her eyes, and her chin quivered unsteadily. It was hard to picture her as the serene, confident noblewoman he had come to know.

At the same time, Holt's heart ached at the sight of her misery. Somehow he found the resolve to reach out, to take her in his arms and hold her. She clung tightly to him, and he felt the tension slowly drain from her rigid body.

"Wh—where should we go?" she asked hesitantly.

Holt had been thinking about that problem. "All the power here seems to be focused in the Source Lodestone. I think the artifact *must* have been drawn to that rock. I think once we find the lodestone, we'll find the crown."

They worked their way down the steep slope toward the place where Gazzrick had fallen. No sign of the halfling remained on the ground, nor anywhere they could see. Danis slumped in despair.

"You—that is, you're not the only one who's sorry," the Daryman said awkwardly. "I owe you an apology."

"Why?" asked the princess, looking at Holt in genuine puzzlement.

"When we first started out, I thought . . ." His voice trailed into silence. How could he tell her that he had scorned her as a selfish brat? That he thought she felt nothing for her brave and loyal companions? He couldn't. "It's an honor—a true honor—for me to have the chance to serve you," he said in uncomfortable explanation.

"I suppose it is," she said listlessly, looking about as if she had barely heard him.

Her reply drove through Holt like a dagger of ice. He remembered the feelings that had swept over him as they lay hiding together, of the sympathy and comfort he had wanted to offer. How could he have imagined that she would have welcomed such attentions from a Daryman—from a mere farmboy?

His own throat hurt from a new kind of pain as Holt rose to his feet. He turned toward the darkened cavern so that Danis wouldn't see the anguish that burned in his eyes.

"Come on," he said, his gruff tone concealing his pain. "We don't want it to get too far ahead."

21
First Daughter of Vanderthan

Holton set a murderous pace, trotting along the rough cavern floor. He looked around continually, certain the Source Lodestone's brilliance would be easily visible in the darkness. Yet, as he heard Danis gasping and stumbling behind him, he had to wonder if he hurried really only to strain her endurance.

In his mind the reality jangled: to the princess he was a farmboy, a mere subject of her father's crown. He flushed again with embarrassment and anger as he recalled the tenderness and affection he'd allowed to creep into his heart.

The winding cavern twisted and curved, always descending. The Source Lodestone, they guessed, would be near the center of the tunnel network—but would doubtless be very far under the ground. Fortunately, frequent patches of the glowing lichen cast enough illumination to allow them to find their way. The leafy crust on the rocks was so bright that Holt felt no doubt the stuff was in fact enchanted by its proximity to the lodestone; the brighter the lichen, the closer the crown, he hoped.

Close-set walls restricted the passage they now followed. Both Holt and Danis were grateful for the confined space since it provided them some protection against the nightshade.

Dropping to his hands and knees, Holt crawled beneath a low-hanging section of the cavern ceiling, rising to his feet and hurrying on as he heard the princess scrambling behind him.

"Wait!" she called, her voice a hoarse whisper. Gasping for air, she climbed to her feet and leaned against an outcrop of rock. "I've got to catch my breath," she wheezed.

Greenish lichens crusted the walls and floor, shedding a bright glow through this portion of the caverns. Holt looked scornfully at the young woman. His emotions showed clearly in his face, and she recoiled from him as if he had slapped her.

"What is it?" she demanded, glaring back at

him. "Why are you looking at me like that?"

Her face was streaked with mud, and Danis angrily pushed a sweaty strand of hair behind her ear. Her green eyes flashed, and as he met their fiery gaze, his anger abruptly vanished. She only acted like the person she had been raised to be, he told himself.

"It—it's not you," he stammered. "I was thinking about the nightshade . . . about Fenrald, and Gazzrick, and Tellist."

Immediately her face softened. She reached a hand out and clasped Holt's shoulder in a surprisingly strong grip. "I understand," she said.

"Are you ready to go?" he asked gruffly, uncomfortable with his minor deception—as if he feared that she would read his mind and learn the truth.

"Yes," she replied with a nod. She drew a long breath, fortifying herself for the walk, and once again they started deeper into the cavern.

They passed around additional corners and ducked underneath countless stone arches. Gradually their surroundings darkened as they reached a place where none of the luminous lichens grew. Groping slowly through the utter darkness, Holt reached back to take the princess's hand. Several times his feet released cascades of pebbles over an unseen drop, but he kept his left hand firmly anchored on the cavern wall.

After a seeming eternity of darkness, they came around another bend and saw a pale, florescent wall. The lichen-coated rock cast enough light to once again illuminate their surroundings.

A long, steep slope dropped to their right. The bottom of the incline was lost in shadow, but Holt could see that the surface consisted of loose gravel and a few large boulders. The top of the slope formed a treacherous, narrow trail, with the cavern wall rising steeply to their left. A single misstep, Holt knew, could send them plunging into the shadows below.

Though they could see again, Danis didn't pull her hand out of the Daryman's grip, and for his part Holt made no effort to let go. He told himself that this way each helped the other to maintain balance, but in his heart he knew that the touch of the princess's hand gave him the courage to continue forward.

Abruptly the stones shifted underfoot, and a clattering of rubble tumbled down the long, steep incline. Holt grabbed an outcrop of rock with his free hand as he felt Danis slide away behind him. Desperately he turned and pulled, swinging her toward him as the ledge beneath her feet crumbled. For a moment she dangled over a perilous drop, but then Holt heaved with all of his strength, hauling her back to safety.

"Ouch!" she cried, as she bashed into a large rock. Grunting from the strain, Holton pulled her up beside him. She tried to step back but immediately collapsed. The Daryman threw both of his arms around her, barely preventing a dangerous plunge.

Pawns Prevail

"It's my ankle!" Danis hissed, frustration welling upward in her voice. She leaned her head against the cavern wall and squeezed her eyes shut. After a moment she opened them and looked at Holt. "Thanks," she offered, with a faint smile. "I think you just saved my life."

"Can you walk?" he asked.

She probed the ankle, which had already begun to swell. "I—I think so. Let's give it a try."

They rose to their feet, Danis leaning heavily on her right leg. As soon as she tried to take a step she groaned, and once again Holt's arms prevented her tumbling down the slope. She shook away tears of frustration and sank once more to a sitting position.

"We'll wait," the Daryman said.

The Princess of Vanderthan shook her head firmly. "No—you'll have to leave me here and go on alone."

"But—"

"The crown is too important—it matters *far* more than me, or my pain!" she declared, her jaw set in the stubborn pose he'd come to know so well.

"In a little while we can both go!" Holt insisted, surprised—and a little awed—by her courage.

Again she shook her head. The solid clench of her teeth remained firm, but her eyes softened as she looked at him. "Find the crown!" she said, her voice pleading. "*Then* we can worry about getting me out of here. But go, now—there's no time to waste."

Douglas Niles

Holt looked miserably down the winding cavern. At his feet a long slope descended through a smooth slide. Every instinct within him objected to the idea of leaving Danis here, alone. Rationally, he knew that if the nightshade found her there was little he could do to protect her. He hung his head, realizing that even that pathetic thought was too grandiose. *Nothing* he did could shield her from the awesome, chilling power of the beast.

"Holton Jaken," the princess said, laying a hand on his arm. "I've never known a man like you before. You're not afraid of me! I could order you to proceed on your own, but you would just ignore me if you wanted to."

Mutely he nodded.

Danis sighed. "You're *so* stubborn!"

He was forced to smile. "I was just thinking the same thing about you," he admitted.

"You made me angry—even furious—at first." The princess turned her face away from him, lowering her voice as she looked back to meet his gaze. "Now, I guess . . . I don't know. It's the way you are. I can't order you to go after the crown. It has to be something you'll do on your own."

"I *want* to!" he said through clenched teeth. "But I can't just *leave* you here!"

Her grip on his arm tightened. "I'll wait—I can do it. Remember, Holton, that crown is not just a trinket for myself. It's a force of extreme power, and if it falls into the clutches of the nightshade, it's a terrible threat to all Karawenn. Even Oxvale."

"I wish the accursed thing had never been made!" he declared bitterly.

"So do I," she acknowledged quietly, once again surprising him. "But will you go?"

"I guess I don't have any choice."

"Your idea was right, you know," Danis said through teeth gritted against a sudden spasm of pain. "Find the Source Lodestone—and there you'll find the crown! It *must* be the place!"

"I *will* find it!" he promised.

He helped the princess to a niche between two rocks, where she could at least have some protection. They were high above the cavern floor, near the curved edge where the wall and ceiling of the chamber began to arch overhead. Looking below, they could see a narrow gap where a passage opened into the next chamber. The steep slide of loose rock and gravel extended downward from the hiding place all the way to that tight passageway.

A slight whirring of air gave Holt a split second's warning, and he drew his sword and ducked as a giant bat winged past. The fang-studded jaws snapped an inch away from the Daryman's ear, but the huge mammal glided off before his blade could slash outward.

Holt looked up in time to see the second bat plunging downward. Stabbing, he felt the tip of his blade tear into the leathery wing. At the same time, savage claws reached outward to rake his cheek.

"Go!" Danis cried, sheltered in the tiny niche behind him. "I can hold them off!"

He ignored her, hacking at a third bat that nearly took him by surprise when it dived from the darkness overhead. Jaws clamped onto his shoulder, and he grunted in pain—but another hard chop of his sword drove this attacker into momentary flight.

"The crown!" the princess urged. "You must go after it!"

Stubbornly he shook his head, eyes scanning the shadows in the center of the cave. He saw the trio of dark, winged shapes as they swooped together, quickly climbing back toward him.

Abruptly he felt a foot drive firmly into the small of his back. Shouting in surprise and outrage, he toppled forward, driven by Danis's kick away from the narrow entrance to her niche.

Loose stones slid from under his feet, and Holt pitched forward, losing hold of his sword as he clawed for purchase on the sliding, tumbling gravel. In a clatter of loose stones, he bounced, tumbled and rolled to the bottom of the long, steep slope. Something solid clanked nearby, and he quickly snatched up his weapon. In fury he looked up the cavern wall, toward the shadows concealing Danis.

"Go!" she commanded once again.

He looked in frustration at the incline and knew

that he could never climb back up to her—at least, not with the bats ready to dive at his back. He saw Danis's sword flash, driving the flying creatures back from her shelter, and he tried to convince himself that she would be safe.

The dark hole yawned nearby, and he turned and plunged through, furiously determined to complete the quest for the crown. Rough walls immediately pressed close to Holt's right and left. The cave twisted through several narrow turns, with only the pale glow of infrequent lichen to light the way. In many stretches, the corridor twisted into total darkness; then the Daryman groped his way along, feeling the sides, cursing silently as he repeatedly scraped his knuckles and shins against unseen obstacles.

Abruptly he crashed headlong into a wall of stone.

Wincing, Holt probed the bruises on his cheek and forehead. He forced himself to slow down, searching carefully with his hands for obstacles before him, and checking the ground with a toe before each step.

The jagged stone walls closed in even farther until Holt had to turn sideways and squeeze through a very tight spot. As he stepped out of it, he felt the sides of the passage spread beyond the reach of his groping hands. The Daryman felt a slight breeze tickle his face, and the scuffing sounds of his footsteps echoed for a moment. Holt sensed that he had once more entered a large chamber in this network of caves.

Yet here, unlike the bigger caverns he had previously traversed, no glimmer of light showed anywhere in the smothering cloak of gloom. He was tempted to make noise, to learn the size of the cavern by echo, but he dared not attract attention to himself. The nightshade was abroad in these tunnels, and the full blackness of Holt's surroundings made that knowledge more terrifying than ever.

Holt sagged, a sense of complete hopelessness draining his energy. He believed he was doomed, whether the nightshade swooped at him in the next minute or he remained lost in darkness until he starved—or went raving mad.

* * * * *

An immortal play once again fluttered into the pool. It was the subtle, quiet power of the greenleaf. In response to the command, plants took hold of the bare rock . . . and began to grow. The lichen spread rapidly, and in the near presence of the Source Lodestone it glowed with enchanted light.

The game was almost done—the most potent tokens had been played. Still one remained, but it could be of little consequence. After all, it was merely a gust of wind.

22
Darkness and Light

As Holt lingered there, paralyzed with indecision, minutes or hours passed—he couldn't be sure. Once he tried to walk, but his first footstep slipped from a narrow ledge, and he swayed sickeningly over an unknown drop. Desperately he clawed for handholds, clinging to the rocks while he listened to stones and debris clatter below for a very long time.

After the echoes died away Holt remained immobile. Cramps seized his arms, but he dared not let go of his precious handholds. A wave of nausea surged through him, and he was forced to scramble back from his precarious perch, collapsing against the cave wall and straining for breath in long, ragged gasps.

In the darkness, Holt's mind created pictures for his sightless eyes—memories of the forest, of a squawking pheasant or startled, fleeing deer. He saw the outlines of distant mountains, rising in a series of ridges before him. Rippling lines of terrain soared into a wall of looming heights.

Then he blinked, and the imagined horizon vanished until he opened his eyes and saw it again. He closed his eyes, and once more the undulating terrain disappeared! But when he peered through the darkness, he could see!

No—he must surely be mad! How could he see a mountain range when he was trapped in a lightless, subterranean cavern?

Yet the images returned, defying the logic of his dark-struck brain. The first ridge rose only to the level of his eyes. The crest was outlined in a pale, greenish, glow. Beyond that line another, rougher barrier climbed higher, with more and more of the steep, jagged ridges appearing in the distance beyond. Each of them was limned in that unworldly illumination.

Then, in a flash of insight, he understood: these weren't mountains—they were small hummocks of stone that extended across the cave floor! They were outlined in the subterranean lichen that had lit his way before, which now seemed to sprout, as if by magic, across the entire base of the immense cavern. Stalagmites, framed in green light, stood in stout forests on the floor while stalactites extended down from the ceiling like the sharp fangs of some impossibly huge beast. Though a crevasse yawned black and apparently bottomless on one side of him, the way straight ahead was clear.

Hesitantly the Daryman started across the undulating floor. His slow pace was dictated not by fear, but awe. Gaping upward with wondering eyes, he saw that the lichens sprouted so fast that he could actually see them grow. Then, as he studied them further, he saw that the tiny plants not only outlined the floor below his feet, but actually seemed to form a pathway leading him around the tortured terrain of this vast, rock-strewn cavern.

Unconsciously he quickened his pace until he jogged along the carpet of crisp, leafy growth. The pathway led him around the edge of the great chasm and toward a narrow tunnel exiting the far side of the massive chamber. Holt's senses tingled. He wondered about the strange pathway—why did it appear now under his feet? For a second he considered the prospect that he was being led into a trap, but he intuitively knew this wasn't the case. The Daryman drew his sword, and the weapon felt light in his hand, like a natural extension of his arm. His boots barely brushed the ground, making no sound even though he was practically running.

Entering a narrow side cavern, the Daryman raced along, ducking beneath a low-hanging stalactite and twisting sideways to worm through an especially tight passage. The glowing pathway beckoned, and now he scrambled upward, eagerly using his free hand to pull himself over a series of rising stones. Vaguely he sensed that the passage grew brighter around him—illuminated by a light source more powerful than the magically sprouting lichens. He was close, now . . . *very* close!

Abruptly the tight confines opened again, and Holt blinked against a glare as he entered a huge, circular grotto. Blinded by the glow coming from the center of the room, the Daryman turned sideways. Dazzling gems sparkled in the chamber's walls, while pale lichens sprouted everywhere, their glow fully overwhelmed by the brilliance in the center of the chamber.

The Source Lodestone gleamed before him, large as a cottage. The stone rose from the bedrock like a massive diamond placed in a setting of raw steel. Smooth facets streaked by gray-blue covered its face while pulses of magical light flared beneath the translucent surface.

Yet ultimately neither lodestone nor lichen captured the Daryman's attention. Instead, they

glimmered as mere background to the central feature of this chamber—the thing that had drawn him to World's End, that had cost the lives of so many brave men.

It rested upon the rounded crest of the Source Lodestone, reflecting from a thousand shining surfaces. Delicate tines jutted from the platinum circlet. Emeralds the same pure green as Danis's eyes . . . diamonds of immaculate crystal, all sparkled around the rim. The artifact had suffered no visible damage in its plunge from the upper spheres.

Slowly, reverently, Holt approached the stone. Reaching out, he lifted the Crown of Vanderthan in a strong and steady hand.

23
Lodestone Blade

As he held the crown in his hand, Holt's attention shifted back to the Source Lodestone. The mottled pattern of color on the rock seemed vaguely familiar, and in a flash, the resemblance came to him. He raised his sword and gasped as he examined the weapon he held in his trembling hand.

The surface of the blade was the same rippling blue-gray stonework as the Source Lodestone.

True, the sword lacked the pulsing sense of *life* that seemed inherent in the boulder itself. Still,

Holt knew immediately that he had found the origin of his unusual blade. It was only natural that the power that had once infused the weapon was gone now, so many centuries after it had been chiseled from the Source Lodestone.

Hesitantly, reverently, the Daryman extended the weapon, touching the tip to the Lodestone. Sparks flashed through the cave, blinding him and filling the air with smoke. He tried to pull the sword away, but it was stuck fast to the great rock, the hilt of the weapon tingling in Holt's hand. Heat baked his face, rising in intensity until he knew it must sear the flesh from his bones.

Strangely, he felt no fear—and no pain.

Gradually the light faded, and Holt regained control of his weapon. He pulled it back and sheathed it, his eyes still flash-blinded and a thousand questions swirling through his mind.

Yet already that wonder was yielding to explanation and understanding. The answers to his questions, he realized, lay in a battle that had been fought four hundred years before. He remembered pieces of the tale he'd heard in Elkhorn's glade. . . . It had been a company of Darymen who were first over the wall in the assault on the Graytor Castle. . . . A lone warrior had broken a sliver from the lodestone to replace his lost weapon. . . .

And what had his father said when he gave Holt

the sword? "It has belonged to the village for a *very* long time!"

With a growing sense of awe and reverence, Holton Jaken understood that he bore the Lodestone Blade, fashioned by a heroic Daryman during that ancient battle.

A sudden sense of urgency possessed him, and though he could make out few details in the darkened passageway, Holt turned and stumbled from the cave, holding the crown in his left hand and using his right to feel for obstacles before him. In a few moments, he knew, his night vision would return.

Carefully he tried to retrace his steps. He felt no doubt he could return to the place where he had left Danis. At the same time, he feared that it would take a long time to make the reverse climb.

The glowing carpet of lichen again became visible before him. Awestruck, he realized his discovery of the crown had been no feat of luck: mighty forces were at work. Silently he thanked the spheres that those powers had worked to his advantage.

The narrow chute that had led him down to the crown's chamber proved even steeper than he remembered. Loose stones slipped from beneath his feet, and he fell roughly against the cave wall, absorbing the blow with his shoulder so that he wouldn't strike stone with the crown.

Looking upward, he saw a steeply climbing succession of broken rocks, and knew that he would need both hands to make the climb. He needed to place the crown where he could free his hand.

Holton set the gleaming artifact on his head.

Immediately he froze in shock and wonder, staring around at surroundings that looked very different. Subconsciously, he knew that the *cave* hadn't changed—the *man* had. Yet he could not banish the sensation that he had been transported instantly to a new and magnificent place.

The overall outlines of the cavern remained the same. His eyes, however, perceived more details than he could have previously imagined. Holt could see through the darkness, even into shadow-cloaked niches where no illumination penetrated. Holt's hands and feet moving with certain strength, he resumed the climb. When he examined the broken rock of this narrow passage, he seemed to see *through* some of the stones. He saw several teetering precariously, on the brink of falling, and took pains to avoid these as he hastened upward.

Aided by the power of the crown, he stepped around more treacherous footholds, swiftly working his way over a series of firmly grounded rocks. He even imagined that he could see around corners, anticipating the end of the narrow corridor several moments before he saw it.

Once again he entered the large chamber where stony fangs jutted upward and down from floor and ceiling. Across the expanse he saw the steeply sloping pile of stones and the niche where he had left Danis.

Even here, hundreds of feet away—and staring through heavy darkness—Holt could see that the princess was no longer there. The discovery might have provoked despair a few minutes earlier, but now he started resolutely forward. If she wasn't here, he knew that the crown would help him find her.

Another sense, this one a warning, tickled in his scalp. He whirled, raising his sword, anticipating attack.

The giant bats soared into the cavern through a great tunnel. They were still a long distance away —once again the crown had remarkably enhanced his senses, warning him of the monsters well before he could have noticed them on his own.

In fact, as he watched the bats weave and swirl through the air, he saw more than their mere presence—he actually sensed their *intentions!* They searched for him, sniffing the air with their foxlike nostrils, peering through the gloom with their dark-sensitive eyes.

When he drew his sword, Holt was shocked to see blue ripples of light flickering beneath the surface of the stony blade. Brightness suffused the cavern, revealing every feature in clear outline.

A shrill, ultrasonic squeal pierced the air. The bats dived, all three in line, and the Daryman placed his back to a large stalagmite, ready to fight

Douglas Niles

for his life. He felt no sense of fear—just a taut
readiness, and the courage to battle these creatures.

The first bat's jaws gaped as it plunged toward
his face. Holt's sword slashed, but at the last
instant he knew that the creature intended to veer
upward and use its claws. A fang-studded maw
surrounded by white whiskers snapped in the air.
The Daryman reversed his parry, and the tip of his
glowing blade scored a cut across the giant bat's
belly. The creature flopped, squealing, to the
ground. But it would rise again.

The second and third bats separated in their
descents, one diving from each side. He thrust his
blade at bristling chin whiskers, forcing the first
bat to veer away, but the last—and smallest—of
the savage flyers hit. The nimble creature raked
sharp claws through his tunic and across the skin
of his shoulder before the Daryman could whirl
back. Slashing and spinning, Holt drove the third
bat momentarily away.

In his brief respite he realized that he felt no
pain in his shoulder. Wonderingly, he probed at the
torn shirt, feeling his skin barely scraped underneath. The monster had struck him, but the talons
had not penetrated to muscle or bone.

With a flash of insight, Holt knew this was
another of the Crown of Vanderthan's potent pro-
tections; like a supple, armored cloak, it had
deflected the brunt of the creature's attack.

Enraged, the three bats swooped toward the Daryman again, filling the cavern with their high-pitched shrieks. The keen sword danced this way and that as leathery wings flapped around Holt's head. He felt the weapon cut flesh again, and the smallest of the bats dropped, flopping awkwardly, to the ground. A long gash gaped in its wing, and it hissed and spat in fury, unable to take to the air.

Further infuriated by their companion's wounds, the two flying bats rushed desperately toward Holt's head. The Daryman's sword flew back and forth, carving deep cuts in each of the creatures. Teeth and talons tore at him, and though blood trickled from numerous scratches, none of the blows cut deep.

One of the bats, the white-muzzled one, settled to earth, wounded too badly to fly, while the other circled, keening in fury and frustration. Angrily Holt watched, wanting to get on with his search for Danis. Yet in the momentary pause, his crown-enhanced vision revealed to him that the bats were not inherently evil. In fact, they had been compelled against their will to serve a powerful creature of entropy.

"Stop!" he cried in frustration as the third animal swooped back toward him. "Leave me alone!"

Immediately the bat flew upward, hissing at the Daryman but making no attempt to attack. Instead, it winged away, toward the depths of the cave. The animal had obeyed his command.

"Come here," he ordered, holding the blade ready before him.

The flying bat returned, settling to ground beside its two wounded cohorts.

"Now, approach me," Holt commanded.

Awkwardly walking on their short legs, all three bats hobbled toward him.

"Stay there," he said when they were about three paces away. Again the creatures obeyed, lowering their heads and staring up at him with dark, glittering eyes.

Holt glanced at the unprotected necks, knowing that three quick blows would allow him to continue his search completely safe from the threat of the bats. But then those black eyes caught his attention.

He expected to see hatred and rage there, but instead the bats looked at him with expressions that seemed almost pleading. Holt's intentions softened. Their obedience to evil had been total until broken by the Crown of Vanderthan, but now the Daryman did not see them as dangerous enemies.

Holt could not slay them out of hand.

"Wait here," he said firmly. The gleam in their dark eyes convinced him that the creatures understood and would obey.

With a few cautious, backward glances, Holt started toward the niche where Danis had been hidden. The bats remained as he had left them.

Pawns Prevail

Needing his hands free for climbing, the Daryman was again forced to sheath his sword as he crept up the slippery slope toward the hiding hole, but even then the bats showed no inclination to move. By the time Holt reached his destination, the animals far below had shrunk to tiny spots of darkness.

Once again the power of the crown came to his rescue, for although the princess had left no actual evidence of her passage, the Daryman's tracking eye could see softly glowing outlines of the soles of her boots. Holt could even see the scuffing where she had been forced to drag her injured foot.

The young farmer's sense of awe continued to grow. He couldn't tell how old the prints were, but they didn't seem to fade as he followed them.

Why had she left the shelter? He didn't waste any time agonizing over that frustrating question. Instead, he jogged easily along the precarious rocks of the steep trail. His eyes unerringly recognized the unstable spots, and he was able to move at a loping sprint through the chambers of the subterranean maze.

A series of nagging question hissed their way into his mind: *Why* should he bother to find Danis? Hadn't she sacrificed enough of her companions on this quest? Did she need to sacrifice Holt as well? If he found her, he would only have to carry her to the surface and fight skeletons and the nightshade all at the same time, and probably die in the attempt. There seemed little point in that.

Then his thoughts took a darker turn. Had she shown him anything but distrust and disdain since this quest began? Was he only another tool of hers? He had the crown now—a crown that made Danis seem like the peasant and him like the king. If he found her, she would only try to take the crown away and put it on her own head. Was she worthy of wearing it?

But one final realization kept him looking for Danis, one thought Holt knew was cold, perhaps heartless, even selfish, but he strangely did not care. He thought, I could easily prevent her taking the crown from me. Even minions of the nightshade have the sense to obey me now. Perhaps the crown will teach Danis a little respect for me, too. . . .

Danis's footprints worked their way through a torturous network of tunnels. Holt followed the trail into another of the huge, looming caves that made up so much of this cavern network. Trotting across it, he gazed in wonder at the spires of rock jutting from the floor or dangling from the ceiling. A gentle breeze flowed past his face, and his keen senses told him that this was fresh air, only recently captured by the walls of stone.

Abruptly the cavern wall opened to reveal a vast expanse of clear, night sky. Holt stepped forward onto an open shelf of rock on the very brink of

Pawns Prevail

World's End. The cliff extended both above and below him, and somewhere up there, he knew, stood the keep of the giants' castle. The wide shelf was a mere niche in the cliff wall, and from here, as from a lofty balcony, he could look into the night sky of an infinite horizon.

He sensed the deadly chill of the nightshade even before the icy cloak descended. Looking upward, he saw the vast, dark form, floating with deceptive gentleness down from the sky. Apparently it had left the caverns—perhaps by this same ledge—and now it swooped back to the attack.

Sword in his hand, Holt awaited the beast without fear. He didn't know if the crown would protect him against the monster—nor did he know if he could hurt it. Yet now it seemed right to him that he would wear the crown and bear the sword, facing the beast in a fight only one of them would survive.

Then icy fear *did* grip his heart—but not fear for himself. He saw movement across the wide shelf of rock—Danis Vanderthan. The princess had emerged from the inner cave, and she struggled, limping, toward him across the rocky ground.

"Holt!" she cried, unaware of the diving horror overhead. "You found it!"

With a tilt of its great wing, the nightshade veered its dive. Now it plunged straight toward the Princess of Vanderthan.

24
Sword of the Daryman

"I challenge you, Beast—come to me!"

Holt shouted the only words that entered his mind, hoping to command the nightshade with the same power as had subjected the bats to his will. He raised his sword and charged across the cave toward the massive nightshade. "Face me if you dare!"

If his command had any effect on the creature, the Daryman saw no clue. Instead, the massive, winged shape continued its plunge, straight toward the Princess of Vanderthan.

Pawns Prevail

Warned by the penetrating chill of the night-shade's presence, or perhaps by Holt's cries of alarm, Danis looked up and gasped in dismay. Hobbling awkwardly, she tumbled into the scant shelter between a pair of towering stone spires.

The beast struck the tops of those stalagmites and snapped them off like dry twigs. Danis covered her head against the resulting shower of debris.

Her stony refuge proved at least minimally effective—the huge creature tried to push between the stubs of the spires, but they were too close together for its massive bulk. Instead, the great wings flapped and the beast soared upward again, veering back toward the Daryman.

"Stay where you are!" Holt called to Danis while he scrambled toward the cavern wall, wanting to place his back against the barrier. Even now, with the horrendous monster filling his vision, he felt none of the stark terror that had earlier paralyzed him.

The crown rested firmly on his head, and the sword of his fathers felt light and deadly in his hand. As the nightshade swooped lower, he clearly saw the midnight black face, the widespread, tooth-studded jaws—and the bizarre lack of eyes and ears. Yet this time that visage held no terror for him—instead, it aroused every ounce of his determination and rage.

As the creature closed, the Daryman for the first time got a full impression of its size. The two black

wings filled the cavern, and the mouth gaped wide, huge enough to swallow him whole.

"Holt!" screamed Danis, her voice shrill with terror for him. Her fear gave him strength, and as those massive jaws lunged toward his face, he drove the sword upward with all the power in his shoulder and arm.

The beast's weight smashed Holt against the cavern wall and forced the breath from his lungs. Slumping to the ground, he felt a tearing pain in his chest, felt the jagged prodding of broken ribs. Even worse, his rippling blade was deflected by the force of the nightshade's attack, the blade not so much as contacting the black skin. As splintered rock fell around him, fetid breath made Holt gasp and choke—but then the monster passed, flapping upward for another assault.

As Holt climbed to his feet, he reached upward to reassure himself that the circlet remained on his head. Even the beast's powerful, raking claws couldn't knock it off!

The nightshade circled outward from the wide ledge and over the abyss of World's End before it soared back for another attack. Holt advanced to stand at the edge of the great, cliff-side cave, at the brink of the precipice that plummeted to the unknown depths below the world. He wondered at the fact that he didn't feel pain—logically he knew that his chest should be racked with agony. The

Daryman sensed a slight hesitancy in the beast, and that knowledge gave the man a sense of confidence.

Across the shelf of rock, he saw Danis. The princess hid under the layer of broken stone and dust that had been knocked down in the beast's first dive. Holt knew it was only his heightened perception that enabled him to see her, for the camouflage effectively rendered her invisible. Now, however, he could feel her eyes upon him, hear the straining gasps of her breaths as she tried to remain utterly still.

The nightshade veered back toward the Daryman, and once again Holt met the diving attack with an upraised blade, legs braced in a widespread stance. He no longer had the cave wall to his back, but the beast showed no inclination of maneuvering for a rear attack. Instead, it swooped downward, the wind of its passage rising to a shriek. The nightshade uttered a single, thrumming cry—a wail like the tortured moaning of a million lost souls. The sound chilled Holt's blood, but even that fearsome noise could not bring back his earlier terror. Instead, loathing fused his determination.

Again the Daryman chopped, and again that huge body collided with him. Mighty claws raked toward his face and shoulders with rending power, but this time they made no passing strike. Instead, they seized Holt's shoulders in a powerful grip, lifting him bodily from the ground. The Daryman stabbed upward at the creature's black, oily belly, but only succeeded in scraping the blade along one of the scaly legs.

Holt twisted painfully in the claws of the nightshade. The ground dropped away as the beast labored upward. Abruptly, the Daryman saw the vast abyss of World's End plunging below.

The monster released its grip, and for a sickening instant, Holt floated in the air, the bottomless well of space yawning beneath his feet. Desperately he reached out, grasping the creature's leg in his left hand. He swung sideways with a wrenching twist, feeling a tearing in his chest that was frightening—though not particularly painful. Grimly he kept his one-handed grip until he sheathed his sword.

The nightshade glided back toward Danis, toward the stony ledge in the cliff side. Jagged rocks lay strewn across that surface, interspersed with numerous cracks, splinters, and rough columns of stone. Abruptly the beast veered to avoid a tall spire rising like a tree trunk from the broad shelf.

Holt knew he'd never get a better chance. He let go of the monster's leg and smashed into the pillar with bone-crushing force. He hugged the shaft with enough strength to keep him from tumbling free, while he skidded and bounced ten feet down to the ledge.

The monster keened in outrage, veering back toward the man. With a shriek of fury, it dived toward Holt, jaws gaping and talons extended. The Daryman strode forward again, meeting the beast at the brink of World's End. This time he ducked under those deadly claws, springing upward in the next instant. His sword flashed, sorcerous blue light surging along the blade, and he lunged for the nightshade with all the hunger of a starving predator.

All the power in Holt's body lay behind that attack. The sword cut deeply into the nightshade's hideous shape, and its shriek of pain and fury knocked stones free from the cliff. The howl rang in a thunderous echo for long seconds, finally fading into a gurgling gasp. The massive body thrashed powerfully as the Daryman pulled free his blade and fell backward.

The beast's monstrous wings suddenly collapsed. For a moment it struggled for purchase at the cliff edge, but then it stiffened and slipped and tumbled lifelessly into the yawning vastness beyond the end of the world.

The unworldly shriek still echoed through the cavern as Holt limped away from the edge, slowly making his way to the Princess of Vanderthan.

25
Reunion

A flying creature soared past Holt, and he instinctively ducked, then cried out in recognition as he saw the barrel-shaped owl come to rest beside Danis.

"I say—that was rather well done, my good man," said Sir Ira with a dignified nod to Holt. The owl's feathers had been thinned by battle, but after a moment's preening they all pointed more or less in the right direction.

"I thought you were killed by bats," Holt admitted. It occurred to him that he ought to feel some joy at his companion's return. Instead, he was curiously numb, lacking any emotion.

"Killed? Bah—though I'll admit that one of the creatures did get a mouthful of my feathers. I led them on a merry chase, and none of them were able to get much else out of me!"

Danis crawled from beneath the rubble, and Holt stepped forward to take her hand, helping her to a sitting position on a nearby rock. The Daryman was acutely conscious of the crown on his head and very reluctant to remove it. He looked around, still amazed at the clarity with which he sensed his surroundings, and he knew that acute sensation would be gone if he relinquished the crown.

The princess shook her head, and Holt was surprised to see that her face was streaked by tears. Why was she crying? Her response seemed odd to him, fascinating, almost funny.

"Was it worth it?" she asked, between her tears. "Was it worth the loss of Tellist, of Gazzrick and Fenrald and all the . . ." She couldn't finish.

"Tut, tut—it takes some getting used to, this business of walking again." The reedy words came from the depths of the cavern, and Danis whirled to stare in surprise and disbelief.

"I'm sick and tired of wings!" huffed a voice that could only belong to Fenrald Falwhak. "I don't care *how* sore my feet get—I'm going to stick to walking!"

Pawns Prevail

Holt's eyes penetrated the darkness, and he recognized three familiar figures coming slowly toward them.

"I don't care about wings *or* feet," Gazzrick Whiptoe added, hastening between Fenrald Falwhak and Tellist Tizzit. "I'm just glad to be doing what *I* want, instead of what the nightshade commands!"

"Over here!" shouted Danis, waving wildly. The trio quickly scrambled over the rough cave floor to join them. Danis embraced the halfling in a wild hug while the Daryman nodded coolly to the wizard and the dwarf. All the time the princess shook her head in disbelief.

"How did—? That is, I thought you were—what happened?" he finally blurted.

"Bats!" spat Fenrald, as if he tried to get an unpleasant taste out of his mouth. "That nightshade turned us into giant bats!"

"All three . . . ?" Holt was intrigued. "Those bats were *you?* I almost—"

"We know," declared Gazzrick. He showed the Daryman a deep cut on his arm. "That was a wing when you stabbed me."

"Tut, tut—it's a good thing I'm nearsighted even with bat eyes. Else my teeth might have taken more than a nibble out of your ear. I'm really quite sorry about that," Tellist noted with a frown of chagrin.

"But—*why?* What made you attack us?" Danis asked.

Douglas Niles

Fenrald flushed with embarrassment. "It was the strangest thing. Once the nightshade got to me, it was like going to sleep—but with your mind still awake. I lay there on the ground, looking up, but I couldn't move a muscle." The burly dwarf shuddered. "I don't mind telling you it was the spookiest thing that ever happened to me!"

"It was like that for me, too," said the halfling. "I even *felt* myself changing into a bat. Growing wings, legs getting even shorter. Then, when I took off flying, it was like the nightshade hovered at my shoulder, gripping my mind itself, telling me exactly what to do."

Miserably, Gazzrick looked at the princess and the Daryman. The halfling's face twisted with guilt. "I would have thought that nothing could make me betray you," he told Danis. "But I was wrong. The power of the nightshade was too great —I couldn't begin to resist the compulsion."

"We're all quite glad, actually, that you weren't hurt—seriously, in any event," Tellist noted apologetically.

"And I could have killed you," Holt admitted flatly. "I don't know why I didn't, really."

"Yes, well . . . tut, tut. We really owe you a bit of thanks on that one. How did you know you could break the thrall of the nightshade?"

"It's the crown," Holt explained, suddenly conscious of the silver circlet on his brow. "It allows me—the wearer, I should say—to see things, to understand the mysterious."

"And it carries a compulsion, stronger even than the nightshade's," Gazzrick noted. "I found it impossible to disobey when you gave me the command to stay put."

"Aye," the dwarf agreed. "That was a kindness, lad, when you could have cut our heads from our shoulders without a second's worry."

"Holton wouldn't kill in cold blood," Danis announced, firmly. She met the Daryman's eyes with her own.

"And you?" Holt asked the princess. "Why did you leave your hiding place?"

"I . . . I went looking for the crown," she said sheepishly. "I thought, perhaps, if I looked in a different place, we'd have a better chance."

"You didn't think I could find it." Holt stated the fact, understanding Danis clearly. Perhaps it was the power of the crown that enabled him to penetrate her awkward explanation, or else he merely remembered the scorn with which she had treated him.

"I'm sorry," she said quietly. "I was wrong."

Holt looked around at his companions. Although he could see them more clearly than ever, in extremely sharp detail, it was as though he looked at canvas paintings of each of them. The crown heightened so many of his perceptions, but it also seemed to place a distance between him and his companions.

With a wondering dread, he experimentally reached up and lifted the crown off his head. Immediately his surroundings became darker, but now he saw the tears that glistened in Danis' eyes. Emotion rolled over him like a warm ocean wave, and he realized how cold and heartless the crown had made him. He now sensed the joy that Gazzrick and the others felt in their reunion—happiness that had been terribly remote while he wore the crown.

"My friends!" he gasped, anguished that he had allowed the crown to numb his own joy. Wordlessly he clasped them all, weak with relief.

Then the wave of pain swept through him, dropping him to his knees with a gasp of agony. He felt each broken rib as a fresh puncture, and his head rang with a concussive ache that the crown had somehow deadened. *I'm dying!* was his last thought as the world went black around him.

He awoke to the gentle touch of Sir Ira's wingtip stroking across his face. His chest still hurt, but the pain was the familiar ache of recovery—not the fresh stab of a near-mortal wound. His vision was clear, his breathing deep and regular.

"That was a near shave," Sir Ira admitted, blinking seriously. "You'll be your old self in little bit. Apparently it was only the crown that held your wounds at bay."

" 'Tis a potent artifact," the halfling noted, looking at the silver circle still clutched in Holt's hand. "What does it feel like to wear it?"

The Daryman slowly rose to his feet. He looked at the crown, the emblem of the sword and scepter of Vanderthan in the center of the crown's forepeak. There could be no doubt in his or anyone else's mind that this artifact was intended for Danis.

"It's very powerful," he began. "Perhaps the most powerful thing in the world. While I wore it, I saw things—*some* things—more clearly than ever before. The darkness lightened. When the bats attacked, I knew you were coming—even before you came into sight."

"And when you gave us a command, it was impossible not to obey," noted Gazzrick with a low whistle. "That's a *very* powerful artifact."

"Yes. Almost . . . *too* powerful," Holt added. "When I wore it, all of you became like *things* to me. I could see you, and I knew what you were thinking. But, as to the way you were *feeling*— well, that just didn't seem important. It's not so much that I couldn't sense your emotions. More like the crown made me just not *care*."

"Give it to me," Danis said, extending her hand. "I want to see what you mean."

He looked at the young princess. Now that he had removed the crown, her beauty struck him with a new force—like something he had never noticed before. In truth, perhaps he hadn't. The firm set of her jaw, the proud curve of her cheeks, and the tangled golden hair strewn like wheat around her head, all seemed an image of perfection.

At the same time he remembered her cold arrogance, the ruthless drive with which she had pursued the crown. He thought of what the crown might do to her. If it removed her sense of empathy, would she become utterly intent on her ambitions?

He had no doubt that, aided by the Crown of Vanderthan, Danis could rule all Karawenn if she wanted—and he suspected that this would indeed be her ambition and her desire.

Danis's expression darkened as she sensed his reluctance to give up the treasure. Her eyes flashed, and she allowed a cold edge to creep into her voice.

"You shall be well paid for it," the princess declared. "Name your price."

Holt looked back, anguish in his eyes and in his voice. "You think I want *riches?*"

"I should think that life on the farm could become considerably more comfortable," Danis declared icily.

Holt understood the real fear that grew in the back of her mind. She feared that *he* would keep the crown, and she knew that she would never be any match for his power. But to the Daryman, that idea was now even more repellant than the thought of giving the artifact to her.

"The crown is an artifact of the immortals," he said pointedly. "As such, it's too powerful for humankind—*any* human—to hold."

He looked at his companions, all of whom watched with wide, staring eyes. Carefully, he hefted the crown, looking again at the brilliant diamonds, the impeccable, gleaming platinum.

"Let it go back the way it came," he stated with powerful determination.

In one smooth gesture, he turned toward the sweeping cliff of World's End, hoisted the crown behind him, and then hurled it with all of his strength into the infinite expanse of space.

* * * * *

The final immortal token, the gust of wind, floated across the waters of the pool. The breeze swirled outward and down, sweeping into Karawenn.

26
The Crown of Vanderthan

The crown winked and sparkled in the light of the rising sun, arcing skyward and then starting into the long, downward plunge.

"No!" shrieked Danis, lunging toward the cliff edge. Gazzrick and Holt each seized one of her arms, hauling the kicking, struggling princess back.

"Oh, my—look!" announced Tellist, pointing into space.

Holt's jaw dropped as a strong breeze suddenly blasted them, driving them back toward the wall of the cliff-side ledge. He watched in astonishment and disbelief as the crown veered back toward the precipice. The wind drove the metal ring through the air, until it clanked to the stones perhaps thirty feet below their position. There it rested securely on a wide, flat boulder.

"Perhaps *that* will teach you some manners!" gloated Danis to Holt, too overjoyed to remember her fury of a few moments earlier. "Your rope," she added, turning to Fenrald. "Lower me down there."

With a sigh, the dwarf uncoiled the line from around his waist. Holt sagged weakly against the cliff, appalled by a sense of futility and failure. His decision to throw the crown had not been an easy one, but once it was made, he knew it was the proper course.

Yet now that course had not only failed, but failed in a way that would have to cause Danis to regard him as a traitor and a fool. A voice in his mind whispered the fact over and over. Surprisingly, the reaction of the princess seemed more important to him than the crown's retrieval.

All the same, he couldn't now try to talk them out of recovering the artifact. Perched where it was, it would be easy pickings for any creature or person with the means to divine its presence. If Danis didn't claim it today, he knew that someone—or something—else would before much time passed.

In a matter of moments Fenrald had a secure

knot tied around Danis, and he and the Daryman held the rope while she scrambled down the cliff and took the crown in her hand. She held it high while the pair hoisted her back up again.

As the princess rejoined her companions, her eyes quickly found Holt's. A flush of shame crept across his features, but he didn't lower his gaze. Her next words surprised him immeasurably.

"I understand why you did that," she said quietly. "It was more an act of friendship and loyalty than of betrayal."

"You—you don't know how powerful that artifact is," he replied. "In the wrong hands, it could be a terrible danger to Karawenn."

"Then we'll have to keep it out of the wrong hands, won't we?" she retorted, a mischievous light in her eyes.

As the others watched in awe, she placed the platinum circlet upon her head and looked around. The crown's emeralds of rich green and sparkling diamonds glittered in the sun. It seemed to Holt as though Danis suddenly stood taller, a more imposing figure. Though his chin was at the level of the crown, he felt as though he looked *up* at her—at a profoundly awe-inspiring presence.

Yet he no longer saw the glow of delight that had shined in her cheeks and eyes a moment earlier. Her upwardly curving lips might have been smiling, yet they conveyed no sense of real happiness.

Instead, her mouth suggested an expression of aloof, regal satisfaction.

"It *does* open your eyes," Danis said quietly. Holt knew she was experiencing the same sense of miraculous transformation that he had. "I feel as though I can see *past* the end of the world, even to worlds beyond. . . ."

Her voice trailed away. Silently, as if her companions were no longer present, she turned and entered the cave. The princess, no longer limping, walked rapidly through the dark chambers. The others struggled to keep up, tripping and stumbling often. At last, Holt thought to draw his sword to light the way, enabling them at last to catch up to Danis.

She didn't turn around as they joined her. The companions made their way in silence through the winding caverns, back to the original cave, and finally to the base of the long throne room staircase. Holt's chest was tight, and he had noticed Tellist and Gazzrick staggering with exhaustion. When Danis climbed immediately onto the first, giant-sized step, the Daryman could no longer hold his tongue.

"Your Highness," he said loudly. "We need to rest."

The princess continued to the second step, but then stopped and turned, as if she had just remembered some vague and unimportant fact.

Douglas Niles

"Danis . . . " Gazzrick's voice was weak, pleading. "Please—let's stop for a bit!" The halfling leaned against a rock and sank to the floor with a groan.

"We might have to fight," Holt reminded the princess. "The skeletons broke through the portcullis—remember? They could be waiting at the top of the steps."

Danis looked up the stairway, then turned to the Daryman. "The undead are gone," she declared. "Gone with the nightshade."

Knowing the perceptive power of the crown, Holt believed her. Yet he saw that Tellist had slumped to the ground, and Gazzrick already began to take off his boots. "Wait," he urged her.

For a moment Holt wondered if the princess would continue up the stairs. Then she nodded, as if confirming a decision she had made somewhere in the distant reaches of her mind.

"Very well," she agreed.

She touched the crown uncertainly, then looked away from the companions. Finally she raised her hands again and slowly lifted the artifact from her head.

An expression of shock came over her face. She looked at Holt, at Gazzrick and the others as if they had just appeared beside her. Lowering her head in shame, she spoke through a tremor in her throat.

"I would have *left* you there," she said. "Not

because I wanted to, but because I just *forgot* about you!"

"The crown raises one above such concerns as friendship and loyalty," Holt said softly. "It's—it's what I tried to explain before."

Tears came into her eyes. "I can't wear the crown—I can't live with that kind of loneliness! I *need* you—all of you!"

She turned to Holt. "Now I understand why you would have cast this crown away—but I can't do that. There must be a reason for it, a time when it will be needed."

"As much as I needed it against the nightshade," he agreed, knowing that without the artifact his wounds would have doomed him early in that battle.

"Indeed. I shall take it back to Vanderthan with me—but in my saddlebag, not on my head. In the castle we'll keep it under tight guard, locked away in our deepest vault."

With that, she held the artifact in one hand— and took Holt's hand with the other. Together, side by side, they started up the long climb, back to the world of light and sun and air.

* * * * *

The farms of Oxvale came into sight as the path toward Vanderton veered away from Holt's route home. He reined back on Old Thunder while Danis brought Lancer to a halt. They heard a glad whoop from below, and saw Derek Jaken waving from the farmyard. Holt turned to say good-bye to the princess, surprised at the way his throat grew tight.

Walking on the trail behind Danis and Holt, Fenrald coughed awkwardly, and then turned to Tellist and Gazzrick while the man and woman searched for the words of their farewell.

"You'll be welcome in the castle—anytime you want to return," Danis said quietly. "I hope you can forgive the rough treatment you received the first time you came."

"It's forgotten," he replied. "I'll be there by midsummer. Fenrald's going to stop at the farm for a while. Then he's invited me to Graywall in the autumn to study swordsmanship under one of the dwarven masters. You can be sure I'll come through Vanderton on my way!"

"Until then, Daryman—farewell!" She smiled, and the sun sparkled in her green eyes. For the first time Holt understood how much he was going to miss her.

Gazzrick and Tellist fell in behind the princess, all of them waving. The last thing Holt saw as they started down the trail was the proud, pompous figure of Sir Ira Hsiao, perched on the shoulder of the Princess Danis, First Daughter of Vanderthan.

Epilogue

The water in the immortal's fish pond clouded, the image of Karawenn vanishing as the power of the mortal game faded. The white-bearded sage pushed himself back from the water's edge with an indignant snort.

"A complete lack of ambitions and imagination," Pusanth sulked. "How could he hold victory in his hand—and then throw it away?"

Dalliphree shrugged with a delicate buzzing of her wings. "Who knows what makes these mortals work?" Then she smiled, her eyes teasing—and a little bit gloating. To the faerie, the garden looked a little brighter, the rose petals smelled a trifle more sweet.

Douglas Niles

"Who cares about all that?" she asked lightly. "I think it's so much fun to play a game—and win!"

The sage's expression softened. "I'll admit the match was a good one—and, in truth, my mortal did things of which I'm proud."

"Mine, too!" Dalli squeaked. "And now she'll be able to do anything she wants!"

Pusanth's smile was tolerant, even sympathetic. "You think so? It could be that the crown presents more of a burden than a blessing."

"Ha! You're just jealous!"

"Not at all," the sage demurred. "You won the game, and I accept that . . . for now."

Pusanth looked at the pool again, and then regarded the faerie, his eyes sly as he reflected on the game and his opponent. "Are you ready for a rematch?"

LOVE AS IT WAS MEANT TO BE

"No matter how it came about, I am so very happy you agreed to become my wife. The rubies were my father's wedding present to my mother and have come to be called the Montrose Bridal Set." He paused again, then his voice grew soft with emotion. "Noramary, from the moment I met you, I felt, even then, something. I think, I believe—I have been waiting for you all these years."

"Well, here I am," she replied in a whisper.

Her lovely eyes seemed to reflect the shining thing suspended between them, fragile as a butter-fly wing, a silken thread that might, in time, become a strong, sure bond.

∾

Look for these other titles
in the Brides of Montclair series

Ransomed Bride
Fortune's Bride
Folly's Bride

published by HarperPaperbacks

of HarperCollins*Publishers*
 Street, New York, N.Y. 10022

on of this book was published in 1989
 division of HarperCollins*Publishers*.

ick Johnson.

 printing: February 1994

ates of America

colophon are tra emarks of

HarperPaperbacks   *A Division*
                    10 East 53r

A trade paperback editi
by Zondervan Books, a

Cover Illustration by R

First HarperPap   backs

Printed in the Unit   d S

HarperPaperbacks a   d
HarperCollins*Publish*   e

❖ 10 9 8 7 6 5 4 3 2

To Irma Ruth Walker, my friend,
whose faith in me and this series contributed greatly
to its creation

Part I

Boast not thyself of tomorrow; for thou knowest not what a day may bring forth.

PROVERBS 27:1

Chapter 1

"Well, William, whatever shall we do *now*?" demanded Elizabeth Barnwell of her portly husband.

But all Squire Barnwell seemed capable of doing at the moment was to stare into the empty fireplace of the parlor in their Williamsburg home and to shake his head, a bewildered expression on his ruddy face.

While waiting for some answer from him, Betsy reread the note she held in her hands. Then, looking up at her husband again, she tapped it against her palm impatiently.

Betsy frowned, eyeing her husband's appearance, which was in sharp contrast to his usual meticulously groomed state. Today Squire Barnwell's powdered wig was askew and the buttons of his waistcoat had been fastened hastily, as if a five-year-old had been practicing. *And it is no wonder!* Betsy sighed. The shock they had just received would unsettle the most staid of men.

Indeed, both of them had been badly shaken by a totally unimaginable domestic crisis. Practically on the eve of her wedding, their eldest daughter had eloped with her French tutor, leaving only a scribbled note for them to find after she was safely away.

Who would have ever believed it of the girl? Even though Winnie was prone to flightiness at times, to behave in such an irresponsible manner was inexcusable!

Really! It was almost too much to bear. Betsy smoothed out the wrinkled scrap of paper clenched in her hands and read for the tenth time the hastily written explanation. Her eyes misted with tears of frustration and indignation more than grief. A mother with four marriageable daughters prepares herself all their lives for the bittersweet moment of parting on their wedding days; and Betsy had been particularly proud of the good match Winnie had made with Duncan Montrose, a wealthy planter.

"Well, 'pride goeth before a fall,'" Betsy quoted. That foolish girl had allowed her infatuation with the suave foreigner to render her witless, and she had run off with him. By now they were probably in Yorktown, perhaps already aboard a ship sailing for England.

Betsy bristled, setting her ruffled cap atrembling. Winnie had gone with not the slightest care for the havoc she left behind nor the wrecked plans for the wedding only two months hence, not to mention her jilted fiancé.

William glanced over at his wife. Never in the twenty years they had been married had he seen her so upset. He himself was at a loss as to what the next sensible step should be. The silence between them lengthened. Suddenly they heard the sound of lightly running feet on the polished floor along the hall. Then followed a tap on the closed parlor door, and the familiar voice of their orphaned ward, Noramary Marsh asking, "May I come in?"

As if on cue, Betsy's eyes met William's in a long, measured look. No words were needed to convey the thought that was born in that instant. Noramary, William's niece whom they had taken into their home when she was twelve, was now an appealing seventeen—only a year younger than Winnie.

Quickly Betsy gave William an imperceptible nod, then, tucking Winnie's note into her apron pocket, she called, "Yes, dear, come in."

The door opened slightly and around its edge peered an enchanting face. The coloring was perfection—the pink and porcelain complexion bestowed on country-reared English girls by a benevolent Creator. Masses of dark curls framed her forehead and fell in disarray about her shoulders. Her eyes were deep blue and darkly lashed, her smile radiant. She was wearing a simple blue muslin dress and a wide-brimmed straw gardening hat that had slipped from her head and now hung around her neck, suspended by wide ribbons exactly the color of her eyes. She was holding a flat wicker basket filled with spring flowers.

Noramary was unaware of the charming picture she made, and of the silent appraisal her foster parents were making of her assets.

"I just wanted to show you the flowers I picked, Auntie." Noramary smiled, holding the basket out so her aunt could see her choice. "The pinks will be perfect for the centerpiece tonight. Or do you like the daisies better?"

"Oh, yes, tonight—well, dear, they are lovely, but there is something—" Betsy paused, lowering her voice. "Come in, Noramary, and close the door, please. Your uncle and I must talk with you."

The Barnwells' eyes met again, and this time there was no mistaking the message that passed between them. *Of course! Noramary!* Why had they not thought of her at once? Noramary would be the most suitable substitute for her cousin as Duncan Montrose's bride. Thus the family honor would be saved and disgrace averted, not to mention the sizable dowry already paid to the Montrose clan by the Barnwell family, the latter not to be dismissed lightly, considering the Squire's recent financial reverses.

William Barnwell cleared his throat, turned toward the empty grate, and absentmindedly extended his hands to a nonexistent fire. He decided to let his wife handle this delicate matter. Although usually quite direct, she could, when the occasion required, be very diplomatic. *An admirable woman,* he thought gratefully, *equal to any situation.*

Noramary stepped into the room, closing the parlor door quietly behind her, never imagining that this conversation was to change her life forever.

"Sit down, dear," Aunt Betsy said gently, gesturing toward one of the needlepoint-covered chairs. "A most distressing thing has happened," she began solemnly, "and we want to tell *you* before we tell the younger girls."

Chapter 2

Less than an hour later Noramary came out of the parlor into the hall. Stunned by what she had just heard, she felt slightly light-headed and leaned against the closed door for a moment to steady herself.

The shock of the news of Winnie's elopement sometime during the night had been followed almost immediately by a second—the staggering request of her foster parents that she step into her errant cousin's place as the bride of Duncan Montrose!

"So you see, my dear, why we must ask this of you?" Aunt Betsy's voice rang in her ears.

Noramary closed her eyes, bringing back the scene which had just taken place. As her aunt explained the dilemma Winnie's irresponsibility had brought about and what must now be done, Noramary had sat very still, eyes downcast, hands folded in her lap, hearing but not fully absorbing her aunt's words. Now those same words burst upon her, strong and clear, exploding in her head.

"—marry Duncan Montrose!" *Marry Duncan Montrose!*

Distractedly Noramary set down the basket of flowers she had picked up and carried out into the hallway with her. Moving woodenly, she crossed over to the staircase and, clinging to the banister, mounted the steps with weighted limbs. She felt strangely burdened, frightened, and confused. Suddenly all the joy, the lovely, comforting warmth she had found here in the Barnwells' home was slipping away. Once again, in her short lifetime, she was experiencing that sense of aloneness—like a little boat adrift without its mooring.

When she reached the top of the stairs, she went swiftly down the hall, passing Winnie's bedroom as she did, wondering how her cousin had managed to slip out of the house in the middle of the night with no one the wiser. Pausing at the door of the room she shared with her other cousin, she listened for sounds of Laura's moving about within and then opened the door cautiously. To her relief, she found it empty. Then she remembered that Laura had gone for a final fitting of the bridesmaid's gown she was to wear at Winnie's wedding.

Will she wear it now—at mine? Noramary drew a long breath. The enormity of what had been asked of her swept over her. To marry a man who had been betrothed to her cousin—a man she barely knew, practically a stranger!

But how could she refuse to do as they asked? When as a twelve-year-old child she had been sent from England to Virginia, the Barnwells had opened their home and hearts to her. When there had been no place for her with her half-brother Simon, newly married to the haughty Lady Leatrice, they had welcomed her here. There was so much for which she could never repay them. To Noramary, her duty was clear.

Shakily she sat down on the edge of one of the maple spool beds, trying to bring to mind a clear image of Duncan Montrose.

The first time she had ever seen him was a year ago at Christmastime on the night of the Barnwells' annual holiday open house. Winnie, who had met him at another party earlier in the season, had boasted to Noramary of "the attractive Scotsman" whom she had invited to her home. Winnie was forever falling in love. None of the infatuations ever lasted for very long, so Noramary paid little attention to her cousin's enthusiastic description. Besides, she was much too preoccupied with thoughts of her own beau, Robert Stedd. That evening, however, she had gone into Winnie's room to borrow some ribbons for her hair, when suddenly Winnie had called her over to the window.

"Come quick, Noramary! Duncan Montrose has just arrived! You must see how handsome he is!"

Curious, Noramary had rushed to Winnie's side. Peering over her shoulder, she watched below as a man dismounted from his horse. It was already dark and, with only the light streaming out from the downstairs windows and the meager illumination of the street lamps, she had only the impression of a tall, broad-shouldered figure moving with easy grace across the cobbled courtyard.

He had tossed his reins to the boy stationed outside to attend to the guests' horses, then stood for a minute, brushing the falling snow from his caped greatcoat with his tricorne hat. Then, almost as if aware that he was being observed, he had lifted his head and looked directly up to where the two girls were peeking at him from behind the curtains. Startled to be caught so handily, both girls had jumped back, giggling.

Later, downstairs, Winnie had brought him over to be introduced to Noramary.

At close range, Duncan Montrose was taller than he had appeared from her vantage point at the bedroom window, was Noramary's first thought. Her second was that he was every bit as handsome as Winnie had claimed. His strong features were classically molded, with skin bearing the bronzed glow of a man much outdoors. Although elegantly attired for the occasion, he was not the least foppish. His fine blue broadcloth coat was superbly tailored. The pleated cravat and ruffled shirt of white linen boasted exquisite lace trim, and the crested buttons on his gray satin waistcoat were of silver.

But there was something else about Duncan Montrose that Noramary now remembered. Something Winnie had never mentioned. Something compelling—a directness, an inner confidence without affectation, a maturity that belied his years. His was a strong face, a magnificent face, full of character, she decided. And then there were his eyes—clear, gray, thickly and darkly fringed, strangely searching.

But does anyone recognize a moment of destiny in life? Noramary asked herself as she recalled that first meeting. They had exchanged the usual pleasantries and yet, now that she thought about it, she remembered there had been something unusual about that first encounter.

As he acknowledged their introduction and bent over her extended hand, his eyes had held hers intently for a few seconds. In that fraction of time, everything surrounding them—the laughter, the music, the guests—momentarily dimmed, and something infinitely important passed between them.

Recalling that long-ago evening, Noramary remembered something else she had almost forgotten. When Duncan's lips brushed her fingertips, her heart had lifted lightly. Duncan had held her hand a little longer than necessary, raising his eyes to linger on her face. Noramary had turned away quickly, glad to see Robert crossing the room to claim her for the next reel.

Robert! With a sudden clutch of panic, Noramary realized that in all the confusion of the morning's events, she had completely forgotten Robert! It seemed unimaginable that her first thought was not of him!

A half-sob escaped Noramary's tight throat. Robert—whom she loved so dearly and who loved her, too. From a childhood friendship, their relationship had progressed into a romantic attachment special to both of them. And at Christmas, Robert had asked her to marry him. Of course, it was their secret. Robert still had to finish his studies at nearby William and Mary College before entering medical practice with his guardian, Dr. Hugh Stedd.

Robert! He would have to be told of these startling new circumstances which would affect their future. Even now he was probably waiting for her at their meeting place. He was free now during these days of spring holiday, and during his visit at the Barnwells last evening they had made plans for this afternoon.

Thinking of last evening, Noramary shook her head in remembered amazement. Winnie had seemed her usual self, not betraying by a single telltale look or word or action her own secret plans. And Monsieur, dropping by so casually, all respect and circumspect behavior toward the Barnwells, whom he was to place in the most awkward position imaginable. What a wily pair they had been! Noramary wondered if her pretty cousin had acted upon whim or impulse. It seemed unlike Winnie to plot such an escapade while in the midst of fittings for her trousseau and the flurry of pre-wedding festivities. The whole episode defied understanding.

But now Noramary was to pay the piper for the tune Winnie had danced to!

Slowly, hot tears rolled down Noramary's cheeks. How was she ever to tell Robert? How could she explain her obligation to the Barnwells? How could she make him understand what she must do?

Although the families were longtime friends, neither suspected that Robert and Noramary had discussed anything so serious as marriage. Noramary had purposely delayed saying anything to Aunt Betsy and Uncle William because it was an unwritten law of Williamsburg society that the eldest daughter must be wed before the younger daughters followed suit.

Noramary's own plans must be deferred until Winnie was happily settled, though she had never doubted that both families would give their blessing to the match. After Winnie's wedding to Duncan Montrose, Noramary and Robert had planned to announce their engagement. Now everything had changed.

Noramary could no longer restrain her tears as she thought of how much Robert meant to her and how painful it would be to give him up.

Almost from the first they had been drawn to each other by the parallel circumstances of their lives. Noramary and Robert were both orphans and, so, set apart. Unlike Noramary, who was penniless and without family or fortune, Robert had an assured future. The only relative of the prosperous physician, he had been adopted by Dr. Stedd and made his sole heir. Besides this, at age twenty-one, he would inherit the combined legacies of wealth, land, and property of his own parents.

Well aware of her own precarious position as a young woman without the dowry required to attract a suitable husband, Noramary was particularly grateful for Robert's devotion. This fact also assured her of the Barnwells' approval when the time came to declare their love and desire for marriage. But aside from all practical considerations, they had loved each other with a shining, incandescent affection that transcended the thought of dowries or property or inheritances.

She knew Robert loved her unconditionally. He teased her, made her laugh, plied her with compliments, set her at ease. Now she was being asked to relinquish the one person in the world who made her feel cherished and needed. Because of her childhood pain, the rejection she had felt at the hands of her imperious sister-in-law, there resided a deep insecurity beneath Noramary's tranquil manner. This feeling stemmed from the time she had been sent to live in a strange land, among strangers, though her sense of isolation had gradually diminished in the busy, cheerful Barnwell household.

Instinctively, Noramary equated love with being lovable. She concluded if she were helpful, well-behaved and sweet-tempered, she would win the love she yearned for. It was this wistful longing to belong that drove her to be *more* obedient, *more* generous, *more* gracious than any of the other children and so earn a place for herself.

Since the Barnwells had treated her with the same affection and tenderness they had for their own daughters, Noramary felt she could refuse them nothing—not even her life.

She must go now! Noramary wiped away the tears. Robert would be growing impatient. How to break this terrible news to him? She knew she could not put off any longer the painful task that lay ahead of her.

Unconsciously she ran her fingers through her hair, and, feeling the silky strands catch in the straw hat still hanging from its ribbons, she loosened the ties and took it off. Then she went over to the dressing table to brush her tangled curls.

Appalled by the ravages of shock and tears reflected by her image in the mirror, she set about to repair them. As she did, her gaze fell upon the framed miniature of her mother. Noramary picked up the small portrait, a copy of the life-size painting hanging over the massive fireplace in the library of Noramary's ancestral home in Kent, England.

The artist had captured all the legendary Celtic charm of Eleanora Cary Marsh—her graceful figure was shown to advantage in the fitted green velvet jacket of her riding habit, the glowing complexion, intensely blue eyes, the masses of dark curls spilling out from under the small plumed hat. In the background was her prancing black horse upon whose curved neck she rested one graceful hand; in the other she held a riding crop. Every detail was expertly executed, even to the exact rendition of the Tara brooch worn on her shoulder, its emerald and diamonds sparkling.

Noramary studied the painted face in the ivory oval, then looked searchingly at her own reflection. The words of her old nurse, Nanny Oates, came to her.

"You're the image of your sweet mother, darlin', and you'll be just like her when you're a young lady."

Noramary recalled that a variation of these words was given to her later as an explanation as to why her brother Simon was sending her to live with the Barnwells in Virginia. Why must she leave Monksmoor Priory forever? Cross the vast ocean alone? she had demanded tearfully.

"It's because you're beautiful and *she's* jealous," Nanny Oates had told Noramary bitterly as she packed her little trunk for the journey.

The old memory stirred uneasily as she examined her reflected face. *Had* Noramary, as Nanny Oates predicted, grown up to look like her beautiful mother? Her face seemed quite ordinary to Noramary. In her naïveté she did not realize that even a work of art viewed daily begins to appear commonplace.

She had never known her mother, for Eleanora had died giving her birth. Instead, she had been reared in a house that mourned its young mistress, the second wife of a deeply grieving master. Nanny Oates had done her best loving Noramary as dearly as she had loved Eleanora before her. Simon, a half-brother and older by twelve years, had inherited everything at their father's death—the palatial manor house, the vast lands and properties. There had been no provision in the will for Noramary. It was simply assumed that, when the time came, Simon would arrange a dowry and a suitable marriage for his little half-sister.

No one had counted on Simon's marrying a woman who would bring such drastic changes in the heretofore rather careless life of the Marsh home and eventually send away the girl child whose promising beauty she feared.

Now Noramary pieced together the truth and was learning that beauty can, indeed, be a curse—a cause of unhappiness in the life on whom it is bestowed.

"But why must I go?" the childish Noramary had demanded of Nanny.

The old woman's face contorted as she replied, "Because not many can stand the sight of beauty that's not their own. Ofttimes it brings out the worst in people—lust in men, envy in women." She had jerked her head meaningfully in the direction of the suite occupied by the Lady Leatrice Marsh.

"She's jealous, she is, my pet. She can't abide the thought that in a short time, you'll outshine her. Hers is the kind of beauty that fades quickly. Give her a few years of childbearing—and she must have at least three bairns, a boy among them—and her looks will go. *You* have the bones and bearin', the inner glow, that makes beauty real, makes it last!"

Thinking back to that long-ago day when all the arrangements had been completed for her departure for America, Noramary remembered when the reality had struck her full force. It was when she realized Nanny Oates would not be coming with her! She had flung herself into the old nurse's arms, sobbing.

Rocking her as she tried to comfort her beloved charge, Nanny had murmured over and over, "It's God's will, dearie, God's will. 'Tisn't ours to question. We must accept it."

Now Noramary wondered, was this, too, God's will for her? Turning from the mirror, Noramary threw herself onto her knees beside the bed and buried her face in her hands as she hugged the miniature to her breast.

"Oh, why must it be like this! Dear Lord, help me understand!" she cried.

Then Noramary recalled what she had so often seen Nanny Oates do in times of stress. She raised her head and glanced at the small Bible the old nurse had packed into her belongings to bring with her to Virginia. She picked it up and turned the pages slowly until she came to a passage she had heard Nanny pray many times: "Thy Word is a lamp unto my feet, a light unto my path. Dear Lord, give me the guidance I need this day."

Opening the Bible at random, she slid her finger down the page, her eyes following it to the fifth verse of the first chapter of Joshua: "I will not leave thee nor forsake thee; take courage and be strong. . . .Take courage then and be very *valiant*.

Obey my laws and do not depart from them."
Noramary thought quickly of the commandment,
"Honor thy father and thy mother." Surely Aunt
Betsy and Uncle William had been like parents to
her. She read on: "Fear not and do not be dismayed,
because the Lord thy God will be with thee in all
things wheresoever thou shalt go to."

Noramary closed the Book. Certainly those
instructions were clear enough. She straightened
her slender shoulders. Now all that was left was to
tell Robert.

Chapter 3

Noramary could see Robert waiting for her as she hurried along the path toward the meadow. He was leaning against the gnarled old oak tree which, when they were younger, they had used as a hiding place for secret messages. Sometimes, even recently, Noramary had found a note from Robert hidden in one of the knotholes there.

At the thought that now there would no longer be such notes, no longer the camaraderie they had shared through the years, Noramary felt a wrenching in her heart. It was so unfair! Hers and Robert's life irrevocably altered. All because of two irresponsible people.

What would Robert say when she told him? He had always thought Winnie a silly, empty-headed flirt. And when he found out that she would bring about a drastic change in his own life, his whole future—change everything—Noramary halted, chilled by the thought of Robert's reaction.

Noramary stood there a moment longer, unconsciously delaying the telling. She watched Robert stoop, gather up a handful of pebbles and send them skipping over the smooth surface of the pond at the end of the meadow.

How handsome he is, she thought, how free and graceful the movements of his lithe body as he tossed the stones, the full sleeves of his white linen shirt billowing, the sun glistening in tawny lights on his brown hair.

Noramary's heart felt sore and heavy within her. How could she give Robert up to marry a stranger? Robert, who knew her better than anyone else, who loved her with all her faults, who made her happier than she had ever been!

Knowing Robert's enthusiastic, impulsive, intense nature, Noramary dreaded his reaction to the new circumstances that would change their future plans. His situation with his uncle was entirely different from her own with the Barnwells. Would he understand her sense of obligation, her conviction that it was her duty to fulfill their request? All she could do was try to make him see what to her was a clear and certain path.

As she stood there uncertainly, Robert, spinning around to fling another pebble, saw her and waved both arms in greeting. He tossed the pebble, then started running to meet her.

"Noramary! What took you so long? I've been waiting for ages!" he demanded, the twinkling brown eyes belying the stern tone of his voice.

"My aunt and uncle . . ." she began hesitantly. "They wanted to talk to me. . . ."

"Well, no matter, now that you're here at last!"

He caught both her hands in his and smiled down at her, his square, white teeth contrasting with the glowing tan of his lean face, his dark brown eyes shining with happiness. His arm went around her waist. At his touch a familiar tingle, swift as quicksilver, coursed through Noramary. She dared not look up at the tall boy who led her over to the shade underneath the sprawling limbs of the old oak. He knew her too well. She needed still more time to gather the courage to tell him what must be told.

There had never been anyone like Robert. Up to now all their times together had been happy. From childish play and games, they had grown to enjoy so many of the same things, shared so much—the love of music and dancing, poetry and plays. They had laughingly called themselves "kindred spirits." They had laughed much together, Noramary thought wistfully. Robert had always been able to make her laugh even when she was a little melancholy.

"Let's sit down here for a minute," Robert suggested.

He spread his jacket on the grassy bank for Noramary to sit upon, then scooped up a handful of pebbles and tossed them one by one into the water. Watching as the circles spread wider and wider, one circle making another and another, Noramary suddenly thought how much like the circles on the water life was. In life everything affected everything else—one's words, one's actions touched everyone else's. As the poet John Donne had written—"no man is an island." Careless Winnie never imagining how her action would shatter all Robert's and Noramary's hopes, dreams, plans, like a pebble tossed thoughtlessly into a pond.

When Robert put his arm around her shoulder, took her chin in his other hand and gently tilted it upward to kiss her, she drew back.

"What is it?" he asked, the hurt showing in his voice at her unexpected movement.

She swallowed over the rising lump in her throat. "Oh, Robert," she began, her distress making it difficult to go on. "Something has happened at home, something that affects you and me . . . *us*. My aunt and uncle have asked something of me that I have no right to refuse, and . . ." She stumbled awkwardly through the difficult recital while he stared at her in growing disbelief.

Even though Noramary had anticipated his dismay, she had not expected him to react so violently. When her stammering explanation trailed off with a plea for his understanding, Robert jumped to his feet.

"No! I can't understand! Noramary, you love me, I know you do. How can you think of marrying another man? You must wait for me, darling. Another year and then I shall be of age. I'll have my inheritance—a house in Williamsburg and property besides. I'll be a physician, an honorable profession. We'll have a place in society. You will have everything I can give you. What more could the Barnwells want for you? Of course, Montrose is a wealthy planter, I know that, but they have three other daughters. Why could not one of them take their sister's place as his bride? Why you? Blast Winnie and her fancy French tutor . . . what right has she or anyone else to rob us of our happiness?"

Noramary shook her head sadly. "Robert, dear, listen . . . please listen. I've given my promise. I can't do anything else. No matter how *we* feel, my darling. I *do* love you, I shall always love you. . . . But, Robert, they gave me a home when I had no home. They were my family when my own family turned me away . . . they have treated me as their own daughter. . . . I can do no less than give them the same obedience and love I would give my own parents."

"Respect, gratitude, obedience—to a point! I can understand *that!* What I cannot understand is blind obedience—giving yourself as the sacrificial lamb!" Robert declared furiously.

With that, he turned to Noramary, reached down and grasped her wrists and pulled her to her feet. His face was very close to hers, so close that his eyes seemed almost black, the pupils dilated with anger. His voice was harsh and bitter.

"And is *our* happiness to be sacrificed then?" He grabbed her shoulders. "Doesn't that mean anything? Noramary, I love you! You can't do this to *us!* I won't let you!" he said with desperate intensity.

Then he crushed her against him, his arms holding her fiercely, and kissed her with a passionate urgency neither had dared reckon in themselves before.

As he held her and kissed her, she felt for the first time the fire flaming up in them both, that promise of a rapture that would blind them to anything else. It had always been there, she knew. Perhaps both sensed it; yet, knowing instinctively that it was for later, they had been willing to await its fulfillment.

Now, suddenly, there would be no tomorrow for them, no future, only this day, this moment.

In spite of her brave words, all of Noramary's resolve melted as their kisses deepened, intensified. It was with immense effort that she finally broke away, breathless and shaken. "Oh, Robert, we can't—don't make it harder for me. . . ." With a broken sob, she turned from him quickly and, lifting her skirts, she started running back toward the house, a slim, graceful figure, fleeing like some woodland creature—from danger.

On and on she ran, stumbling at times on the hem of her gown, sobbing helplessly, the sharp pain in her side matching the one in her heart.

Behind her, she could hear Robert's pleading voice calling her name. "Noramary, wait! Noramary!"

But Noramary never stopped until she reached the garden gate—and never turned back.

Chapter 4

A curious pall seemed to descend upon the usually cheerful Barnwell household in the days immediately following Winnie's elopement. Even the younger girls, Sally and Susann, seemed strangely subdued in the wake of their older sister's rash action. Laura, on the other hand, reacted with rare excitement at the unexpected event that had plunged her parents into such a dismal mood, and she wanted to talk of it endlessly.

Noramary, usually Laura's willing confidante

and indulgent listener, was quiet and uncommunicative. And in the face of Laura's protestations that the turn of fate casting Noramary as Duncan's bride was highly romantic, the older girl maintained her stoic silence.

Behind closed doors, there was constant discussion between the older Barnwells as to how to break the news of their daughter's betrayal of her promise to Duncan Montrose and how most tactfully to suggest to him the idea of Noramary as his substitute bride.

"The sooner done, the better!" declared Betsy emphatically.

It was Squire Barnwell's unhappy task to be the bearer of such tidings. So at the end of the week, armed with a miniature of Noramary to refresh Duncan's memory of Winnie's pretty cousin, William left Williamsburg for Montclair.

Even though Montclair was situated on the James River, a hard day's ride from Williamsburg and thus removed from the possibility of quickly circulated gossip, the Barnwells, nevertheless, wanted to be sure the news of their daughter's folly was delivered to the jilted suitor with as much dignity as the situation afforded. Thereby, it was fervently hoped, the news would be received with understanding and forgiveness by Duncan Montrose.

Although Squire Barnwell's pride made him reluctant to set out on such an undertaking, he agreed with his wife that no time should be lost. Too, he was anxious to make the trip before late spring rains might worsen the wretched country roads, which was in places little wider than a trail for a single horseman.

In spite of the unforeseen event of the elopement and the aftermath of despair they had felt briefly, both Barnwells were fairly optimistic of the outcome of the journey. Actually, both Squire and Mistress Barnwell secretly agreed Duncan would be getting a far better bargain with Noramary than with their own daughter. Not only was the younger girl beautiful, but a sweet-tempered, gentle girl with a delightful disposition, in contrast to Winnie, who could be petulant and willful. Noramary was also gifted musically, accomplished in needlework, painting, dancing, and spoke French fluently. Yes, Noramary would make an ideal wife for the wealthy planter. Truthfully, she was much better suited to the role than Winnie would have been, they concurred.

Still, even with this hopeful outlook, William had a few nagging doubts as he left for Montclair. What if Duncan, insulted by Winnie's rude and thoughtless act, should refuse their offer? Worse still, what if he considered the dowry already paid simply a debt of honor as compensation from the Barnwells for their daughter's dereliction of duty? Given his recent business losses, that would be a disastrous turn of events, indeed!

"Drat that headstrong girl! And that despicable Frenchman!" grumbled William as he jogged along the rutted road toward Montclair.

A much more cheerful William returned from the Montclair plantation. To his anxiously waiting wife he reported that Duncan, although greatly surprised by the news, had received William's apology with admirable restraint. It was his sister, Janet Montrose McLeod, a "formidable Scotswoman," lately arrived from Scotland for the express purpose of helping her brother prepare his newly built home for his bride, who had evidenced the most indignation. She seemed to take it as a personal affront to the entire Montrose clan.

However, when William and Duncan had an opportunity to discuss the situation in private, and Will had suggested that he might consider transferring his marriage offer to Noramary, Duncan had had a most favorable reaction. He told Will he was very pleasantly impressed when he had met Noramary and recalled her as being "a young lady both comely and gracious."

However, he insisted he would consider such an arrangement only if Noramary herself was willing to receive him as a suitor, and that a proper time of courtship should be maintained in which they could become better acquainted. Then, if mutually agreeable, a wedding could be planned.

"Montrose is a most estimable gentleman," William told Betsy in conclusion. "Any girl would be lucky to have such a husband."

Betsy was quick to relay this observation to Noramary, who listened carefully to her aunt's recitation of all that had transpired between her uncle and Duncan Montrose. And, later, when Duncan sent a formal note asking permission to call on her, she replied affirmatively.

Betsy Barnwell breathed a mental sigh of

relief. Everything was working out for the best. Noramary was being dutifully amenable, and in the end she would be grateful. True, she had seemed unduly quiet, almost melancholy, but that was surely due to natural maidenly timidity, Betsy assured herself.

Still, there was something odd in the way Noramary had suddenly refused to see the Stedd boy. Betsy felt sorry for him when she had sent him away, crestfallen. Strange, Betsy puzzled, the two of them had always seemed such good friends, always taking walks together, laughing merrily, finding pleasure in simple activities. Why, surely these children had not been seriously— romantically—involved with each other!

But how absurd, Betsy continued her thoughts. Robert still had his medical training to complete, and he was only a year or so older than Noramary. Both of them were so very young—they had simply been affectionate companions. Marriage could not have been considered so soon. She denied the very possibility, though she had to admit it had crossed her mind.

If this unfortunate thing with Winnie had not happened, Robert Stedd would have been a fine prospect for Noramary. But it had, and that was that. Noramary was being sensible and obedient—and, in the end, she would thank her aunt and uncle for arranging such a prestigious marriage when she had no reason to expect anything half so fortuitous!

Chapter 5

The next few weeks brought spring in a blaze of beauty to Williamsburg, but for Noramary, moving through her own private grief, the world around her seemed gray and bleak. Hard as she tried to be cheerful, it was an effort to get through each day. At night, her pillow was often wet with the tears she had held back during daytime.

A letter from Winnie finally arrived. In it she begged her parents' forgiveness for the pain her elopement may have caused them and for any embarrassment resulting from her broken engagement. She went on to assure them of her happiness and health, and asked for their belated blessing. In closing, she sent love to her sisters, naming each, and including Noramary. As the letter was passed around to be read within the family, Noramary could not help the hardening of her heart. Winnie's own excuses seemed so superficial, considering the havoc and heartbreak her action had left in its wake.

The more Noramary considered it, the stronger was her conclusion that Winnie had used her courtship with Duncan as a foil for her real romance with Philippe Jouquet. She knew her parents would never countenance her marriage to a man ten years her senior, one who had no money to offer except that which he earned. But it was so like Winnie, with her romantic, rebellious imagination, to plunge headlong into such an attachment, the element of danger giving it even greater appeal.

Often in the past Noramary had had to pick up the pieces after one of Winnie's thoughtless deeds, but never before had there been one with such serious implications.

Now that Winnie was gone, Aunt Betsy's indefatigable energies were focused upon Noramary, helping her step into the role her daughter had so foolishly abdicated. Duncan Montrose, a man of wealth and power, was too important to lose as a son-in-law, and Betsy was determined that it should not happen. Therefore, on the day Duncan was to pay his first formal call to

Noramary, Betsy fluttered about her anxiously.

Tense and pale, Noramary stood in front of the dressing table mirror, tying the drawstrings of her second starched petticoat around her tiny waist.

Noramary was well aware of her aunt's desire that everything should go well on this first visit and that Noramary should make a favorable impression on Duncan. She herself was apprehensive enough, and Betsy's fussing over her did nothing to assuage her fears. She tried not to show her irritation, for she sympathized with Betsy's understandable nervousness. The fact that this meeting was very important was emphasized by Betsy's insistence that Noramary should have a new dress for the occasion.

"You're much too thin, Noramary. I don't think you've been eating properly." Aunt Betsy frowned as she helped fasten Noramary into the bodice of the blue faille. "This dress fit perfectly when we tried it on ten days ago. Now it needs taking in!" she said with a sigh.

Noramary studied her reflection in the mirror, trying to see herself through Duncan's eyes. If he particularly favored Winnie's type, he would be disappointed in her, she thought.

Winnie was plump, with doll-like features and flaxen hair. In contrast, Noramary was tall for a girl, wand-slender, with masses of dark hair.

"Blue is certainly your color!" declared Betsy, standing back to admire the effect of the lighter blue overskirt embroidered with forget-me-nots. "Do you need help with your hair?" she asked.

"No, thank you, auntie," Noramary replied, taking up her brush.

"Then come downstairs when you're ready, dear. Duncan should be here in a few minutes. I remember him as being very punctual," Aunt Betsy said as she went out the bedroom door.

Noramary took a deep breath. This meeting would be crucial. She knew how much her aunt and uncle were counting on it to go well. She closed her eyes for a moment and said a little prayer. When she opened them, she regarded herself critically in the mirror. She *was* pale and thin. She leaned forward and pinched both cheeks to bring some color into them, just as she heard the sound of hoofbeats outside on the cobblestone street. Duncan arriving! She would have to go downstairs now. Aunt Betsy would be annoyed if she kept him waiting.

At the top of the stairs, Noramary paused, hearing the murmur of voices coming from the parlor, recognizing her uncle's jovial one, Aunt Betsy's light patter, and a third, deep and resonant, that must be Duncan's. She strained to hear what was being said.

"In answer to your question, ma'am, the house is nearly completed. I have incorporated some of my own ideas with the plans of the architect my father commissioned. I have some fine artisans among my own people, and they are hard at work on the carpentry and cabinetwork. I hope you will see it for yourself when you come as guests to Montclair."

"From what William told us upon his return from his recent visit, it will be one of the most impressive of all the manor houses built along the

James River," commented Aunt Betsy. "Is that not right, William? Is that not exactly what you said?"

"Indeed it is, my dear!" This from Squire Barnwell, emphatically. "I must say, Duncan, it is a magnificent place!"

Noramary knew they were discussing the house being built on the Montrose land, the home intended for Duncan's future bride, the mansion to which he had planned to bring Winnie!

Noramary moved quietly down the stairs, still listening as Duncan continued.

"It has been my preoccupation for the past two years, I must admit. That is the reason I haven't come to Williamsburg more often. I wanted to be sure the house was ready—" His voice broke off and there was an awkward silence. Everyone knew the unspoken ending of his sentence would have been, "by June"—the planned date of his wedding to Winnifred Barnwell.

Graciously, Aunt Betsy shifted the subject to a more pleasant topic. "And I have always been curious as to the derivation of the name 'Montclair,' Duncan. Is it a family name?"

"A combination actually, Mrs. Barnwell," he replied, "the first half from the first half of our surname; the second, from my mother's Christian name. Many of the ideas for the house were hers; she made sketches from which our architect drew his plans. Of course, sadly, she didn't live to see them realized. As you know, she suffered delicate health and never moved to the plantation from our town house. In recent months I've been living on the property in the architect's model, a small cottage on the other side of the creek that runs through the land. Since my sister Janet arrived from Scotland, we have been using that part of the house that's finished while the rest is being completed. That way, she can oversee the workmen, arrange the furniture—" Again Duncan's voice trailed away significantly.

Just then Noramary stepped into the doorway and stood there hesitantly. Duncan saw her first, and Aunt Betsy, following his glance, nodded and smiled encouragingly. "Why, here's our Noramary now! Come in, my dear."

As Noramary entered the room, Duncan rose and she was again struck by his impressive height. She came forward and curtsied as he took a few steps toward her and bowed over her proffered hand.

Noramary, who before had only regarded Duncan with the natural curiosity given her cousin's intended, now saw the man from an entirely new perspective. He was impeccably dressed in a tan coat, immaculate white ruffled linen, yellow waistcoat. His russet hair, unpowdered and smoothly groomed, was tied with a brown swallow-tailed grosgrain ribbon.

As she looked up at him, she again noticed the nobility of his features, the steady gaze of clear, gray eyes.

She took a seat beside her aunt on the loveseat opposite Duncan, and the conversation began to flow once more. Noramary observed, with interest, that his manner was genuinely warm and unaffected.

"Montclair is not as isolated as it seemed in

earlier days, for many Williamsburg families have built magnificent homes along the river convenient to load their tobacco on barges to take to market. My closest neighbors and good friends are the Camerons, whom you may know." There was a murmur of assent from the Barnwells. "Although the plantation social season is not quite as lively as in Williamsburg, there is much visiting back and forth and partying, a celebration for any and every occasion." Here Duncan laughed. "Like most Virginians we planters enjoy good times, and get-togethers are frequent. In winter, the roads do get rather difficult, but then our winters are short."

Although Duncan's conversation was directed to her aunt in answer to her questions, Noramary got the feeling he was trying to reassure her that life with him at Montclair would not be a dreary exile.

Uncle William then asked Duncan about his crops and the conversation turned to a discussion of the agricultural and commercial aspects of the plantation. During this business talk, an area Noramary was vaguely aware was of great significance to her future and thus of interest to her uncle, she noticed Aunt Betsy casting glances in her direction as if trying to ascertain her reaction to the prospective suitor.

When Duncan took his leave, he asked if he might call again at the end of the week before returning to Montclair to oversee the spring planting. Aunt Betsy assured him he would be most welcome. As Duncan again bent over Noramary's hand in farewell, he said, "A pleasure to see you again, Miss

Marsh. I shall look forward to our next meeting."

Thus began a series of well-chaperoned visits signifying a courtship between Duncan and Noramary. Of course, Aunt Betsy was always present on these occasions and often, to Noramary's acute discomfort, would insist her niece play the harpsichord for Duncan or would point out one of her watercolors or a piece of needlepoint Noramary had completed.

It was during one such episode that Noramary gained an insight into Duncan's nature that she might never have guessed.

At Aunt Betsy's insistence, Noramary had agreed to play a new piece she had just learned. Fearing that her memory might fail her, however, she was moving with some reluctance to the harpsichord when she caught Duncan's sympathetic glance and, at the same time, noticed a twinkle in his eye. It surprised and comforted her to know her prospective husband was a man of consideration and sensitivity, and an answering smile of amusement touched her lips.

Indeed, the more she was with Duncan and the better acquainted with him she became, the more resigned she became to the inevitable outcome of this arrangement. Beyond his courtly and gracious manner was a man of intelligence and wit. She began to admire his forthrightness, and what she had once judged aloofness she now determined to be only an innate reserve. She liked his lack of superficial conversation, his disinterest in gossip. In fact, he had absolutely none of the affectations or airs of some of the young dandies so prevalent in Williamsburg social circles.

Besides these calls in the Barnwell parlor, Duncan had escorted Noramary and her aunt to a musicale and to a supper party hosted by mutual friends and, once, he had even purchased tickets for all the family to attend a play presented by a traveling theatrical troupe, much to the delight of the younger Barnwells.

During the first weeks of summer Duncan called often at the Barnwell house and, in time, Aunt Betsy discreetly withdrew into an adjoining room, leaving the door ajar and Noramary and Duncan to themselves. It was on one such afternoon that Noramary sensed Duncan was struggling to phrase the formal request for her hand. Though Noramary felt they both knew it was a foregone conclusion that she was expected to accept his proposal, she still felt a certain degree of reticence in the tall man she had come to appreciate. Perhaps he entertained second thoughts about the agreement. Well, she would give him the opportunity to back out if he so chose.

"It's such a lovely day, perhaps we should go out to the garden where it's cooler," she suggested.

Solemnly, his hands clasped behind his back, Duncan followed her out into the soft balmy air, fragrant with the scent of many flowers. As they strolled along the narrow, gravel paths between the flower beds, Duncan at last broached the subject on both their minds.

"Your aunt and uncle have told me that you would not consider it unthinkable—I mean, if I were to . . ." Here Duncan paused and made a great show of studying some tulips as if they were a rare, exotic specimen. He suddenly seemed so vulnerable that Noramary felt sorry for this proud man who had been placed in such a position by her cousin.

"I am aware, sir, that you have been approached by my uncle and given permission by him to speak to me . . . of marriage."

"I would be honored if you would then consider my proposal . . . not simply because of the circumstances that have brought it about . . ." Here he paused, a flush reddening his face.

"I have already given my consent to your suit, and we have their blessing," she said.

Duncan still seemed to hesitate.

"I am, you know, twelve years your senior, ma'am—a man not too much at ease in society . . ." Again he paused.

"I am aware of the honor you do me, sir, for I am alone in the world." Noramary made the statement simply, for she wanted Duncan to know that with his proposal of marriage, he was offering her position, a home, and wealth, none of which she now possessed.

He looked at her solemnly, then said quite humbly, "I am alone, too. And have been for too long."

They walked a little farther along the flower-bordered path before Duncan spoke again.

"Then you will marry me?"

"Yes, Duncan." Her answer was so low that he had to bend near to hear it.

Noramary looked past the low garden wall to the meadow beyond, where she had so often walked with Robert. She closed her eyes for a moment. Now that she had promised to marry Duncan, from this day forward she must put all thoughts of Robert out of her mind. There must be no looking back, no regrets. If she made this free choice, she must try to forget what might have been and to accept her life as it was. She thought of the flood of letters from Robert, letters she had finally stopped opening, being unable to endure reading his anguished words, letters she dared not answer.

"Are you sure? I would not have you act against your will, Noramary." There was a thread of anxiety in Duncan's voice.

Sure? Her thoughts echoed his question. *But how can anyone be sure about anything in life?* She had thought hers and Robert's future was sure. Now, she couldn't be sure whether what she felt for Robert was true love or merely the yearning to belong to someone.

When she had timidly questioned Aunt Betsy as to whether her lack of romantic feeling for Duncan might be wrong, her aunt had replied briskly, "Of course not, my dear. If the truth be known, *most* marriages are actually amicable arrangements made for reasons of property or mutual benefit."

Was Aunt Betsy right? Or was there possibly something more? Noramary remembered vividly that flaming moment in the meadow with Robert when they had kissed for the last time, and the world had stood still. The possibility of what they might have together had trembled between them. Then it was forever lost. Duty had robbed them of knowing the ecstasy that was now beyond their reach. Would pondering "what might have been" haunt Noramary for the rest of her life?

"Noramary?" Duncan's voice prompted her answer.

She blinked as if from the bright sunlight, then clasping her hands tightly together, she took a deep breath and turned back to Duncan. She looked into the face so earnestly waiting for her reply. How strong he seemed, how steadfast.

One could trust that face, believe the message in those eyes, Noramary was certain of it. Perhaps if she could not yet love him—at least not with that rush of fire and excitement she had felt for Robert Stedd—she could at least return that honest affection.

As Noramary met Duncan's eyes, she realized if she were to accept his proposal, follow the expectations of her aunt and uncle instead of the longing of her heart, it must be done with no mental reservations. It must be done with full knowledge that with her acceptance, she put away the past with all its promise, all its possibilities, and relinquish her dreams of romantic love.

Perhaps the future with Duncan Montrose would yield a richer, deeper experience than she had ever known before. In any case, she had decided this marriage was God's will for her and, in obedience to Him and to her beloved aunt and uncle, she would do it.

Decisively Noramary placed her hand on Duncan's arm and said very softly, "Yes, Duncan, I would be proud to be your wife."

With those words Noramary was rewarded with a special look in Duncan's eyes. It came to her with sweet surprise that Duncan felt a warmth for her that had nothing whatever to do with his prearranged agreement with the Barnwells!

Chapter 6

The wedding was set for late September after the tobacco crop at Montclair was harvested and Duncan was free to come to Williamsburg for a few of the prenuptial festivities.

Although Noramary had wished for a small wedding, the Barnwells were too well-known, too highly respected to avoid a large guest list. Too, Betsy was anxious to offset any unfavorable gossip that might still be circulating about Winnie's elopement by doing everything surrounding Noramary's marriage to Duncan with dignity and decorum.

Noramary seemed peculiarly indifferent in the midst of the swirling activity surrounding her, but if Betsy was aware of it, she chose to ignore it. If Noramary seemed quieter, paler than usual, more passive, Betsy chalked it up to the normal apprehensions of any bride, but nonetheless sent up a frantic prayer: "Please, no last-minute problems. Just let me get her safely married—"

She suppressed any stirring of panic, reminding herself that Noramary, for all her fragile appearance, was a strong, sensible girl, and her word, once given, could be counted on.

Inevitably, however, a crisis did arise, and at a moment when Betsy least expected it and was least prepared to cope.

The week before the wedding, Noramary seemed to have regained her composure. She attended several parties, gone about her small household tasks with her usual sweet calm. Then, quite suddenly, the dam burst.

Two days before the wedding, a servant from Dr. Stedd's brought a letter to Noramary, which she took up to her room to read, away from her aunt's sharp eyes. Only a half-hour later, the seamstress arrived to make a last-minute fitting of the wedding gown. It was after the woman left and Betsy was helping Noramary down from the stool on which she had been standing to have the hem measured that Noramary burst into tears. Still in her lovely gown, she sank down on the rug, the creamy satin skirt billowing out around her.

"Whatever is the matter, child?" gasped Betsy.

Noramary could not answer.

"Dear child, whatever is the matter? Are you ill? In heaven's name, tell me." Betsy got down on her plump knees beside Noramary, patting the girl's slim shoulder.

"Oh, Auntie, I'm sorry! But it's just everything! This dress—"

"The dress? It's lovely, dear. Don't you like it? It's French satin, Belgian lace—"

"No, no, the dress is beautiful! I was just thinking—everything was intended for someone else—hand-me-down wedding gown, hand-me-down bride, hand-me-down husband! Nothing really belongs to me, and I don't really belong to anyone!"

Noramary's face was buried in her hands and she continued to cry, while Betsy stood by, watching helplessly.

Betsy knew she must attempt to stop the storm before it became a full-blown hurricane. If Noramary were having any second thoughts about the wedding—nay, even worse, the marriage . . . she, Betsy, would just have to do something and do it quick!

At the back of her mind was the letter that was so recently delivered—the letter from Robert Stedd. That's what had upset Noramary so. Well, she'd see about that! And Betsy set her chin determinedly.

Inwardly she strengthened her resolve to firmly support Noramary, to see that she kept her pledge to Duncan, fulfilled her promise. Noramary would be richly compensated for any sacrifice that her marriage to Duncan would require. She was, after all, becoming the mistress of a mansion, with servants and wealth, the wife of one of the most prominent men in this part of Virginia. There were certainly worse fates for most girls in her situation, a penniless orphan.

She patted Noramary's quivering shoulders comfortingly and spoke in a cheerful tone of voice. "Now, now, my dear. You're simply worn out with all the excitement. We'll just stop now and have a nice cup of tea, and you can rest and tell me what's bothering you."

Betsy rang the needlepoint bell-pull by the fireplace, and soon Essie, the housemaid, stuck her head in its muslin mobcap around the edge of the door.

"Bring us some tea, Essie, and be quick about it. Miss Noramary is feeling a bit faint."

She eased Noramary gently into one of the chairs and took a seat opposite her, peering with concern into Noramary's sad face. The girl did look peaked, she thought. Violet shadows under the wide eyes indicated sleeplessness, the droop of the sensitive mouth bespoke melancholy. Betsy frowned anxiously.

"Now, what is it, Noramary? You can tell me."

"It's about R-Robert," Noramary whispered.

Betsy's blood chilled. Oh, not at this late date! Surely Noramary was not planning to back out of the agreement!

"I want you to do something for me, Aunt Betsy," Noramary continued in a tremulous voice. "Something I cannot ask anyone else to do. Will you promise me, please?"

Oh dear! Betsy felt herself tense even as she impulsively responded, "Anything, child. You know all you need do is ask."

Immediately she wondered if she had spoken too quickly, rashly agreeing to something it might be unwise to accomplish.

Noramary rose and went over to the small applewood chest, touched the hidden spring that released the catch to the secret drawer at its base, and brought out a packet of letters tied with a blue hair ribbon.

Noramary stood, holding them to her breast for a long moment. Then, hesitating a second longer, she opened a small wooden box on the top of the dresser and brought out another envelope. Then she turned to face her aunt.

"These are all the letters Robert has ever written to me. A few years ago, maybe two, we began leaving them for each other in a hole in an old oak tree in the meadow. It was a kind of game at first. A secret hiding place that made it special." She paused, biting her lip. "I'm not sure when we first began to know we . . . loved each other."

Her eyes, bright with tears, regarded her aunt solemnly.

"Did you know Robert and I loved each other, Aunt Betsy?"

"Well, of course, dear," Betsy nodded, her chin bobbing, "we *all* love Robert. He's always been like one of the family. Dr. Hugh has been our friend for years—"

"No, no, auntie!" Noramary shook her head,

her dark silky hair falling about the pale oval of her face. "Robert and I loved each other differently. Maybe at first it was like brother and sister, but later . . . we wanted to marry, auntie. Of course, we were planning to wait until he finished college, until he came of age, received his inheritance, and went into practice with Dr. Stedd. And until Winnie ran away—" she stopped short. Two tears rolled down her cheeks and she brushed them away with one hand and bravely went on. "But now, things are different. I've given my promise to Duncan and nothing can change that. Robert will have to get over this—as I'm trying to do."

With some effort Betsy got up from her knees and eased herself into a chair. Noramary came over, knelt beside her and put her head into her aunt's lap. "Oh, auntie, forgive me for causing you grief, but I must ask you to do me this one small favor. . . ." She handed the packet of letters to Betsy. "I want you to keep all Robert's letters for me. I tried to burn them, but I just couldn't . . . they mean too much to me . . . it would be like cutting out part of my life. . . . Oh, auntie, I really loved Robert so. I shall always love him!"

Betsy's generous heart contracted at the sob in Noramary's voice. Her instant reaction was to gather her niece to her bosom and say, *"All right, Noramary, you don't have to go through with it. We'll call the wedding off . . . no matter that we'll be disgraced, possibly not able to hold up our heads ever again in Williamsburg society . . . never face Duncan Montrose. You can marry your Robert. Be happy, Noramary. Life is short . . . love, fleeting. . . ."*

But Betsy's innate practicality prevented the impulsive words from being uttered. Much as she loved Noramary, she knew the wedding to Duncan must take place. The family's reputation was at stake; with three other daughters to be married well, Noramary could not be allowed to jeopardize their chances. Who would risk betrothals into a family if two of its members broke their promises to a man of honor?

"You must promise me, auntie, that you will keep them safely, marked that they must be destroyed without being read after your death—or mine."

"Oh, Noramary . . ." Dismay crept into Betsy's voice.

"*Promise,*" Noramary insisted.

Betsy looked into the sad, lovely face of the girl beseeching her. It was such a beautiful face, a face Betsy had often felt eclipsed the ordinary prettiness of her own daughters. But its tragic expression now touched her sympathetic soul. If there were only some other way. . . . Then her common sense asserted itself once more. There *was* no other way. The marriage *must* take place as planned. She drew herself up and said firmly, "Of course, my dear, I promise."

There was a tap at the bedroom door and after Betsy's acknowledgment, Essie entered with a tray. Betsy poured Noramary a cup of the steaming hot, fragrant beverage and handed it to her.

"Now, drink every drop, Noramary, then lie

down and have a nice rest. Things will seem much better later," she soothed.

After Noramary finished her tea, Betsy helped her out of the "hand-me-down" wedding dress, thinking fleetingly that perhaps they should have had a completely new one made for Noramary, then led her over to the bed, fluffed the pillow under her head, drew the quilt over the still quivering shoulders, and murmured, "There, there, dear. Rest well, now."

At the door, she paused and looked back at the small figure in the tall, canopied bed. *Surely Noramary will be happy . . . if not happy, content, comfortable, provided for. . . . She'll have a house of her own, servants, a husband of good family, of means. . . . I could not wish more for one of my own blood daughters.* And almost unconsciously, as an afterthought, *And may she forgive us . . . if she is not.*

Chapter 7

On Noramary's wedding day the sky was overcast with heavy clouds threatening rain.

When Betsy entered her niece's bedroom quite early to bring her a breakfast tray of tea and toast, she found Noramary clad only in her nightgown, a thin shawl around her shoulders, huddled forlornly on the window seat, looking out into the gray morning.

A tiny flare of alarm rose in Betsy at the sight of Noramary's woebegone figure. The possibility of rain and no sunshine bode ill for a wedding day! A vague premonition of something unpleasant stirred within her, a feeling she had tried to banish all morning with busyness.

"Come away from there at once, Noramary!" Betsy said sharply. "You'll catch your death of cold. Bare feet, indeed! Where is your robe?"

She bustled about, setting down the tray, finding Noramary's slippers, her warm wrapper. She held it out for Noramary to slip into, then poured a cup of steaming tea.

"Now drink this, dear. Then you must start to get dressed. Remember the ceremony is earlier than we had planned, since Duncan wants to reach Montclair before nightfall. . . ." Her voice trailed off anxiously as she observed her niece.

The girl was chalk-white and had to lift the teacup with both hands to bring it to her pale lips to drink. Her hands were shaking so that the cup rattled in its saucer when she set it back down. *Oh, dear Lord, don't let her have a fainting spell!* Betsy prayed. Unconsciously she groped in her skirt pocket for the small bottle of smelling salts she kept handy.

Any further pursuit of what might be troubling Noramary was silenced by the briefest tap at the door. Laura's head in curl-papers looked in. "Good morning, Noramary! Mama!" she sang out gaily. She danced in and bounced on the bed where Noramary was perched.

"Well, how is the happy bride?" asked Laura, her eyes sparkling with excitement. Not waiting for an answer, she turned to Betsy, declaring, "Oh, Mama, my dress is perfect! I absolutely adore it!"

"Very well, Laura, I'm glad you're pleased," said her mother with an air of dismissal. "Now run along and see that the other girls are up and dressing."

Laura sighed, but hopped off the bed. "You're lucky, Noramary," she called out in parting. "Your hair's naturally curly. My poor head is sore from sleeping in these!" She shook her paper-wrapped head with an expression of mock pain, contradicted by her happy little pirouette.

After Laura had skipped out the door, Betsy turned again to Noramary.

"I'll go now. But I'll be back to help you with your headdress and veil." She turned to leave, but paused. "Are you sure you don't want to have your hair powdered? After all, it is the vogue. . . ."

Noramary shook her head. "I'd rather not, auntie. There wouldn't be time to wash it out before we start on our journey."

"Yes, I suppose so. I wonder if it is a good idea to agree to an afternoon reception at the Camerons? It will give you such a later start for that long trip to Montclair. But they are such good friends of Duncan's and so prominent, it would have been unseemly to refuse such a generous gesture . . . I suppose."

The Cameron plantation bordered Montrose land on the James River, and both families had pioneered what had once been wilderness territory. Their fathers had been close friends and the friendship was a close and loyal one into the second generation. The Camerons also kept a town house in Williamsburg, where they stayed when James Cameron attended meetings of the House of

Burgesses, of which he was a member. It was a large, impressive, pink brick house, where they were known to entertain lavishly. They had offered, rather insisted, on giving a festive party for the newlyweds after the wedding breakfast at the Barnwell home, to which only a limited number of friends had been invited. Jacqueline Cameron, James's glamorous and young second wife, a beautiful French woman, had tactfully pointed out to Betsy that the Montrose family had many friends who might be offended even if they understood they could not be accommodated in the Barnwells' smaller residence.

"We would consider it an honor," she had told Betsy when she called on her a few weeks earlier to request that the Barnwells allow them to give the party specifically for their dear friend, Duncan, and his lovely bride. "Duncan is so dear to us, and we are happy he has made such an admirable choice in the beautiful Noramary."

She had leaned close and, in a confidential voice, had told Betsy, "We have often been concerned for him, so magnificent a man to live alone. Your niece will make him very happy, we are sure."

An hour later when Noramary descended the stairs, Uncle William, preening before the hall mirror, resplendent in a purple velvet knee-length coat, lavender brocaded vest, white silk stockings, and shiny silver-buckled shoes, looked up and emitted a long "Ah-h-h. My, my Noramary, my dear. You're a veritable picture!"

Noramary was touched by the soft look in his eyes, now somewhat brightened suspiciously. Uncle

William had never been demonstrative, but his kindness really needed none. Noramary could see it in his expression as he gazed at her fondly. She felt a terrible tightness in her throat. He was the only father she had ever known, and, for the first time, she realized he regarded her as a daughter.

The tender moment lasted only briefly, then Betsy bustled out from the parlor, magnificent in mauve taffeta, elegantly bewigged, and wearing her pearls. She was pushing the two younger girls, Sally and Susann, ahead of her. At the sight of Noramary in her wedding finery, they all stopped, and the children rushed over to her.

"Oh, Noramary, how beautiful you are!" they exclaimed.

She leaned down to gather them up in hugs when Betsy's voice rang out in a warning. "Careful, girls, you'll crush Noramary's gown!"

"Oh, auntie, I don't mind crushes like these!" and she held each of them a second longer. Her younger cousins were especially dear to Noramary. They had been her charges upon her arrival in Virginia, when Sally was five and Susann only three. It had been one of her duties to take them to their dancing class, call for them at Miss Spencer's Dance school, and put them to bed at night when Betsy was receiving visitors or was otherwise occupied. She had read many a Bible story to them, played with them, taught them songs, corrected their sums. Perhaps their care had made her feel most a part of the Barnwell family. Now she held them close to her, experiencing the first real pang of homesickness.

Susann wriggled out of her embrace, spinning around holding out her yellow silk skirt, then making a deep curtsy. "Look, Noramary! Ain't I elegant?"

"And look at *me,* Noramary!" chimed in Sally, turning so Noramary could admire her twin yellow dress. She tossed her head, setting her coppery-gold curls bobbing.

"You're both sights to behold!" Noramary declared, clapping her hands.

"Enough of this! We must start or we'll all be late, and Duncan will be wondering what's become of us!" Betsy said briskly. "We'll go on ahead, Noramary. You and William will follow in the other carriage. Where's Laura, and where's Noramary's bouquet?" she asked no one in particular.

Almost as she spoke, Laura appeared, lovely in peach taffeta, holding the bridal bouquet.

There were several minutes of confusion and chatter as the ladies entered their carriage and pulled away. Then Uncle William solemnly offered his arm to Noramary and they went outside where the handsome gilt-trimmed carriage, hired for the occasion, stood waiting. A misty wind was blowing, and bending their heads against it, they allowed the liveried coachman to assist them.

Taking her seat, Noramary arranged her voluminous skirts. Her headdress and veil required her to sit well forward, holding her head erect. William sagged heavily into the luxurious uphol-stered seat opposite, beaming at her encouragingly.

"Well, my dear, so we're on our way."

Noramary could think of no reply. She merely smiled politely and looked out the small window at the gray morning, hearing the sound of the clopping hooves on the cobblestone street. "On our way," Uncle William had said. But in truth, it was only Noramary who was on her way—to marry a man who was still little more than a stranger, on her way to an unknown future.

Her hands were icy under the lace mitts, yet the palms were clammy as she gripped the holder of the starched ruffle surrounding the bouquet of white roses and mignonette. She stared without really seeing as they traveled down the familiar streets, passed the houses of friends, and at length turned into the courtyard of the mellow-brick church where she had worshiped ever since coming to Virginia.

The horses came to a halt with a jangle of harnesses, and Noramary felt the movement of the carriage as the coachman jumped down from his place and, a moment later, opened the door for them.

"So here we are, my dear." Uncle William's voice nudged her gently.

Noramary started. She slowly came out of her numbed abstraction. She turned wide, frightened eyes on her uncle, but he did not see the panic in them for he was already exiting the coach. He stood at the door, offering her his hand. Hesitating only a split-second, Noramary carefully stepped down.

For just a moment she rearranged the wide panniers of her gown, adjusting her headdress with her free hand as Uncle William fumbled with her tulle veil. It was then that Noramary became conscious of a movement in the grove of trees at the side of the church.

Instinctively she turned her head, in time to see a figure, half obscured behind a flowering shrub, duck out of sight. It was so fleeting that she was not sure at first she had even seen anything. Then she *knew!* She had recognized the swift, graceful stride. *Robert!* Here? Had he come to the wedding?

Noramary trembled. A faint, giddy feeling swept over her. Drawing a ragged breath she turned toward the place she had seen the darting figure. But there was no one in sight.

By now the mist had turned into a fine rain, and she felt Uncle William's hand under her elbow urging her forward.

"Come, my dear, it's starting to rain. We don't want your lovely gown to be ruined. Come along then."

Like an automaton, Noramary put her hand through his arm and leaned on him to steady herself as they walked toward the entrance of the church, past the shadowy clump of trees. Noramary's face, hidden by the gauzy veil, was tense, its sad expression unseen.

From the moment they entered the hushed vestibule, Noramary moved as in a trance. She felt detached, remote, removed from the crowd of well-wishers, yet keenly aware of everything about her.

Moving slowly down the aisle toward the tall man standing at the altar, Noramary was strangely conscious of the rustle of her taffeta petticoats, the squeak of Uncle William's new leather shoes, the guests in the pews they passed, the scent of flowers and candlewax.

Through a haze she saw the smiling faces of her cousins, who had proceeded her to the altar and now faced forward awaiting her arrival. The little girls with their flower baskets; Laura, in a posture of unaccustomed dignity, ready to relieve Noramary of her bouquet after she reached the chancel rail.

Above all, Noramary was aware of Duncan Montrose—looking distinguished and handsome in a nutmeg brown velvet coat, creamy vest, ruffled jabot. When he turned toward her as they halted at the altar steps, his eyes held a new expression, something she had failed to see there before. Could she define it, it might have been—*worshipful?* No, that couldn't be, she thought, though she could think of no other suitable word. But there was no more time to ponder, for the minister began to speak.

Noramary did not glance at Duncan again, although she was very aware of him standing beside her as they took their places. She never raised her eyes from the starched surplice the Reverend Mr. Hewlitt was wearing. She stared straight ahead as he began the ceremony. The words struck deeply into her uneasy conscience. Desperately she tried to forget that fleeting glimpse of the figure in the churchyard, to concentrate on the minister's words, to pray to God to still her confusion, calm her errant heart.

"You are about to enter into an estate that is

most sacred, and so should not be entered into rashly or ill-advisedly, or without the full acknowledgment of both its sacrifices and its blessings."

Everything grew hazy to Noramary—the white flowers and flickering flames of the tapers on the altar, the drone of the minister's voice. Then he came to that part of the ritual she had been most dreading and his voice took on a deeper tone.

"If anyone knows of any reason why these two should not be joined in holy wedlock, let him now speak, or, as he will answer on the dreadful day of judgment . . . forever hold his peace."

I do, thought Noramary, horror-stricken, as a breathless sort of hush fell over the congregation following the Reverend Hewlitt's words. *I know why we should not marry, for I love someone else. . . . Dear God, is it a sin to marry someone you don't really love . . . for whatever reason?*

Noramary swayed slightly, her knees threatening to buckle under her. Immediately she felt Duncan steady her with his firm hand.

The moment after the minister had uttered this solemn question seemed to lengthen interminably. Noramary did not move or breathe. *What if Robert is here, in this sanctuary? What if he should come forward, speak, deny the truth of my vows?* Noramary's thoughts collided tumultuously as the agony of waiting stretched endlessly in the too-quiet church.

"Duncan Montrose, will you have this woman to be your lawful wedded wife—to love, honor, protect, cherish her . . ."

Duncan's answer rang out with strength and conviction. "I will."

Then the minister was speaking directly to Noramary. "Will you, Eleanor Mary Marsh, take this man for your lawful wedded husband . . . from this day forward . . ."

Her throat was dry, and she had to swallow before she could respond, "I will," her voice barely more than a whisper in contrast to Duncan's clear response to the same pledge.

"The ring, sir, if you please," he directed Duncan, then to Noramary, "Place your hand in Duncan's, Noramary. Now . . . sir, as you place the ring on your bride's finger, repeat after me—"

Duncan's voice came steady and sure. "With this ring I thee wed, and plight unto thee my troth, and with all my worldly goods do thee endow . . ."

"Bless this ring, O Lord," the Reverend Hewlitt was saying, "that she who shall wear it, keeping faith unchanged with her husband, may abide in peace and obedience and live in mutual respect and love."

The minister now concluded the service as he covered their clasped hands with his and intoned solemnly, "If you undertake to live the pledges you have taken today one for the other, and have made them with pure intentions, true love, and right spirit, you may expect the greatest measure of earthly happiness allotted man in this vale of tears. The rest is in the hands of God."

Chapter 8

At the second crash of thunder the horses reared, whinnying in fear, and the carriage swayed precariously. Inside, Noramary looked over at her new husband as she clung to the swinging hand-pull to keep from falling against him. His profile was sharply defined by the intermittent flashes of lightning that slashed the blackness of the night. In that brief bit of illumination she could see the stern, almost angry set of his features.

Noramary shrank back into the corner, shivering,

and drew the velvet hooded cloak more closely about her. Duncan turned, aware of her movement.

"You're cold, aren't you?" It was more statement than question. He quickly removed his greatcoat and put it over her lap, tucking it around her feet. "I'm very sorry about this, Noramary. We should have stayed at the Camerons as Jacqueline requested, but I was too anxious to reach Montclair. I wanted us to spend our first night together under our own roof. I apologize for my rashness."

Noramary sensed that Duncan was a man to whom apologies and the admission of poor judgment did not come easily and murmured, "It's not your fault . . . the storm . . ."

"Yes, but I should have known these storms at this time of year can be treacherous. I blame myself," he said brusquely.

It had been raining steadily ever since their departure from Williamsburg late in the afternoon, and now the downpour had turned the rough country roads into rivers of mud. Duncan had been forced to leave the carriage several times already to help the footman push the wheels through the thick, oozing stuff.

Noramary huddled miserably in her corner. The relentless swaying of the carriage had aggravated a nagging headache that had begun soon after they left Williamsburg. It had probably been brought on by fatigue and hunger, for she had slept poorly the night before and had only picked at the sumptuous buffet hosted by the Camerons. After the toasting and the farewells, she had rushed to change into her traveling clothes because Duncan was adamant they get started on the long trip ahead.

Perhaps adding to her discomfort was the growing sensation of homesickness as each jolting mile carried her farther from everything dear and familiar. Noramary was transported back in time to another separation, another beginning when, as a frightened child, she had traveled alone to her new home in Virginia. She felt much the same now, except this time there was an added inexplicable sense of foreboding.

Stinging tears welled up in her eyes as Noramary pictured the warm, cozy parlor at the Barnwell home, where she had spent so many happy evenings, and a painful lump rose in her throat. When would she ever see them again?

She remembered when she confessed to Aunt Betsy how unsure she felt about marrying Duncan, and her aunt had held her comfortingly, said, "You must realize, Noramary, that it is much wiser for our heads to rule our hearts, to accept things as they are. Life, dear child, is full of pain and partings. Love is one thing; life, another altogether. If one is fortunate," here she had paused, "you may live out your life with someone for whom you feel a passionate affection, but for most of us, life is simply doing one's duty." This advice left no doubt that for a girl with no dowry, no inheritance of her own, Noramary must take the course of duty.

With a sudden lurching the carriage came to a standstill. There was some shouting from the coachman and the footman, but their words were not discernible in the howling of the wind.

Duncan swore under his breath. "What the deuce is it now!" he exclaimed, opening the door and jumping out.

Noramary, her heart pounding, her whole body aching with weariness, leaned forward and tried to peer out into the driving rain. This journey was taking on a nightmarish quality. The carriage had come to an absolute halt. One side seemed to be slowly tipping, as if the wheels were sinking into the mud. Terrified, she could only make out the three figures of the men moving awkwardly, hear the muffled sound of their shouts. There was a strong tugging sensation, a sudden, shuddering lurch—then, no movement at all.

They must have unhitched the horses, she thought and, just then, the carriage door was jerked open and Duncan stood there, rain dripping from the corners of his tricorne, his clothing sodden and muddy.

"It seems that it is worse than I thought. I'm sorry my dear, but the creek is flooded just ahead and washed out the footbridge we have to cross to continue on to Montclair. I'm afraid we are going to have to spend the night elsewhere."

"Not *here!*" exclaimed Noramary in dismay.

A slight smile twitched the corners of Duncan's mouth.

"No. The little cottage I told you about, the one I lived in before the big house was complete, is just this side of the creek. We won't be able to get the carriage moving tonight. The men will ride the horses to shelter, and I'll take you on mine. There's a small barn where we can stable them, with a loft above for the men. We can spend the night in the cottage. It's quite livable, I assure you." There was a trace of a smile on his lips as he added, "And as they say—any haven in a storm!"

Duncan reined his horse beside the open door of the carriage and spoke in a calm, even voice. "Just put your foot in my hand. He'll not move. I'm holding him steady. Now, don't be afraid," he directed her.

Noramary lifted her skirts and did as he had bade her, feeling his hand firmly on her waist. She was hardly seated in the saddle when he mounted behind her, fitting his feet expertly into the stirrups.

"I shall keep my arm around you so you will be secure and not lose your balance. Try to relax. My horse knows the way and will take us safely there."

Galloping through the rain-dark night could have been fraught with terror had not Duncan been such an expert horseman and held Noramary so securely. Just as they reached a latticed shelter, the rain sliced down in sheets. Leaning forward slightly, Noramary saw that they were in front of a small gabled house.

Duncan dismounted, then his hands encircled Noramary's waist and he lifted her down as easily as if she had been a child.

"All right?" he inquired solicitously.

"Of course." She nodded, but she was shivering and her teeth had begun to chatter, for the rain had penetrated her cloak and she was chilled.

"We'll be inside in a minute," said Duncan. Getting out a ring of keys and finding one, he unlocked the door. "Come, I'll have a fire going in a minute."

He held the door open for her to pass before him and Noramary stepped inside. Then he followed her, shutting the door and bolting it against the fierce wind. She stood to one side as Duncan walked through the house, his boots echoing in the empty rooms. She heard the sound of cabinet doors being jerked open, drawers being pulled out, the sound of rummaging as Duncan searched for candles. Then, after a short pause, he reappeared, holding before him two tall candlesticks, shedding a pale, wavery light. He set them on the mantlepiece above a wide, stone fireplace.

While Duncan busied himself laying a fire with logs from a woodbox beside the hearth, and kindling and pine cones from a big basket, Noramary looked around curiously.

So this was the house Duncan had lived in alone for years before moving into the mansion she had yet to see. The walls were paneled and painted blue. The few pieces of furniture were gracefully made and finely crafted. There was a deep wing chair and footstool on one side of the fireplace, a gateleg table and a ladder-back armchair. Patterned draperies were drawn across the windows.

"There," said Duncan, standing and brushing his hands. The flames had begun to leap and the dry wood crackled as the fire took hold. "The fire should be going well in another few minutes and soon this room should be cozy and warm." He turned to Noramary. "I'm going out to the barn now to see that the men rub down the horses and give them oats, and bed down themselves. I shall be back as soon as I can. Will you be all right until then?"

He started to the door again, then stopped abruptly. "Are you hungry? I can find something for us to eat, I'm sure, but—"

"Please. Do whatever you have to do. I can wait until you return."

He hesitated a moment longer, as if unsure whether to leave her. "I'll hurry then." And he was gone.

A gust of cold wind blew in as Duncan went out and Noramary shuddered, not only from the sudden chill but from a kind of nervous reaction. Here she was, still miles from her destination, virtually alone with a man she hardly knew. Another wild thrust of wind flung the rain clattering against the windowpanes, and Noramary moved closer to the fireplace where the roaring flames now sizzled and sputtered.

Her wedding night! Noramary felt a wild urge to laugh. What bride had ever found herself in such bizarre circumstances! But her innate sense of the ridiculous was edged with apprehension. There was really nothing very funny about spending this night in an isolated cottage with a husband who was almost a stranger.

Noramary moved even closer to the fireplace. As she held out her hands to the fire's warmth, the light from its flames glinted on the gold band of her new wedding ring.

It felt heavy and unfamiliar on her slender finger. As she twisted it thoughtfully, she remembered a day last summer when Robert had fashioned a ring of buttercups and slipped it on the same finger with a smile. "Someday," he had promised, "this will be a band of gold uniting us forever!"

How little they had known in those carefree days of summer how soon their dreams would end. *Oh, Robert! Robert!* Noramary's heart cried. *I thought I would spend my wedding night with you! I imagined we two would explore the mysteries and sweet intimacies of marriage together! I never imagined marriage with a stranger!*

Chapter 9

The sound of the latch lifting and the bolt shoved back made Noramary jump. She whirled around as the door was flung wide and, with a chilling blast of rain and wind, Duncan strode back into the room. She was instantly jolted back to reality.

Duncan was her husband now—not Robert. They had taken vows before God and man "for better or for worse until death" parted them. All thoughts of the past and Robert must be put behind her. She straightened her shoulders, wiped away the few tears, and turned to greet him.

As Nanny Oates had darkly predicted when Simon had sent her away at Leatrice's demand, "Every debt in life must be paid somehow, the cost of everything exacted, in this life or the next." Would Winnie someday have to pay for what she had done?

Noramary quickly prayed that her cousin was as happy as she had hoped to be. She would not wish anyone remorse. She had been brought up by Aunt Betsy to believe that whatever happened, you made the best of it.

Still, a girl's wedding night should be . . . Noramary bit her lip and clasped her suddenly clammy hands together tightly.

"Well, all is well out there!" Duncan said heartily. "Luckily, there's plenty of hay and the men had stashed some provisions of their own in their pockets," he laughed, "scavenged from the wedding feast by way of the kitchen maids, I'll wager."

He looked at her with concern. "Now, we must see about some food and something to drink for ourselves. You must be hungry as well as tired."

Noramary shrugged slightly. "If I had known where to find things, I could have—"

Duncan interrupted her. "Nonsense! I wanted you to stay close by the fire and warm yourself. I didn't expect you to do anything. Actually, I don't know what we'll find. I come here very rarely nowadays, sometimes only at midday if I happen to be riding this part of the plantation."

Duncan lighted another candle and took it with him into an adjoining room. When he came back, he was juggling a round loaf of bread, something wrapped in cheesecloth, and a basket of small russet pears. He slid them handily onto the gateleg table and pulled it over to where Noramary stood.

"It's a meager enough supper, I'm afraid. Certainly not the welcoming feast I'm sure my sister Janet had planned for our homecoming this evening!"

"Will she be worried, do you think?"

Duncan halted for a moment, cocking his head toward the sound of the storm raging without, then with a slight smile, shook his head. "On a night like this? Janet probably supposes I was wise enough not to have left Williamsburg! There she misplaced her confidence, to my chagrin!"

"Duncan, you are not responsible for the weather! Nor for the storm or the muddy roads or even the carriage wheels!" Noramary admonished, with a hint of teasing laughter in her voice.

He looked at her, frowning, then gave a short laugh.

"You're right! I have taken too much credit, haven't I?" A smile tugged at the corner of his mouth. Then a curious look flicked in his eyes as he gazed at her. "You know, you're really quite remarkable. Most women would have been in a fine temper by now with all this!" He threw out both hands in a gesture of futility.

"But it's no one's fault," Noramary insisted. "It

couldn't be helped. After all, only the Lord controls the weather."

"True," said Duncan solemnly. He paused and Noramary was surprised by a broad grin spreading over his serious features. "Actually, we've been praying for rain. The woods around here are like tinder and we've been worried about forest fires."

"Really?" Noramary exclaimed, putting her hand to her mouth in a spontaneous burst of laughter.

"That should teach me to be careful how I pray, eh?" Duncan joined in her laughter, and Noramary realized it was the first time she had heard the sound. It was a rich laugh, deep and hearty.

That bit of shared mirth seemed to break the stiffness between them, and the tension she had felt so strongly in the forced intimacy of the long carriage ride from Williamsburg eased considerably. By the time he had gotten down pewter plates from the pine hutch cabinet, set them on the table, found woven napkins and pottery mugs, the atmosphere was decidedly more relaxed. Duncan had also found a jug of apple cider.

"Only about half full," he declared, holding it up and giving it a shake, "but it will quench our thirst and take the chill off, no doubt. Come, you must be famished. You hardly touched anything at Jacqueline's party," he said sternly.

Noramary was both embarrassed and oddly touched by the knowledge that he must have been watching her at the Camerons' reception.

She took her place opposite him at the little table and was surprised when he reached across it and took her small hand in his.

"Let us ask a blessing on this first meal we eat together as husband and wife," he suggested in a low, almost shy voice.

Noramary nodded, bowed her head, and closed her eyes as Duncan prayed reverently, "Good and gracious Father, we ask Thy blessing on this food we are about to partake of at the beginning of our life together. And on that life, whose path is known only to Thee, we earnestly beseech Thy help and grace. We ask this in the name of Thy Son, Our Lord, Jesus. Amen."

"Amen," whispered Noramary.

When she opened her eyes, Duncan was gazing at her. Her cheeks, warmed by the fire, flushed a deeper rose. The hood of her cape had slipped back, its shimmering blue satin lining framing her face and her dark, rain-dampened hair that curled in fetching tendrils about her forehead. Her skin had a dewy freshness and her eyes—he drew in his breath unconsciously. Those eyes—deep, sparkling like sapphires! A man could drown in their depths, he thought, in a rising tide of emotion.

As if he knew he'd been caught staring, Duncan quickly picked up the knife and began cutting the loaf of crusty, rough-grained bread, mumbling as he did, "This is not at all as I'd planned your arrival at Montclair to be!"

Noramary looked at him curiously. In all their

meetings Duncan had always seemed so sure, so confident. It was surprising to see him so annoyed over this unpredictable turn of events. It also surprised her a little that Duncan must have planned their homecoming carefully. She had been so preoccupied with her own thoughts that she had given little attention to what he must be thinking and feeling about their marriage, about bringing her to Montclair.

"How had you planned it?" Noramary asked shyly.

He unwrapped the large triangle of cheese from its cloth and started to shave wedges from it. "Well, to begin, I had hoped to reach Montclair a little before sunset when the view of the mountains is best. Then when we went inside," Duncan continued, "there'd be fires burning in all the fireplaces, shining on the paneling and floors— newly polished for your benefit, I might add." He looked up, smiling. "Incidentally, all the wood used in the construction of the house is our own timber—white oak—and the floors are heart of pine, rubbed to bring out their golden sheen."

Again Noramary was conscious of another facet of this man that had, heretofore, gone unobserved. Duncan was really quite articulate in contrast to the reserved, rather stilted conversations in Williamsburg. That he was describing Montclair with such pride and affection was equally enlightening. Every detail of the house was of great importance to him.

"And Janet would have a grand supper waiting,

the table set with our mother's English china and crystal, which now, of course, belongs to you—as mistress of Montclair."

Mistress of Montclair—Noramary turned the title over thoughtfully in her mind. Noramary . . . *Montrose* now. The name still sounded strange to her, but one day she would grow accustomed to it, she supposed.

"Tell me, Duncan, why didn't your sister come to the wedding?"

Duncan took a long swallow of cider before he answered. "A number of reasons, actually, the first being that she is officially still in mourning— although Angus has been dead for nearly two years. The second, of course, is that she wanted to have everything in readiness for our homecoming." He paused significantly before adding, "And thirdly, and I'm inclined to believe this may have been the most important reason in her mind, is the fact that after marrying my late brother-in-law, Janet turned Calvinist, and my guess is she felt there might be more wine, music, and merrymaking at a Williamsburg wedding than her conscience would countenance."

"Well of course," Noramary dimpled prettily, "Williamsburg citizens are known for their hospitality. But I can scarce believe that your sister would withhold her attendance from her brother's wedding, when even our Lord enjoyed such occasions."

"The difference, I'm afraid, between strict adherence to man-made rules and rituals, rather than to the loving spirit He intended. But never fear. Even though Montclair is a distance from other plantations, your coming will bring on a spate of entertaining! Everyone I know is anxious to honor my bride."

Which bride? Noramary thought dismally. She could not help wondering how Duncan's friends felt about the circumstances of his marriage. Winnie's running off practically on the eve of their wedding had to have been an embarrassment to him, and now he was bringing home her cousin as her substitute. Would they pity him, feel that the Barnwells had taken advantage of him?

Before Noramary could follow this line of thinking to its conclusion, Duncan said disparagingly. "What a wedding feast! Crumbly cheese, dry bread—slightly turned apple cider!" He sounded disgusted.

Impulsively, Noramary quoted: "Better is a dry morsel with quietness, than a house full of feasting with strife."

"Aha! Proverbs 17:1. My lady knows her Scriptures," Duncan applauded.

"I had a very pious nanny," she explained.

"A *nanny* . . . in Virginia?" Duncan seemed puzzled.

"But that was in *England,* of course. I've only been in America since I was twelve. I was born and reared in Kent."

"I didn't realize. I just assumed you had always lived with the Barnwells."

Noramary shook her head. "I came to them after my brother Simon married." She hesitated, feeling there was no need to tell Duncan now about the circumstances under which she had been sent away from Monksmoor Priory. "My mother and Uncle William were half-brother and sister," she explained.

"Do you . . . miss England? Your home there?" Duncan persisted.

"Well, of course, sometimes I think about it. But it was a very long time ago. . . . Virginia is my home now," Noramary stated firmly.

"And you have made the best of things," Duncan finished.

To her astonishment he put his large hand over hers where it cupped the tankard of cider.

"I hope you will come to feel Montclair is your home, Noramary, that you will come to love it as I do," he said softly.

"Tell me more about it," she urged, eager to change the subject for fear she might display some evidence of homesickness, more for Williamsburg and the Barnwell household than for faraway Monksmoor Priory in Kent England.

Duncan launched into a description of the things he had built into the house to accommodate a climate and weather unknown to the original English architect. Noramary listened with interest until, suddenly, midsentence, Duncan broke off.

"My word! I am talking a great deal!" He held up his tankard and asked quizzically, "Do you suppose this aging cider has loosened my tongue?"

Noramary laughed a light, rippling sound that delighted Duncan with its natural spontaneity. He laughed along with her and rising, said in the pompous manner of an orator, "Let us drink a toast! For, upon my honor, I have never before been known as a brilliant dinner partner. Of course," he added sheepishly, "this is not what might be considered such an elegant dinner, either."

Noramary laughed again, pleased to discover Duncan's sense of humor. "I never dreamed you were such a thespian!" she teased.

"Madam, I am *many* things you never dreamed!" he retorted with a broad smile that transformed his usually serious demeanor.

Noramary looked at him in astonishment, realizing that what Duncan said was true. In these few hours—in this outrageous, unforeseen situation—she had learned more about this man than in all the weeks of their decorous courtship. Duncan was not just the dignified, rather aloof, courteous but cool suitor he had seemed, a man of conservative opinions, a prosperous planter. He was a man of many layers. A man who could laugh at himself, as well as at circumstances, a man of consideration and kindness, a man of faith and humor. He was complex, with myriad emotions and feeling underlying the reserved façade. He was, in fact, very much like herself.

Amid much merriment they ate the simple fare, and the shared meal became a feast as if the dry bread were a light, moist cake and the slightly turned cider the finest champagne. The unpredictable circumstances in which they found themselves, and what their family and friends would think if they knew about it, produced more mild hilarity.

Their initial stiffness with each other had long since disappeared, and by the end of supper they were both surprised to discover the other to be a most amiable companion.

Duncan filled the black cast-iron kettle with water to boil for tea and hung it on the crane, where its rising steam sizzled on the still crackling hearthfire.

"Have you had enough or too much of this poor supper?" inquired Duncan.

"Just enough, and I do feel better, thank you."

"You know, just now when you so aptly quoted from the book of Proverbs, another came to mind." He smiled. "I, too, was taught the Scriptures by my mother."

"And what might that have been?"

"Two came to mind, actually. First, Proverbs 15:10. Do you know it?"

Noramary's dark winged brows came together over her smooth forehead as she pondered. "Hmmm. Fifteen, ten, did you say?" And she quoted slowly, searching her memory, "Better a dinner of herbs where love—" She stopped short, blushing.

Duncan finished it for her. "—a dinner of herbs where *love* is than a fatted calf with hatred."

His eyes were twinkling and Noramary smiled. Love was a word that had never been spoken between them until the wedding ceremony earlier that morning: "love, honor, cherish." So beautiful, but love had to be more than words, Noramary thought wistfully.

For a few minutes there was silence in the room. Only the sound of the wind and rain blowing against the sides of the cottage, clattering like pebbles on the roof and windows, disturbed the peaceful moment.

Duncan refilled their tankards with cider and began speaking again in a more serious tone of voice. "When I started planning my house—*our* house," he amended, "I wanted it to become one of the finest of the James River manors. Only the best materials would be used in its construction—elements from our land itself. I wanted to build a splendid house that would endure for years, that would stand for our family . . . and those who came after us." Again Duncan paused, his eyes holding Noramary in an unswerving gaze. "Our family has been greatly blessed in property and possessions. Our land was originally a King's Grant deeded to my father and his brother. Unfortunately, my uncle died before reaching his majority and his part came to my father and his sons." A shadow seemed to pass over Duncan's face as he continued. "But my older brother James died of fever when he was still a boy and so . . . I'm the only Montrose left, the last of the family. The land is now mine and . . ." He left the rest of the sentence incomplete, its implication clear.

As the only male surviving, the owner of vast properties and wealth, it was understandable that Duncan hoped for an heir to carry on the proud name of Montrose. It was important, therefore, really necessary, for him to marry, Noramary mused, if not the bride of his choice, then a substitute. She lowered her eyes, crumbling the piece of dry bread in her hand.

A sudden clap of thunder caused them both to start, and Duncan nearly toppled his tankard of cider with the involuntary movement of his hand. In the ensuing moment, they rose from the table and Duncan strode over to the door to bolt it securely against the rising wind.

The interruption seemed to break the amiable intimacy of their mealtime, and as Noramary moved to stand beside the fire, she sensed an awkwardness between them once again.

She began to feel intensely weary. It had been a long day filled with tension and excitement, as well as the unforeseen hazards encountered on their journey. She had had little sleep the night before, she recalled, spending a good part of it apprehensive about *this* night.

Her wedding night! Here?

Before her thoughts became more agitated, she heard Duncan moving around behind her, his boots sounding on the bare wooden flooring of the rooms beyond. Curious to see what he was doing, she turned about just in time to see him returning with an armload of quilts.

"There are no sheets or pillows in the bedrooms, and the mattresses have been removed, but I found these in the blanket box and I'll fix you a place on the settle in front of the fire. You should be fairly comfortable there. By morning the rain should have slacked enough for us to ford the creek and get to the house on horseback. Later, I'll get help to move the carriage out." Duncan spoke briskly as he shoved the wooden high-backed settle at an angle to the fireplace and proceeded to fold quilts upon it. "Maybe the water will have receded and we can use the bridge." He turned to her with a teasing smile. "But, as they say, 'we'll cross that bridge when we come to it,' eh?"

Noramary attempted a weak smile. She felt worn out, but relieved at the makeshift sleeping arrangements. She was almost too tired to think of anything but curling up before the fire and closing her heavy eyelids.

"Come try this. See if you can manage to sleep on it," urged Duncan.

She gathered up her skirts, let herself down to stretch out on the narrow bench. To her surprise, the quilts felt amazingly soft.

"How is that?" asked Duncan with concern.

"Fine," she murmured drowsily, her eyes already beginning to close.

"Then, I'll bank the fire a bit, and it should burn through the night."

Through her half-closed eyelids, Noramary saw the flames sending patterns of light dancing across the ceiling. Then the firelight was temporarily blocked by a tall figure standing over her. She felt a light touch as Duncan placed the back of his hand against her cheek and said very softly, "There is another Proverb, Noramary." His voice was very low. "The most important one, more important than land or property or possessions . . ."

"Which one?" she asked, her voice husky with sleep.

"Proverbs 19:14," he replied.

She mustered a small laugh. "Duncan, I'm too sleepy to think what that could possibly be," she said, and sighed sleepily.

"Houses and riches are an inheritance from fathers, but a good wife is from the Lord." Duncan's words were the last she heard as she drifted off to sleep.

Before Duncan himself bedded down on the opposite side of the fireplace, he stood looking down at his sleeping bride. She was infinitely more beautiful than he had ever seen her—dark wavy hair tumbled about her flushed cheeks pillowed on small, dainty hands; her black lashes, shadowy crescents against her flawless skin.

Noramary, so gentle and sweet, so warm and laughing . . . Duncan felt a sensation so sharp, yet tender, that it was almost pain. Hope flared brightly within, and the conviction grew that in her he had found the thing for which he had been searching all his life—love. The marriage had been carefully considered and, while he thought he had based his decision on the most practical of reasons, he knew now he was wrong. By the most unforeseen, the strangest of circumstances, this lovely creature had become his wife. Now, all at once, she was the most important thing in his life.

How was it possible that he had entertained even a brief attraction to her cousin? Because he now knew without a doubt that he had fallen in love—madly, wildly, inexplicably with Noramary, his bride by default!

Thanks be to God! Duncan's heart pumped gratefully. He, who had always thought love was for poets, the writers of ballads and sonnets and romantic plays, a kind of madness that a practical man like himself would never experience. How wrong he had been and how thankful that he would not, after all, miss this glorious insanity!

Now looking at Noramary, he was overwhelmed with the passionate desire to possess her. But he must proceed carefully, gently, so as not to frighten her in any way. The right time would come. In the meantime he must simply be patient and wait. . . .

A log broke apart in the fireplace, sending up spirals of sparks and scattering red embers. Duncan turned to tend the fire.

Outside, the elements raged on, but oblivious to both the storm and her new husband's adoring vigil, Noramary slept.

Chapter 10

Faint gray light seeped between the edges of the curtains. Noramary stirred, sighed, and opened her eyes. She felt stiff and cold, then fully awake, confused. She sat up and Duncan's cape slipped off her knees. Realization of where she was and what had happened came quickly. She saw Duncan's long figure stretched out on the high-backed wooden settle opposite.

As quietly as she could she got up, stretching her strained muscles and arching her back a little.

The room had chilled, for the fire had smoldered into a few glowing red chunks of charred wood. She pulled the cape around her shoulders and crept over to one of the windows and peered out.

Although it had stopped raining, steady streams of water dripped from the overhanging eaves. As far as she could see, the cottage was surrounded by a deep wood. Its depth was somehow overwhelming. Noramary had heard this part of Virginia was practically wilderness, but until now that fact had not particularly frightened her. But on this dreary morning it somehow seemed threatening.

At Cameron Hall the afternoon before, she had not had the feeling of isolation she had now. In the luxurious drawing room, illuminated by dozens of candles in crystal chandeliers, its yellow damask draperies, white marble mantel, graceful furniture and French wallpaper, they could have been in any elegant Williamsburg home. Here, however, a feeling of isolation assailed her, and Noramary shivered involuntarily.

"Good morning! I did not expect to sleep this soundly." Duncan's voice startled her. "You are awake and up already, I see. No doubt it was the comfort of your accommodations last evening!" he said with a trace of humor.

Noramary felt a little self-conscious, newly aware as she was of their relationship. The merriment with which they had accepted their predicament last night became somewhat diminished in the cold light of day.

"We'll have a cup of tea, then I'll ride ahead and take a look at the creek, see if we can get across it,"

Duncan told her. "I'll make up the fire before seeing how the men and horses have fared through the night."

With his back to her, he began placing fresh logs on the grate, stirring up the coals. Over his shoulder he said, "There's a bedroom at the end of the hall, a mirror, the necessities, if you care to freshen yourself."

Noramary gratefully followed his directions and found herself in a large bedroom. She surveyed it with interest, knowing Duncan had lived here during his bachelor years. It pleased her to see with what taste it was decorated. A huge high bed with carved pineapple posters, covered in a plain, tufted woven spread. A fine English desk with a slanted top, a shelf of books, and two fiddle-back armchairs on either side of the fireplace, which was bordered by colorful tiles.

Noramary did the best she could with her small brush to untangle the damage done to her hair by wind and rain and a night curled up on the settle. She wanted to be at least presentable when she met Duncan's sister when they arrived at Montclair.

Janet McLeod had agreed to stay on another few months after Duncan's engagement to Winnie ended with the prospect of a substitute bride coming to Montclair. Noramary was grateful that there would be someone knowledgeable to help her assume her new role as plantation mistress, for she knew very little about running a household, especially a house as big as Montclair with a number of servants to supervise.

She felt some timidity about meeting this lady

whom she had heard Uncle Will describe as "formidable," whatever that meant.

Having done all that was possible to repair her appearance, Noramary rejoined Duncan in the front room.

He handed her a cup of strong and unsweetened tea that made her eyes water as she swallowed it, but sent a comforting warmth all through her chilled body.

They stood facing each other by the now roaring fire. Both acknowledged, although unspoken, an intimacy, evolved from enduring together an unexpected but surprisingly interesting adventure. It was as if they had taken a new measure of the other.

All at once, Duncan felt overcome with emotion and turned away to stare into the fire to ease his own consternation. The words he wanted to say stuck in his throat. He finished his tea and set down the cup. When he turned back Noramary was still looking at him, a little smile lifting the corners of her pretty mouth.

He moved toward her, took the teacup out of her hand and, placing it on the table, searched her face as if seeking some certain response.

At that very moment there was a loud, insistent knock at the door. Impatiently Duncan took a few quick steps and jerked it open. It was Josiah, his groom, standing on the porch. He whipped off his hat and bowed low. "Horse ready to ride, Master Duncan."

"Be with you in a minute," Duncan said

crisply. He snatched up his cape and flung it over his shoulders.

"This shouldn't take long, my dear. I'll check the carriage to see if we can get it out of the rut. The sun's shining fairly strong now. Perhaps the mud has dried some."

With that he was gone, leaving Noramary both touched and bewildered by the little scene that had just taken place between them. She could not imagine what her future with Duncan would hold. He was, she could tell, a man of quickly changing moods. A man who would be hard to know, but possible to love.

By noon they had freed the carriage from its muddy rut and were back on the road. He had gently deposited her in the carriage, not letting her feet touch the rain-soaked ground, saying to her, with eyes shining in anticipation: "I'll see you at the house." He seemed to want to say something else, then changed his mind and just touched the brim of his tricorne in a little salute, sprang upon his horse, and rode away.

The sun was out full now, breaking through the clouds in a brilliant burst of light, turning the raindrops still clinging to leaf and shrub to sparkling diamonds.

Noramary leaned forward, looking from window to window, as the carriage jogged along the rough road. The country through which they rode was spectacularly beautiful, if wild. Through the rows of dense pines, flashes of scarlet maples could be seen. Purple asters and flaming goldenrod flourished on either side. As they came into a clearing Noramary saw a ribbon of gleaming light that must be the river sparkling in the autumn sun.

After what seemed a long drive, Duncan rode back beside the carriage, ordered the driver to halt the horses, then opened the door and leaned in to tell Noramary that they were now at the edge of their property.

"This is the beginning of 'Montclair,'" he said with evident pride, as if he wanted her to take special notice of the landscape from this point on. "It won't be too much longer. The house is just two miles from the gate."

"I'll ride on ahead," he said and with a wave was off again. "We'll soon be home!"

Home! That word had meant two places to Noramary in the short span of her lifetime. Now she was asked to call another strange place *home*. She wondered if Montclair could ever mean to her what it obviously meant to Duncan. A fierce longing for a place of security, comfort, protection—a place where she truly belonged—swept over Noramary. Would she ever know such a place! Would Montclair fulfill that yearning in her?

She leaned her head against the carriage cushions and closed her eyes, struggling against a wave of nostalgia threatening to overwhelm her. A picture of her childhood home in Kent formed in her mind—as she had seen it the day she left.

Monksmoor Priory—piercing the sky with its

pointed gables, the sun glinting on the diamond-paned windows, the rosy stone. The house had been in the Marsh family for generations, its first stone laid in the fourteenth century. There was a topiary garden and terraced lawns and wide meadows stretching for miles. She had ridden her pony along the chalky cliffs down to a rocky beach and then the sea. There had been a vast expanse of sky and the ocean thrusting out as far as the eye could see. It had not closed in upon one like these dark woods, Noramary thought, opening her eyes again to find the carriage edged on both sides by a thick stand of pines.

Leaning forward again, she looked out the small carriage window to see Duncan riding ahead, and beyond him, a wide gate flanked by fieldstone posts. Noramary drew in her breath sharply. Soon she would arrive at Montclair, get her first glimpse of the great house of which she was now mistress.

Duncan should be with her now, she thought. Yet, when at last Montclair came into view, she was glad he was not, so keen was her disappointment!

The house stood on a knoll directly ahead as they approached by way of the winding road. It was austere to the point of severity, an unpretentious square building of new, raw brick, rising three stories, with a sloping slate roof and massive twin chimneys at either end. Peaked dormer windows marched across the top; six windows along the second row, shuttered with dark green louvers; and, on the first floor, long narrow rectangles with matching shutters. The grounds, except for the surrounding elm trees, were not yet landscaped—not a flowering bush nor any sign of a garden was in evidence. Noramary, who loved flowers dearly, was dismayed.

She had to remind herself quickly that Montclair had only recently been completed, and it still bore the stark look of newness. There had not been time enough to acquire the gracious patina of the older manor houses along the James River. Neither had there been Flemish masters to design intricate brickwork, nor landscape artists to plan formal gardens with Italian statuary. As Duncan had told her earlier, he himself had done much of the planning of the house.

And, in a way, the house reflected the man. Those qualities she had begun to observe in him were an integral part of the building before her—honesty, simplicity, a certain quality of reserve and dignity. All it lacked was warmth.

In time, that could change. Perhaps all the house needed was someone to bring it charm, vitality, a personality uniquely its own. Perhaps she, as its mistress, could do just that.

And, of course, the setting was beautiful. *If only it weren't so isolated,* she thought. But then Noramary's natural optimism rallied, for she had a child's heart, eager, expectant of good, hopeful of joy.

As they neared the house, a chill crept into the air. There was the smell of woodsmoke, and, somewhere in the distance, Noramary heard the harsh cawing of rooks. As she leaned out the carriage window, she saw several black menservants emerging from a side door, and a group of fine hunting dogs running alongside Duncan's horse, barking.

Then, finally, the carriage came to a stop, and a moment later Duncan opened the door and held out his hand to help her out. Noramary started to adjust her hood and gather her skirt to descend when she saw, over Duncan's broad shoulder, the front door opening and a tall woman in black step out onto the porch.

Instinctively Noramary drew back. A terrible feeling of dread swept over her. An unbidden warning flashed through her mind, each word unmistakably clear: "In this house you will know your greatest happiness and your deepest sorrow."

Then Duncan's voice, warm and encouraging, broke in, dispelling that frightening prophecy. "Come, Noramary, we are here at last—at Montclair!"

Struggling not to reveal her sudden chilling experience, Noramary put her hand in his, at the same time calling forth a passage of Scripture Nanny Oates had insisted she commit to memory before she left England: "Take courage, therefore, and be valiant. Fear not and be not dismayed: because the Lord thy God is with thee in all things whatsoever thou shalt go to."

Part II

He who finds a good wife finds a good thing and obtains favor from the Lord

PROVERBS 18:22

Chapter 11

Janet Montrose McLeod stepped onto the broad porch of Montclair, shivering in the chill wind that whipped her fine worsted shawl around her thin shoulders. She watched the arrival of the carriage bearing her brother's bride with mixed feelings of relief and cautious expectation.

Relief, because she was anxious to return to her own home in Scotland. She only came to Virginia in the first place to help her brother ready his new home for his bride, bringing with her some of their mother's silver, china, and furniture that had come to her as the only daughter in the family at her mother's death. She did not need them herself, for she was the widow of a prosperous Scot with a country house full of his family's antiques and other fine furnishings.

She never meant to stay this long. Janet disliked the Virginia climate she remembered from her own childhood here. The humid summers, the damp winters, even the blindingly beautiful spring and the lush brilliance of autumn were not compensation enough. She longed for the Scottish coastal weather and the heather blue hills. If it had not been for the scandalous behavior of the Barnwell girl, she would never have remained these many months.

Watching her brother dismount, Janet thought how handsome Duncan was, what a splendid man. A fortunate girl, this Noramary Marsh, and it was profoundly to be hoped she was of some finer and more honorable character than her fly-by-night cousin. Janet had been strongly opposed to Duncan's agreeing to marry into the same family. Blood will tell, she brooded. Likely as not, one girl was as flighty as the other. She had shaken her head and set her mouth in a tight line when Duncan tried to tell her that Noramary was different. In the end Janet had said nothing. After all, her brother was twenty-nine, and if he were ever to take a bride, it must be soon. Here, in this part of Virginia, still verging on wilderness, a man needed a wife, companionship, warmth, and if he were blessed indeed, affection . . . not that that always came with marriage, as Janet herself well knew.

Janet had hoped her brother would marry a woman trained and capable of taking over quickly. When she had seen Noramary's miniature, however, she had put those hopes aside. A mere child, if the picture was any proof. And when she questioned Duncan he had told her, albeit reluctantly, that the girl was "barely seventeen." *Humph!* Janet snorted to herself. *Barely out of the schoolroom!*

With any luck the new Mrs. Montrose would be a fast learner. There was much to managing such a large plantation house. Its mistress had many duties other than presiding at a tea table, which was rumored to be all the young ladies in Williamsburg were taught. But Janet, ever one to do her duty, was determined to teach Noramary everything she needed to know before she departed.

Duncan opened the carriage door and was handing the girl out carefully. Her blue-lined hood fell back, and dark curls tumbled on either side of a delicate oval face. A tremulous smile turned up the corners of a full, sweet mouth. For all her glowing youth, Janet thought, she looked fragile, and Janet felt a momentary foreboding. Would this delicate young girl be capable of shouldering the responsibilities of mistress of Montclair, physically strong enough to survive the demands of this isolated life and to bear the children Duncan so wanted?

Repressing her serious doubts, Janet hastened forward to welcome her new sister-in-law as Duncan led her up the steps.

"Welcome to Montclair, my dear," she said. "I am sorry not to have been able to attend your wedding, but I am, as you see, still in mourning for my dear husband." Turning to Duncan, she greeted him with a smile. "Come inside. You must be tired and hungry."

Duncan's sister was a very handsome woman, her features much like his, though cast in a feminine mold. Her lips were drawn more tightly, but her eyes were as keenly penetrating and kind. Her hair, the same russet brown as her brother's, was covered by a black lace widow's cap.

Pleasantly surprised by the genuine warmth of Janet's greeting, so different from that suggested by her stern appearance, Noramary stepped into the wide center hall. In contrast to the rather forbidding austerity of the outside, the interior of the house was cheerful and inviting. The wide-planked oak floors were highly polished and reflected the glow from a dozen candles burning in two wide-branched brass chandeliers. From the hall, Noramary could see through an arched doorway into the parlor, where an open fire in the wide hearth was burning brightly.

"This is Ellen, my housekeeper, who has been helping me with the preparations for your arrival." Janet acknowledged the spare, sharp-featured woman who stepped forward and bowed slightly. She was wearing a gray dress, starchly collared, and a ruffled mobcap over carrot-colored hair.

"Mistress Montrose," she addressed Noramary, who started at the sound of her new title.

"And these are the houseservants," Duncan

said. One by one, two shyly smiling black women, wearing blue homespun with starched aprons and colorful turbans, came forward and made awkward curtsies, followed by two black men in white pleated shirts and black breeches. "Delva, Maysie, Thomas, Jason," Duncan introduced them.

"Would you like to see the house now?" Duncan asked Noramary with unconcealed eagerness.

Before she could answer, Janet interjected, "Perhaps Noramary would first like to go to her room and freshen up after her long journey."

Suddenly conscious of her probably untidy appearance, Noramary put her hand to her hair and murmured, "Yes, perhaps that would be best. Thank you."

"Then we can have a nice tea," Janet said briskly.

"Forgive me, my dear. I wasn't thinking," Duncan apologized. "There will be plenty of time to see Montclair."

"Come along then." Janet nodded, then turning to one of the women, directed, "Delva, go and fetch Mistress Montrose some hot water and fresh linens."

Noramary bowed slightly to Duncan, and followed his sister's tall figure across the wide hallway. Janet opened the first door to the right, stepping back to allow Noramary to precede her into a large, high-ceilinged room.

If this room had been especially planned with her own tastes and comfort in mind, it could not have suited her more perfectly, Noramary marveled. In front of the fireplace, where a cheerful fire crackled, were two wing-backed chairs covered in crewel-embroidered linen and flanked by candlestands.

The windows were recessed, curtained in indigo blue, with cushioned seats. Before one of the windows was a small curved desk and chair, and against the opposite wall, a dainty dressing table with a tilted mirror and toilette box on top. An enormous tester bed with blue and white hangings and a quilted coverlet occupied the most prominent space.

"What a lovely room!" Noramary exclaimed.

"I'm glad you're pleased. Duncan had it completely repainted, the draperies and bed curtains changed after your cousin . . ." Janet halted abruptly. "Forgive me, Noramary. I just meant to say that Duncan wanted it done over in colors he felt would be more to your liking."

Duncan's thoughtfulness removed the sting of the reference to Winnie and the implication that the master bedroom had been originally planned to suit the tastes of another bride. It was a relief to Noramary that her room at Montclair was not simply another "hand-me-down."

To cover her confusion Noramary moved over to one of the two other doors in the room. "Where do these lead?"

"That one is to Duncan's dressing room; the other, to your own, but there is another door inside. Why don't you see for yourself where that one leads?" Janet suggested.

Noramary walked into the dressing room equipped with a slipper chair and large armoire

reparation for the long festive evening ahead, a
arewell party given in Janet's honor. And though
the two women had gotten on admirably,
Noramary could not truly say she was sorry to see
her sister-in-law go.

The following day Janet was to depart for
Yorktown, there to embark her ship for her return
to Scotland. Ever since Noramary's arrival at
Montclair, Janet had been instructing her on her
duties as mistress. Contrary to Janet's fears and to
her own astonishment, Noramary had been an apt

and then pushed open the small inner door to
reveal a narrow winding staircase. She turned
questioningly to Janet, who stood at the door
watching her.

"In the original plans for the house, this
stairway led to a nursery. This plan gave the mother
privacy and easy access to the child, and also the
baby's nurse could come and go through the upstairs
central hall without disturbing the parents. A very
convenient arrangement, don't you see?"

Noramary nodded but made no comment.

"Here comes Delva now with your water and
towels, so I'll leave you. Tea will be served promptly
in a half hour." Janet swept out of the room, closing
the door behind her.

The tall, slim black girl entered smiling, her
delight in having been chosen to serve the new
mistress undisguised.

Noramary tied back her hair and washed
herself, enjoying the refreshing sensation of the
warm water and fine lavender-scented soap. She
changed into fresh linens, relieved to be out of the
blue woolsey traveling costume she had worn for
the past twenty-four hours. Delva helped her into a
cinnamon-colored bodice and gold overskirt looped
in velvet ribbon, then helped arrange Noramary's
hair in a shiny fall of rippling waves secured with a
velvet ribbon.

When she joined Janet and Duncan in the
parlor, she found an abundant tea table. At her
appearance Duncan lifted the glass he was holding,
saying, "To your first day at Montclair, Noramary.

May it be only the beginning of a lifetime of happiness under its roof."

Duncan's words reminded her of that moment in the carriage when she had been gripped by the strange premonition. Nevertheless, she quickly banished it and acknowledged Duncan's toast.

"I pray God it will be so."

Chapter 12

A blue haze of early autumn hung in the stillness of the afternoon as Noramary left the house. Once out of view she picked up her skirts and ran lightly along the woodland path. The crispness in the air was exhilarating, and the feeling of freedom from Janet's constant supervision, intoxicating. Noramary ran until she was breathless. On this particular afternoon Janet had retired for a nap—an event unprecedented in the three weeks Noramary had been at Montclair. The nap was in

These had been intense weeks, each day filled with learning, adjusting, absorbing all Janet was trying to teach her about the management of a huge plantation house. There had been a constant flow of callers, Duncan's neighbors, if one could call them such, separated as they were by great distances and hundreds of acres. Nevertheless, everyone had been eager to meet Duncan's bride, the new Mistress of Montclair.

And tonight would be her first time to entertain them officially in her new role, Noramary thought, half in anticipation, half in apprehension.

Noramary had learned, however, that being mistress of such a large manor house was much more complicated than playing the gracious hostess. It was a role she had never imagined would be so demanding. At first Noramary was nearly overwhelmed by the duties detailed by her new sister-in-law: overseeing the houseservants, fourteen in all, each with different duties to supervise.

Daily, there was the cleaning, dusting, waxing, and polishing required to keep the twenty-room house sparkling. There were menus to discuss with the cook, then supplies to be measured and brought from the storehouses; the available fruits and vegetables in season, to be picked from the gardens and orchards. Since all the fabric for the servants' clothing was processed on the plantation, there was the supervision of wool-carding, spinning, dying, and weaving. The linen for bedding and table use was made from flax grown on the land.

Since candle-dipping and soap-making were important to the smooth operation of the household, the mistress must keep close check on the progress of these activities so that supplies never ran short.

It seemed there was no end to the list of responsibilities Noramary would assume upon Janet's departure. The very thought of it left her dizzy. The Barnwell household, with fewer servants, had seemed to run itself. Now, however, Noramary realized that was probably due to Aunt Betsy's efficient management with the lighter chores divided among all four girls.

At the end of the first few days, following Janet as she made rounds, Noramary was nearing exhaustion. She found she could barely keep her eyes open throughout the late dinner hour and fell asleep the instant her head touched the pillow each night.

Guiltily, Noramary knew she would not miss her sister-in-law's cold, patrician face, the fastidious manners, the tedious way she had of explaining things. Nevertheless, Janet's efficiency and swift dispatch of duty would leave a gaping void.

Thank God for Ellen, Noramary thought gratefully.

It had been decided that Janet's own housekeeper, Ellen Anderson, whom she had brought with her to Virginia, would stay a while longer to assist Noramary.

Noramary liked Ellen, who was bright and cheerful, with an unexpected and delightful sense of humor. Most importantly, the brisk Scotswoman was wonderfully proficient in all the household tasks.

By the time Noramary reached the rustic bridge spanning the creek, she was breathless, both from her brisk run and from her turbulent thoughts. Since the night she and Duncan had been stranded by the flash flood, the little bridge had been repaired. She paused, leaning on the rail, and looked down to the sun-dappled water rushing over the rocks and swirling into opalescent eddies. She had had no time to herself for weeks and now she felt a sudden, heart-catching loneliness.

These had been strange weeks since her arrival on that stormy night. Strangest of all, perhaps, was her puzzling relationship with her new husband. Husband? Perhaps not, for they were not yet husband and wife in the fullest sense, and she was puzzled why that was so.

Her very first night at Montclair, he had escorted her to the master suite. There he had bowed over her hand, kissed it, and told her gravely that, after his two-week absence, there were plantation records that needed reviewing. He bade her good night and a pleasant rest, and left her staring after him in bewilderment.

The next morning when she had awakened in the bed alone, her curiosity piqued, she had tiptoed over to the dressing room door and looked in. The room was empty. There was evidence, however, that Duncan had slept on the narrow couch in the recessed alcove.

Since then, he had continued to sleep in the adjoining dressing room. Duncan seemed fond of her, was unfailingly courteous, seemed ever interested in providing her with any number of things for her pleasure and happiness. With eager pride he had shown her the music room, where a small harpsichord stood waiting. No doubt he had purchased it especially for her after hearing her play, for Winnie was not musical. On another occasion he had taken her out to the stables and presented her with the gift of a gentle, sweet-tempered black mare.

"She's yours to name," Duncan had said, smiling down at her.

"Cinders" had become a delight and a welcome respite on several mornings when Noramary managed to escape Janet's relentless tutelage.

Though Noramary was innocent, as were most of the other unmarried young women of her acquaintance, still she was troubled. Surely by this time her marriage to Duncan should be more than affectionate consideration and lavish gifts.

Of course, there were doubtless many practical reasons for his frequent absences. This was harvest time at Montclair, and Duncan spent long days in the saddle, riding over the acres and acres of land, while her days were crowded as well. And then there was Janet's constant presence—at meals, in the parlor, in the kitchen, wherever Noramary turned. There was little opportunity for romantic intimacy with her husband under these unusual circumstances.

Fleetingly Noramary recalled those few hours of laughter and unique camaraderie she and Duncan had shared so unpredictably on their wedding night in the warmth of the little cottage. Perhaps . . . after Janet was gone . . . Noramary mused.

Noramary stretched out her hand, surveying the ring on her finger alongside her wedding band. Only that morning Janet had called her upstairs to the room she had been occupying while at Montclair. Her trunks were open, and she was doing the last of her packing. Noramary had expected some last-minute instructions. Instead, Janet had taken off a large ring from her own finger and handed it to Noramary.

"This is the traditional Montrose betrothal ring," she explained. "It came to me upon our mother's death. But I think you should have it, wear it, as the first Mistress of Montclair."

Noramary had often noticed the dark purple amethyst on Janet's finger, but had never examined it closely. Now, as it lay in her palm, she saw its exquisite craftsmanship, the stone in a heart-shaped setting, held by two sculptured hands under a tiny crown.

"It's very lovely, Janet. Are you sure I should have it?"

"I have no sons to inherit it," Janet said firmly. "And it is my belief that it should stay in the Montrose family to be handed on to your son to give to his wife, then down through the family."

To your son . . . Janet's words came to her now as she held out her hand, turning the ring this way and that to catch the sun and split its rays into a million lavender lights.

Noramary left the bridge and walked on, still lost in thought. She came to a clearing in the woods and there, on a little rise, she saw the cottage where she and Duncan had stayed the night of the storm. Something real, something tender and strong had sprung up between them; a bond had been forged, tenuous perhaps, but in it there had been an unspoken promise given, but not yet fulfilled.

She stood there for a while, looking at the small house nestled in the trees, then she turned and started slowly back along the path leading to Montclair. Perhaps Duncan was waiting for some sign from her—that she was willing at last to make their marriage a true union. Maybe, just maybe, it was up to her. . . .

Tonight would present her first opportunity to show him that, even though she had not been his first choice, she was the right choice.

Tonight she would make Duncan Montrose proud, happy that she had become his bride— even if the substitute bride.

Chapter 13

Seated at her dressing table Noramary, brush in hand, considered the possibility of letting Delva powder her hair for the evening's festivities.

The candles in the sconces on either side of the mirror cast flattering light, reflecting her serious expression as she weighed her decision. Delva, anxiously awaiting her mistress's directions, stood behind with the horn-shaped paper face mask and powder bowl, ready to dust Noramary's rich dark hair if she was directed.

"No," said Noramary finally, "it's much too much bother." *Besides,* she thought, *Duncan never powders his hair, even for formal occasions.* And tonight, standing by his side to receive their guests, she wanted to complement him.

"Now, Delva, if you'll put that messy stuff away, you can help me with my gown."

Noramary stood while the girl carefully dropped the damask underskirt over her head and tied it in the back. With the width of the three starched muslin petticoats Noramary was wearing, her tiny waist looked even smaller. Then the puffed taffeta paniers were attached, adding more fashionable breadth. Next came the shirred satin bodice with the tiny buttons to be fastened down the back. Stiff lace ruffled the square neckline and elbow-length sleeves.

"Oh, ma'am, yo' does look mos' beautiful! Jes' wait 'til Marster Duncan sees yo'." Delva stepped back, smiling, head cocked to one side in admiration.

Noramary surveyed herself critically, thinking with some satisfaction that, although this modish creation was also one of those hand-me-downs made for Winnie's trousseau, then altered for Noramary's taller, more slender figure, it was extremely becoming. It was blue, the color of a peacock's feather, chosen to enhance Winnie's blonde prettiness. Nonetheless, the gown proved spectacularly becoming to Noramary's blue eyes and rose-tinted complexion.

She hoped that Duncan would be pleased with her appearance. She had seen him ride in from his field inspection earlier. From her window she had watched as he swung himself out of the saddle, moving with careless grace, then took the steps into the house, two at a time. A little later she had heard his voice mingled with that of his manservant's from the dressing room and knew he, too, was getting ready for the evening.

Noramary felt an excited little tingle at the prospect of her role as hostess for the evening. Many times she had helped Aunt Betsy entertain guests, but never before had she enjoyed the privilege of overseeing an elegant party in her own magnificent home.

Even as she was thinking these thoughts, a knock from Duncan's dressing-room door startled her and she turned just as he entered the bedroom, handsome in a saffron satin coat, fluted neckpiece and cuffs, creamy breeches.

"Good evening, Noramary," he said, his sweeping glance taking note of every detail. "How truly lovely you look."

The spontaneous compliment seemed to surprise him as much as it pleased Noramary, for he reddened slightly under his tan. Then, he took a few steps toward her, extending a rectangular velvet jewel case.

"I'd be pleased if you'd wear these tonight. They belonged to my mother." He pressed the spring lock, and the lid snapped open to reveal a magnificent ruby brooch surrounded by diamonds and a set of matching earrings of teardrop-shaped rubies, also surrounded by tiny diamonds.

"Oh, Duncan, they're exquisite!"

"There is a gold chain so that you can also wear the brooch as a pendant if you'd prefer," Duncan explained. "Here." He handed her the box.

She lifted them carefully from the box, fastened in the earrings, then turned to Duncan, holding out the fragile chain on which she had attached the brooch.

"Will you fasten the clasp for me?" she asked. With one hand she lifted her curls and bent her slender neck. As his fingers touched her bare skin, she felt a little shiver. When he had secured the catch, his hands moved tentatively along her neck to her shoulders, lingering there for a moment. She turned slowly around to face him.

"I'm afraid you and Janet are spoiling me," she teased. "Why only today she gave me this— another Montrose jewel." She held out her hand so he could see the betrothal ring. "With all these family treasures, I am truly beginning to feel like your wife!"

The minute the words were out of her mouth, she regretted them. But Duncan's eyes seemed to blaze with sudden fire, and then he caught both her hands and brought them to his lips.

"Not quite, Noramary," he said huskily. "There is something important I want to say to you—that I've meant to tell you for some time. But there hasn't been the opportunity . . . nor could I find the words." He paused, struggling to go on.

Duncan was gazing at her with such tenderness that Noramary felt a warm melting sensation. Meeting those clear gray eyes, she experienced a sense of intimate communion between them. Then Duncan spoke again.

"No matter how it came about, I am so very happy you agreed to become my wife. The rubies were my father's wedding present to my mother and have come to be called the Montrose Bridal Set." He paused again, then his voice grew soft with emotion. "Noramary, from the moment I met you, I felt—*even then*—something. I think . . . I believe—I have been waiting for you all these years."

"Well, here I am," she replied in a whisper.

Her lovely eyes seemed to reflect the shining thing suspended between them, fragile as a butterfly wing, a silken thread that might, in time, become a strong, sure bond.

At that very moment an insistent tapping came upon their bedroom door, and Janet's piercing voice intruded.

"Duncan, Noramary, a carriage is coming up the drive. Your guests are arriving!"

Duncan groaned under his breath, sighed heavily, and smiled—a smile that did unexpected things to Noramary's heart.

"Later . . ." he said. "When everyone is gone . . ." The implication dangled as he drew her to him, framed her face in his hands, and bent to kiss her. Her lips yielded sweetly to his kiss, and it left her strangely stirred.

"Come, Mistress Montrose. Our guests are waiting." Duncan took Noramary's hand and slipped it through his arm. "There will be time for us . . . we have a whole lifetime ahead of us."

The evening was a gaily festive one. Virginians in this part of the country knew how to enjoy themselves, Noramary discovered, finding the company as cultured, the conversation as spritely, the ladies as elegantly gowned, the gentlemen as suave as any she had observed in Williamsburg circles.

Throughout the evening she kept glancing at Duncan, thinking of the unforeseen intimacy of their earlier encounter, his eloquent declaration. Noramary was deeply moved to know he had cared for her so long ago. Duncan, she was learning, was a man of many moods, an intriguing, fascinating man.

With renewed resolution, Noramary determined to put the past behind her forever and, not even by a random thought, betray the trust and honor this good and gracious man had given her. She would be to Duncan Montrose the best wife it was in her ability to be—with God's help!

The Camerons had brought with them their houseguest, Cecil Brandon, a well-known English artist who had been commissioned by James to paint the portraits of Jacqueline and their two young sons, Bracken and Brett.

After their introduction, he was bent over Noramary's hand, and she felt scrutinized by his lingering gaze. If she could have read his thoughts, she would have been quite overwhelmed.

What an exquisite creature. And how incredible to find such a vision in this vast wilderness. Of course, Jacqueline Cameron is a great beauty, but it is to be expected. She is from France—a sophisticated, worldly woman. On the other hand, Mistress Montrose is hardly more than a girl, with the radiant innocence of childhood still upon her—the heart-shaped face, the delicate ivory skin, the magnificent violet eyes, slender figure, cloud of dark hair . . . entrancing!

All through dinner Brandon could not take his eyes from her, while all around him the conversation flowed almost unheeded.

Even though Noramary was unaware of his observation, it did not escape the notice of Jacqueline and Duncan. They exchanged a knowing glance. Duncan himself followed the direction of the artist's focus and smiled, joyful that this treasure belonged to him.

Indeed, Noramary did look lovely in the mellow candleglow, Duncan thought, the gleam of her dark hair pulled high, exposing her tiny ears with the bobbing flash of the ruby earrings and the creamy expanse of throat and shoulder. She seemed to him even more beautiful than the first time he had met her. How strangely things had turned out! Duncan recalled his bitter frustration after that first meeting at the Barnwells' party, the despair when he realized he had met Noramary too late—that he was already engaged to her cousin!

As he looked down the table-length, he could hardly believe his good fortune. A man might wonder if there really were a planned purpose for life . . . if he and Noramary had really been destined for each other, after all.

Suddenly Noramary caught his look and smiled at him. Hope leaped afresh in Duncan's heart. He and this woman *would* build a wonderful life together at Montclair. What had once seemed a vague dream now appeared to be reality. Duncan could not believe his good fortune!

Brandon impatiently endured the traditional ritual of brandy and conversation among the men when the ladies withdrew after dinner. However, as soon as they rejoined them in the drawing room, Brandon sought out Noramary immediately.

"Madam, I must compliment you on the delicious dinner, the beautifully appointed table. I cannot remember when I have enjoyed a gathering more," he began. Then, unable to contain his enthusiasm, he blurted out, "Madam, I must paint you . . . if you would permit it."

Noramary was completely taken aback. Then, as if by appointment, Duncan was beside her and Brandon was directing his request to her husband.

"Sir, I would like very much to paint a portrait of your wife. Indeed, I would consider it a privilege to do so."

Noramary turned to Duncan and was surprised to see the look of pleasure and pride in his expression.

"I see you appreciate beauty, sir," he said.

"Beauty, yes, but not just beauty for itself, sir. Only when it is coupled with an inner sweetness of soul, unspoiled and pristine . . . that is when I want to capture it . . . before it is corrupted in any way." He made a slight gesture to Noramary. "As this lady can surely testify, too much beauty can be a burden . . . unless it brings peace, tranquility, and happiness."

Noramary made a small movement as if in protest to Brandon's extravagant phrases, yet at the same time she was moved by his perception. Had she not felt the weight of just such a burden when, even as a child of twelve, that stunning, sensitive beauty had caused her heartbreak?

Then Duncan was speaking. "Perhaps when I return from accompanying my sister to board her ship in Yorktown, we can make some arrangements about having Noramary's portrait done. How long do you expect to be in this part of the country?"

Noramary did not absorb much of the rest of their conversation; she was too bemused by Duncan's eagerness to comply with Brandon's suggestion. She was even more aware that while they had been talking to the artist, Duncan's arm had circled her waist, its gentle pressure sending a tremor of pleasure through her.

Finally the evening came to an end. The guests began to leave, with many thanks, return invitations, and promises to visit, as well as farewells and Godspeed to Janet.

As was his custom, Duncan rode to the gates alongside the carriages of his departing guests. Janet, pleading weariness and need for sleep before her long journey the next day, took her candle and retired.

Noramary lingered, walking back into the dining room, admiring once again the elegant table, flowers, and candelabra still in place. Then she wandered into the drawing room, feeling a new pride in its handsome furnishings, the quiet dignity of its atmosphere. This was her home now. She was mistress here. And, to her amazement, she had enjoyed her role as hostess more than she had imagined possible. Duncan, too, had seemed pleased.

What an evening it had been! She had felt more like herself than at any time since . . . well, since long before she had left Williamsburg. It was as if some heavy weight had fallen away and she could now take a long breath without pain.

Was it possible that something had transpired between herself and Duncan tonight that bode well for their relationship? Could the growing respect and affection she had for him be turning to love? Did such things really happen?

Tonight they had seemed a real couple. She recalled how, arm in arm, they had moved among their guests before dinner, stopping to chat with this group and that. Noramary had felt relaxed, and Duncan had seemed to take delight in her every word. She had found it easy and natural to visit with Duncan's friends, even to bringing off a bit of humor now and then. Later, at dinner, she could feel Duncan's eyes on her from his place at the opposite end of the table, and she had experienced an instantaneous rush of pleasure. Something intangible tingled in that silent communication, something that made her pulse race, brought flaming color to her cheeks, set her heart beating so fast that it was hard to breathe.

Delva was waiting for Noramary in the bedroom. But after she had helped her mistress out of her elaborate gown and into her blue panné peignoir, Noramary sent the girl away.

Thoughtfully Noramary replaced the rubies in their case. The Montrose Bridal Set. Her hand stroked the velvet lid, remembering the poignant moment when Duncan had given them to her. The promise in his eyes when he had kissed her. Would this be the night she would truly become his wife?

Noramary looked at the high, canopied bed, its silken coverlet turned back invitingly, the mounds of ruffled pillows offering peaceful repose. But Noramary was far too stimulated by the events of the evening to be sleepy.

She brushed her hair, giving it long, vigorous strokes until it crackled. She sat for a long moment, regarding herself in the mirror with a kind of curiosity. What had Brandon seen in her face that compelled him to paint her portrait? And why had Duncan acquiesced so readily?

Sighing, she blew out her candle, crossed to the window, thrust it open, and leaned on the sill, looking out into the night.

The air was cold, with the snap of autumn; the moon glistened on the early frost that coated the grass and outlined the tender saplings Duncan had planted along the drive.

Duncan! A little tingle coursed through Noramary. How long would it take him to ride to the gate with the last guests . . . and return?

Chapter 14

Dawn's faint blush stained the pale gray morning with shimmering light and gradually stole into the master bedroom at Montclair.

Duncan leaned down to kiss Noramary's eyelids, still closed in sleep, and gently brushed back the dark strands of silky hair from her forehead. She stirred in his arms, half-waking.

"It's time to get up, dearest," he whispered regretfully. "Janet will be up and anxious to leave as soon as it's fully light."

At that Noramary's eyelids fluttered, then opened. She looked up into Duncan's face, and her eyes widened as if in surprise. Then, in a rather drowsy remembrance, a tiny smile turned up the corners of her rosy mouth and she sighed contentedly. As awareness sharpened, she recalled how infinitely tenderly Duncan had made her fully his wife.

That's what he had murmured over and over, *beloved wife.*

He gathered her close, and, as Noramary put her arms around his neck, he buried his head in her sweetly scented hair. That she could return his love filled Duncan with a sense of gratitude and tenderness so sharp it was almost pain.

"I hate to leave you, my darling," Duncan said, releasing her reluctantly, "but I'll only be gone long enough to see Janet safely aboard her ship and settled. I'll be away only a few days."

Only a few days, Duncan had said, but as soon as Noramary saw the carriage disappear at the bend of the drive, she felt a strange emptiness. And as the days passed, she was amazed that she could miss him so much.

Of course, Noramary was not used to solitude. The Barnwell household had been a lively one, with five girls coming and going constantly, and a steady stream of company besides. It had been a home filled with noise, chatter, the sound of running feet, laughter.

Here, with only the houseservants for company, Noramary experienced an altogether new kind of loneliness. To her amusement she found she missed Janet as one would miss an aching tooth when it has been pulled! She was, however, more grateful than ever for her sister-in-law's rigorous instruction, for the household tasks filled many of the lonely hours and provided a welcome pattern to the days Duncan was away.

As the day of Duncan's expected return drew near, Noramary found herself anticipating his homecoming with equal portions of joy and reserve. Their intimate relationship was still so new that she had to wonder if the days apart had changed him. She still did not know Duncan well. Now, for some reason, Janet's admonition came to mind.

They were putting out the elaborate silver flatware that was to be polished for use at the farewell dinner party when, pausing in the act of counting the place settings, Janet had spoken in a low, serious tone.

"I hope you will not misunderstand what I am about to say, Noramary. Please try to accept it as an older woman's advice to one just starting out in married life. I do not know how well you think you know my brother, but I feel I should give you fair warning.

"You have heard the saying, 'Still waters run deep,' haven't you? Well, that could have been written of my brother. On the surface, he may appear calm, controlled, but he is a complex man. A man of strong passions, of fierce loyalty, unswerving honor, lasting love. But I have also witnessed his anger, sudden, violent as summer lightning, followed by cold, implacable unforgiveness and ruthless retribution. I say this not to frighten you, but to warn you.

"You are very young, and the young sometimes act thoughtlessly, behave recklessly, or take carelessly things that older people cherish or venerate. I would caution you to be aware of the fragile quality of most relationships . . . especially the one between a husband and wife."

Noramary had been tempted to pursue the conversation, to ask Janet about those times when she had seen Duncan's darker side, but something had kept her from doing so. Still, she could not help wondering if one of those times might have been when he learned of Winnie's elopement.

Such an event could be devastating to a man's pride, fill him with feelings of anger, resentment, a desire for revenge.

Yet, it was hard to picture the Duncan she had come to know as unforgiving. He seemed compassionate, understanding, gentle, as only a strong, confident man could be.

Because Janet was not inclined to discuss the matter further, Noramary tucked the information in the back of her mind, hoping that she herself would never have to witness this terrifying anger of Duncan's or, worse still, be the cause of it.

Duncan certainly had none of Robert's impulsive charm, boyish gaiety, mischievous sense of humor, Noramary mused, then quickly chided herself for making such a comparison.

She had not wanted to think of Robert. But in those long, lonely afternoons, when she walked alone through the autumn woods surrounding Montclair, thoughts of him came to her despite her resolution to thrust him forever out of her mind. They had often walked together in the woodlands near Williamsburg on just such golden, Indian summer days.

The nights during Duncan's absence were even more unmanageable. Even though she had fallen asleep only once in his embrace, the secure comfort she had felt within his arms now made it difficult to sleep soundly in the bed they had shared.

Each night Noramary tossed and turned, then drifted into a shallow slumber, troubled by dreams. To her dismay, the dreams had been of Robert Stedd! Two mornings she had awakened with his name on her lips, shaken by memories she thought long since erased.

Earnestly Noramary tried to discipline herself to keep her mind occupied.

Aunt Betsy had started her on a sampler when she first came to Williamsburg. All the cousins were at work on similar projects, as it was deemed essential for all young ladies to display not only their skill with a needle, but to present the important events of their lives, express their ideals with appropriate Scripture verses. Since coming to Montclair, however, Noramary had neglected it because of new demanding duties required of her as mistress.

Now she found that the solitary evenings gave her time to take up her needlework again, and she had made good progress on the line of Scripture to embroider at the bottom of the sampler.

On the morning of Duncan's expected return, Noramary rose early to see the servants' tasks supervised, then by early afternoon, she dressed in one of the most flattering of her "at home" dresses, a coral wool bodice with a cream tucker and skirt embroidered with wild rowan berry blossoms.

Afterward she made a final inspection of the house, satisfied with the polished perfection of each room. There were fires burning in all the fire-places; the scent of candlewax and the fragrance of flowers mingled pungently with the smell of applewood logs. It was a bright and cheerful house—a house awaiting its master's return.

As the afternoon shadows lengthened, Noramary became more restive, frequently looking out the window to peer down the drive for some sign of the returning traveler.

At length she settled herself at her frame and diligently applied herself to her sampler, trying to suppress her nervousness. Her needle was poised over the canvas when she started at a sound outside. Carriage wheels? Yes, it was! Noramary flew to the window as the carriage rumbled into sight. Duncan—home at last!

She ran from the room and down the hall. But when she saw Titus, one of the houseservants, opening the front door, she halted, assuming the more dignified stance expected of the mistress.

She held her breath as Duncan stepped inside, handed his caped coat to Titus, and glanced past him to Noramary, standing in the archway to the drawing room. Seeing her, he beamed with pleasure.

"Welcome home, Duncan," she said demurely, dropping a little curtsy.

"It's good to be home," Duncan said heartily,

his eyes feasting upon her until her cheeks flamed.

"Shall we serve dinner now, Mistress?" asked Titus.

Noramary glanced at Duncan with lifted eyebrows.

"In another half hour, Titus. Tell Cook," Duncan ordered. "I want a few minutes with Mistress Montrose." Again his glance swept Noramary. "Let us go into the parlor, my dear. I have something to show you."

Tucking her arm through his, he led her through the arched doorway. Once inside, he cupped her chin with one hand and kissed her mouth lightly, then with his other hand, he drew a small package from his waistcoat pocket and handed it to her.

"A gift!" Noramary gave a cry of delight. "Oh, Duncan, you are spoiling me terribly!"

"Perhaps I like spoiling you," he said, smiling at her with great tenderness.

Noramary had received few presents in her life, and so it was with a child's eagerness that she opened the little box. When she lifted out a dainty folded fan, her face lighted up.

"Duncan, how lovely!"

With a flick of her wrist, she unfurled it, displaying the arch of creamy silk on which a spray of tiny red roses was handpainted. The sticks were of filigreed ivory, with a crimson satin tassel dancing from the guard. She held it up in front of her face in a coquettish gesture, fluttering it flirtatiously.

Duncan laughed at her nonsense. "I'm glad it

pleases you. So then, what have you been doing with yourself while I've been gone?"

"For one thing, I've accomplished quite a bit on my sampler," Noramary announced much like a little girl reporting on her schoolwork. Still fluttering her new fan, she walked over to the frame and tapped it with her fingers. "It's almost finished."

"I shall have to examine it. I understand a sampler is supposed to be representative of a young lady's achievements in needlework as well as a revelation of her ideals, her thoughts, and her spiritual state." His voice held a teasing quality, although he maintained a serious expression.

"Come see for yourself!" Noramary challenged.

He walked over to the tapestry frame and with great solemnity appeared to be studying it carefully.

The sampler was uniquely the story of Noramary's life thus far. At the top she had outlined Monksmoor Priory, her childhood home, and the date of her birth. Coming to Virginia by ship had, at the time, been the single most important event in Noramary's life, so she had traced the "Fairwinds" in colorful yarn. Next she had added her rendition of the Barnwells' yellow clapboard house and a row of flowers, new to her, found in the garden there. All these symbolized her new life in America. Recently she had stitched an outline of Montclair and added to her signature, NORAMARY MARSH, the letters of her new married name— MONTROSE.

Duncan slowly read the words aloud, placing significant emphasis on the last name. He looked up and smiled at her. Then he continued, reading the Scripture verse she had worked on during the last week: "Delight thyself in the Lord; and He shall give thee the desires of thine heart—Psalm 37:4."

The candlelight softened the angular planes of his face as he regarded Noramary silently. "And what *are* the desires of your heart, Noramary?"

She returned his steady gaze, her eyes sweetly grave. "My heart's desire is to please God, Duncan, *and* you," she said at length, lowering her head so that he could not see into her eyes through the dark veil of her lashes. "To be your wife . . . in every sense of the word . . . to belong to you . . . really belong. *That* is the desire of my heart."

Almost as if speaking to himself, he said, "That has been the desire of my heart, too."

At his words a sudden joy seized Noramary and tears sprang to her eyes. She saw Duncan's face and realized that it was true.

If she were his second choice, the substitute of the bride he had first desired, she no longer cared. At that moment the past seemed to fade away, and only the growing eagerness to love and be loved dwelled in her heart.

She held out her arms to him, tenderness and expectation spreading through her in a warm, enveloping glory. He drew her to him, enclosing her in his arms, his chin resting atop her silky head.

"Darling Noramary, you have made me happier than I ever dreamed possible."

Her slender body swayed closer and, sighing her name, he gathered her to him.

Chapter 15

At daybreak the distant sounds of birdsong broke the stillness. Pale light, filtering through the louvered shutters of the windows, banished the night shadows.

In the large canopy bed Duncan stirred and awakened, propping himself on one elbow to observe his still sleeping wife. He was not sure how long he had slept, nor what had disturbed his slumber, but something had roused him.

Just at that moment Noramary moved restlessly.

Her head turned from side to side; a frown drew the smooth brow into a pucker. Duncan leaned closer, but could not understand the words she was mumbling.

Poor darling, he thought. *Having a bad dream perhaps.* He touched her shoulder, gently pressing it. At his touch she uttered a few incoherent words, and with her eyes still closed, reached up and drew his head down against her breast.

Duncan's arms went around her, holding her close. "I'm here, darling," he whispered comfortingly. "Dearest Noramary, I love you."

Noramary smiled as if with some secret joy. "And I love you. . . ."

At the name she whispered, shock like a saber thrust pierced Duncan's heart. It reverberated in his brain, settled into his consciousness.

Robert! I love you, Robert! Robert?

Who was this Robert whose name Noramary had spoken with such passionate tenderness? Noramary, to whom he had opened himself with a surrender, an intensity he had never thought possible. Noramary, in whom all his inner loneliness had been assuaged. Noramary, with whom he had found an ecstasy beyond his wildest imagining. She had deceived him! She had dreamed of another man while in his—Duncan's—arms! *Robert.*

Stiffly he loosened Noramary's clinging arms, withdrew himself from her embrace, and dragged himself from the bed. His hands clenched into fists as he stood staring down at her in a kind of disbelief that she could look so innocent—her dark hair, feathered out against the white linen pillow; her cheeks, flushed with sleep; her lips, slightly parted as if expecting to be kissed.

The blood roared in Duncan's temples; his heart thudded heavily; he felt as if he couldn't breathe. In his mouth he tasted the bitter gall of disillusionment. How quickly their joy had turned into a kind of heartsick despair.

He dragged on his clothes, moving wearily, like a man twice his age. He pulled on his boots and walked over to the fireplace. The fire that had glowed so brightly when he and Noramary had entered the bedroom the night before was now a heap of crumbled logs, mostly ashes. Like his own hopes and dreams, he thought dully.

Duncan felt a tremor of suppressed fury course through his veins.

How could he have been so deceived? So taken in by her apparent innocence. What a clever actress, how devious.

He thought of their courtship during the summer just past, how restrained he had behaved with her, never taking the slightest advantage, afraid he might importune her delicate nature, frighten her if he revealed the depth of his love and desire for her.

And all the while, perhaps even up until the wedding day, she had been seeing, perhaps carrying on a clandestine affair with this—this Robert, whose name she had uttered with such tenderness. Duncan felt cheated, betrayed by his own emotions as well as the falseness of the one to whom he had allowed himself to be so vulnerable.

More fool he! And what was God's design for them now?

Duncan put on his jacket, searched for his neckpiece which he had carelessly dropped somewhere last night in his haste. As he moved about, he stumbled against the small candle table and set it to rocking noisily.

Noramary awakened. Coming slowly out of a happy dream of childhood days, she raised herself on her elbows and looked around drowsily. Still half-asleep, she was smiling, for her dream had been the first one for months not plagued with sad memories or vain regrets. She had dreamed of the days when she and Robert had played together, along with the Barnwell girls—a time when they had all been young, carefree, unburdened.

Seeing Duncan, Noramary felt the newly awakened love for him like an embracing warmth.

"Duncan," she called, sitting up and holding out her arms to him.

Duncan whirled around, steeling himself not to succumb at the sight of her—the tumbled dark waves falling about her sleep-rosy face, the smile trembling on her lips.

"Duncan?"

This time it was a tentative appeal, her eyes widened at his fixed stare. She shivered involuntarily and huddled under the covers, drawing them up to her chin. "What is it, Duncan? Is something the matter?"

Noramary waited for him to speak. When Duncan made no move toward her, she remained poised in a questioning attitude, trying to read the cold anger his eyes seemed to hold.

What could she possibly have done to deserve that look of withering scorn? Noramary searched his face, seeking some reassurance for the sudden coldness she saw in his eyes.

The chilling silence was finally broken when Duncan, visibly suppressing rage, spoke in a toneless voice.

"I have only a few things to say to you, madam, and they are of immense importance. First, I believe we can both agree that I never importuned you nor unduly pressured you to consummate our marriage."

An unknown fear gripped Noramary as, bewildered, she dreaded hearing what he was going to say next.

"Whatever you chose not to reveal to me before our marriage was your privilege. However, it is inexcusable that you would pretend a passion you did not feel, when there was another man in your life. You have profaned the vows we took together, vows which I held sacred.

"It was clearly understood by me that you entered into this marriage of your own free will, under no duress from me or your aunt and uncle. Now I have reason to believe that I have been doubly deceived."

A frightened Noramary gave a protesting cry, but Duncan cut her short. With clenched teeth he spoke harshly. "But we have made a commitment, you and I, a pledge, promises made before God and witnesses. These shall remain. As far as the rest of the world is concerned, we are pledged to each other for life. I shall never break that bond. You are my wife and shall always be, but . . . our marriage will be in fact what it has become, a mere façade; in reality, the sham *you* have made it."

His voice was hoarse, and the mouth that had lingered so lovingly on hers twisted into a cruel line.

With that, Duncan turned and stalked toward the door.

Noramary, who had been paralyzed by the flood of Duncan's angry words, threw back the covers and jumped out of bed, running after him on bare feet. Recklessly, she grabbed hold of his sleeve.

"Wait! Duncan, wait!" she pleaded. "I don't understand. What have I done? Why are you so angry with me?"

"For God's sake, Noramary . . ." He paused significantly. "Yes . . . *for God's sake*, and mine, don't make it any worse!"

He shook off her clutching hands and strode out of the room without a backward glance.

Part III

*Wrath is cruel, and anger is outrageous;
but who is able to stand before envy? Open rebuke is
better than secret love.*

PROVERBS 27:4-5

Chapter 16

For weeks afterward, Noramary relived that dreadful scene, and the one that took place later that same evening. Neither seemed real to her.

When Duncan stormed out of the bedroom, leaving her in anguished bewilderment, Noramary collapsed in spasms of uncontrollable weeping. What had she said, what had she done to deserve Duncan's heartless rejection?

All her new happiness, the joy he had awakened in her at the passionately tender lovemaking was replaced with a numbing emptiness. That beautiful flame that had touched both of them burning so brightly, yet so briefly, was gone. Destroyed by some reason known only to Duncan.

The rest of that day she had wandered about the house as if in a trance of misery, waiting for Duncan's return to plead with him again for an explanation.

But when he walked into the house, he gave her only a cold glance and walked straight into the drawing room without greeting her.

She followed him, saying, "Duncan, we must talk."

"Well?" Duncan demanded impatiently. "What do we have to talk about?"

"Please," she said in a low voice, "I do not care to be overheard." Noramary inclined her head slightly toward the dining room, where the maids were setting the table for dinner.

"Very well. Come in then."

She entered the drawing room, closing the French doors behind her. He stood facing her, frowning, slapping his riding gloves on his palm, his whole attitude intimidating. But Noramary was too desperate not to attempt some understanding.

Determined to pursue the mystifying cause until she got an answer, she asked as quietly and calmly as she could manage, "Duncan, I must know what I have done to anger you so. How can I apologize if I don't know . . . ?"

But he interrupted her, "I thought I made myself clear this morning. I have nothing more to say. The subject is distasteful in the extreme to me, and I will not discuss it further."

Rebuffed, Noramary struggled not to lose her composure. But when she spoke, her voice betrayed her emotion. "If you will not give me the chance to defend myself, what is there for me to do? Nothing left for me but to assume that you deeply regret the agreement you made with my aunt and uncle to marry me; that, for some reason, you *now*, desperately wish you'd never accepted a substitute bride."

Getting no answer, Noramary turned to leave.

"One moment, madam." Duncan's command halted her as her hand touched the door handle. "I will be gone most of the time for the next ten days or so. The tobacco crop is being harvested and I must oversee its cutting, drying, and tying at the other end of the plantation. So, do not expect me for dinner in the evenings. If I should come, have my meal served on a tray in the office."

Her back still to him, Noramary asked, "Is that all then?"

"One thing more, madam. You may rest assured that I will never again assume my so-called marital rights. As far as I am concerned, we live under this roof as man and wife—in name only."

Noramary, biting back the tears that threatened to blind her, opened the double doors and, holding herself erect, walked out to the hall. She could not see the sudden slump of Duncan's broad shoulders as he watched her small, dignified figure disappearing through the door into the master bedroom.

*   *   *

The next two weeks passed in a blur of meaningless days and sleepless nights for Noramary. Day after day she searched her mind and heart, trying to discover the key that would unlock the source of Duncan's blind rage.

Janet's words came back to Noramary tauntingly. Her description of her brother's "ruthless unforgiveness when betrayed" took on new meaning. If Duncan, for whatever reason, thought she had betrayed him, how could they ever be reconciled?

A pervasive gloom hung over Montclair, diminishing the cheerfulness Noramary's endearing personality had brought to the household. The servants seemed to feel it, too, and went about their daily work as if on tiptoe. Ellen, from whom Noramary found it difficult to conceal anything, observed her mistress with characteristic sharpness, and set her mouth in a tight line as Noramary's growing unhappiness became more apparent. But Noramary, unable to explain to herself what had happened, could confide in no one.

Feeling lonely and abandoned, Noramary threw herself on her only hope, her faith that God had brought her to Montclair for His purposes and, no matter how it might appear, would continue to uphold her if she trusted Him. Even as she wept, on her knees, face buried in her hands, she told herself He was always true to His Word, and clung desperately to the Scripture promise: "I will never fail thee nor forsake thee." It was her lifeline, that thin thread holding her back from the brink of despair.

November, with its bleak, gray days, brought with it a dreary sameness that Noramary found almost unbearable. The strain of the estrangement imposed by Duncan was gradually wearing her down.

Then something happened to break the awful monotony of Noramary's days and shed a ray of light on the darkness that had threatened to engulf her. An invitation to the annual pre-Christmas party came from Cameron Hall. Noramary received it with delight. But if she had entertained any hopes that the prospect of a social outing at Cameron Hall would soften Duncan's attitude or thaw his unremitting coldness toward her, they were dashed at once by his indifferent comment.

"Well, I suppose we have to go," he said with a shrug. "We can't offend my best friends, but I have no taste for it." And he turned away.

In spite of her disappointment at Duncan's reaction, Noramary continued to hope that once in the festive atmosphere at Cameron Hall, seeing friends and neighbors alive with the holiday spirit, Duncan might realize the pointlessness in maintaining his stubborn silence. How could anything breach the rift that daily widened between them unless he told her the source of it?

All she could do was try, Noramary decided. She would look her best and pray that the affection he had once felt for her might be revived. That as Scripture exhorted, "a wife's sweet spirit" might win over her husband.

And, on the night of the Camerons' party, if Noramary were to believe the adoring Delva, she did indeed look her loveliest. The dress she was wearing was not one of Winnie's cast-offs but had been a gift from Aunt Betsy. Cut from a length of crimson velvet, its low, square neckline was edged with lace stiffened with gilt; the underskirt and draped paniers, of brocaded satin.

"Jes' wait 'til the Marster sees you!" declared Delva. "He'll be that proud!"

If only . . . thought Noramary wistfully.

Just as she was putting the finishing touches on her hair, there was a tap on the door from Duncan's dressing room. Surprised, Noramary turned from her mirror expectantly. He had not entered the bedroom for all these weeks.

Noramary held her breath as Duncan, looking handsome in a dark broadcloth coat, buff knee britches, and ruffled shirt, stepped in. He brought from behind his back the jewel case Noramary recognized as containing the Montrose rubies. She had not worn them since the night of Janet's farewell party.

Perhaps this was a gesture on Duncan's part to bridge the chasm of their estrangement. Her heart fluttered hopefully. But one look at his stony countenance killed that foolish notion.

"For you to wear tonight," he said brusquely. "The rubies."

"Oh, I was not sure you'd want me to wear them," she said in a low, controlled voice. She had left off the betrothal ring in the past weeks, feeling it was a farce. She now felt the same about the rubies.

"It is simply that people will expect to see them tonight," he said and paused. "As soon as you're ready, we can leave," he called over his shoulder as he turned away.

Wordlessly Noramary watched him walk back into his dressing room. Quickly gathering her injured pride around her like a ragged shawl, she felt Delva's eyes upon her, she tried to hide her hurt. It wouldn't do to give the servants more to gossip about.

Her hands trembling, Noramary fastened the brooch to the shoulder of her gown, then slipped the earrings into her earlobes. The deep color of the jewels, caught in the light from the candles on the dressing table, shimmered like claret wine in crystal or . . . more like heart's blood, for her own heart seemed to be bleeding. Would Duncan never speak to her with tenderness nor look at her with love again? It seemed a cruel reality.

At Cameron Hall Noramary mounted the steps eagerly, grateful that their silent ride in the forced intimacy of the carriage was over.

Jacqueline greeted her affectionately, exclaiming over her, complimenting her costume. Looking at Duncan, she shook her finger playfully.

"Shame on you, Duncan, for not bringing Noramary over to visit us more often! Do you keep her prisoner at Montclair, for your pleasure alone?"

Duncan looked uncomfortable, but Jacqueline never noticed. She was too busy signaling one of the maids to take their cloaks. Then, slipping her arm companionably through Noramary's, she insisted on taking her around personally to meet the other guests.

The house was beautifully decorated for the occasion. Garlands of galax leaves were wound between the banisters of the curved center staircase, crimson ribbons tied at the posts. Vases of nandina, cedar and pittosporum, and shiny holly boughs bright with berries, adorned every table. On the mantelpiece were vivid arrangements of pine cones, evergreens, and candles, and in the dining room, where candles shone in crystal-prismed holders, a wreath of fruit, bayberry, nuts, and cones centered the polished mahogany table set for sixteen.

For all the gaiety that surrounded her, Noramary found herself hard put to keep a smiling face. All her anticipation of this evening, her hopeful expectation that it might be a turning point in her relationship with Duncan, faded in the face of his indifference. He kept his distance from her and spent the entire evening talking with others, ignoring her completely.

When dinner was served, Noramary found herself seated at James Cameron's right, with Duncan far down the table beside Jacqueline. The table was laden, the dishes grown in the plantation's gardens and orchards. Noramary, distracted as she was, could only pick at the succulent food before her.

For Noramary, the evening lengthened interminably as an endless round of toasts began. It seemed each gentleman felt obligated to offer a toast, not only to the ladies present, but to each couple as well. Noramary's apprehension mounted as Duncan's turn approached, though it was James Cameron's toast she dreaded most.

James had been flatteringly attentive throughout the dinner hour, telling Noramary what a blessing she was to Duncan, how happy his friends were that his lonely bachelorhood was ended, that he had taken to wife such a beautiful bride. As he got to his feet to propose the next toast, Noramary felt herself go rigid.

"My dear and honored guests—I want to propose a toast to a special man, one whom I regard as my closest friend, my neighbor," he began, raising his glass. "Duncan Montrose, of Montclair.

"Montclair has always been esteemed for its splendid crops, its fine horses, its excellent hospitality—" He paused as "Hear! Hear!" and the tinkling of silver being gently tapped against the wine goblets rose in chorus from the company; James continued—"From now on it should be known for its beautiful mistress as well. . . . To Noramary!" The gentlemen rose to their feet as one, lifting their glasses to her, and a murmur of approval circled the table. She colored prettily, wishing nothing so much as to disappear.

But the judge was not finished. He turned in Duncan's direction and bowed slightly. "My fervent wish is that, in the years to come, there will be many children to bless this charming couple and to fill their home with great joy."

Noramary's hand, holding a long-stemmed goblet, began to tremble. His words numbed every thought except to know what Duncan was thinking and feeling. She controlled the impulse to steal a quick glance his way, see his reaction.

But she had no opportunity, for James was leaning toward her, diverting her attention. In a stage-whisper he asked mischievously, "Can you guess what Jacqueline has planned for tonight's entertainment?"

Trying to appear interested, she listened politely. As a memento of the evening, each guest would carry home a profile of himself or herself, cut from black paper by a professional silhouettist. It was a skilled art, and the guests were delighted when the plan was announced.

"What fun!" exclaimed one of the ladies to Noramary. "I've always wanted to have my silhouette done. They're really quite an amazing likeness, I understand."

Noramary watched with fascination as the little man carefully surveyed his subject with narrowed, measuring eyes. Then, folding a sheet of black paper, he began to cut with sharp scissors, turning the paper carefully in his hands as he snipped. It was an astonishing thing to see.

Before she was quite prepared, it was Noramary's turn to sit for the artist. Because everyone gathered around the subject, watching the master silhouettist at work, she struggled to overcome her natural reluctance to be the center of attention. However, she decided if the portrait turned out well, it would make a nice Christmas gift for her aunt and uncle.

She took her seat as instructed, her body turned so that a lighted candelabrum threw her profile sharply against the white wall of the paneled parlor wainscoting.

"Ah, what an enchanting profile!" said the artist, and for a few minutes there was absolute silence as he worked.

When he had finished, he held it up for Noramary to see, then quickly dabbed some mucilage from a small pot beside him and applied the silhouette to a stark white stiffened paperboard. "Voilà!"

Jacqueline leaned over Noramary's shoulder to admire the artistry. "It's lovely, Noramary—a surprising likeness, don't you agree?"

"Perhaps I shall give it to my aunt and uncle for Christmas," Noramary said.

"I notice you cut two at the same time, Monsieur Varny," Jacqueline remarked.

"Yes, it is my custom. Two thicknesses provide a firmer material with which to cut," he explained.

"May I have the extra one of my friend, then?" Jacqueline asked, smiling at Noramary.

Shortly afterward, Duncan appeared. "It's time

for us to go. I'll wait here while you get your cloak, then we'll say our good nights and be on our way."

The words were so terse, so unlike Duncan's former courteous consideration of her, that Noramary felt again the wound of their estrangement. But she went to get her cloak and muff, pausing only long enough to gain her composure before returning to the drawing room.

At least she had something to look forward to, something pleasant to occupy her thoughts on the ride home, she reminded herself: She and Duncan would be going to Williamsburg for the holidays. He had promised Aunt Betsy. Surely he would keep his promise.

Chapter 17

Since it was a Christmas Day tradition at Montclair for the master to distribute gifts—bolts of bright calico, indigo cloth, new hats and scarves, jugs of molasses, flour, and candy—to the servants, Noramary and Duncan did not leave for Williamsburg until the following day.

The entourage left Montclair before daybreak, and even though the country roads were rutted by winter rains and hardened by freezing weather, they made good time.

There was the hint of snow in the crisp air of the December dusk when their carriage rumbled through the streets of Williamsburg, and Noramary's heart lifted with anticipation.

As the coachman slowed the horses to a more sedate pace through the residential part of town, Noramary felt a surge of nostalgia at the sight of the lighted candles in the windows. Here, at least, things were as they had always been. Families gathering to share the happy season, carolers raising voices in familiar hymns at each door, party-goers on their way to holiday festivities. At Christmas, Williamsburg was at its best.

When they passed a house marked by a wooden sign at the gatepost: HUGH STEDD, PHYSICIAN, Noramary's heart pinched sharply. The familiar figure of Robert's uncle emerging from the front door brought a rush of memories—memories too dear, too sweet not to recall.

Noramary had locked away thoughts of Robert as the bittersweet keepsakes of a love best forgotten, but recently, in her loneliness, she found herself thinking of the past, of Robert, of the innocent love they had shared.

As they drew up in front of the Barnwells', Noramary was already on the edge of her seat, ready to alight as soon as the carriage door swung open. But Duncan put out a restraining hand, enclosing her wrist in a hard grasp.

"I hope I do not need to remind you that our private difficulties should remain just that," Duncan said in a voice intense with warning. "I don't know how much of a confidante either your aunt or your cousins are to you; however, I do not wish to have our problems discussed with anyone. Is that understood?"

Stricken by the harshness of his words, Noramary was momentarily shaken. When she could speak, her voice trembled.

"I understand *what* you are saying, Duncan, even though I still do not understand *why!* Whatever has made you so angry with me?" She shook her head as if to clear it. "Duncan, it's Christmas, a time for forgiveness, for joy, for love. In the spirit of this blessed season let us forgive one another, let us love . . ."

His grip only tightened on her arm. This time his tone was gritty with irony.

"Must I repeat myself, Noramary? Can you not understand that to all *appearances* we are a happily married couple, home for the holidays?"

Noramary closed her eyes for a second, then opened them and looked at Duncan with sorrow. "Yes, Duncan, I do understand," she said wearily.

She did not have time to say anything more, for at that moment the carriage door was opened, and at the same time the Barnwells' door flung wide, enveloping them both in the cheery glow from the house. The excited welcoming cries of Sally and Susann as they bounded down the steps for a hug were followed quickly by Laura, then Aunt Betsy and Uncle Will's glad greetings. All swept Noramary up in comforting warmth.

But there was more for Noramary to endure,

to accept with a bravado she could not feel. Over the clamor and chatter of her little cousins' welcome, Duncan's words to her aunt and uncle fell like stunning blows.

"I shall be staying at our town house while we're in Williamsburg," he was saying. "I have some pressing business to attend to while I'm here—lawyers to consult about some recent land acquisitions and . . . some other matters. My hours will be erratic. I felt it would be best to spare your household this inconvenience, Aunt Betsy."

This, then, was Duncan's solution to the problem of sharing a room with her! Noramary realized, with a sinking heart, that there would be no reconciliation during this festive holiday, after all.

Though she was not sure her aunt and uncle believed Duncan's explanation, they accepted it graciously. So, as Duncan had requested, Noramary played her role of a wife home for a visit, hiding her secret sorrow under a smile and a cheerful countenance.

On New Year's Eve, as was their custom, the entire Barnwell family attended the early evening church service. Sitting beside Duncan in the family pew, Noramary was overcome with sadness. In this church . . . at that very altar . . . they had pledged their hearts and lives "from this day forward" in the sight of God and the gathered company of friends and loved ones.

There had been a promise of love in Duncan's eyes then, Noramary remembered, where now there was veiled contempt, almost as if he could not bear the sight of her. He stood a breath away from her as they rose to sing the opening hymn, but he might as well have been a thousand miles distant.

Noramary tried to control the urge to weep by focusing on the beautifully decorated interior. This little church, so like the small stone chapel near Monksmoor Priory, meant so much to her. In that other time and place, Nanny Oates had taken her as a very little girl to morning services and vespers.

Upon arriving in Virginia, suddenly surrounded by everything unfamiliar, Noramary had found a sense of identification in the recognizable ritual, the scent of candles, the old songs. It was here, when all else was confusion and frightening, that Noramary had found that comfort and true peace "that passeth understanding."

As the service proceeded, Noramary realized how much she had missed going to church regularly since moving to the country. When she needed it most, she had been deprived of this kind of strengthening help.

The music seemed particularly melodious and inspiring, the sermon appropriate and thoughtful. Yet, because of her inner turmoil, Noramary felt bereft. Her mind wandered and all she could seem to relate to was one brave, sputtering candle among all the other steadily burning candles, struggling not to go out. *Like me,* she thought, her throat aching with unshed tears, *just trying to survive!*

Duncan said they must return to Montclair on New Year's Day, explaining to the Barnwells that duties awaited him at the plantation. But there would be one last event before they left—a New Year's Eve party at the Langley home.

Noramary had brought the crimson velvet dress she wore to the Camerons' Christmas party, and some of the old excitement returned as she dressed for the evening. She took great pains with her hair and, at Laura's suggestion, wore it piled high, with curls falling behind each ear.

When she fastened in the ruby earrings Duncan insisted she bring to Williamsburg, Laura gasped, "My goodness, Noramary! I never saw such jewels! They are magnificent!"

"The Montrose Bridal Set," she explained in a toneless voice. "It's traditional for Montrose wives to wear them on special occasions."

Laura touched the brooch with a tentative finger. "Diamonds and rubies . . . they must be priceless!"

Noramary gave a short, mirthless laugh. "Like the valiant wife?"

Laura looked blank.

Noramary shook a playful finger at her cousin. "Don't tell me you've forgotten all the Proverbs we had to memorize! Remember 31:10? 'Who shall find a valiant wife, for her price is above rubies'?"

"And so you are!" responded Laura loyally. "Duncan must know how fortunate he is. Well, they're gorgeous and will look perfect with your gown. Don't keep him waiting too much longer!" And blowing Noramary a kiss, she skipped gaily out of the room.

When Noramary came downstairs moments later she found Duncan, looking splendid in a royal-blue jacket, black breeches, white ruffles at throat and wrist, waiting for her. Uncle Will was also in the hall.

"How lovely you look, my dear!" declared her uncle. "Duncan should be the proudest gentleman in all of Williamsburg tonight, escorting such a beauty."

She darted a quick glance at Duncan, who made no comment at all, although his eyes swept her from the top of her head to the tips of her tiny, satin-shod feet.

A short coach ride later, they arrived at the Langleys' doorstep, where the sound of spritely music and lighthearted laughter floated out into the crisp December night air.

In the entry hall one of the scarlet-coated servants helped them off with their wraps. Noramary felt her heart lift as she and Laura, like two moths drawn to a flame, followed the flow of music to the doorway of the ballroom.

Tapping her foot to the lively lilt of the music, Noramary was intent on watching the musicians perform when suddenly Laura clutched her arm and said under her breath, "Why, there's *Robert Stedd!* I didn't know he and his uncle had returned. They've been in England and Scotland since last fall. Robert is to attend medical school in Edinburgh, I understand."

Noramary felt as if she had turned to stone. All the noise of merriment, the shimmering candle-light, the music and dancers all seemed to dissolve, leaving her alone with only the echo of her heart's wild beating.

Robert! The possibility of running into Robert here at the Langleys' party had not even occurred to her. She vaguely remembered Aunt Betsy's mentioning, in one of her letters, the fact that he and his uncle had gone to England. But since then, her own life and its unexpected complications had occupied her attention.

Suddenly Noramary was aware of Duncan standing directly behind her and, at the same time, of Robert catching sight of her as he turned to speak to a friend.

The orchestra started up again, this time for the Roger de Coverly, the riotous reel Virginia had adapted for itself from the more sedate English version of the dance.

"Would you do me the honor, ma'am?" she heard Duncan ask Aunt Betsy.

"With the greatest pleasure!" replied her aunt, who still liked to dance.

Noramary, frozen in uncertainty, saw Duncan lead her aunt onto the floor. Laura was quickly claimed by a partner, and Noramary found herself standing alone, riveted by Robert's intense gaze. And now he was making his way toward her.

He moved with the same easy grace she remembered, but in his stylish English-tailored clothes he had lost his boyish look. His expression was serious as he approached. No smile softened the gravity of his mouth. Only his eyes spoke volumes as he came closer. Then he was standing in front of her and, with a kind of ache that bruised Noramary's tender heart, she realized Robert looked older. But then she was older, too. It was a long time ago since last spring when they had both been very young.

Frantically Noramary's eyes moved around the room, seeking an escape. But before she could flee, Robert was speaking her name softly, fervently.

"Noramary . . . what unbelievable luck to find you here."

All the old emotions rushed up in Noramary. All the memories merged into a dizzying blur. All the happy times they had known together as beloved companions—sharing, laughing, teasing, confiding, dreaming, planning, the hidden notes, the secret meetings. It had all been so innocent, so carefree, so loving.

Feeling that many eyes must be observing this reunion, Noramary's breath came shallowly as she held out her hand to him. Robert took it, raised it to his lips.

"Robert, how well you look," Noramary murmured, knowing how inane the words must sound.

"And you, Noramary, are more beautiful than ever." Robert raised an eyebrow. That gesture left much unsaid, but his insinuation was clear to her.

"I would ask you to dance, but I'd rather talk. Could we find some quiet place . . . just for a few minutes?" he asked, his eyes never leaving her face.

She found his intensity disturbing. "I think it better if we converse here," she replied formally, although her heart was pounding.

The music, enhanced by the sound of the dancers' feet, suddenly seemed louder. His fingers still held her hand and she felt an increased pressure.

"Surely two old friends can slip away to find a peaceful corner to renew acquaintance. . . . I don't think anyone would find that unseemly," he persisted. Then, with more gravity, "Noramary, I must talk to you . . . alone. Is that too much to ask after all these months?"

"Robert, I am a married lady now. I cannot leave the dance with you. The gossips would have a field day!"

"In this merry crowd, filled with holiday cheer and punch as well? Come, Noramary, we'll dance this one minuet together, if that will satisfy your sudden penchant for propriety . . . then we'll find a convenient doorway and . . ."

Before Noramary could protest further, Robert took her hand and led her out onto the dance floor. The slow, measured precision of the minuet allowed for ample opportunity to look into her partner's eyes, and Noramary found it difficult to avoid his magnetic gaze. They followed the dance to its finale, when each couple in turn bent low to sweep through the arch formed by the clasped hands and uplifted arms of the other dancers. With a skillful maneuver, instead of escorting Noramary around to the other end of the line to form another link, Robert whisked her off the floor and out into the hallway.

Never relaxing his firm grip on her elbow, Robert rushed her down the corridor and into one of the small rooms opening off the center hall. As if in a dance step, he whirled her through the door and spun her around, then closed the door behind them.

The minute she heard its click behind them, Noramary knew the folly of Robert's ploy. Although in the society of the day, light flirtations were regarded with amusement, in her heart Noramary knew this was different. She and Robert had meant too much to each other to render meaningless any such meeting.

In a torrent of pent-up emotion, Robert burst forth: "Forgive me, Noramary! I had to do this. It was all I could do not to take you in my arms the minute I saw you!" She took a step backward, but he continued. "I've missed you beyond telling, Noramary. Did you ever think of me, knowing how much I loved you, how I was missing you all these months? I didn't realize how much until tonight, when I turned and saw you coming through the door."

"Robert . . . please! What if someone saw us

coming in here together? Can you imagine what a scandal . . ." She looked around the room for another exit. But there was only one door and Robert was leaning against it, barring the way. "Robert, how did you know I'd be here?"

"I *didn't* know, Noramary. I haven't had much stomach for social life . . . not since . . . not for some time. . . . And now that I've been back with Uncle, I've been helping him in his practice. I wouldn't have come tonight except for the Langleys. Please, relax. There's no harm in a quiet chat."

Noramary's agitation eased somewhat with Robert's calm reassurance, and she took a moment to catch her breath. *This must be the Langleys' music room,* she thought, noting the harp standing in one corner. Like the rest of the house, this room was decorated for the holidays, with wreaths at the windows, garlands and candles on the mantelpiece, and the traditional Christmas kissing-ball, which was a beribboned, clove-studded orange, hanging from the brass chandelier in the center of the ceiling.

Both she and Robert saw it at the same time. Noramary stepped away, blushing furiously. But Robert gave a low chuckle and moved toward her, grabbing both her hands before she could put them behind her back.

"Ah, Noramary, you didn't used to be so shy. It's only a holiday custom. Come, for old times' sake," he said, the old teasing quality in his voice melting her resolve a little. "It's little enough between two dear friends. 'Dare I not ask a kiss nor beg a smile'?" he quoted pensively.

And with a sharp tug of nostalgia, Noramary remembered how Robert had often read poetry to her. His eyes held such an irresistible plea, such pain, that she was overwhelmed by a longing to comfort him and experience for herself that old affection, that nonjudgmental, unconditional love only Robert had ever given her.

What harm could one kiss do? she thought, as she took a step toward him and lifted her face, intending to press her lips against his cheek, but Robert encircled her waist with his hands and drew her to him.

Suddenly the door burst open, followed by a peal of laughter. Noramary and Robert jumped, startled, and turned to see another young couple at the door, evidently seeking a little privacy themselves. Their shocked expressions at finding the room occupied might have provided a shared moment of hilarity had not Aunt Betsy and Duncan been passing in the hallway at that precise moment.

Turning to see what the commotion was all about, the two standing in the hallway saw Noramary and Robert in the incriminating embrace. To her horror, Noramary realized it must appear as though they had been surprised in a lover's rendezvous.

Aunt Betsy was the first to recover. Always the diplomat, she bustled forward as if nothing were amiss, and said, "Oh, there you are! I thought you two would be off somewhere reminiscing over old childhood mischief." She shook her finger at Robert. "You were always the naughty one, Robert, teasing Noramary and tricking her into leaving her chores so she could run off and play." She laughed merrily and, turning to Duncan, put her hand on his arm. "What a time I had with these two children, Duncan. And now here's Robert all grown up and almost a full-fledged doctor." She prattled on while the three other people in the little scenario stared at each other, speechless.

Then Aunt Betsy stopped her chatter and asked in all innocence, "But, Robert, I don't believe you've ever met Noramary's husband, have you, dear boy? And Duncan, this is the nephew of one of our oldest friends, Robert Stedd."

At the introduction a dark flush spread rapidly over Duncan's face, and a muscle tensed in his jaw.

"*Robert?*" he repeated. "Robert Stedd?" There was a steely quality in his voice as he repeated the name.

"Your servant, sir," Robert acknowledged, bowing slightly.

Noramary looked from one to the other as the two men evaluated each other icily. A tangible tension crackled between them. It was as if they recognized each other as adversaries—*rivals*. For under the veneer of polite exchanges seethed the truth that she belonged to Duncan in name; to Robert, by virtue of his steadfast love for her.

Finally Aunt Betsy broke the dreadful silence. Moving over to Robert, she slipped her hand through his arm. "Now, Robert, I do want to hear all about your plans to study in Scotland. Your uncle was just telling me and Will . . ." She steered him tactfully to the door, calling back over her shoulder to Noramary and Duncan, "Come along, you two. Supper will be served soon."

Duncan gave Noramary a stiff little bow and offered her his arm without a word.

Noramary moved distractedly through the remainder of the evening. All she could think was how the scene he had happened upon must have looked to Duncan. Surely now it would be futile to hope that he would ever understand the circumstances.

Outside, church bells began to chime the hour of midnight; inside, the wooden clackers, whistles, and horns given to the party guests began an ear-splitting cacophony, welcoming in the new year.

But Noramary's heart knew no joy. How could she join in the riotous celebration? For her, the year ahead held only the promise of bitterness and pain.

Chapter 18

New Year's Day dawned dreary and bleak. Noramary stared out the window of her bedroom at the Barnwell home, sipping her morning tea and reliving the events of the days just past. Parting with the Barnwells would be difficult enough, knowing the loneliness that awaited her at Montclair, but the long ride from Williamsburg with the grimly silent Duncan would be almost unbearable.

He had not spoken an unnecessary word to her since leaving the Langleys' party the night before, seeing her with Robert in what she felt sure he had mistaken as a romantic rendezvous.

Even more than that, a note that had been delivered to her that morning weighed heavily on Noramary's heart. Essie, the upstairs maid, had brought it to her with her breakfast tray.

"A little boy who b'long to Dr. Stedd brang this earlier, Miss Noramary. Say I was only to gib it to yo' when you wuz by yo'self."

Noramary recognized Robert's handwriting even before she tore open the envelope. The first few lines set her heart beating, flooded her face with color.

My darling Noramary,

What bittersweet joy to see you last night, and what sadness overcame me at so brief a meeting, and so soon a parting. Are you happy, my dearest? If only I knew that you were, *without any doubt*, without any uncertainty, then perhaps I could reconcile myself to having lost you. If that were a certain fact, I could then . . . somehow . . . go on with my life, assured that the one I care most for in this world was happy. Because I do not know if this is true, I have to live without that knowledge, and without you. The world indeed looks gray and without hope or cheer, and sometimes even without purpose. I will always hold you in my heart, since I cannot and never again will hold you to my heart. I pray you are happy, that God will bless you richly.

Forever . . . your most affectionate,

Robert

Noramary glanced out the window. The day was gray, heavy with snow clouds rolling across the wintry sky. A blustery wind whipped the branches of the bare trees, and Noramary shivered. Before she could sort her confused thoughts, a little tap at the door was followed immediately by Aunt Betsy's rosy face.

"Are you almost ready, dear? Duncan has arrived and is anxious to get under way before the weather worsens. Do you need any help with packing?"

Guiltily, Noramary wondered if her aunt could possibly read her mind. Rising, she tucked Robert's note surreptitiously in the jewel case lying open on the dressing table. Then she snapped the lid shut and turned quickly to answer her aunt's inquiry.

"No thank you, Aunt Betsy. And, yes, I'm nearly ready."

Her heart was pounding crazily. Could the expression on her face in any way betray her state of mind? Nothing much ever escaped her aunt's keen observation.

Noramary folded a chemise and placed it inside a small portmanteau she had been packing. Then she stood for a moment, distracted, trying to compose herself.

"I suggest you hurry, dear. Duncan is not a patient man," Aunt Betsy reminded her gently.

There seemed to be some special significance in that remark, Noramary thought, glancing at her aunt. And indeed there was, as Aunt Betsy's next words confirmed.

"My dear Noramary, it pains me to speak of this, but I feel I must. It was foolish and indiscreet of you and Robert to go off by yourselves as you did last night. I know neither of you considered the possible scandal such action might bring, but surely you remember your upbringing—the things your Uncle Will and I have tried to teach you. Christian ladies should not give even the slightest appearance of wrongdoing."

Noramary felt the sting of tears. To be so rebuked by her aunt cut her to the quick. There was no need to try to explain. She knew she stood accused of, if not deliberate flaunting of convention, certainly at the very least, irresponsible behavior. Such indiscretion was inexcusable, she knew.

There was another knock at the door. This time it had a peremptory sound and, when Aunt Betsy opened it, Duncan stepped into the room.

"We must leave at once, Noramary, if we are to avoid getting caught in a snowstorm," he said curtly. "Are you ready?"

Noramary quickly closed her portmanteau.

"You forget your jewel case," Aunt Betsy reminded her.

Remembering Robert's note hidden inside, Noramary's heart nearly stopped. She started to reopen the latches of her luggage when Duncan moved quickly to the dressing table and picked up the velvet box. "I'll take it."

Noramary felt as though she might faint. She knew Duncan kept the Montrose Bridal Set, along with other valuables, locked away in a strongbox in the library at Montclair. There was little chance he would open it before putting it away . . . but how could she retrieve Robert's letter? What if Duncan found it?

Sick with apprehension, there was nothing Noramary could do but watch helplessly as Duncan slipped the narrow case into the inside pocket of his coat.

"Ready?" he asked her, holding out her cape.

Noramary allowed him to place the jade green wool cape around her shoulders. With hands that shook she fastened the braid frogs, then reached for a beaver muff and slipped her suddenly clammy hands inside. Silently she passed through the door he held open for her, preceded by her aunt.

Feeling dizzy, Noramary endured the farewells at the bottom of the stairs, then, on Duncan's arm, went out to the waiting carriage.

On the long journey to Montclair, Noramary huddled in one corner, pretending to sleep. Her mind, however, was racing. Every once in a while she glanced over at Duncan, who was staring out the carriage window, lost in his own dark thoughts.

Besides the pressing problem of recovering Robert's note, how, she asked herself, was she to endure this loveless marriage, this cold indifference?

It was late when they finally reached Montclair, barely ahead of the first real winter storm, and Noramary awoke at dawn to a world blanketed in snowdrifts.

She had slept only fitfully and, during the night, startled into wakefulness by nightmares, had lain staring into the darkness. Her every thought, waking or sleeping, was of Duncan and what might happen if he opened the jewel case and found Robert's note.

Housebound by the blizzard for the next week, Noramary lived in an agony of fear, praying constantly for God's mercy—and for Duncan's.

At the beginning of the third week in January the snow began to melt, making the roads passable once more. With the moderating temperatures came a message from Jacqueline Cameron offering Noramary a change from her prison of doubt and fear. It was an invitation to visit Cameron Hall.

"It will be a ladies house party," wrote Jacqueline in her flowing script, "although husbands are welcome! The fashion dolls I ordered from Paris have arrived, and I thought you would enjoy seeing the latest Parisian styles."

For ladies in the Virginia colonies, the arrival of the so-called fashion dolls, actually small manikins dressed in the height of fashion, was always a high point of the year. From these tiny models wearing miniature clothing, they could view the latest in fashionable attire, cut patterns from them, and have them copied by skilled seamstresses. Noramary remembered how Aunt

Betsy had always anticipated the twice-yearly event in Williamsburg.

After receiving the invitation, Noramary's initial enthusiasm waned as she wondered what Duncan's reaction would be. Would he allow her to make such a visit? Would he allow her to go?

She gathered her courage and went to find him. He was in the library, sitting at his desk with a sheaf of papers in his hand. At her entrance Duncan looked up with a frown. Few words had passed between them since their return from the holidays. Noramary knew the incident with Robert Stedd had not been forgotten. This, compounded by whatever else had embittered him, made the wall between Noramary and Duncan even more impenetrable.

When she mentioned Jacqueline's invitation, his only reaction was to inquire when she would be leaving.

"Jacqueline says she will send her carriage for me tomorrow afternoon, if I can go. Her man, Len, is waiting in the servants' quarters to take my answer back to her."

"Then by all means, do as you wish," Duncan said indifferently.

"Thank you, Duncan," she said in a small voice. She stood there another minute, twisting her hands nervously while she pondered the advisability of making another request.

"Yes? Is there something more?" he asked in an annoyed tone of voice.

"Well . . . I was wondering, Duncan. Since

there will be a festive party . . . might I wear the Bridal Set?" Noramary's heart was beating wildly. What if he had already checked the jewels and found Robert's note among them?

Duncan said nothing at first. Then, he pushed back his chair, stood, and went to the locked cabinet where he kept the strongbox.

Breathlessly Noramary watched as he unlocked it and withdrew the rectangular case. Her mouth went dry in terror.

Please, Lord, don't let him open it!

Duncan stood for what seemed an endless moment, simply holding the case thoughtfully. Then, without a word, he turned and handed it to her.

Noramary's legs managed to propel her through the door and out into the hallway without giving way. But once she was safe in the haven of her bedroom, she fell to her knees beside the bed, unable to stem the torrent of tears. She opened the case with trembling hands. To her immense relief Robert's letter lay, undisturbed, on the top.

Noramary got up from her knees and, taking the letter, she hid it carefully under her lingerie in one of the dresser drawers. When she was calmer, when she could think exactly what to say, she would answer the letter, she told herself weakly.

Recalling the scene as she rode to Cameron Hall the next day, Noramary thought ruefully that it might have been better if Duncan had refused her request. At least that would have shown his interest in whether she came or went. Even that small knowledge would have been some consolation.

Noramary pressed her fingers to her throbbing temples. Her constant tension brought on nagging headaches.

If it had not been for her desperate need to escape the oppressive atmosphere at Montclair, she might not have made the effort to go. Lately Noramary had experienced some troubling physical disturbances to add to her emotional distress.

Just this morning she had awakened with the dull headache and a general feeling of malaise. Only the prospect of Jacqueline's delightful company had prodded her into overcoming her lethargy and following through on her plans.

There was no sign of Duncan upon her departure. It was not surprising. He had taken to riding out to the fields very early in the morning, not returning until late. Some days, when he was surveying a distant part of the plantation, she knew he stayed over at the cottage at night instead of returning to Montclair. But his not giving her the courtesy of seeing her off on a week's absence was yet another wound to be concealed beneath a bright smile when she arrived at Cameron Hall.

By the time her carriage drew up to the door, she had assumed her usual cheerful outlook, and no one, not even Jacqueline, who knew her well, would have suspected the pain she harbored in her heart.

Noramary was greeted with great warmth by her hostess and introduced to the three other houseguests, ladies from neighboring plantations, all of whom she had met at the Christmas party. Each of them, liberated from the stultifying isolation of the long winter and icy roads that had kept them from the company of congenial friends, was eager to enjoy the pleasant interlude, and the mood was soon one of frivolous gaiety.

The next two days at Cameron Hall were a delightful blend. The mornings were spent in examining the fashion dolls, making sketches of the various costumes, consulting each other about patterns, fabrics, and adaptions of the styles. After the midday meal, they retired for a long afternoon nap.

But it was the evenings, when they gathered in the drawing room for more conversation or music, that Noramary found most enjoyable. Here, amid friends and a relaxed atmosphere of cheerful repartee and laughter, Noramary thrived. Here, she did not have to watch her every word, fearful of saying or doing something that would bring a frown to Duncan's brow or a cool stare. For Noramary, it was a time of pleasant diversion— feeling amused and amusing and, above all, accepted. More than anything, she felt herself again after the dreary winter in Duncan's reluctant company.

On the last evening of her visit, Jacqueline came into the guestroom where Noramary was dressing for dinner.

"Ah, *cherie,* it has been such a pleasure to have you here these past days, but I have not had a moment for private conversation. I thought you looked a bit pale and peaked when you arrived, and the thought crossed my mind that perhaps . . . ? *Mais non,* I'm sure it is only my imagination, for you seem rosy and radiant now. You have enjoyed yourself here, *n'est-ce pas?*"

"Oh, it's been wonderful, Jacqueline. I've had such a good time, I hate to . . ." Noramary checked her impulsive words before she admitted that she dreaded going home.

Jacqueline did not seem to notice, but continued smoothly, "But then, the handsome Duncan must be pining away for the return of his bride, *oui?*" Without waiting for a reply, she went on: "I shall never forget how excited Duncan was after you became engaged. How anxious he was that the house would be in perfect condition for your arrival, everything finished for you!

"You are a very lucky girl, Noramary, to catch such a man! You know half the mamas in the county were hoping to have him for a son-in-law!" Jacqueline laughed at Noramary's puzzled expression. "You didn't know that? Well, let me tell you. I can't count how many friends tried to select just the right bride for Duncan. All the daughters, nieces, sisters who have been trotted out for his approval! Ah, la! But let me tell you a secret—I never saw him so happy as when he rode over to tell us there had been a change of plans, that instead of the Barnwell girl, he was marrying her cousin. The look on his face, *cherie!* Oh, it was good to see! Duncan is a wonderful man . . . and I have seen many, but none better than he!"

Suddenly Noramary felt hot and sick and dizzy. Blood rushed into her face, then drained from her head as waves of nausea swept over her. Jacqueline's face became a blur and the whole room tilted crazily. She tried to stand, but a smothering black mask came down upon her, choking off the air, and she slipped to the floor in a faint.

The next thing Noramary knew was the stringent aroma of smelling salts, the pressure of a cool cloth against the back of her neck, the support of gentle hands. As she regained complete consciousness, she saw that she was lying on the chaise lounge, with Jacqueline's anxious face hovering above her. Nearby stood a black maid, holding a cup of steaming, fragrant tea.

"What happened?" Noramary asked weakly.

Jacqueline's worried pucker changed to a teasing smile. "But why didn't you tell us this happy news? Or were you keeping it a secret for a while? Do not worry, *cher* Noramary, soon you will feel better, you'll see. It is the first few weeks that are sometimes trying."

Noramary stared blankly at her hostess for a moment, bewildered. Then slowly, understanding came, followed immediately by dismay.

"Oh, no!" she covered her mouth with one

hand. "I *can't* be! What will Duncan say?"

"What! Haven't you told him?" Jacqueline demanded in amazement. "But what *should* he say? Duncan will be beside himself with joy, of course! Oh, yes!" she hastened on over Noramary's protest. "He adores you, and now even more, since you will bring him an heir to his vast lands and to his name!"

"But you don't understand!" Noramary shook her head forlornly, slow tears rolling unchecked down her cheeks.

"What is to understand? Duncan will be so happy at this news. Did you not see his reaction when my husband toasted him at the Christmas party? There is nothing Duncan wants more than many fine sons to follow him at Montclair."

Noramary continued shaking her head. But she knew she could not confide in Jacqueline what she did not know herself. Perhaps Duncan had once been happy to have her as his bride. Perhaps even once he had loved her. But now everything was different, everything was changed.

"You'll see, Noramary. What I'm saying is true. I only wish I could see Duncan's face when he hears his good fortune."

As she rode back to Montclair from Cameron Hall the next day, Noramary felt the news she carried to Duncan was more a burden than a blessing. She dreaded the moment when she would know his reaction, for of course he must be told.

It was Ellen rather than Duncan who greeted

Noramary upon her return. The delay only fueled her apprehension. Perhaps it was for the best, she reassured herself. In the morning she would be more rested, better able to confront Duncan's anger or disdain, whichever it might be.

Still, as the hours passed, Noramary grew more and more distracted. When the strange weakness and nausea assailed her again, she went to lie down, telling Delva to tell her the minute Duncan came home.

She must have drifted off, for her bedroom was shadowed when she heard the dogs barking, always a signal of Duncan's homecoming, then the sound of his boots on the polished floor outside her room.

The door opened and he stepped inside.

"You wanted to see me?" he demanded. Approaching the bed, he frowned. "Your maid tells me you're feeling unwell. What is it?"

Noramary struggled to sit up. "Oh, it's nothing . . . really," she murmured hesitantly.

"It must be *something* . . . otherwise you wouldn't have asked to see me." His voice was stern. "Perhaps it is simply an attack of melancholy after your visit to Cameron Hall. Perhaps coming back to Montclair is the cause of your malaise. It is sad, but true, that life at Montclair can hardly rival that of either Williamsburg or Cameron Hall."

"Oh, no Duncan . . . it isn't that. Indeed, under the circumstances . . . my coming back to Montclair should be a time of *rejoicing.*" Noramary forced herself to ignore his irony and to speak steadily and cheerfully. It was, she felt, a chance to right all the wrong between them, to end forever this state of bitter misunderstanding.

He turned to stare at her, bewilderment, doubt, and uncertainty mingled in his expression.

Noramary took a deep breath and proceeded, "Duncan, we are to have a child."

The sudden silence that fell over the room was devastating in its totality.

Then Duncan spoke and his voice was edged with steel. "Correction, my dear!" Here he paused significantly. "*If* your condition is as you imply, it is *you* who are to have a child . . . not *we*. What kind of a fool do you and your close, loving, and oh-so-clever family take me for? First, they offer—as a 'substitute' to one flighty daughter—her more beautiful, brighter, more amiable, more charming cousin, as if she were some prize that I, the rejected suitor, should feel fortunate to win. Never a word that it would be convenient—nay, helpful, in fact—to get this lovely young woman off their hands before she did something indiscreet. . . . Or perhaps they were aware of other indiscretions that might have led to a less . . . shall we say . . . suitable marriage! At any rate, I admit I was taken in by this cleverly arranged substitution. More than that, I fell under the spell of this charming 'substitute bride.' Ah, yes, her demure, unassuming manner did quite beguile, and I fell prey to every well-planned move until—" He halted abruptly.

"So, Noramary, you find yourself with child.

So be it. We are married. You bear my name. I should not disgrace either of us by disclaiming the child that you are carrying. But never . . ." and his voice deepened in cold intensity, "*never* insult me by insisting it is *mine*."

His words fell upon her like stinging blows.

"Duncan, you are wrong!" Noramary burst out. "Why can't you believe me? I have not . . . there has never been . . ."

"Don't add to your shame with more lies. I have eyes! I saw you and Robert Stedd in Williamsburg. There was no mistaking the relationship between you. Nor did it escape my notice that you took the first opportunity to be alone with him, regardless of how it might look. . . . Please, spare me any more . . . spare us *both* more of these distressing scenes."

With that he spun on his heel and stalked out of the room, leaving Noramary quivering under the lash of his words.

Chapter 19

The first of March was bitterly cold, ushering in a series of storms, each one worse than the one before. Rain, sleet, and sudden snows followed one another in rapid succession.

Noramary, morning-sick as well as heart-sick, felt imprisoned and isolated. Duncan's unrelenting attitude numbed every emotion except the anguish of his constant rejection, the reason for which still remained a mystery to her.

What bothered her most was that there was no

joy in the coming baby. The child of their supreme moment of love had found no welcome in the home he would inherit, none in his father's heart.

Because of the depressing sameness of her days, Noramary was tempted to daydreams of Williamsburg, of Robert, of what might have been. She prayed to be rid of them, for she knew they only added to her unhappiness and did nothing to give her hope of an eventual reconciliation with Duncan.

Seated at her escritoire at the window of the master bedroom one morning, Noramary tried once again to answer Robert's letter. She had taken it from its hiding place that morning and reread it through tear-blurred eyes. Poignant memories of all their happy times together now seemed so long ago. Another lifetime!

She took out stationery, dipped her quill into the inkwell, and with pen poised to write, searched her mind for the words.

How could she answer truthfully Robert's question? Was she really happy? Anything she might say could give him false hope. To allow Robert to harbor hope was wrong. To let him linger in regret of what might have been was destructive. To prolong his yearning for her love was cruel. As long as he kept thoughts of her burning in his heart, he put his own soul in jeopardy. Didn't the Commandments themselves prohibit such thoughts? "Thou shalt not covet thy neighbor's wife." It was clear enough there. Even clearer in the New Testament. There was no other way than to write gently, firmly, and finally to

Robert, telling him he must forget her once and for all.

Determinedly she started to write, but each time she tried, the words sounded so stilted, so false, she scratched them out, crumpled up the paper, and started again. On about the fourth try she happened to look up from her desk and see Duncan ride by on his dapple gray horse.

With a heart sore with longing she watched them pass. The graceful beauty of the animal matched the proud bearing and set of the head of the rider. A powerful yearning wrenched Noramary, a desperate longing that the terrible misunderstanding could be solved, that they could know once more that soaring rapture. But it had been as brief as a candle flame, she thought sadly, and as quickly extinguished.

For a few minutes Noramary stared out the window. Although the severe winter storms had passed, the landscape was bleak. The rim of the mountains seemed like grim prison walls, locking her within this unhappy place.

As she looked a pale sun struggled through the pewter-colored clouds, and although a blustery wind was bending the bare tree branches, Noramary felt a sudden urge to go outside, get out of the house, out into the fresh air. A walk would do her good after the weeks she had been confined by the inclement weather.

She flung her cape around her shoulders, paused briefly to tell one of the servants she was leaving, and went outside. The wind whipped the folds of her cape like billowing sails, but the sharp bite of the wind felt invigorating.

Patches of snow still clung to the brown meadow, and icy drifts were piled under the low-hanging branches of the evergreens along the path to the woods. Noramary took long breaths and drew the crisp, exhilarating air deep into her lungs.

She walked along briskly, more conscious of her troubled thoughts than of the direction she was taking. When she found herself at the rustic bridge that curved over the creek that cut through the meadow, she stopped and paused to catch her breath. Inevitably she was reminded of that stormy night when this bridge had been washed away, forcing her to remain with Duncan in the little cottage overnight. That night when they had made those first, tentative moves toward understanding each other, getting to know each other. Everything had seemed possible then. Even learning to love each other.

The memory was bittersweet. Noramary stared hypnotically into the crystal clear water rushing over the stones, wishing she could somehow turn back the clock. Almost unconsciously, she continued on the path toward the cottage, as if following some inner leading. Soon she was on the little rise just above the hollow where the cottage nestled into the protective shelter of the trees. The next thing she knew, she was standing in front of the door. Moving as if in a dream long-remembered, or by the deep longing in her heart, she put her hand on the latch and lifted it. The door opened easily to her touch, and Noramary walked inside.

She went over to the fireplace, remembering

the festive supper she and Duncan had shared in front of it. At least it had seemed so. She thought sadly of the strained dinners they now took together in the vast dining room at Montclair— each seated far apart at either end of the long table, with only a few words spoken in the presence of the servants waiting on them.

Ironically, she recalled how they had happily quoted the psalmist over their meager supper that night. "Better a dry morsel with joy than a feast where strife dwells."

Noramary wandered about the little house, noticing the tasteful furnishings. Just as Cameron Hall bore the indelible stamp of its mistress's colorful personality, so this place where Duncan had lived for several years reflected his quiet dignity.

On the night of the storm, she had remained in the front room near the blazing warmth of the fireplace. The next morning she had gone into the bedroom only long enough to make a brief toilette. Now she moved through each room taking note of everything. It was a miniature of the great mansion down to the most minute detail. Everything was of the finest quality, the most precise craftsmanship. Duncan demanded perfection in everything.

There was also evidence of the more recent times when he had chosen to remain here rather than ride back to Montclair, the house where love had ceased to be, Noramary thought sorrowfully. A heavy, woolen outer jacket was hung carefully over a chair, a linen shirt discarded, a scarf flung onto the wooden settle.

Noramary stepped over to the door leading into the bedroom and pushed it open. As she might have expected of a man of Duncan's meticulous habits, the bedcovers were smooth, the quilt folded at the bottom of the four-poster bed. She was starting to leave when something caught her eye. Hanging over his graceful English desk in one corner of the room was her silhouette—the one cut by the artist at the Camerons' Christmas party!

Noramary went over for a closer look. There could be no mistake. It was the duplicate of the one she had given Aunt Betsy. But it was Jacqueline who had asked for the copy. Had she given it to Duncan? Or, and something like hope leaped in Noramary's heart, had Duncan asked for it?

If Duncan had come to despise her as much as it seemed, why would he want an image of her where he could see it often? It was a tantalizing question, one for which Noramary had no answer.

She sat down on the chair at the desk, staring at her silhouette, trying to make sense of this puzzling discovery.

How long she remained there, lost in thought, she never knew. But suddenly the rattle of rain against the window startled Noramary. Looking up, she noticed that the day had darkened considerably. She had come a long way from the main house. She must start back right away.

The wind had come up and she heard it keening down through the chimneys of the empty fireplaces and around the eaves. She stepped outside onto the porch. In the midst of these dense woods, it appeared as if evening had already descended. She pulled up the hood of her cape, drew its strings, and tied them under her chin. The rain was spasmodic as she started out, but the wind was fierce and she bent her head against it and began to walk faster.

It seemed that she walked for some time at a brisk pace when her legs began to tire. She stopped, arching her back and pressing with her fingers to relieve the ache. Looking around, she frowned. She should have come to the clearing that led into the meadow above Montclair by now, but she was still in thick woods.

Had she turned the wrong way when she left the cottage? Perhaps she had missed the path. She paused for a few minutes, trying to remember how she had come. Maybe it had been from the other direction. So she reversed her course. But this did not lead her to the opening she had hoped to find, either.

Feeling her legs quivering with exertion, she leaned against a tree to rest. By now the rain was threading through the trees, increasing steadily, so that soon the ground was soaked. In spite of her warm cape, Noramary, too, was drenched.

No matter, she would simply have to plow on. This must be the way back to Montclair, she told herself, stumbling forward again.

She couldn't have gone so far that it would be impossible to find her way back, she encouraged herself, though she had heard of people who traveled in circles through the wilderness, became lost, gave up in despair, and were eventually discovered only a few yards from their destination.

The rain turned to icy needles of sleet. Noramary ducked her head and forced herself on. Her thin slippers were already wet, and she was almost blinded by the freezing rain slicing in front of her and upon her, the wind slashing against her.

She bit her lip, trying not to cry out in fear and panic. Her feet slipped and slid on the now sodden ground. Once or twice she fell to her knees. She staggered up—her skirts, now heavy from the rain and mud, slowing her progress. The sleet had turned to snow. Driven by the mounting wind, the flakes struck her face in rapier-sharp particles. She stumbled on, stopping only to draw a ragged breath and rest, her hands clinging to the rough bark of the pine trees, fighting fatigue and a growing desperation.

It was then that she saw a light swinging in an arc, as though from a lantern. Breathless with hope, she watched as it grew brighter, stronger.

Then through the dark and the cold, she heard a familiar voice, rough with anxiety, calling . . . calling her name, hoarsely, over and over. . . .

"Noramary! Noramary . . . answer me!"

The light was a blinding square now directly in front of her. She held up one hand weakly and answered with utmost effort, "Here I am! Oh, Duncan, thank God!" before she felt her knees give way and she sank to the ground.

The next thing she knew, she was swung up in strong arms, the hood of her cape falling back, her wet hair streaming into her face.

She did not remember much about the jolting horseback ride in front of Duncan's saddle, his arms holding her tightly as he spurred his horse forward through the sheet of whirling snow.

She recalled being carried into the house, the circle of fearful dark faces around her, hearing Duncan's voice say harshly, "Ellen, get her out of these wet clothes and into a warm bed as fast as possible. She's soaked to the skin and already shaking with fever."

She roused herself enough to try to control her shivering and whisper guiltily, knowing she must have caused great concern and trouble by her absence in the storm, "I'm sorry. . . ."

"Never mind that, dearie." That was Ellen's voice with its soft Scottish burr. "We'll have you warm and cozy soon so's you won't catch your death of cold."

Noramary opened her large eyes, now unnaturally bright, and murmured, "It's nothing really . . . a slight chill."

Ellen gently helped her undress, while a frightened Delva was busily running the warming pan between the sheets. Two other maids heated bricks in the fireplace, then wrapped them in thicknesses of flannel to place at her feet. Noramary alternately shivered and felt fiery hot, but protested that she would be fine in the morning. Soothingly, Ellen guided her over to the bed and, as tenderly as if she were a child, half lifted her aching body into bed.

Outside, the storm continued to rage, but no more so than did the fever in Noramary, who tossed and turned with troubled dreams. It was the same one she had had over and over in the past few months. She always seemed to be running, as if searching desperately for something or someone. There seemed to be a river rushing wildly between her and the object of her search. A mysterious figure stood on the other side, just out of reach, beyond the sound of her voice as she called his name. He never looked in her direction, and she would awake, sobbing and breathless.

Time after time, when she woke choking and hoarsely calling that name, Ellen was there. It was the same throughout the night—the fitful sleep, the dream, waking to Ellen's ministrations, then falling again into troubled sleep. Never once did she see the tall, shadowy figure standing just outside the half-open bedroom door.

The next few days were a blur to Noramary and were followed by weeks of slow recovery. She slipped in and out of consciousness as her fever mounted, aware only of the muted sound of movement around her; of hushed, yet urgent voices; of hands, blessedly cool on her burning skin; of a headache pounding so persistently that she could not think.

Then there was the night she awoke to an agonizing stab of blinding pain like the thrust of a sharp knife. She remembered crying out as a rushing shudder shook her frail body, and then she sank into oblivion. The pain was the last thing she remembered. It was days before Noramary was conscious of anything else.

Much later, she learned from Ellen the other part of the story: Of how, when she had not returned by dark, the frightened servants and a weeping Delva had gone to Ellen, who had sought Duncan in the plantation office. Hearing that their mistress had gone out early in the afternoon for a walk and had not yet returned, he had jumped to his feet.

"You are sure she didn't take her horse or get the small carriage from the stable, perhaps to ride over to Cameron Hall?" he demanded of the cluster of houseservants and Ellen standing in a frozen line, awaiting the master's decision. They all shook their heads. "In that case, send word to the stables to saddle my horse, and get two of the men mounted to go with me. We must find her before it gets any darker or colder."

Noramary opened her eyes and turned her head slowly on the pillow to gaze out the window. Outside, the sky was blue and, on the branches of the trees, fragile green leaves shimmered in the sunlight. Somehow spring had come at last, she thought in surprise.

Vaguely she wondered what day it was, for she seemed to have lost all track of time. She tried to raise her head but felt rather lightheaded and weak. Tentatively she moved, and in an instant Ellen's kind, worried face bent over her.

"You're awake, dearie. I'll get you some broth. The doctor said you must try to eat something soon. You've dwindled away to a mere nothing, you have."

"Ellen, what happened? I know I must have

been ill, but I don't remember. . . ." Noramary's voice was faint.

For a moment Ellen's blue eyes misted with bright tears. "You've been *very* ill, dearie. We were that afraid that you might slip away altogether. But the Lord was good. Except, dearie . . ." Ellen's hand covered Noramary's small, thin one with a sympathetic gesture. "You've lost the bairn. . . . The doctor said it was the high fever . . . it could not be helped. But you're not to be sad, dearie," Ellen continued briskly, plumping the pillows behind Noramary's head. "You weren't that far along, and he says there's plenty of time for babies!"

Part IV

Hope deferred makes the heart sick,
but when the desire comes, it is the tree of life.

PROVERBS 13:12

Chapter 20

Aunt Betsy, accompanied by Laura, arrived at Montclair in response to Duncan's urgent summons. She was shocked at the drastic change in Noramary's appearance. Her vibrant, glowing look was gone. Her skin, pale, almost transparent. Her slender body, wasted.

Within hours of her arrival, Aunt Betsy had come to the decision that Noramary must return with her to Williamsburg to be nursed back to health.

"I must say, Duncan, I am gravely concerned. To be very blunt, I fear for her life."

Duncan paled. "But the doctor has assured me Noramary is out of danger. . . ."

"That may be. However, the girl has suffered not only physically, but the other effects of losing her child may not yet be known. Unless we do something right away, Noramary might still slip away from us."

"Then, madam, I can only agree to whatever would be best for her," Duncan agreed.

"Right now she needs the bright company of her cousins and the activities of our busy household to distract her from her sorrow over the baby," Aunt Betsy continued firmly. "Noramary is much too young to bear the natural depression she feels in this solitude. It will do her a world of good. Mark my words, we must all help her to get well, and we must begin now."

The decision was made and, while it was met with some reluctance and not a little resentment by Ellen, who had nursed Noramary so faithfully, she relented when Duncan convinced her it was all for her beloved charge's good. Even Ellen could see that Noramary was getting no better, in fact, seemed to be losing ground each day.

Ellen helped bundle Noramary warmly into the carriage and, amid the flurry, the strangely formal farewell between husband and wife went unnoticed.

As they started down the drive from Montclair, Noramary turned and looked back through the oval window, and her heart was suddenly wrenched at the sight of the tall man standing on the porch. His shoulders were slumped in an uncharacteristic posture of dejection and defeat, and she thought of what Ellen had told her.

"He never left your bedside, ma'am, not for all those days you were sick. When I had to go take some slight repast or for some other necessity, or when he insisted I have a short nap, he would stay right there until I returned. Tender as a woman, he was! When you were out of your head, tossing and turning and calling out, he would soothe your head with cool cloths. He never seemed to tire. And when you lost the baby . . . why, I never saw a man so grieved!"

Grieved? Duncan, over a child he did not believe was his? Noramary could only shake her head in bewilderment.

For Noramary, the next few weeks passed in a peaceful montage of long, leisurely, sun-splashed days. She slipped back into the framework of life in the Barnwell house as easily as if she had never left, and the longer she stayed, the less real seemed her life at Montclair.

Spring had come to Williamsburg in a burst of delicate color of blossoming fruit trees and flowering bushes. The gardens of the town behind the neat boxwood hedges were rainbows of bright blooms. Noramary enjoyed sitting in the sunshine of the pleasant walled garden behind the Barnwells' home, in the lounge chair that had been placed there for her.

When she was relaxing there one day while Aunt Betsy filled her basket with mint leaves, Noramary sniffed the spicy fragrance appreciatively.

"You should plant an herb garden at Montclair, Noramary," Aunt Betsy remarked.

"Yes, I suppose I should," Noramary agreed passively.

Unknown to Aunt Betsy, her words pierced Noramary's heart. With aching remembrance, she thought of that night at Montclair when she and Duncan had sat together at the window of their room, and he had asked her, "What can I do to make you happy?"

"But you have already made me happy, Duncan."

"I want to do something special for you! Isn't there something you would like to have?"

"Well," she had replied thoughtfully, "I would really like to have a garden."

"You shall have it, my darling!" he had declared emphatically, kissing her tenderly.

But there had been no garden. After that night there had only been a wasteland at Montclair.

Then one day the quiet stream of days was broken by two unexpected events.

Noramary was alone in the house one afternoon while Aunt Betsy and Laura were shopping. The little girls were in school; Uncle William, at his business office.

She had just come in from the garden and settled herself in the small parlor with some knitting when she had the sudden impression she was no longer alone. A shivery tremor tingled down her spine so positive was she that someone's gaze was upon her.

Lifting her head slowly, her eyes widened upon the figure standing in the doorway.

"Robert!" She dropped her knitting and gasped his name.

He came into the room and stood there gazing at her with a look of such longing that it touched the very depths of her heart. The bond of years embraced her in warmth, and she held out both hands in greeting. Remembering the carefree happiness they had known together, all her desolate loneliness faded, the weary emptiness of the past months fled.

For a few minutes her hands remained in his, and there were no words for all that was in each heart to say. Then Noramary, realizing the danger of this innocent meeting and what was in both their minds—the close companionship growing into innocent romance, the summer kisses, the impulsive promises—gently withdrew her hands. She needed to remind Robert—and herself—that everything was different now, everything changed.

"Sit down, Robert. I was about to have my tea and you must join me." Her voice trembled slightly.

"There's no need for that." He dismissed her suggestion with a gesture. "I came only because I heard you had been very ill, and I wanted to see for myself that you were all right."

Noramary reseated herself, picking up her

knitting again. Perhaps the activity would still the shaking of her hands.

Robert stood by the fireplace, looking down at her. She felt uncomfortable under his close scrutiny, for one did not have to be a physician to see the changes wrought by her illness. Yet it was the more subtle changes carved into her face by her unhappiness that Robert noted. Her delicate-boned slenderness now verged on thinness, the rosy-cheeked roundness of her face had been replaced by a pale oval, the eyes that had once danced with mischief and fun were smoky blue pools of haunting sadness. Noramary knew he had not missed any detail.

She cast about for some topic to relieve the heavy silence that hung between them, but it was Robert who spoke first.

"I have been talking with your uncle, Noramary. He is writing some letters of introduction for me. I am leaving shortly to go to Scotland, where I will study for a year with a friend of my uncle's—a surgeon with an excellent reputation. He has been developing some new methods of surgery that I hope to learn so that when I come back . . ." His voice trailed away.

Noramary glanced up from her knitting to catch the look of grief in his eyes. She spoke quickly to mask the awful silence that was descending once more. "That sounds very interesting, Robert. I'm sure your studies will be most fascinating and . . ."

But Robert interrupted. "Oh, Noramary, surely

we can talk of other things than my medical studies. There is so much I want to say, so much I need to know, so many unanswered questions. ."

"They are better neither asked nor answered, Robert," she said softly.

"Why cannot there be truth between us, Noramary?" Robert asked. "I realize you could not respond to the note I wrote you at Christmastime, but it would still mean so much to me to know . . . to be *sure* . . . that you are happy."

Noramary looked directly into Robert's earnest eyes, remembering with regret the day she had tried to write to him, the half-written letters she had left on her escrittoire just before leaving for that ill-fated walk in the woods. She had gone to the cottage that day, had found her silhouette over Duncan's desk. Then the storm had come and . . .

"Well, Noramary, are you? Have you been happy these months?" Robert's voice broke in upon her reverie.

She looked over at him. He was bending forward, his hands clasped on his knees, the clear, truth-seeking eyes searching her face.

Just then the door opened and Thomas, the Barnwells' butler, entered, bearing a silver tray. It took a few minutes for him to set it down and bring the serving table over in front of Noramary. She willed her hand not to shake as she lifted the heavy silver teapot to pour the steaming tea into delicate cups. They were both silent until Thomas left the room, leaving the door discreetly open as befitted the situation of a married lady entertaining a gentleman.

But still Robert's question begged an answer.

Noramary's thoughts were in turmoil. She knew Robert deserved an answer. Yet how could she give him an answer that would satisfy him, yet remain loyal to her wifely vows to Duncan? To reveal the secret she had borne so long alone now seemed a betrayal.

In spite of everything that had happened, Noramary still believed her marriage vows were sacred. She recalled the words the minister had read from the book of Hosea on their wedding day.

> I will betroth thee unto me *forever*,
> Yes, I will betroth thee to me
> In righteousness and justice
> In lovingkindness and mercy.
> I will betroth thee to me in *faithfulness*.

The words themselves, echoing in her mind, brought instant understanding of what she must do. Much as she loved Robert, would always love him, he was part of her past, her childhood, the other life she had put behind. That is where he belonged—in her past. She had to help him put *her* in *his* past, too. What they had once had together would never really end. It would be a lovely memory always. To try to make anything now of these chance meetings would only spoil those memories. He must understand that they both had to go on to other lives, other loves. Only if she freed him could Robert do that.

So when Noramary answered Robert, she spoke very gently but very positively. "Yes, Robert, I am happy." And by that affirmation she believed she was willing that happiness into existence.

With God's help I will find a way to be happy, she resolved, *and if not happy, then content.*

"Then I, too, am happy, Noramary," Robert said solemnly. He tried to smile. "I suppose there is nothing more to be said. I shall take my leave."

Noramary rose from her chair and, with a rustle of skirts, came around the tea table, holding out her hand to him. As she did so, her wide skirt brushed the knitting basket by her side, toppling it and spilling the contents onto the floor. A ball of yarn rolled toward Robert, stopping somewhere midway between them.

At the same time both Robert and Noramary moved to retrieve it, bending down simultaneously. Robert was quicker and collected the yarn ball, placing it in her cupped hand. Their fingers touched and, for a moment, all the old memories flowed back. Suspended in nostalgia, they stood looking into each other's eyes.

At that very moment a tall figure stepped into the doorway, blocking it and casting a long shadow into the sunny parlor. Startled, Noramary and Robert turned to see Duncan standing there, regarding them coldly.

"Duncan! What are you doing here? I didn't expect you!" exclaimed Noramary, flushing. Even as she spoke, she realized how the scene he had come upon could easily be misread and that her words had only served to confirm his suspicions.

"Obviously not," Duncan replied icily. "I've come to take you home." Turning to Robert, he made a stiff little bow. "My apologies, Mr. Stedd, if I have interrupted another reunion of old friends." He paused to let the reference to New Year's Eve take effect. Then, addressing himself directly to Noramary, he said, "My arrival is untimely, I see. It was not planned, but prompted by a surprise visitor at Montclair. In the press of all the events of the winter, I'm afraid we failed to remember the portrait we commissioned Cecil Brandon to paint when he was at the Camerons' last fall. He is at Montclair at this moment, waiting to begin. So we must leave for home at once. The Camerons have graciously consented to entertain him until our return. This will explain why I had no opportunity to warn you of my coming."

Noramary tried to ignore the emphasis he put on the word *warn.*

"Of course. I will get ready right away," she murmured.

Over Aunt Betsy's protests, they left for Montclair the next day—Noramary, comfortably cushioned with afghans and pillows in the carriage, Duncan riding his horse alongside. Noramary was grateful for that. At least they would not have to endure the long ride in the chill atmosphere of Duncan's displeasure and suspicion.

The countryside she had left still locked in the

bleakness of winter had erupted into glorious springtime color, Noramary discovered. Upon her return, the woods around Montclair were a fairyland of pink and white dogwood blossoms. Even so, the old familiar feeling of dread swept over her as the carriage rolled into the drive. She felt almost like an escaped prisoner who had been captured and returned to gaol.

After a night's rest, Noramary sent word to Cecil Brandon at Cameron Hall that she would be ready to sit for him the following day.

Ellen laid out the crimson velvet gown for the sitting. As she helped Noramary with the buttons, she clucked in dismay. "Oh my, madam! This will have to be pinned to fit properly—you've wasted so! We must get some flesh on your bones. Some hearty Scotch porridge should do it!" she declared emphatically.

Brandon had dispatched a note to Noramary with directions for her to wear her hair very simply, adding with his flourishing hand: "Anything else would be gilding the lily." She put the finishing touches to the classic style he had requested, put in the ruby earrings, and clasped the pendant on its chain around her neck. Without preamble, Duncan had simply sent in the case containing the Bridal Set.

Delva came to announce that Mr. Brandon had come and was setting up his easel in the drawing-room corner that he had chosen because of its light.

Ellen beamed at her mistress. "Oh, madam,

you look truly lovely. A picture, indeed!"

"Thank you, Ellen," Noramary said, smiling at her loyal housekeeper. "I don't fancy this whole thing much, I confess, but if it gives Duncan pleasure . . ."

"But, madam, you are the first bride to live in this house. He wants your portrait to hang in the front hall, like in the grand manor houses of England and Scotland. Then . . ." She paused and her eyes twinkled merrily, "the portraits of the brides your sons bring home will be hung next to yours."

For a moment the old pain seized Noramary's heart. But of course Ellen did not know that there would never be any Montrose sons! Why Duncan should insist on this portrait Noramary couldn't fathom.

Cecil Brandon surveyed his subject through narrowed eyes. Then he seated her in a high-backed chair where the light streamed in through the windows. He took great pains arranging the folds of her gown, her hands with her unfurled fan just so. He tilted her head, moving it a fraction of an inch to the left, then, stepping back, moved it a little to the right. At last he stepped over to his easel, picked up his brush and palette, and announced, "Now we are ready to begin. I only hope I can do justice to your great beauty, my dear lady."

For what seemed a very long while to Noramary, there was no other sound in the room but that of the brush moving rapidly on the canvas as Brandon began blocking in her portrait. It was hard to sit so still. Her chin began to quiver from holding it at the angle in which he had positioned it. Her back began to ache and her fingers, holding the fan, to tingle. It seemed an eternity before Brandon put down his brush and said, "We'll take a short break now."

"May I see?" she asked, standing and arching her back to ease the stiff muscles.

"No, I never let my subjects see a portrait in the working stages—a rule I adhere to very strictly, in spite of the wiles of many beautiful ladies," he said, chuckling. "And you, my dear, are among the most beautiful it has been my pleasure to paint."

Noramary blushed. She could never really think of herself as beautiful, despite this noted artist's use of the word. Beautiful women had life handed to them on a silver platter, did they not? All the beautiful married women she knew, at least, had the love of their husbands—Jacqueline, Leatrice. . . .

Cecil Brandon was a man of cosmopolitan tastes, one who had traveled extensively and was as knowledgeable of many other topics as he was of painting. He was also a man of considerable sophistication, yet he was not in the least condescending. Noramary had, at first, been awed by him, knowing his prestige as a painter of the great as well as of the nobility of England. But, as the sittings progressed, she lost her timidity in his presence and began to ask questions about his profession.

"Painting portraits is a very specialized branch of art," he told her. "One cannot improvise as an artist can in painting a landscape or still life; that is, put in a light or shadow or even add a piece of fruit or a flower if it will enhance the composition. A portrait painter must be true to what he sees. . . . Oh, I admit to having eliminated a wart or a wrinkle at times." He chuckled. "But in painting such perfection as yours, I'm hard put not to make the viewer think the artist has idealized his subject!"

Again Noramary felt uncomfortable. The compliment seemed too lavish for her own estimation of her looks.

She started to protest, when Cecil fixed her with a studied, penetrating look. "I have a feeling you don't like being beautiful. Perhaps it has caused you unhappiness?"

Noramary stared at him. It was almost as if she heard Nanny Oates speaking again. How could he know?

"Perhaps you find your beauty too heavy a burden? Perhaps it makes your husband jealous?"

Noramary looked at him incredulously. How had he discerned this?

As if reading her thoughts, he continued. "Ah, I suspected there was some cause for the decided change I find in you after only a few months' time. When I was here in the fall, you were radiant . . . all the glowing happiness of a bride newly wedded to a man she loves, who adores her! I find so great an alteration in you, there must be a deep, abiding problem. . . ."

Noramary was suddenly quiet, too quiet.

All at once it was too much to bear. Duncan's

continued coldness, his distrust, his suspicion. It was too heavy a burden to carry alone any longer. Her eyes filled with tears. Speechless, she stared at Brandon. Sobs ached for release. She dropped the fan to put two delicate hands to her throat, as if she were choking. Tears rolled unchecked down her cheeks.

"My dear lady," exclaimed Brandon. "What is it?" Little by little, haltingly, Noramary poured out her story.

"I have come to believe that Duncan was still in love with Winnie when he married me. I don't think he realized that fully until . . ." Here Noramary broke down again. "In the meantime, I had fallen deeply in love with him." She paused, then said in a voice that betrayed her bewilderment, "He thinks there is someone else in my life. A childhood friend, a very dear person whom I hold in great affection. But since the day I accepted Duncan, I have not tried to communicate with him nor to see him, except by chance. Somehow, no matter what I've said, my husband believes me to have been unfaithful!" she burst out. "I swear to you I have never been! He will not believe me, although I have told him over and over. I married him under circumstances that might have led him to think I did not love him. Perhaps I did not. I did not know what real love was then, though I took vows that were, and are, sacred to me. Perhaps, for a time, those vows were all that bound me to him— a promise made, a covenant to be kept. That, too, has changed. I have learned to love Duncan

Montrose with a deep, abiding love, for I have seen him in moments of tenderness and gentleness. It is *that* Duncan I will go on loving, whether or not he ever believes that love . . . or accepts it."

Noramary put her head in her hands and wept brokenly.

"My dear lady, I have made you weep! Forgive me, I should have said nothing . . . but there was such a marked difference, not only in your demeanor but in your whole expression . . . the eyes, the very mirror of the soul, are so sad. They reflect the pain in the heart. . . . I have not painted portraits for so many years for nothing. I could not help but observe . . ." Brandon said in some distress.

When her hard sobs finally lessened, Brandon lent her his clean linen handkerchief to wipe her eyes, and pressed her hand gently.

"Dear lady, sometimes one needs only a sympathetic ear to release healing tears. Perhaps our conversation has been fortuitous. I believe tomorrow the sitting will go better. Your candor and innocence will show forth. I will paint you so no one can question the shining beauty of your virtue." He smiled and gently touched the ruby earrings swinging from her ears, and quoted softly: "'And who shall find a valiant wife, for her price is above rubies?'"

"Even your stern husband will not be able to deny the fulfillment of the Bible's definition of a 'fortunate man.' He will read in your face the truth he has not been able to receive from your lips. Trust me, dear lady. Your portrait will be the finest work of my career."

Brandon quickly packed up his painting case and bid Noramary good-afternoon. He had been invited to the Camerons' for dinner, and Jacqueline had sent her carriage for him, which was even now waiting. He kissed Noramary's hand and left her sitting alone in the drawing room.

The afternoon sun was slanting through the long windows, and Noramary sat bathed in its rays, thinking over her confession and the artist's assurances. If it could only happen . . . if Duncan could only be convinced . . . if he could love her again. . . .

There was a noise behind her and instinctively she turned to see Duncan standing in the archway, his height and broad shoulders filling it.

Her eyes, so recently misted with tears, were glistening, her lips parted in surprise, all color drained from her cheeks.

Noramary stood up, hands pressed against her breast where her heartbeat quickened noticeably. She started to speak, but something restrained her. Several swift changes of expression passed over Duncan's face. He seemed to be struggling for words. So she waited. When he finally began to speak, his voice shook with emotion.

"Noramary, please understand that I did not mean to eavesdrop. I came into the house earlier than usual, intending to look in on the sitting, to see what progress Brandon had made on your portrait today. Perhaps it was intended that I should overhear your conversation." He stopped, flinging out both hands in a helpless gesture. "Maybe I should have left after hearing part of it— but I couldn't. I didn't.

"How can I explain? It all began the night we truly became man and wife. It was so glorious. I couldn't believe my good fortune—that the Lord had given me so precious a wife. Then, in your sleep, you whispered a name . . . a name that was not mine. And I foolishly jumped to conclusions." His tanned face flushed deeply. "I believed you and Robert Stedd . . . were more than friends . . . that you were lovers.

"I was mad with jealousy. It seemed that after I'd found what I'd been waiting for all my life, it was no longer mine. I hardened my heart against you, so that everything else that happened met that barrier I'd erected between us. I was ready to think the worst." He halted, shaking his head as if it was almost too much for him to continue. "I didn't dare let you know how much you'd hurt me or how much what I *imagined* had hurt me. It made me too vulnerable. It was easier to build a stone wall around myself. He paused again. "But I couldn't stop loving you. If I couldn't have you as my true wife, I could at least carry an idealized image of you. . . ."

"The silhouette?" Noramary whispered.

Duncan looked surprised.

"I saw it," she explained.

"Yes, the silhouette. . . . I persuaded Jacqueline to give it to me . . . but when . . ."

"I went out to the cottage that day I got lost in

the woods, the day I became ill—"

"That terrible day I thought I'd lost you forever." Duncan sighed, a look of infinite pain on his face. "While you were lying ill, delirious, I stayed beside you, telling you how much I loved you, but of course, you could not hear. Then, in your room, I saw the letters on your desk, the ones you had started to write to Robert, and all my dreams for our life together when you recovered were dashed. I thought they were love letters, that you and he had been corresponding behind my back all this time. Then when I came to Williamsburg and found you with him . . ." Duncan broke off. He hesitated, searching for the words to continue. "Noramary, what can I say? I was wrong. Terribly wrong. About you . . . about everything!"

For a long moment they stood without speaking, gazing at each other—one with eyes begging to be believed; the other, hoping she could trust what had been said.

Then Duncan held out his arms. After a pause he said, "Noramary, my love, forgive me . . . I've been so blind."

There was only a moment's hesitation before she went into those open arms with a sigh, and she felt the strength of his embrace enclose her.

All the sad uncertainty of the past months vanished. All her anxiety lifted. Something deeper than happiness began to grow, filling her with an incandescent gladness.

It was a moment Noramary never dreamed she would know. Before it, every other emotion dimmed to a mere shadow. It was everything known of poetry and music and passion . . . of joy and love and ecstasy. It had no beginning and no end.

At last she belonged, truly belonged. At last she could love and be loved . . . wholly . . . without fear or apology . . . completely . . . until the end of all time.

Epilogue

N oramary stirred, aware of some new sound penetrating the deep, dreamless sleep into which she had slipped, exhausted. The room was shadowy, only the tawny glow from the fireplace gave some light. From her bed she could see out the window that against the gray blue February sky, snow was gently falling. Snowflakes drifted lazily as she watched. It seemed that she and the world were wrapped in a velvety quiet.

Then she heard voices in the hall outside her

door. As it opened gently, letting in a shaft of light, Noramary turned her head slowly and saw Ellen approaching the bed carrying a bundle in a lacy white shawl in her arms.

She came closer, bent nearer, laid the bundle in the curve of Noramary's arm. She felt its light weight against her heart. Her arms felt heavy, almost too tired to lift, and yet as the bundle moved, a kind of excited wonder rose inside her. The baby! The last terrible hours were only faintly recalled as her hand cupped the tiny head and ran a finger over the downy tufts of hair. She felt something expand within her heart: love, happiness, a sort of rapture. Here was her baby.

"A handsome little boy, ma'am," Ellen announced proudly, as if she had produced him herself.

"A boy," Noramary murmured, peering into the little face. "A son for Duncan."

The child was so beautiful, his white skin transparently fine, the pearly shadows of his eyelids, the long lashes, the small, rosy cheeks, the tiny mouth with its short upper lip, the softness of the light brown hair, like a cap on the small, round head.

Afterward she slept for a long time. The next thing she knew, a tall figure was entering the bedroom, now shuttered against the evening, glowing with firelight. Moving lightly, quietly, for such a big man, Duncan came to the side of her bed, then knelt on the mounting steps and cradled her cheeks with his palms.

"My dearest love . . ." she heard him say, and a deep thrill trembled through her at the sound of his low voice.

"Duncan!" she whispered. "Are you pleased . . . a son?"

"*Our* son . . . Noramary. My darling." His voice faltered, nearly broke; his hand groped on the coverlet for her small one, grasped it. "I have never loved you more. You are more precious to me than I can ever say . . . I was afraid . . . I might lose you."

Noramary reached up and touched his mouth with her fingers.

"There is no need for words, Duncan. I know now that you love me. Now we have—everything."

He kissed her fingertips and the palm of her hand as he turned it.

"Noramary, you will always be first . . . always." His voice was very slow, soft.

She must have drifted off again with Duncan holding her hand, because later, when she awakened, she was alone. From the little room above, Noramary could hear a low, crooning song. She smiled. Delva must have finally managed to get the baby away from Ellen and was rocking him in the nursery in the new cradle.

Weak but happy, Noramary floated back and forth from the euphoric half wakefulness to a sort of dreamlike state in which she felt all-knowing, all-powerful, and prophetic.

She was so pleased that their first child was a boy, a son for Duncan, someone to carry on the name, the proud heritage of the Montrose clan with its long lineage going back into Scottish history.

She remembered what she and Duncan had talked about earlier.

"If you agree, darling, I should like to call the baby Cameron. They have been such good friends."

Cameron, she repeated to herself. Yes, she liked the name. It sounded strong and honorable, a fine name for their son and the heir to Montclair.

As difficult as it might be to imagine now, one day that small baby would be a man, and Montclair would be his. And one day he would bring his bride here, and they would have children—sons, who would then bring their brides here to this beautiful house that Duncan had built, which they were making into a home at last.

Perhaps, Noramary thought dreamily, there would be daughters, too, to be betrothed under the spreading branches of the newly planted elms or married in the lovely garden.

Noramary smiled to herself as she closed her eyes. Montclair would become legendary, like the love she and Duncan shared, triumphing over hardships, heartaches, trials. Montclair, like their love, would survive through all the years to come.

She twisted the heavy gold and amethyst ring on her finger, the traditional ring given the Montrose brides, thinking of the other women who would wear it.

She, Noramary Marsh, had been the first bride to come here . . . but not the last . . . no, not the last . . . she sighed happily.

Family Tree

❧

In Scotland

Brothers GAVIN and ROWAN MONTROSE, descendants of the chieftan of the Clan Graham, came to Virginia to build on an original King's Grant of two thousand acres along the James River. They began to clear, plant, and build upon it.

In 1722, Gavin's son, KENNETH MONTROSE, brought his bride, CLAIR FRASER, from Scotland, and they settled in Williamsburg while their plantation house—"Montclair"—was being planned and built. They had three children: sons KENNETH and DUNCAN, and daughter JANET.

In England

THE BARNWELL FAMILY

GEORGE BARNWELL first married WINIFRED AINSELY, and they had two sons: GEORGE and WILLIAM. Barnwell later married a widow, ALICE CARY, who had a daughter, ELEANORA.

Eleanora married NORBERT MARSH (widower with son, SIMON), and they had a daughter, NORAMARY.

In Virginia

Since the oldest son inherits, GEORGE BARNWELL'S younger son, WILLIAM, came to Virginia, settled in Williamsburg, and started a shipping and importing business.

WILLIAM married ELIZABETH DEAN, and they had four daughters: WINNIE, LAURA, KATE, and SALLY. WILLIAM and ELIZABETH adopted NORAMARY when she was sent to Virginia at twelve years of age.

Jane Peart, award-winning novelist and short story writer, grew up in North Carolina and was educated in New England. Although she now lives in northern California, her heart has remained in her native South—its people, its history, and its traditions. With more than twenty novels and two hundred and fifity short stories to her credit, Jane likes to emphasize in her writing the timeless and recurring themes of family, traditional values, and a sense of place.

Ten years in the writing, the Brides of Montclair series is a historical, family saga of enduring beauty. In each new book, another generation comes into its own at the beautiful Montclair estate near Williamsburg, Virginia. These compelling, dramatic stories reaffirm the importance of committed love, loyalty, courage, strength of character, and abiding faith in times of triumph and tragedy, sorrow and joy.

THE SAGA CONTINUES!

Be sure to read all of the "Brides of Montclair" books, available from your local bookstore:

Valiant Bride

To prevent social embarrassment after their daughter's elopement, a wealthy Virginia couple forces their ward, Noramary Marsh, to marry Duncan Montrose. Already in love with another, Noramary anguishes over submitting to an arranged marriage.

Ransomed Bride

After fleeing an arranged marriage in England, Lorabeth Whitaker met Cameron Montrose, a Virginia planter. His impending marriage to someone else is already taken for granted. A story of love, conscience, and conflict.